BLOOD TIE...

a searing conflict between old and new, between clashing cultures and enduring values, between the price of honor and the cost of corruption.

"Dazzling ... ambitious ... splendid." —*Kirkus*

"Mary Lee Settle has written a complex, startling novel ... this story is so real, I felt I was looking at it rather than reading about it; I felt I could reach out and touch it. *BLOOD TIE* is an amazing novel." —Ann Beattie

"In this novel are all kinds of wisdom that matter—political, social, psychological, even anthropological—perfectly dramatized in the interwoven stories of a fascinating collection of characters, told in brilliant, lucid prose."
—Vance Bourjaily

"I stand in awe of this novel. No American writer I know of writes so fully and so beautifully and so lovingly of people today as does Mary Lee Settle. *BLOOD TIE* is a classic, a marvel, a wonder ..."
—Douglas Day, author of The National Book Award Winner, *MALCOLM LOWRY, A BIOGRAPHY*

BLOOD
TIE

MARY LEE SETTLE

BALLANTINE BOOKS • NEW YORK

Library of Congress Catalog Card Number: 77-8373

ISBN 0-345-28154-3

This edition published by arrangement with Houghton Mifflin
Company

Manufactured in the United States of America

First Ballantine Books Edition: July 1979

MY THANKS

To the Aegean Turks for their friendship.

To the Merrill Foundation for recognition
and award at the right time.

To the Colonnade Club at the University of Virginia
for hospitality and silence.

As fairy tales are started in Turkey,
"Bir var mish, bir yok mish."
Maybe it happened, maybe it didn't.

I
The First Sacrifice

Mount Latmos, now called Annadağ, had drawn nearer to the town. Ariadne could tell the time by its closeness, three o'clock. She stared at it, trying to pick out the royal tomb. The sun caught the gash of the high cliff where it was being dug, but the tomb itself was too far away. She thought she could see the rock-cut graves around it, but they might have been only faults in the mountain necropolis where the dead overlooked the city of Ceramos.

Because she was the kind of woman to whom words like life and death came easily, she put her hand to her slightly sagging belly and thought, I am building my death, too, every day.

Staring at the mountain was only an excuse. She was trying not to watch the sacrifice. She thought she ought to feel some repulsion. She was wondering if she really did. She caught the silence around her and it drew her back and made her look again at the prow of the new boat.

The knife gleamed, a sickle moon above her. All around the huddle of people in the shipyard, dwarfed by space, the shipwrights had stilled their hammers, poised, waiting. A fleet of masts of single tall pines rose high above the yard, the furled sails, and the ropes cat's-cradled across the waiting air. The rigging that usually moved and sighed was quiet, as if the breeze itself waited, as still as the half-sunken abandoned hulls, blue-green with age and sea water, slowly disintegrating off the shipyard shore. The children who had climbed the stone wall of the yard to watch no longer beat their feet against the stones. She saw Kemal, sit-

3

ting as usual apart from the rest. Her heart by habit
hungered a little to change his life.

Faintly in the distance, she could hear the blood lust
of the fifes, the drums, the wailing woodwinds of the
Janissaries' march, its delicate minor dirge as brooding
as the castle that commanded the entrance to the outer
harbor. An isolated horn whispered.

Her eyes measured upwards, slit against the hard
blue sky. Airborne, tilting away from her, the white
ship's prow thrust thirty feet high, proud, dry-docked
on a wooden cradle, balanced on great beams of age-
seasoned logs. The evil eye that hung from the polished
bowsprit watched the agha's tomb on the hillside behind her. Its vaulted roof was as white as the ship, but
it was the dead white of washed plaster.

The sun glittered on the knife raised in the young
butcher's hand. He too was etched by sky, kneeling. His
knee rested on the body of a sheep that lay supine
across the prow, its fear-glossed eyes staring, like the
ship's eye, beyond and over them, at the agha's tomb.
Red ribbon, tied to its horns to show it was first-born,
hung down the white prow. Not a sound, bleat or sigh,
came from its half-opened mouth, its lolling tongue.
The young butcher's hair caught the sun like a halo.
He controlled the moment, knowing his own hand-
someness, as some men do, without shame. Behind him
on the new deck, the ship builders prayed.

The knife arched through the sky, gashed deep into
the throat of the sheep. Through the open wound its
death, a long slow arch of black blood, spouted in a
wide arc clear of the hull to the ground, turning the
sand red. The first breeze caught the red ribbons, then
the blood ribbon, and swung it out so that the people in
front of the crowd pushed back to keep from being
splattered. A ship's carpenter behind them rang the first
hammer blow, the shipyard came to life again around
them. The breeze carried the scent of new-cut wood,
pine resin, sun and blood.

The men on deck stood around the hodja from the
local mosque as he dipped his finger in the blood and
marked their foreheads. One by one, marked now with
a third red eye, they climbed down the ship's ladder to

the sand. In turn, led by the captain, they held their open palms under the bloody fountain, and placed their red palm marks on the hull for the sea to lick away.

Those who had watched, astonished at their own awe, refused to meet each other's eyes, as if they had seen a thing so private it transcended the taboo of disgust they felt they ought to show. Someone's hand shook, spilling wine. It mingled with the blood in the sand.

The rigging of the boats in dry dock hummed in the new wind. The men took their places at the oak cradle that held the ship poised above the wooden slipway green with sea algae, waiting to carry her into the water. The chant began, chant and thud of heavy mallets against the log struts. The hull began to move; the chanting quickened, the logs tipped toward the sea. Released, the hull slid fast into the harbor, lifting a wave of spume with her stern. The men aboard ran to the ropes, corralling her as she felt the new freedom of the water under her, plunged, and threatened to turn. As they tamed her, she rode the harbor calmly, smaller than she had been on land. One by one the bloody hand prints disappeared in the water.

The workmen tipped the dead sheep into a wheelbarrow to take away and cook for their feast. The little knot of strangers watched the Ceramians, and the children, who had not yet climbed down from the wall, wondering if it was all over and time to leave. The Ceramians waited for the foreigners to go. It was not polite to hurry them away. On the wall Kemal felt the tears beginning, and hid his face from the others so they would not tease him.

Basil was late. Agonized at the fear of being left behind, he had suffered as if he were late to meet a lover. He stepped back at the entrance to the shipyard to let the wheelbarrow pass, staring at the dead marbles of the sheep's eyes.

"Oh God." Basil didn't know he had spoken aloud until one of the men called back "Merhaba" in Turkish. This worried him, this opening of his private thoughts and speaking them, as out of a door, like a slut. He promised himself to be careful. It was hard to stop looking at the head banging drunkenly against the side of the wheelbarrow. He could think of several people he would rather see dead and bleeding instead of the little sheep.

He caught up with Ariadne, relieved that she was standing where she should be, with Horst and David, not wandering off with some Ceramian friend in that secret way she had, saying nothing. Her hand rested on Monkey's shoulder. Basil liked Monkey. He was very useful for a Ceramian. Also he spoke English of a kind. Beside her preened the fresh and threatening American child Lisa. Privately when he was sober, and publicly when he was drunk, Basil called her the queen of the cats. She played with her long silk hair and scanned the crowd. He wished she were not there, in the middle of all his safety. He could see Lisa's hair trailing, combed with blood along the ground, her head lolling like the sheep's head over the side of the wheelbarrow, her eyes glass marbles.

"Darling," Basil said, especially to Lisa, with a wide, social smile, "you look ravished. Are you sure the sun is good for you? Your sort gets freckles."

"You missed the launching." Ariadne's kindness was habitual and easy.

"I was very nearly killed." Basil began a story. They stood, ready to listen. The thing about Ceramos that Basil loved most was this way of listening. Basil felt as if he had been waiting for years, sixty-eight to be exact, to find it. Instead of waiting for his mouth to stop, they treated the storyteller as if he had come from a long way with news, no matter how many times they had heard it, and Basil was only too aware of his own repetitions.

"A jeep. My dear, I was crucified against the wall. It stopped just in time; the man was playing with me. You know the madness of them. They treat anything with wheels like a chariot, riding down the rabble. Of course the man may have been blinded by all that glitter they hang in front of their faces, prayers, tinsel balls, evil eyes . . ." Basil stopped, realizing that Monkey was one of them. Actually the driver had blown his horn once to push the crowd back so that he could inch his way through the Pazar. It was the horn that Ariadne had heard faintly, as part of the distant heartbeat of the Janissaries' march.

Now that most of the foreigners had turned away, the Ceramians streamed by them, hurrying to find good places along the quay for the parade. A dog licked at the stained sand.

Ariadne was not ready yet for Basil's incessant voice. She glanced around at the space where the death had been to catch once more at the residue of it before it was gone. She let herself be blinded for a second by the sun that beat down on the trampled yard.

Basil caught at her withdrawal. "Ariadne!" He stopped his story.

"I'll be back." Her voice had that vagueness, that shutting out he hated. Before he could grab her arm, she had walked away.

"Ariadne!" Basil called. "We need you. You'll miss the parade. Oh why does she do that?" He said to the others, "Come. Let's go on. We'll miss everything." He was afraid of losing Horst or David, even Monkey. "Oh God, come on."

He clutched at them to keep the afternoon from disintegrating around him. Horst and David had already started toward the gate, following the Ceramian. There was nothing else to do. He loped after them as best he could.

When Ariadne called back, "I'll follow you in a minute," he didn't hear her.

Kemal stood, so small in the sand below the tall masts, the dry hulls, under the vaulted sky, he might have been the last child in some abandoned city. Ariadne knew better than to touch him before he saw her. He could disappear from a touch like a fish. Strange touches were all too often followed by a slap

across the head, and the call, "Ağzi, gel! Here,
dummy," as if he had no mind.

Ariadne had never heard him make a sound, no
rasping of his throat, nor straining groan, neither barks
nor sobs. He was simply and totally mute, as if he had
chosen it.

So she walked in a circle on the periphery of his attention as she would have a lost kitten she wanted to
charm into her hands. She stopped opposite him and
waited. Between them the splash of blood and wine
had almost sunk in the sand. The dog had curled in the
shade of one of the ship's hulls and gone to sleep. Kemal was letting his tears fall. She saw a drop mingle
with the brown blood and redden it again.

Finally he looked up. He was small, even though she
guessed he must be eleven or twelve years old. His
mother was evasive about his age.

"Kemal, merhaba." She said her hello almost in a
whisper, and then added to make him smile, "Hel-
low." She saw his black eyes brighten, the Tartar tilt of
their outer edges deepen. She thought, they are eyes
that remember the sweep of the Mongols, and have
seen the great Genghis Khan—and was ashamed of
being so fanciful even in her mind.

Kemal was glad, as always, to see Ariadne Hanım,
Lady Ariadne, even though he was embarrassed that
she had caught him crying. It was, after all, only a
sheep. It was not even the animal's dying that had
started the tears, it was the dropped blood itself, seeping into the sand. He had no questions, nor even much
sorrow about it. He knew that whenever he saw blood
on the ground the tears came, not out of his soul as
they did when he was hurt, but out of his eyes with
their own life.

Ariadne Hanım was familiar and soft. He always
knew what she was going to say. He liked that. At any
other time he would have been happy to sit beside her
and listen to her funny bad Turkish, and that other
way of speaking she lapsed into sometimes when she
was using him to speak to herself, but it was the wrong
time. He was in a hurry.

The mountain was getting nearer. It was that time of

bright gold across its face that clanged an alarm to
him, time, it is time to go. He had to get to it before
dark, and it was nearly a two hours' climb, even if he
ran most of the way through the fields and the tangerine groves between the eastern walls of the town and
the foothills. But he could not move until Ariadne
Hanim did. That would have been impolite to his
friend.

Ariadne had thought and practiced, making her
mouth into Kemal's mouth, trying to feel the constric-
tion in her own throat, to find the word that would release him into sound.

"Hel-low. Haal-low," she spoke the word again
slowly to heal him, trying to conjure the beginning of a
voice from him, a try, just a try, once. She reached
across the space between them and took his hand,
holding back from letting her fingers try to shake a
sound from him.

Kemal never knew why the lady kept saying "Hele
hele" to him like that, in such a funny way. She never
looked impatient with her eyes as his mother did when
she said it, and took his shoulders in both hands and
shook him and spat quickly, "Hele hele, tell me the
truth!" as if he could. No, Ariadne Hanım's voice was
gentle.

She was leading him between the hulls, up toward
the little hill, Mahtepe, where the cemetery was, and
the old agha's tomb. He would have to stay and listen
to her for a little while. He hoped she would not take
too long. Each minute that they stayed meant that he
would have to run faster to the mountain, and it was a
hot day.

Sweat hung on the lady's lips from the little climb up
the path, and she lowered herself with a slight, fat-lady
sigh into the long purple shade made by the agha's
tomb. He liked the tomb. It was like a little pretty
white house among the red and orange poppies. He
had to look quickly for scorpions before her bottom hit
the ground. She always forgot.

They required a lot of looking after, the strangers
who had come to Ceramos. They crept into a man's
mind like worms, unfinished and white. Only this one,

Ariadne Hanım who loved the stars and could sit quiet
for a long time, seemed sometimes to glimpse what was
true behind all their words and their worming, but even
her he had to mistrust finally. She was too weakened
by loneliness. She took up a man's time helping at him,
but he knew she needed to for some reason, and sometimes he liked it.

He only hoped that this time she wouldn't use too
many words. In the density of too much talk he suspected a lie, oh not the sensible lie that protected what
was true, but the other kind; the kind that strangers
told when they talked too much and took up too much
room and laughed too loudly and didn't go to their
homes until too late in the night. At such times Kemal
felt older than Ariadne Hanım, and ashamed for her
when she tried to talk like the others, like donkeys. He
had, there in the shade, one of those bright flashes of
understanding of God, who had set him in the world
without the false comfort of words. He had such
flashes often, and paid little attention to them.

All around them, above the level of their eyes, the
slim tombstones tilted, crowned with carved turbans
that showed they were the graves of men. Some were
stained with lichen, some still white. Between the
graves the poppies moved slowly in the afternoon wind.
When Ariadne leaned her back against the agha's tomb
and looked up, she could see the cracked plaster, the
incision of the Arabic scroll, arabesques of grace. Once
she had tried to find out what it meant, but no one
knew, no one except the hodja, and she had learned
better than to ask him. The sky was high, pure, and so
blue she felt as if she were floating in it, a sea of air.

She sensed the stillness of the boy; she knew that he
was not yet ready to leave. She could feel it through
his hand, still clutching at her fingers. Such times with
Kemal were never longer than fifteen minutes or so.
She had so much to do, and people called her, as now,
when she could see Basil in the distance. He turned,
waved back at her, and caught up with the others,
walking as usual a little too close to them.

With Kemal she gave herself the luxury of telling
secrets. He was, after all, a perfect listener. He neither

understood her nor could repeat what she told him. She knew he only wanted to see her mouth move, hear the same things over and over that made him smile, and soften for a little from the hard neglect he was used to. Being with Kemal and waking in the morning were something of the same to her, a slow rise beyond the confusion of her privacy, her past, and her dreams.

From the hillside they could see the town quay, a half-mile semicircle around the harbor. Beyond it the white town grew among the green groves, as the turbaned stones grew among the poppies. Across the harbor, jutting out of the sea high above the bay, the medieval castle faced the island of Yazada, the summer isle in the sea a mile away. Together they guarded the narrow sea channel to the east. Inland was Asia, tier behind tier of mountains that protected the little city and its fields in the half-moon of a valley that opened to the sea.

Among the stone houses, the slim minarets of the mosques rose high above the trees. Down below them in the harbor, the newly launched boat bobbed, a tiny and neglected toy.

Kemal read the racing time by the gleaming finger of the minaret in the center of the quay beside Salmakis kahve, by the dark crowds in the Pazar near the northern gate. People had begun to move along the narrow streets toward the wide quay to find places for the parade. Like a bright patchwork at the north gate, the Janissaries and the marchers waited. The band had started to play the march again. The thin wail from where they sat was a disturbance of the wind.

Kemal knew he would have to leave before the crowds and the parade clogged the quayside. He could only motion toward the mountain that towered along the east side of the valley and ended in great cliffs over the sea. His hand jostled Ariadne's, trying to free itself.

Ariadne was pleased that she understood the language of his body so well. She leaned lower against the agha's tomb.

"Yok, no," she said. "I came from there—Orda." She pointed toward the thin rim of islands four miles

away to the west at the edge of the sea circle. She told
herself it was his favorite story.

"I came here in 1969, three years ago. Now it is
1972." She liked to teach him in her slow, considered
Turkish. "I came from Kos, the Greek island." In the
mixture of Ottoman words she had learned from her
out-of-date dictionary, and her mistakes, she soon lost
the boy, but she read the confusion in his eyes as dis-
belief. "Yes," she went on, "far beyond Kos. One big
ocean, and beyond that, Spain, and then another ocean
and beyond that, America. The world is round, Kemal,
and if you go far enough you come back to where you
started from. World round, küre, a sphere."

To Kemal instead of *küre* she had used the word
kuru, dry, withered, and he was sorry she felt like that.
He could see the same place she could; it was wet
green for the spring, and there were secret rivers, and
the vast blue purple sea. He wondered at her blindness.

"I came, I told you this, three years ago. This same
day, you understand? I did not know it was a bayram,
what we call a holiday. I thought every day was like
that. That day there were the camels in their red velvet
havuts, and the people in their wedding clothes, and
the band. It was only a few miles from Greece, but
very strange to me, you understand?"

Ariadne Hanım's voice had that question in it as if
she wanted comforting. Kemal could only smile again,
and he was getting tired of doing that.

But she had forgotten him, and still she clutched his
hand. Her eyes were far away where her soul was, not
sitting beside him any longer. Sometimes he did that,
too, and he understood. Now, he was sitting with the
lady and he was running up the mountain at the same
time. He watched her close her eyes and go to the
other place and her body was as still as a sleeping animal, and he knew she was still speaking, even though
she made no sound. He who could only talk to the
world that way, how could he not know?

"When I stepped ashore, oh Christ, how could I tell
this even to you?" she told him, but said nothing. You
have seen women like me a hundred times. There I
was, another middle-aged, divorced American woman,

brave and half-alive, and let's face it, as Basil says
never doing that himself, ever so slightly comic in my
courageous colors. I stepped ashore from the ferry,
looking like all the others and never knowing it; we
never know that. We think we choose . . . my shoulder bag that's long since worn out, Gucci, even Gucci
wears out, nothing lasts forever. Of course dark
glasses, I'd been warned to do that, and sensible wash-
and-wear.

The heat met me here, and Asia Minor struck a
great single note in me of where I was. I came from
something I still had no name for, searching for something I didn't know then, I thought of it as something I
could find, I thought I could sit down and be quiet
and think things out, and unpack—what did he
say?—unpack my heart with words and fall a-cursing
like a very drab. God knows I needed to do that, but
how could I, a lady.?

But that first day I sat outside the Customs House
kahve alone and I knew that whatever it was, I was in
the eye of it, and it was still as the eye of energy is
still. It was seducing my emptiness. My body still felt
prim on the outside. There I sat, a lone woman in
wash-and-wear, for the first time in Asia, dear God, a
thousand psychic miles from where I had come from
an hour before, slightly sickened by fear and sea drift.

I didn't know what to do. I felt naked. I sat with my
legs crossed tight, and I didn't know then that to cross
one's legs is the sign of a loose woman, a signal. I just
thought the men were friendly when they smiled. I
sneaked a look in my phrase book when they said,
"Hoshgeldiniz, welcome."

How could they know that the tears I had held back
for so long lay heavy behind my good sunglasses that
the zamparalar, the young machos, envied so? What
did my aunt call boys like that? Drugstore cowboys,
candy ankles, and in Italy they call them e vitelloni.
Everything they own is on their backs and they strut
through their fear like fine colts. Because it was a hot
day I hoped that if any of them noticed the tears they
would think they were sweat.

I did not know it yet but I was falling in love with

the fatal atmosphere of clarity that reflected in the sea, the stones, the air. I had sought oblivion and was finding its opposite, for oblivion is not in Ceramos.

Then I knew what was rising through my eyes, because I had been stripped by the place. Suddenly there outside the kahve I needed desperately to be alone before I sobbed aloud. I almost ran, but I couldn't run; there were clots of tourists from the ferry in my way. I climbed up into the castle that began its rise at the end of the quay, and loomed there over the kahve and the Customs and the Police Station, all I knew yet of Ceramos.

I climbed past balustrade after balustrade to the highest stone wall above the sea. There was no one in sight. Far away below me the castle wall grew out of naked gray sea rock, and the quiet Aegean water was so clear that I could see the rocks below the surface, and the dark patches of sea grass. I forgot that I had come to cry. I was calm. My body was separate from me. It was simply and without emotion of any kind, considering, as between possible and probable, the quite objective ease of throwing itself over the wall, two hundred feet down into the water below.

Poised there, coolly considering the act, I saw as a vision, neutral, clear, and shocking, what had brought me as far as the high rock. I wanted to laugh, alone up there suspended in the air, from the shock of seeing my enemy, my Roger, my treasure, diminished from a threatening giant to a neutral, unimportant man.

Then, imposed upon the rocks below, I saw my body, not dead, but embarrassingly wounded. I saw myself with my skirt up around my thighs in dirty underwear after my mother had warned me over and over—she never said things once—would you want to be picked up like that by strangers, always change your underwear. I saw myself as trouble for the American consul.

Then I did laugh aloud, with no one to hear but a raven who flew away and a rabbit who stared at me. I was, for a pause, robbed of my tragedy and left with a mild, sad, killing comedy. Ceramos had stolen from me the essence of what had happened, my own innocence.

Ever since that afternoon, when I have tried to recover
unsullied the searing injustice that had given me my
strength, it has been smaller, more tender, and less important. But before God I have felt robbed of its importance.

Away below me, at the edge of the sea below the
castle wall, something was being towed ashore by the
movement of the water, then nudged against a rock. I
saw it was a sheep's body, swollen, and I thought, I
might have looked like that if I had let myself jump,
and thought then, why it is ridiculous to let yourself
look like that. But I, swelled up with sorrow and self-
contempt, was as forgotten and impersonal, as ridiculous as the sheep's carcass, except to myself, and I
remember saying out loud like a fool, "I'm going to
have to look after myself better, lose some weight,"
and I got up off the wall, and was, for a second,
mother to myself.

I had sat down there in the high air on the castle sea
wall martyr intacta. I got up deflowered by the awful
blue energy that seemed to rise from the Ceramic gulf
that flowed between the mountains. I remembered that
the first Ariadne, abandoned in the same sea, had been
deflowered by Dionysus, and I wondered if I too had
been fooled like that, thought I was leading through a
labyrinth when I was only being led. I was smiling.

I remember that I walked after that a long way up
toward the eastern mountain, Annadağ. I was buoyant,
thinking of myself as having been to confession to the
sea, and in the right place, the first landfall of the Holy
Land. The ground, arid and brown along the paths, the
moving rocks, the dry sound of cicadas, the sense of no
longer being quite alone, reminded me of Eliot. I saw
how sensuous his penitence was and thought I would
discuss this with Roger, before I remembered he had
been gone for four years.

I walked up a narrow gorge, out of sight of the
town, toward the first cliffs of Annadağ, eerie and unknown to me that day. I remember my first sight of
Kemal's village, Eskiköy, poised high above the pass, a
patch of white buildings on the hillside, and decided to
climb to it, but as I turned, I saw, high on my right, a

Christian chapel, its domed Byzantine roof bone-white in the afternoon sun, and thought instead that I ought to pray, as one does after the cleansing of confession.

I found the path up to it among the camel thorn. It rose above me, isolated, anchorite. I stumbled among the rocks and watched for snakes.

Its doorless entrance yawned. Where the cross had been there was only a vague discolored shape high on the pocked wall of the altar. Plaster had dropped from the walls and the vault of its ceiling, and was lost among the weeds and the sheep droppings on the floor. It was empty, even of its old function, and I could not pray. I thought then that the ruin was ancient, safely ancient, as a ruin should be. I did not find out until later that it had been abandoned in 1922, and that the pock marks on the altar wall were bullet holes.

Outside the chapel I saw the wishing well, grown round with ferns, lush from the dampness deep within it, and thought of pubic hair. I did not know then how the women came to throw their coins in and wish for sons. God, I have thrown coins in it since, but not for that, well not quite for that, although I never knew a man that didn't have for me that quality of sonship.

But that day it only reminded me that I was thirsty, and I walked down into Ceramos, hurrying at the last to beat the sun which was dropping so quickly behind the western hills that I seemed to be racing with it to get back to the safety of streets.

Ariadne Hanım had not spoken aloud for so long that Kemal wondered if she had fallen asleep. The lines had gone from her face. She was pretty like a girl. He thought he would like to touch her breasts. He watched them rise and fall. Her breath caught a wisp of her blond hair and it waved. He put a finger toward it to play with it, but when he did she opened her eyes.

Instead he pointed down at the quay street, now black with people.

"Of course, tabiî tabiî. You want to see the parade. Come, gel." She got up and straightened her trousers, the kind men wore that made her behind look so big. Kemal wished she would wear the pretty loose shalvar trousers, all covered with little flowers, that his mother and the women from the village wore, and you could not tell how big they were inside them.

Now she seemed to be as hurried as she had been quiet before. They walked fast together down the hill and through the empty shipyard and along the street, dodging through the crowd. She was trying to find her friends. She had that lost look the foreigners had when they were looking for each other.

They walked along the wide harbor street, through the spaces left between patient groups of Ceramians who stood, self-controlled and dignified, waiting. Calm-faced women from the villages in their huge flowered shalvar trousers kept their faces half-covered with brightly striped cotton kerchiefs, their fingers and palms hennaed for the holiday. Children clung to the lobed branches of the tamarisk trees. Donkeys crowded to the walls of the gardens, their heads down. On the balconies of the rich white houses opposite the harbor, under the sea-colored carvings of the eaves, women sat with heavy, sunburned, dark-eyed men.

Through the mass, here and there, the villagers tried to edge away from contact with the skin of foreign girls, the gavur, undressed like whores in their narrow breast coverings, the fine hair shining on their obscene rounded arms. It was the arm hair that it was bad luck to touch. They pushed too near to the hot crowd, and when they did, the women held their index and little fingers out under their shawls as a charm against the evil eye, in case they should brush against the hair.

Basil, who had managed to get ahead of them so that he seemed to be leading his little world, noticed the kindness of the village women as they gave the foreign girls room. It was the second thing he loved about the Ceramians, thier politeness—a whole society, except for the drivers, knitted together by good manners left from the rule of the Ottomans.

"Islam, my dears, taught us to be what we thought we were. Knights, geauntylmen if you like," he pronounced it carefully always, "learned their—well—

honor? Hairy beasts before they met the infidel. I know. I may be a little manqué for the present due to circumstances, but never mind, I am, after all, a medievalist of some note." And he would cough if there were strangers present and add, "Really. Oxford. Or Oxon if you really care," and couldn't help giggling, "Really. I DO know."

Basil stopped under a tamarisk tree not overhung with children. The first ponderous camel processed by, its head up like an imbecile English dowager, its hump covered with a great havut of red velvet, hung with gold tassels, its wide delicate feet softly touching the ground.

It was led by a rope looped around the elbow of an old man on a donkey, Kachakchi Attila, Attila the Smuggler, his bare wrist bound with a scarf to hide the stump of his missing right hand. His wits, his speed had imperceptibly drifted out of memory. Only the nickname and the stump were left of what he had been. He rode on slowly, leaving the rope slack between his arm and the lead camel. Tied in tandem, the camel train passed in time with the still distant slow dirge. A female had her foal tethered to her, its legs frail still, but its head and neck already high in imitation of the aristocratic, half-smiling stupidity of its mother.

"I hate camels," Basil told their feet, not daring to look up into their beastly faces, for they reminded him of all the people who had snubbed him in his life.

The parade was too slow, all too slow, and the camels passed forever and he thought he would scream aloud . . . flog them forward . . .

And so anon, to save himself, Sir Basil de Montfort Sans Peur and let's face it Saunze Pité, since none had been done him in the corpse of his life, oh Jesu, that perpetually pulled forelock he couldn't help, did array him with the great red cross of Christ Jesu on silk, for Christ knew him for a geauntylman if no one else saw it.

He took horse then to lead them all in the full armor of the Order of St. John, King Anguish of Scotland to his left and King Anguish of Ireland to his right, for

God knows he had never been accompanied by other. Hill and valley they went in a thin line across God's holy tapestry, little tiny graceful things as cool colored as saints' breath toward the holy something he Basil had forgotten what they called it, only remembered that it was hidden from him.

He could hear the clop of his horse's hooves on the stones and the lope of the sweet soft infidel pads behind him, oh the burbley pleasure of the crowd at the sight, so God him help, banisher and banished, Basil, with King Anguish in the wrong street on the wrong day, always did try his best to cheer things up a bit.

He didn't know Ariadne was behind him until she touched his arm. "Stand in the shade," she whispered, and guided the gaunt body, his sleeping eyes, nearer the tiny patch of shade cast by the new short fronds of the tree. She looked around for Kemal, to hoist him up into the tree so he could see better, but he had run away. She knew it was because he was shy with her friends.

Horst looked up toward the mountain, worried that the dig at the royal tomb was unguarded. David, following his eyes, read the worry and smiled. One of the foreign girls opposite saw the two handsome brothers and smiled back, trying to choose between them. She had seen them walking together before, and she knew they were from California by the way they walked. She could always tell. They seemed radiant in the sun, as useless as lilies of the field, their white shirts opened so that the sunlight seemed to glow through their bodies.

Lisa waited for something to happen, someone to look at her, waited through what they all did now together. Later they would wander to David's bar and drink, and that night, or another night, she would find out why she was there.

Until she did, she had to hold on to Ariadne for ballast. Her one fear was that the old woman would write the wrong thing to her father. She had long since decided that David and Horst were gay because they were not interested in her. She could not understand why Monkey, as attractive as he was, stayed close to Ariadne and hardly noticed her own lovely tall body,

her Titian hair. She decided that Ariadne paid him. A
lot of older foreign women did. She had seen them corralling the young poor sailors.

Trader and Miranda, having looked for them all afternoon, not knowing about the ship's launching,
trudged up, in step, as people do who have searched
the earth together, found them there, inviting, secure, a
rich and sacred circle. Ariadne made a place for them,
and hoped that Miranda, for once, would not make interesting comments.

Trader's gray hair hung sparse and neglected to his
thin shoulders. He kept on smiling his leftover smile.
Miranda, hawk-like, glanced around the crowd, taking
it in little pecking visual notes to write down later in
some journal she thought she ought to start. She, bel-
ligerently free to let the sea and sky carve a brave surface to her face, was conscious of her legs, as solid now
as an Amazon's.

So, tight-knit and intimate, they watched the camels
pass, having little in common but the fact that their
separate pasts had brought them there. Ariadne, in one
of the hints of perception she didn't like to have and
had long since learned not to voice, put it to herself as
she often did, distrusting certainty, as a question, "Why
is it that none of us go back?" What she meant by
"back" she could not have explained.

If the hand had not been hidden by the
thick wisteria which had veiled the opposite balcony
for a hundred years, the older men of Ceramos could
have read a whole history in its gesture as it reached
forward to offer a cigarette to the young judge. He was
still so naive in his office that he thought that if he
drove in over the mountains in his old car and sat back
in the balcony corner, shaded by the pendants of the
vine, no one would know he was there.

What the young judge did not know—he was a
city-bred man—was that every move in and out of
Dürüst Osman's house was known and discussed as
soon as the door shut. Dürüst Osman preoccupied the

communal mind of the town. It had to be that way. He was old, he was powerful, capricious as a girl, and the owner of more of the land than anyone else had ever owned. His enemies called him a derebey, derisively, a lord of the valley. Those who worked for him, and there were so many who had to, called him an agha, and tried to make it sound like a term of respect.

The water man had seen the new judge enter between the stone gates of the single pass that ran into the valley. He had told the seller of pistachio nuts, who had told his brother, so that now, as the peddlers of ice cream, pink candy floss, helva, red apples, fruit juice, and cooling cologne wound in and out among the crowd, spreading the news as they paused to pass fruit or sprinkle cologne on the held-out hands, everyone knew not only that he was there, but exactly why, all twenty reasons depending on their own minds.

One thing they all knew in common. The new judge was being corrupted, or he would not be sitting on Dürüst Osman's balcony. With the deep sophistication of people who lived the patterns and carried the loads of earth, seasons, and change, inhuman and circular, they read, hardly caring anymore, the inevitable steps from naiveté through flattery to corruption in that white plastered house.

All the reasons were wrong. Only the young judge knew why he had come.

Most of the women in the crowd below would have marked the hand offering him the cigarette with the sign of the evil eye. It had, manicured and rich, the blood of a son, a father, a friend, an uncle on it, although the man had never fired a shot in his life.

Huseyin lit the judge's cigarette with his gold lighter and sat back, satisfied with his eyes' meeting with the fool before him, and looked down at the street below. He scanned the flower heads of the girls as he had been doing since spring began, slowly, methodically, to choose which foreign girl he would have for the summer.

Huseyin disdained the habits of the other young men of Ceramos, who went from one loose-belted Christian to the next, collecting them and bragging in the kahves.

That, to him, was too easy. They were as undiscerning as the peasant women who collected wild daisies and anemones in the meadows. He preferred—like his own mother, whose jeweled fingers charmed brighter, larger flowers in her walled garden as her twelve-year-old servant held up the pots so that she would not have to bend down—to cultivate one, fondle her, see her grow and bloom for him, teach her to be civilized for the summer. He knew that soon he would have to marry, and that the marriage would not be found in the street, so he looked with special care for what might be his last plucked summer woman.

He had almost chosen Lisa. His eyes kept coming back to her glowing hair, the wild Frankish way it caught the light. He knew, as he knew the history of most of them, that she was the daughter of a very rich American man. He had investigated this with much care. He even entertained the thought—it was the right word, he was entertaining himself with the thought—that she must be there on some hidden business, otherwise why would an important man send his daughter to a place like Ceramos?

If she had not looked up just then, wishing she were on the balcony where it looked cool and important and cultured, and wanting to be out of the hot sun for a while where the awful woman Miranda droned like a bee in her ear, he might have looked on past her. But she saw him and stared back. He received her look into his eyes, let it go deep, and relaxed his hunter body, having made his summer choice. He knew he would have to get rid of the old woman she clung to, but that did not matter. Ariadne Hanim had little money to spend in the town, and she took up with too many undesirable strangers. Huseyin had not let his father have him elected müdür, mayor, for nothing.

As a matter of fact, it pleased him to know all of their incomes. Having a sensitive feeling for such things, he did not, as some of the others did, ask himself political or sexual questions. The scales on which he weighed the strangers were wholly those of money.

Ariadne, for instance, lived on alimony and a small annuity, which came every month from the Chase

Manhattan Bank, 57th Street, New York. It was not much, three hundred dollars, pale living. Basil, to him, was more interesting. His money came from London in spurts, sometimes flood tide, sometimes drought. It came in the form of traveler's checks from Barclays Bank, wrapped in silver paper, and signed with such a trembling hand that Huseyin had never been able to decipher it. Huseyin hated traveler's checks, they told so little.

As for Trader and Miranda, they were not his business. They would leave soon anyway, but to keep his hand in, he had seen to it that he knew that their small stock of traveler's checks were kept in three black folders wrapped in an old nightgown of Miranda's. Why did women always hide their money in their most intimate garments, diamonds in sanitary napkins, gold bracelets with their teeth caught in nylon underwear? Huseyin had seen it all. It told him much about women. But Lisa, pretending to live on one hundred dollars a month, that was really interesting, yes, her eyes . . .

Just at the time he judged to be best, most mysterious, he slowly looked away and beyond her, aloof, and began to count the little boats that belonged to him, working out in his mind what money the day would bring. They were loaded nearly to the gunwales with what to him were crowds of young, fresh, happy, singing, shining coins, as they sailed out of the harbor toward Yazada, the summer island, a mile away across the bay. Already he could see the day's harvest of golden coins piling higher and higher in the coffers of his mind. He never thought of banks. There was no way to run his fingers through a ledger as there was through piles of mental gold, more sensuous to him than women's hair.

It was necessary to keep the judge away from the docks, so as not to embarrass him by facing him with the stupid law of only ten people to a boat, and thus forcing him to take a stand. He thought it better to take him in a jeep up to the royal tomb, safely out of the way of it all. He would find Horst, bind him to him by a surprising official hope of permission to go on with his dig, entertain the judge, and make his first move toward Lisa, all at once. Another geometric puzzle fitted. He could see the lines in the air. He leaned forward to whisper to the judge. Then he slipped away, selâming to his sleeping one-hundred-kilo mother as he left the balcony.

Lisa had forgotten her contact lenses. Her large blind honey-colored eyes saw the vague purple of the wisteria, stared, trying to see the faces of the people behind it, failed, and turned back to the huge blobs passing she knew were the camels. She licked at her cornet of candy floss.

On the balcony, Melek Hanım, Munci's mother, her face carved into the form of strong beauty that only time can carve, sat a little apart from the others, wishing she were someplace else. The shadow that in a lesser face would be called sulking lay across hers, a shifting memory of some ancient sadness. If Medea had survived into her sixties, reconciled at least outwardly to her neglect, she would have looked like Melek Hanım, Lady Melek.

She had been told to come to Dürüst Osman's house. She had come, where the son smoked in front of the father, and the women laughed with their teeth showing. Nothing had been said to her all through lunch, the huge impersonal meze, the tasteless fish, cooked by maids who did not care. She disapproved of it all. To her, hospitality came from the hands rolling, cutting, flavoring, constructing, slowly and lovingly, food that was a message of welcome.

She cooked always consciously, as if God were coming to her house, drawing His water from her well, chopping His red and yellow vegetables, slaughtering His lamb. She knew it was wrong to see God in her mind's eye shaped like a man, but before expulsion on one bloody night, she had lived on a Christian island as a child, and had seen Him once.

She had sat through the long lunch with her eyes down, politely, while her husband, a grand and humorous man, talked to the judge about the sponge fishing. Beside her at the table there had been an American official, Proctor Bey. The men leaned toward him all through lunch, as men do when they want something. She had paid him little attention. They all looked alike. There were the red-faced ones and the square-faced ones. Now this one was watching the parade without seeing it.

Down in the street she saw her beloved Munci there among the strangers, and wondered, as she had wondered for years, why he liked their grating, strident, over-easy ways. She hated to hear them call him Monkey, insulting him and treating him as a friend at the same time. At least he stayed close to Ariadne Hanim and the old English eunuch, who had moved back into the tiny patch of shade.

She felt sorry for the old man they called Basil. Basil meant the overpowered, the trodden on, the germ. She wondered that his parents had given him so defeated a name. He should not be so rootless at his age. He should be protected, as men needed protection when they became toothless grumbling old lions, but needed also not to know it. She had seen Ariadne touch his arm and draw him back, and knew, as if they were sisters, that she too had this old knowledge, even though she was foreign.

For the other couple there she had only the communal disdain the town felt for them. Such women as Miranda should stay in houses, and spread their legs privately behind the closed shutters. Every town had them, the widows, the poor and neglected, the unprotected women, useful for moments of necessary lust. They served a purpose before the young men married. It was her lack of discretion she hated, the hours in the men's kahves, the joggling of her old breasts under a boy's shirt, her bare, used legs.

For the man beside her, she had only a pitying contempt. He had a curse on him, the pathetic and drifting cuckold, with his ignorant, unconscious smile, refusing to know what his wife was. She could see the sea taking him, hiding his shame. She shivered, seeing too much again, and closed her eyes, pretending to sleep like her hostess.

She had seen Huseyin, though, who she thought was still on the balcony, down close to the foreigners, leaning forward to speak to Ariadne Hanım. Secretly she approved of Huseyin, the safety of his princely ways that he had not forgotten among the foreigners as so many of the others had. Melek Hanım loosened her teeth in comfort, and began to doze.

The guerilla fighters were passing slowly, men with long white beards, with their lambskin kalpaks, their long, flared overcoats, ammunition belts across their chests, their hunting guns at the ready, their feet wrapped in rags to commemorate the old war. From their belts hung hand grenades, now carved from wood, and aged and polished by hand before the winter fires. One of them carried a tattered French flag, another fragments of a Union Jack. Behind them, the women came, wrapped to their eyes in black shawls, carrying ammunition boxes on their shoulders under the waving shadows of the tamarisks as once they had carried them over the mountain passes in the white snows. Behind them an officer, in the old uniform of the war of independence, paced his slow horse, his leather saddle polished by years, his stirrups of the shoe-shape that came from the Seljuks, the great warriors.

Lisa did not see them. She was looking up at Huseyin, finding him, what she could see of him, more than passable. He stood beside her, taking charge of her, maneuvering her a step away from the others. He could read her eyes now, as shy as a wild stag's. He approved of the gentle vague fear in them, the huge pupils, the honey circle of her irises, the American vitamin-packed blue of the corneas. He hardly glanced at the parade of beautiful girls, now passing in their maroon velvet wedding clothes embroidered with gold. He did notice the harem girls that followed them, the colors of broken light, their long coats of striped satin, fallen silk, their transparent veils. He heard the rustling promise of their clothes, saw Lisa dressed as they were, her eyes enormous, black-rimmed, over the silk-embroidered veiling that covered her seeking mouth.

He wished she would stop eating in public, licking the damned pink candy floss. In his first act of summer possession, he took it from her, and, not knowing what to do with it, passed it with a smile back to Miranda, who received the gift and lapped at it as if she were lapping at his face. She threw it down in the street in a little gesture of disappointment when he turned away from her too quickly.

The boys to be circumcised, in long white silk shirts that reached to their silver shoes, their silver crowns on their dark hair, tried to keep step to the distant music, stumbling a little in their unaccustomed skirts, trying to hide the fear in their dark eyes.

Now the music was in the crowd, through its body, permeating the street, the slow throb and wail of the Janissaries' march. It roused in Ariadne her own hatred and suppressed anger, old grievances that send the soul to war. She, forty-eight and lingering on the edge of reconciliation and defeat, could feel the knife between her capped teeth. Her anger followed the Janissaries in their huge feathered hats, the brass kettles, the swords, the brass poles hung with horsehair that had once carried the human hair of the defeated, as they marched with the formal, deliberate pace of the most feared soldiers in the world.

They passed, the music faded and left her stranded on the pavement, under the trees. The parade receded into the distance.

Not one of the guerillas, the ladies, the Janissaries had been over eight years old. It was the yearly bayram, the holiday of the children. Later the presents would be given, the family visits would begin, the flags hung out, the loudspeakers for the music of the saz, the davul, and the kaval hung in the trees outside the houses of the boys to be circumcised.

Now there was nothing to do but stroll the wide street with the other straggling couples, the village families, the boys with their arms around each other—

another thing about Ceramos that Basil loved, but sadly, knowing it was a measure of their masculinity, their prowess, that they could do this.

Huseyin whispered to Lisa. Then he turned to honor Horst with his attention.

"The new judge is here." He spoke as if it were a secret between them. "He is finding your work at the dig very interesting. Will you please to take us there?" To soften what he considered a command, he added, "This is important. He is a historian. He will be useful for the permission."

Horst could not help clutching at visions of all his troubles being blown away, even though he knew better. He was too used to the slowness, the unfathomable changes of the official mind, the innumerable papers. He also knew that Huseyin knew that for the permission he would bark like a dog. Huseyin had said so in public, using, delicately for him, the rumor tense.

When the bus from Ankara had rounded the last curve of the descent into Ceramos three nights before the bayram, Horst had found the lights out over the whole town. This was normal. It was spring; the last storms put out the electricity.

With its protecting bowl of night light gone, Ceramos lay frail under the invasion of vast darkness and the wind-driven rain that drenched the windows of David's bar, the Artemis.

There were only two candle stubs alight in the narrow vaulted room that had once been a stable built into the massive castle walls. One cast too little light on the sink where David was washing ashtrays.

The other guttered and stabbed its last light on the bar in front of Horst and tossed his shadow high on the wall behind him. David was saving his hoard of candles for the inevitable emergency that would happen in the middle of the bayram. David glanced around at Horst, who sat down without speaking and began breaking matches in a neat little pile, staring at himself in the mirror behind the bottles.

He knew that Horst's permission to dig had been delayed again. David moved slowly to keep busy and not seem to interrupt Horst's dreaming, his silence an instinct for honoring his friend's trouble. Behind him he heard Horst take a long breath and then his voice for the first time in half an hour.

"As you no doubt know," Horst was explaining to his back, "there are three main facts about Endymion—incontrovertible. He was beautiful. He fell asleep on Mount Latmos, that mountain, our mountain, and the moon saw his face and fell in love with him. Now he sleeps there forever. Tamam.

"I have explained this to the Ministry many times. Together with the fact that I have found the bee, the stag, the double cleft, the goddess, all this in the tomb in the right place on the right mountain—love of God, what more do they want?"

David said nothing. He knew without looking that Horst had not paused for him to answer, but to stare at his glass and reassemble his complaints.

"I explain to them Hypnos-Thanatos, the twins, sleep and death. This is most important, you understand. Together with the proverb *Endymionis somnum dormire*, which uses the inner accusative, you understand. This is generally considered to be only the conventional inner accusative. This is not enough! Add *the*, David, Endymion sleeps *the* sleep. Hmm? What is the sleep we all share—that is death. Now follow this. According to Theocritus, Endymion could have been a king, a shepherd-king. He is in the same tradition as David and Christ, as shepherd-kings. Of course he was. I am in total agreement with Theocritus. Here is all the evidence the Ministry would want that I have found what I say I have found. I have found it mathematically. I have found it mythically. I have found it existentially—AB ORIGINE. This is no pale shepherd boy washed by the moonlight. Jesus no, not that, my friend. You think for one minute that that white marble Greek jungfrau moon-lady would have fallen in love like that? No. Oh my God, this was the goddess Moon that birthed the Nemean lion, and when she split and brought it forth her bellowing shook the mountain.

She came to that boy-king's dreams maybe like thunder and the wild beasts fawned on her. She is as savage and patient as a root."

David could hear him lift a bottle from behind the bar and pour a drink. He knew by this that Horst had not reached the end of his night. He heard him sit down again, the glass rang against the bar.

"We will take first the basic myth. That of course is impossible. When the myth is told it is no longer basic but a metaphor. Behind it, three things. One, what happened. Two, public metaphor. Three, private metaphor. I will take the first first. David, turn around, I am sick of talking to your back."

"One minute until I finish."

"One. If Endymion was a king who made a ritual marriage with a moon goddess priestess, then he would be throttled or hanged, you understand, within a certain time—length of his reign would be moon phased, nine months, maybe nine years. Lucian says that here in this town was once a festival where the sacrificial victims were hanged on the branches of an imitation forest within the moon's temple. Two. The public metaphor, shepherd and moon goddess, very pretty!"

When David turned around at last, Horst was watching himself in the mirror behind the bottles. His head, suspended between rakı and vodka, flickered in the candlelight. When he saw David sit down, he said, "By the light of the candles my face is enchanting. I am extremely fortunate not to be queer.

"Blood. The blood and the shouts are what they forget; the energy flowing into its names. And then to sleep forever, immortal and beautiful, young? I tell you something. Why does it keep alive, this myth? That is Three, private metaphor. You will of course never tell my colleagues, who would consider me unsound, you understand, but I must be fanciful about this, psychic evidence . . ." He spoke so low that David had to lean forward, although he already knew what he was going to say.

"Evidence. It is the only myth that deals with the wet dream. All the evidence, the goddess touches him only in sleep. He dreams climactic sexual intercourse.

According to Pausanias, there were fifty children born of this union with the moon, all daughters. Maybe priestesses. Who knows ..."

Horst's voice was running down at last. "I know we are supposed to want to wake but really we want to sleep in her arms. Waking up is a duty, a challenge, and a terror. Do you know in hell they do not go to that country we all go to or come from, their eyes are always open?" He waited for David to speak, and, satisfied with his silence, went on, "You say, this or that is like a dream. How would you know except that we have all gone to the same dream country, eh?"

David saw that his glass was empty and that he was not moving to fill it. He got up and went to the sink to wet a sponge, last duty of the night.

"Maybe we go to the same woman, too. The touch of the goddess. There are women like that, you know. You long and you are afraid, maybe a little bit awed. That is the sign of the goddess in them."

David, thinking of Ariadne, began to sponge the counter.

"Horst, go to bed," he said.

"I must find it." Horst pounded his fist on the bar, and David caught his glass before it fell.

"Go to bed, Horst," he said, more gently this time.

Horst followed Huseyin across the road, avoiding the camel dung left over from the parade, and into the courtyard of Dürüst Osman's house. The guests from the gallery were crowded in the doorway making their formal goodbyes. "Ideally," Horst decided while he waited to be introduced to the judge, "modern Ceramos should be thrown away." He found himself sometimes, to his own embarrassment, yearning to do this. He dreamed of an army of caterpillars, bush hogs, and cranes to rootle and lift and break and shift it into the outer fields where there had never been much of value but tangerine groves and gardens, so that Endymion's hidden marble city could shine again in the sun.

He wanted to expose a jewel. Somewhere, in some cave, Endymion lay asleep. Sometimes he knew that he had already found the place, in the hieros gamos of the tomb. Sometimes doubts sprang on him out of dark places.

But as Horst's temptation was a bulldozer, his discipline was a toothbrush, and he told himself he had to be content with that.

He knew the city was there, somewhere under him. He had mapped it with the evidence he had. He stumbled over the name on undated stone fragments, he found temple columns split and used as door sills and stelae as tables in obscure kahves. He stood on it on the stone floor at the crest of the hill, still used as the town cemetery. He heard it in the hill's name— Mahtepe, moon hill—here was even a double clue. The older Ceramians remembered that it had been called Mâbettepe, temple hill, but in their ignorance they thought that there had been a Christian chapel there.

Horst had found the remains of old sacrificial feasts in a deep pit behind the floor. It was filled with murex shells that people mistakenly called Aphrodite shells when they had been sacred to Artemis. He saw a hint in faded letters on the window of the pension, misspelled the Endemon Pension. Evidence flirted with him in electric stars above the discotheque in the abandoned Greek villa at the foot of Annadağ, the sacred mountain. Until three o'clock in the morning, when he couldn't sleep for waves of impatience, it winked on and off outside his windows, ENDYMION, ENDYMION, ENDYMION.

But if he could be said to have had a true experience of love, it was in the never-ending catch of ecstasy as a breath, a quickening of his heart, when he stepped through the ruins of the eastern gate onto the road that led to the first cliffs.

Naturally, he suppressed the feeling when he could in the interests of science. "Romanticism," he told David, late at night, "is the German disease. Goethe was right. It is not health." So the language of his love was tufa, peristyle, dromos and tumulus, limestone and schist.

All the summer before, he had sat at the eastern gate, or in the valley below it, facing the mountain and waiting for some clue in the rock face, and for government permission to explore.

Once, at evening, he had come alone in desperation after the cows had been herded to the mountain village. He had lain there, smoking hashish, trying to stop trying to see so that he could see. Then, in his stupor, the face of the mountain had shown herself to him, so clearly that he would have worshiped her had he been able to move.

He had seen her veil flung out over the cliffs, her huge sad face, the hollow darkness of her cave eyes. He had traced her breasts, her stomach. Fortunately he still had consciousness enough to realize that what he saw was an illusion. The vision, he told himself sternly, was of the wrong period—an Ionic drug dream when it should, by his calculations, have been thalassocratic. Afterwards he had found nothing of the great face in the living rock, and he searched, more sensibly, for the mark of the adze and not the dream.

Mistake after mistake later he had finally glimpsed, after the heavy rains of winter, a dislodged rock that had hidden a scar on the cliff. He remembered how he had kept himself from excitement for a while. He had made so many secret mistakes, climbed up to natural rock that had so often taken the shapes of faces, colossal torsos, the broken heads of huge lions, double axes, entwined snakes—all, in fact, that he was looking for—only to find that the images faded as he got near them, became, under his clutching hands, only the natural stone of the seductive cliffs.

Then, as sudden as the breaking forth of understanding after the long dark road of intuition that seemed so often like a dream-laden sleep, he found form in the mountain, this time not imposed by his imagination but exposed by the mountain itself.

He saw that what had seemed a dry stream bed was, in fact, the vestiges of a road of sorts leading eastward from its throat between two cliffs. What had seemed before a natural fall of stones had been placed there by hands. The stones were great stairs up to the scar on the mountainside.

With the same precision of miracle, dur to some unthinking shift in the Ministry (more difficult to shift
than mountain boulders) he had been given permission
the summer before to dig for a few months. Every year
until he ran out of University of Minnesota money he
knew he would have to fight the battle of the permission again, a changeable battle where the enemy had
no name.

He had already been back in Ceramos for a month
waiting for the summer's permission, waiting to tell his
student helpers when to come, bouncing back and forth
on thirteen-hour bus rides to Ankara to wait before
shut doors, and making love from time to time to keep
his spirits up.

"I can wait them out," he told David. "The discipline of the toothbrush is teaching much patience." His
handsome dark Nordic face looked mournful when he
said it.

Now, driving up the valley behind the sea fringe of
houses that was modern Ceramos, past the tangerine
orchards and the lush gardens, he studied the profile of
the new young judge and decided that since he was an
Aegean Turk and a historian, and therefore a natural
poet, it was these hidden feelings that he would understand, and that the technical language of the dig would
be lost on him. It was a cool and judicious decision as
he studied the man's Phoenician, Celtic, Indo-Euro-
pean, Aegean cross-culture head, his dark hair, long
skull, pale face, blue eyes, the classic cornice of his
Aryan eyebrows, the fine Seljuk tilt of his chin.

They had reached the high outcropping that marked
the eastern gate of the ancient city wall. Its huge
squared stones lay half-hidden in the spring grass.

"Dur. Stop," Horst called to the driver, who thought
they were running into a goat and stopped so suddenly
that they were all thrown forward, and the evil eye
hanging from the windshield clattered against the glass.
"We must walk from here," Horst searched carefully
for the simplest English, "to experience the hieratic
quality of the approach as the ancients did." He unstrapped his compass from his wrist. "If you do not
mind, I must explain this in English. I know only
workman's Turkish," he apologized.

Huseyin was furious. He hated exercise, sweat, English, and enthusiasm equally.

Horst bounded up on the high mound of stone that had fallen from the sacred gate, and waited for the judge to climb up after him.

"I have worked this out." He adjusted the compass. "You see the opposite hill there?" He pointed behind them into the western sun to the conical hill behind the shipyard, now so far away that the agha's tomb was a speck of white. "As you no doubt know, it is still called Mahtepe, moon hill, but I believe this to be a corruption of Mâbettepe—temple hill.

The judge could not see the distant hill. The sun was in his eyes. He was thinking of how far a man had to compromise to stay in a position where he felt he was so needed. He brushed aside a wish that he had a fine pair of Zeiss sunglasses like Horst's. But the people in the villages frowned on such things. They thought that only a man with the double pupils of the evil eye would hide his eyes from them. They were right, of course, but for the wrong reasons. The judge dismissed the sunglasses as yet another sign of capitalist decadence, eyes weakened by luxury and drugs, Mafia eyes from American films.

"For a year I studied from there the face of the mountain, then from here at the gate." Horst showed the judge the compass. "You see, it faced due east. We tend," he included Huseyin, who was standing below with his back to them, "to decry the evidence of myth. This is wrong. Myth is a language to explain observed natural phenomena, as is the language of modern physics or mathematics or astronomy. Among the ancients it was acted out before it was written, metaphor as gesture.

"For example, you know of course about the ancient adoption ceremony. There the man, at whatever age he was to be adopted, often as the king, and sometimes as his substitute in the human sacrifice, would crawl through the legs of the queen, becoming, so, her born son. She would suckle him in public ceremony, one of the last ceremonies of matrilineal inheritance . . . but I digress, do I not?" Horst smiled.

Both Huseyin and the judge smiled back, and nodded with the air of concentrated interest that the Ceramians had found replaced understanding of foreign languages beyond their limited vocabulary. Huseyin had paid little attention anyway. He was studying a certain glitter in the rock, wondering if it were gold, and deciding it was only schist of some kind.

The judge's one interest outside his training at the law school (his pigeon, as his instructor from England had called it during his one year of teaching at the university before he was deported) was nineteenth-century political history. He was still wrestling with the English language by slowly deciphering what he could of his most valuable possession, which he kept in a locked box under his bed behind his chamber pot. It was the Little Lenin Library, published by Gollancz in the thirties, which the instructor had left him as a parting gift.

Horst, reading happily their looks of complete comprehension, almost launched into the origins of the circumcision ceremony itself. He could hear the music faintly in the distance coming from the houses where it would be performed, but not wanting to go too far afield, came back to the fragments of the gate that jutted over them, and pointed at it with the compass.

"Sermons in stone, as the English poet said. I prefer to call it metaphor in stone. And so, I worked on the theory that the tomb of Endymion either faced Annadağ, mother mountain, you understand, or, if the sacro-royal tradition was still extant when it was built, would be found on the eastern slope, within the mother—a return to the womb to be born again, resurrected, which," he ended with a happy rush, "explains not only the many stories of sleepers along this coast, from Endymion to the seven sleepers of Ephesus, a symbolic number, naturally, but the taking over of the tradition by the Christians when they ceased to be revolutionary and became dogmatic, in the resurrection of Christ from the rock tomb in the east. The past, informing, you see, from underground . . ."

The judge was pleased. He had understood two words, revolution and underground.

"A reactionary deviation?" he brought out hopefully.

"Well . . . yes," Horst answered, "I suppose it was
. . . Now will you please to turn to the east."

Politely they turned and faced the mountain. Beyond
the last small valley it rose, pure limestone stained by
rain and wind, in a series of unclimbable cliffs. Between them and the first rises of rock a valley nestled,
flower-decked, so green with spring that the olive trees
were blue against it. Two or three cows from the
mountain village grazed below them among the bright
yellow daisies and the blood drops of poppies. It was
bounded by giant round rocks that seemed flung down
in some furious old game by the thrust upon thrust of
rock that rose above them, now so near they had to
look almost straight up to see the sky.

Halfway up the third tier of rocks on the bald face
of the cliff, the square columns of the entrance to the
royal tomb were the golden pink color of a human
blush. The jeep driver thought they were going to pray,
but Horst began to point again instead.

"You see how the rust has made the rock into the
human color. This is *not*," he added sternly, "an accident, you know. Come now." He bounded down from
the wall into the valley, as familiar with the way as one
of the goats, and waited for the two men to climb
slowly down after him. The judge, who had been raised
in the mountains, was slow because he was wearing his
best shoes and could not afford to scuff them, Huseyin,
because he had been on the mountainside only once in
his life and scorned such activity as a vice for peasants.

It took nearly an hour for them to climb
to the dig and rest on the ledge of grass below the cliff
tomb. Now, near enough to touch, lichen and strong
small mountain plants, rain and wind, had painted the
cliff around the tomb gray-blue, white, green, and pink;
what had seemed dead rock was a live vertical garden.
In front of them the lowest deep-cut room was exposed, a dark, square maw. A second square-cut tomb
was cut into the rock above it and to the right. Be-

tween the rooms, cut through the rock, they could see the body-size openings that connected them.

The third and highest had been the royal chamber. It reached deeper into the mountain. Its walls were still faintly etched and painted. Above it a deep, hollow corridor ran upward to the right to the floor of the shrine. The openings had been cut so far back in the tombs that at first glance there seemed no connection between the black square rooms, the corridor, and the shrine above. It was only now that they could see that it was a single labyrinthine house of the dead.

Around them on the grass were neatly piled fragments of stone labeled with numbers. A small hut was almost hidden by a huge rounded rock like those they had passed all along the giant stairsteps of little valleys. Horst knelt and pointed. "You see, the interior of these rocks has been hollowed out for sepulchers, of course long since robbed, probably not long after they were used." He stood up and swept a wide arc with his arm along the steep way they had climbed. "You will find that most of the rocks we climbed over are tombs, probably second millennium. We humans have always wanted to be buried near sacred places."

Looking down to the now tiny valley in the distance, they seemed to be standing on another mountain. There was no sign of the rejecting cliffs. Eons of topsoil had washed down and lodged behind the outcrops to form a series of gentle green slopes all the way to the valley floor. It could have been a series of secret gardens, this other face of the mother mountain.

"These," Horst pointed to the numbered stones, "camouflaged the entrance, except for a small gap behind them, probably used by worshipers. Initiation? Perhaps. You will have to step back to see the goddess."

Huseyin tried not to look down as they teetered on the edge of the shelf.

"My God, you should have been here the day we took away the stones before the image. She had been hidden from the weather, but the mountain damp had rusted the iron in her, and she seemed almost human—the color of her skin. Artemis as the mother-lover of Endymion."

She was slightly larger than life-size. She stood in deep relief in a square niche between the two columns of the shrine. She was so primitively cut it was as if the rock already had made her, and was only aided here and there by the bronze adzes that had formed her. The sightless hollows of her eyes seemed to stare straight west at the distant low hill on the western edge of the town. The stumps of her handless arms rested on crouched lions on either side of her. They were so eaten and pocked by time that they had almost shed the marks of men's craving, and returned to the boulders from which they had been formed.

"What saved the royal tomb," Horst was ignoring Huseyin and spoke only to the judge, "was that it was not behind the image, as you would, of course, have thought, but in the secret chamber below it. Even so, tomb robbers had found it, probably the pirates that for so many centuries infected," he corrected himself, "infested this coast. But they were looking only for gold. They left the other artifacts. You will see them in the castle. The first time we saw her . . ." He wanted to keep speaking of the moment, as a man in love will keep speaking a name, to relieve the time and gaze of it.

The judge, while he had long ceased to pay attention to what Horst was saying, caught his lurch into ecstasy like a blow. He was surprised at such physically transmitted excitement, which to him seemed almost sexual, in a man who he had already been told was a member of the CIA. The dig was only a cover. He knew that. After all, why else would the money for it have come through an American university to a German national? The naiveté of it appalled him. He retreated into an official smile.

Horst read it with the old fear. As a new left student in Berlin he had seen such smiles all too often, seen them close doors, uproot, destroy with their benign and dangerous, consciously misunderstanding. The light went out of him. What could he expect when he knew that half the officials in Ceramos were in the pay of the CIA?

"It will," he said, trying to hide bitterness, "be a draw for tourists."

The judge nodded. "Yes, I think so," he said, not believing it. Tourists, that strange breed, liked the big Roman ruins, the frail Greek temples, not this archaic, heavy, brutal tomb he wanted suddenly to get away from. He turned to Huseyin and said in Turkish, "I must go back. I am expected at the Police Station."

Huseyin had been staring down at the thin rim of the modern town around the bays, not seeing it, deep in fury that the sculpture that was even more valuable than gold had been found by Horst, the young fool, and stored away in the castle without a hope of it being sold. He looked back and swore to himself. All afternoon, having promised his friend, the Captain of the Gendarmes, he had been steering the young judge away from the Chief of Police. "Why not?" he said, with a deep despairing shrug of his shoulders.

Horst was no longer beside them. He had darted behind the shed. He brought out Kemal, holding him tight by the hair. The judge saw a frightened boy who looked about ten years old. He stared up at the men, his eyes completely still, like a caught fox.

"Empty your pockets," Horst said, in his curt Turkish. The boy hunkered down and began to dig at his pockets.

"He is a crazy boy," Huseyin said. "He is mute—a dummy. He steals whatever he can get his hands on."

Kemal obviously had understood Horst. He laid out on the grass slowly, one by one, a rusty nail, a crumpled pack of cigarettes, a key, a box of matches, a sweetmeat stuck with tobacco, a terra-cotta arm, a votive lamp, five small Ceramian coins, an iron stud, three stubs of candles, a dirty piece of string.

Kemal kept very still, kneeling within the circle of the men like trees over him, ready to lower their branches with a clout. He would not cringe. He had learned that it brought on the fist, the thrown rock. He had long since learned, too, never to lift his eyes to their faces. He had been caught in such circles since he was small. Always the circle was tree-tall, hovering, attacking from star level. So he had learned to read danger in a different way, judge it, think it out, read it coolly, with the country quickness that seemed slow. It worked with animals, too. The snake he inspected, keeping as still as the snake, would never bite him.

He lifted his eyes up the column of legs as far as the genitals. The genitals of the German, Horst, he trusted. They bulged, boy cock-proud on the body of a man. He wore tight, bright red trousers that showed them off. He wore his balls as some of the gavur girls wore their breasts, thrust out proudly, but somehow unused. He knew that Horst could not hold a woman and he was sad for him. He had heard that from the men in the cafés, who said he would fuck a chicken and so only got women as stupid as chickens. But he trusted him anyway because of his deep love for the mountain, even though he took too many of the stones away, put numbers on them, and so killed them, as when his brother would stretch out frogs on a board and study everything about them but their slow cleverness and pulse.

The genitals of Huseyin were always hidden, coiled under his Frankish coat. It was hard not to cringe before them. Huseyin, whenever Kemal's brother was not there to protect him, had always made a game of him. He had given him hot peppers and made him eat them. Once he had offered him a drink he thought was sage tea but it was piss. He used him now that his brother was no longer able to help him to show off to tourists.

"Crazy boy," he would call in English and clout him on the head or make him dance or send him for er-

rands and throw his tip on the ground. Once, when he
was young, he had grabbed Huseyin's leg in his teeth
and hung on like a furious dog while Huseyin danced
him up and down within a jeering circle. When he was
loose he beat Kemal so badly on the head that he
learned never to attack him again. Kemal had roused
laughter, though, that was at Huseyin and not at himself, and he had defended himself without his brother's
fist. He was proud of that, too, although later it was his
brother and Munci who had walked through the town
and had found Huseyin and beaten him in front of everyone.

He never understood why his brother had never
fought again after that. All the men knew better than
to anger him. It was only when he had gone away to
the University, a place Kemal knew nothing of, somewhere beyond the mountains, that the teasing had begun again, worse than ever. Huseyin said that he stole.
He did now, but he had never done it before, and
Huseyin made it sound as if he had done it all his life.

The other genitals, the strange ones, he knew nothing of them. They too were hidden behind the kind of
official dark suit that men wore when they went to
court or to a wedding. He saw beyond the neatness,
now ruffled by his climb, that this man was poor. His
shoes had been repaired. His socks cost twenty-five
kurush in the Pazar. The hands that hung down by the
sides of his coat were quiet hands. Kemal liked them.
They were not hands that hit, but hands that turned
the pages of books, hands that had too little sense in
their tips, unused, unblooded hands. He felt sorry for
the hands. They knew too little.

Kemal was fourteen, and even though younger boys
were as big as he was, his genitals had grown. He was
proud of them. He thought them wise, how they sought
out and stirred at the sight of girls as if they had their
own eyes.

Horst's knees bent, and he was beside him on the
grass. His fingers picked out the lamp, the arm, one of
the coins from the little pile of his treasures. Kemal
hoped they would not touch the iron stud. He had a

use for that. But they did. "Kemal," he heard him say.
He liked the quiet, patient way he said his name, not
screaming as his mother did sometimes or sounding
ashamed of him like his father. Horst took him by the
chin and turned his head toward him.

"You must show me where these things came from.
I have told you that. It is wrong to take them from
their places." He turned away from Kemal to the others. "The boy is a deaf-mute. I have to be gentle with
him. He knows the mountain like an animal. Now," he
said slowly, turning back to Kemal and forming his
words carefully with his full lips, "tell me where these
things came from."

Kemal felt tears come into his eyes. He had not
known before that, like the others, Horst thought he
read lips, that he was deaf as well as dumb. Now he
was treating him as the others did, as if he could not
hear or feel because he could not speak. Often, because he liked him, Kemal had shown Horst more of
the mountain than he wanted to. Now, with the small
betrayal in front of Huseyin, he knew he had been
fooled by his longing for a friend into misreading his
easy kindness.

One thing comforted him. He knew that even when
the tourists struggled up the mountain, the old ladies in
their sneakers, the puffing curious men who talked so
much, they would be satisfied with what he had shown
Horst and would not seek any further. It would be part
of his protection, as it was of the mountain. They
would be knowing and satisfied, as they were satisfied
with the polite faces of the Ceramians behind which
they hid.

For the first time he lied to Horst about his
treasures. He pointed down the mountain toward the
line of hollowed rocks.

"Which one?"

Kemal held up three fingers and pointed with his left
hand.

"You see," Horst passed the harness stud up to the
judge, "the incision of the double axe."

He held the tiny clay arm out, and Kemal raised

four fingers, lying with his eyes to make sure Horst believed him, and pointed to the right.

"We must go," the stranger said.

For a long time Kemal watched them wind their path down through the tiers of valleys, no longer like men, but smaller. When they were far away, dog-size, he spat a gold coin from his mouth to his hand, polished it on his pants, and inspected it. The double axe. A man had to live. He gathered the cigarettes, the matches, the coins, the rusty nail, the string, and shoved them back into his pocket.

It was five o'clock by the sun that sat, huge and red, above the opposite side of the hand of hills that held Ceramos in its palm, by the faint lines of cooking smoke from the chimneys, above all, by the direction of black dots of boats, homebound as sea cattle, patiently riding the glass-calm dark bay toward the harbor to tether to the small circle of the quays.

Kemal read safety from the time, crept behind the shed, picked up the bread, the white cheese, the beer he had hidden there and slung the string bag over his shoulder. He climbed into the first chamber tomb of the mountain.

He had felt sorry for Horst before for his controlled ecstasy when he had found the false front to the shrine. Out of pity he had shown him the right-hand labyrinth through the front chamber tombs, the series of cut holes that linked them. They were the camouflage for the true path of the mountain, her hidden, holy chambers. Sometimes, when they had been friends, he had felt guilty at misleading Horst, but he had seemed so pleased, even at the false façade he called his discovery, that Kemal had put away his guilt.

Now that they were no longer friends, he began to smile as he lay flat in the corner of the third of the connecting cave rooms and brushed a surface of sand and pebbles several inches deep from a large round stone that lay in what seemed a natural niche beside the connecting passage. He lifted it easily. It was a hollow lid. On its underside there was a deeply incised carving of the labyrinth, the octopus, the thalassic god. Kemal set it against the wall of the niche and covered it with debris. Below lay what looked like a shallow well.

Kemal entered its black maw like a snake, head downwards. The passage sloped for the length of a body, then curved upwards until Kemal's fingers found the carved toeholds that led upwards like a ladder. He began to climb through the jet-black dark, his body brushing rock as smooth as glass, running with damp. His fingers knew that if there were light on it, it would shine. He could feel his body moving left into the true labyrinth. He thought how now and always there was that lie that protected the truth, as the iron stud protected the gold coin in his mouth, the discovered secret that protected the hidden one, the counterclockwise world.

He crawled upward through a narrow chimney, knew with his body the way around the turnings, reached a small black chamber, slid up into it, his fingers feeling his way around the runnels of a carved rock in its center, felt around the walls until he came to the first jutting stone step of the last labyrinth and began to climb again. The beer bottle clinked faintly against stone. He shrank, gathering his intelligence in his fingers.

It had taken him half an hour to climb three hundred feet up through the familiar blackness of the mountain arteries. At first, when he was still afraid, it had taken him longer. When he was nearly at the top, and could see the first glimmer of pearl light, and smell the faint smell of urine, faeces, and the uncured lamb and goat skins he had stolen from behind the butcher's, he made the only sound he could, a faint, sweet whistle of a song.

Timur heard the whistle and knelt to help his brother up the last carved rung into a large chamber, opened to the outside air by two circular cave eyes as big as windows, the eyes that Horst had seen in his drugged vision. They kissed and held each other. Timur struck one of the matches that Kemal put into his hand, and lit a cigarette, safe now that for a time the setting sun would blot out any tendril of smoke from the eyes.

Kemal emptied his pockets again, this time on the slab of live rock, carved into an altar. As busy as a housewife, he dumped the candle stubs and the string into a wall niche where, under the faint painting of a red new moon, there was already a pile of wax fragments. He stood, not knowing what to do, the rusty nail in his hand. He had been pleased to think of bringing it, but now, looking around the familiar walls, streaked and runneled by damp that formed figures of its own, green, black, glistening with nitre, he was ashamed. There was nowhere to use it, not the bare cave surface, not the traces of plastered wall, painted red and yellow, not the jutting bull horns where Timur hung his jacket, or the horned moon, or the women with their legs spread, their arms grasping leopards, the face of the lion being born from their damp, streaked clefts, or their mouthless faces staring blind-eyed at the late sunlight. He was embarrassed.

Timur, as he always had, read Kemal's easy shame that showed more clearly than in other faces because he could not speak, took the nail, and began to clean the spilled wax away from one of the votive lamps. He made a pile of it, and threw it on the fragments in the niche.

He set the lamp down on the floor at the entrance of the great woman-shaped cavern at the back of the room that disappeared deep into the black belly of the mountain. In its entrance a chthonic guardian figure stood as natural and mysterious as a stalagmite. It reached up into the shadows beyond the light of the sun.

"That was what I needed." Timur said the first words of the evening. He lay back on the skins of his bed on one of the stone benches, where he had cleaned away the bones of a man. He had laid the bones carefully on the floor in their right order. It amused him to think that he was keeping up with his study of anatomy with the perfect skeleton of a young man, dead three thousand years. There was something humbling about the fact that they were the same, nothing changed, developed, evolved, in all that time. The man had been hanged or garroted. The third cervical vertebra was bitten deep by the gold-torqued snakes that still lay around the neck bones when he had moved them. The gold mask over its skull, the great bronze double axe, the sword and greaves, the bronze anetlopes, the two great age-green bronze shields with their faint swirling octopi, he had set in the corner carefully to wait until he could sell them, but the round gold helmet it pleased him to drink from. He lay smoking, with the setting sun piercing the cave eyes with two gold arrows of dust that now lit the altar table, his pile of books and papers, the busy hands of his brother cutting the bread and cheese. He felt domestic, and almost happy.

Kemal waited until he had smoked, and handed him his supper. He poured the beer into the helmet and presented it to him. If Timur was only contented at this time of the evening, Kemal's happiness was perfect. Watching the black-bearded face of his brother, the long, thick hair, he did not understand why he had to stay hidden in this place, and he could not ask. His dumbness sealed all but the simplest questions that he could act out.

In the night six weeks before, Kemal had heard the scratch at the wooden shutters of the window of their house. He had gone out past his nodding parents, who had heard nothing but the high wind of March that was growing into a storm. His brother crouched in a shadow of the stone stairs.

Kemal acted out no questions. He thought that it had something to do with the fact that Timur was a university student. He knew the army did not like students, but the whys of it were dim. His father's radio, the holy radio, used words he did not know. It sat in the place of honor in their house with flowers beside it, and no one but his father ever touched it. Some students had killed people with bombs. He had no idea why. There was something called an anarchist, but whether you ate it or hunted it or shot with it he did not know. He had seen pictures of students with beards and hair like Timur on a big poster at the Gendarmerie when he carried tea there from the café. The Captain of the Gendarmes had put a large red cross over the face of each one reported killed, and a blue cross over the face of each one captured. He was a very meticulous man. His father said all the students ought to be burned, but he did not know why.

That wind-lifted night his brother had not looked like one of them. He had been clean-shaven, handsome in his city jacket, but it was no protection from the cold. He kept shivering as he whispered, "I must hide. Tell no one. I will go to the mountain. Come at dawn and be sure no one sees you. You must hide our entrance. Have they started the dig yet?"

Kemal clicked his tongue and nodded no. Turning his face and hands to the moon where his brother could see them, he acted out four workmen only, no foreign students, and Horst. When he acted Horst, the innocent sexual swagger, the orders, he heard Timur laugh softly in the shadow.

Then, after he watched Timur slip away, carrying nothing but a bag of books and a piece of bread his mother had put out for the chickens, he went back into the house buttoning his pants so his parents would not question him. At first he took it for granted that Timur had killed a man, but then he remembered that Timur had sworn never to fight again, and Timur never broke a vow. It was the only thing that disappointed him about his brother. He loved it when he fought.

In the first days his mother complained so much that a fox was stealing eggs from the nest that his father sat out all night with his shotgun. After that Kemal had to range farther and farther afield for food. It was easier finally to leave the village and go down into Ceramos, play the fool, hang around the quays, no matter how many blows he gathered. The pickings were good, and he was honored by the fact that he was doing it for his brother.

Now, six weeks later, he watched this shaggy man who seemed to be going to live inside the mountain forever, had, in fact, made it comfortable with the trash, the pickings he had gathered. Kemal saw himself as a flying father bird that brings old rags, string, wool, wood shavings to build into the perfection of a nest. There were already evening rituals, habits of home, like the one he always waited to begin until he couldn't wait any longer. His brother would not ask, he would not show, until finally, supper over, the time came and he unbuttoned his pants and from the seat of them brought out the newspaper he knew Timur would hide behind, forgetting him while he read it. He kept putting it off while Timur drank his beer and the gold helmet flashed in the last of the sun. He knew Timur would be angered or saddened; the day would be over. There was something he was searching for in the paper, and when he did not find it, or when he found something that made his fist clench, he would sit, staring at nothing, leaving Kemal to a kind of darkness.

He handed him the paper, and lost him.

The setting sun had climbed up the stalagmite form that guarded the cavern behind them, its delicate inset hands, its hanging breasts, and lit the face of the goddess. Time and water had rusted the marble the color of young flesh. From the deep empty caverns of her eyes, where centuries of blown rain and the living damp of the cavern had washed out the lapis of her pupils, she stared now, aloof at evening, almost cruel. Her eyebrows, carved deep above the empty sockets, were black streaks of shadow. Only fragments of their inlay were left; the rest was lost in the thick dust of the cave floor. Her small, changeable mouth was calm. Faintly over her body, and flung behind her on the cavern walls, the ochre streaks of her robe soared upward toward her carved and painted hair, as if she had flown down to light, for a moment, in the arch. Neither of them saw this miracle of movement made, only for a minute, by the fast-falling sun. Tımur was too intent on the paper, Kemal was too concerned with how his brother would be for the last of the best time of his day.

At last Timur folded the paper and put it with the others under the skins to make a softer mattress for his bed.

Kemal knew it would come, the question. Hanging his head didn't stop it, he had tried that. "I'm not blaming you," Timur said when he did that. "I know you are trying."

He was trying, trying to follow Timur's orders, every sentence of them. "Find Lale. I have told her about you. As soon as you can see her alone, walk with her to the beach. Write T with your finger in the sand. Nod no to her. Now. That is all you do. Understand?"

Every day he followed her. She was always with the others, this dark lady, this hanımefendi with the painted nails and mouth. How could he make such a lady look at him so she would see he was like his brother? How could he do that? When they sat at the kahve table, there were too many students. In the boat there were too many. He wasn't even sure it was the right Lale—so many Lales, so many tulips, so many flower girls at the bayram. Yesterday he had thought up a story to make Timur a little happier, how she had gone to his father's house. Today he could think of nothing.

Timur knew by Kemal's face that there was no use in asking him if he had made contact. He asked instead, "What was she doing?"

Kemal ran to the eye of the mountain and pointed to Yazada, the summer isle.

"How many did she go with?" Kemal held up his hands twice, twenty.

"Had she come back when you left the town?" Kemal threw back his head and clicked his tongue, no.

Timur could see Lale, the sad wonder of her face, the downward tilt of her head. It was an agony to him that he could not send her a note to tell her he was safe, but he was afraid she was being watched. All he dared was the T in the sand. All he could rely on was

Kemal's muteness—the police could not question him.
He knew what happened to girl students the police
caught, the thrust of the baton into the vagina, the release of secrets and blood. He knew she had come under the protective camouflage of the bayram to meet
him, and all she would find was a T in the sand, and
the nod—no—until the wind changed, and amnesty
was announced in the dirty newspaper that Kemal
picked up every day in the street.

He knew she was searching for some hint of news
from him. Only yesterday, Kemal had acted her walk
up to his village from the town, alone, watching behind
her for fear of being followed. She had stood for a long
time outside his father's house. When his mother saw
her, she covered her face. The strange city girl in her
western clothes had knelt and drunk from the fountain,
and then walked through the ruined gate toward the
mountain, drawn there. Kemal had followed her, but
when he tried to catch up to her, she had ran back
toward the town again, afraid of being alone with the
strange boy, too afraid to see that he looked like his
brother, young and silent. Kemal had acted all this for
him, first Lale, then his mother. Timur did not know
that it was no longer Lale's face that he recalled when
he longed for her, but the face of the goddess behind
him as it looked in the first light of dawn, its yearning
shadowed sadness.

The sun sat for its final flaming moment on the opposite hill, then plunged behind it, leaving the sky
glowing, the clouds the strident pink that is only beautiful when it rides the high air and is gone. It was time
to leave. Kemal took the urns, one half-filled with his
brother's dirt, and disappeared down the long passage.
Now, at deep twilight, he was safe. No villager would
set foot on the mountain at dark for fear of the evil
spirits. By the time he had gone to the spring, buried
Timur's dirt and washed his chamber pot and filled the
other urn with water, and made two trips back to the
room in an ecstasy of care to leave no traces, the sky
was already deep purple.

Kemal set the round stone back into its place and
piled the sand and stones over it and smoothed them
flat. From the eye where he sat, Timur could only

faintly see Kemal's shadow among the black rocks as
he disappeared, elusive as an animal, and he was left
alone.

T imur set the shields over the windowed
eyes, lit the votive lamps, and forced himself to work.
Dreams dulled his mind, anatomy fragmented into
visions. Kemal returned, now so small in his mind that
he was still plunging around the courtyard of his father's house, with the blind bravery and trust of a baby
learning to walk. When Kemal moved into his mind
like that, Timur saw him in motion always, his early
agonized attempts to speak, his retreat from his father,
who treated the boy as he would have a defective animal that could not, by some thin taboo, be killed.

He knew that his father and the village men, who
treated Kemal with the mixture of kindness and teasing
they did with holy naturals, would have turned him
into the imbecile they thought he was. Timur, instead,
had seen something more than the gulf between the
child and the world. He had seen his silent pleas across
it. So he had taught him to read. He remembered the
day when Kemal acted out the whole of Ali Baba for
him. He had fought for him, fought for the intelligence
and trust he knew were in his eyes. Kemal in return
had given him ambition.

The silence, the grace he found in him, the questions
that could not be answered, had driven Timur to study
into the cold nights before the one dying fire, while the
blanket-wrapped boulders of his parents and his
brother lay asleep on their floor mats in the room's
shadows. The geometry, the grammar, the reading,
was, each night, each day in the village school, a step,
a step away from ignorance and cruelty and taboo and
toward this night and this book, the anatomy of the
tongue, the throat, the vocal cords.

When he won the scholarship to the secondary
school, the schoolmaster came and argued long into the
night with his father. He could hear the rumble of their
voices, now as loud as separate words, now a murmur

as they drank coffee and smoked and bargained like men in the Pazar for his future.

When he and Kemal had discovered the cave tomb, they had kept their discovery as a secret, that instinct for secrecy bred into them by punishment of the muteness of one and the alien intelligence of the other that his father called the bidat—the sin of his questioning mind.

It had not, even then, been quite real, a thing that happened to Alladin, not to him. They had squeezed themselves behind a boulder on the mountain, hoping to find the old coins the foreigners seemed to like, and in the dim light that filtered through the rock fissure had found the empty square tomb, and dug like two dogs with their hands along the floor to where the earth was a little softer. At first Timur thought they had hit the rock floor, then his fingers followed a line, a circle around the stone.

They had brought back a pick from Munci's house—Timur's father and his uncle only owned one shovel between them, and they would have missed it, even for an hour. Timur could still hear the pebbles slide down the rock as he pried, and fall into space below as they lifted the great disk, surprisingly light. They had carried it to the streak of daylight and examined it, brushing with their hands the octopus, as new as the day it was carved.

Kemal, he was six then, had gone back and pointed down into the black hole. His total faith in Timur was like a dare. Timur lowered himself into the hole. He could feel again the directional turn of his body, the self-dare now to climb on, and, so much fear later, the faint light in the distance above him.

When he left to go to the University, he had never once crossed his legs or smoked a cigarette in his father's presence and he had never in his life slept in a room alone.

His father had given, grudgingly, his formal blessing, the kiss to eyes and forehead. After it Timur had stood while his mother cried and threw water behind him, splashing his new socks, so he would return. It had been his last look at the familiar whitewashed courtyard, the house so rooted it seemed grown out of the

rock, the rock cave of the stable where the fall calf
cried, tethered away from its mother's milk, the purple
and red masses of flowers his mother raised in whitewashed gasoline cans, the round stone well, the old
apple tree with its clenched fist of a trunk, the grape
arbor heavy with bronze pendants of grapes.

His father followed him out and stood beside him,
now scarcely as tall as his shoulder, though the boy in
Timur still felt a twinge of fear when he came so near.

"If you do not pray," his father had struggled with
words he was unused to, "if you join people who hate
our ways, may you weep over the grave of your first-
born son."

That sea-gnarled man, time-broken, afraid of any future he could not eat or milk or catch like a fish or
fashion with his hands, despising any god he could not
name, called after him again from the courtyard door
with all the bitterness of a man shut away from his
own first-born's future, "May you weep over the grave
of your first-born son!" and his voice was full of old,
rusty tears.

Timur left behind him all he had known with his
senses and the pride of his body and temper that was
the only virtue he had been taught a man should have.
That, the fear of the other boys of provoking him, their
admiring awe, he had grown ashamed of as something
to shed before he ever knew why. When he had beaten
Huseyin unconscious, all the zest of his anger for Kemal, his bitterness for his own struggle, had been behind his fist as it smashed into the rich, cruel face. He
knew, seeing him lying on the quay, seeing the grins of
his friends, the ignorant darkness of their admiration,
that it was part of what he had to turn from, in them,
and in himself.

Until Timur had begun to study the anatomy of the
throat, and realized that Kemal was condemned forever
by ignorance and poverty to the life of a half-man, he
had not understood why his father had threatened to
curse him. It was then, ruthlessly, he had cut the vast
red umbilicus of his inheritance and entered with his
heart and his sorrow for his brother into a future that
had no past.

He was a lonely, awkward country-bred boy among

the fast-talking Istanbul boys with money clinking in the pockets of their rich jackets. Then he had found his friends, like himself medical students from the villages, with the marks of struggle on them. One of them spoke to him for the first time outside of the classroom, took him by the arm, and he was swept into the bright future as into a fast-flowing river. When he had been knocked unconscious once by a charge of the Gendarmes, new friends had taken him home, fed him, and cared for him like a brother.

He fell, or plunged rather, with all the pent-up fury of his loneliness into love with Lale, the city girl, the equal girl, whose ways he had never seen in a woman before. Hers was the first live woman's body he had ever seen, an enchantment of flesh. She had listened, and he remembered her listening as more eloquent than speech, and more wise, to the spate of words he never knew he had, and it made him feel foolish and happy to talk so much.

The page before him swam in the lamplight. Loneliness engulfed him before he knew it was coming. It never came like this in daylight, empty and heavy and dark. Then he could hear the workmen, men he had known and grown up with, hear them call to one another beyond the hidden labyrinth that in certain winds made itself into a bullhorn for their voices.

He blew out the lamps and opened the eye windows to breathe the night. There was no town. The moon rode high. Its light obscured the stars and made the sea, surrounded by the black mainland and the distant islands, like a great leaden silver lake. The clover curve of the land was black, etched with little galaxies of fallen stars. Ceramos was only a thin cluster of pin-pointed lights reaching around the two harbors, its starfish shape defining the invisible hollows between the hills around it. The castle towers were brushed with a dim mist of diffused light. Across the great gulf, the Greek island towns were thin fine threads of light in the distance.

At the end of Yazada, and along the coastal hills, he could see the navigation beacons. At the shallow cove he knew so well at Yazada, the riding lights of clustered boats made a faint galaxy of their own as they moved in the water. He could see Lale there, staring out into the darkness, her contained self apart from the others. He longed to be with her, free of this running that had begun so innocently, free not to care.

When he had seen all the violence he had hated in himself grow among the students, the blood violence with a new face, he had had to leave them as he had left everything before and go on alone. He found their acts, the kidnappings, the blind anger, the bombs in crowded neutral streets, sympathetic, terrible and naive. They seemed not to know that there was another way, slower, knitted as a bone knits. There were no words to tell them. They had forgotten how things grew; they had never been condemned to patience.

When the police roundup had begun, he had been on the list. His scholarship had been withdrawn. That was in the first wave; the second, as at sea, was bigger. The arrests began. He had stood in the city street, afraid to appear at the job he had found loading trucks.

It was an ordinary tea kahve in an Istanbul street, too narrow for cars. There was a fish head in the gutter the cats had not found. There was a dirty spoon on the table, and two paper napkins under a water carafe. Lale picked up the spoon and kept playing with it, turning it over and over. Neither of them dared to cry for fear of the police.

"At the children's bayram when there are so many students we will not be noticed in Ceramos. We will meet there. Make your way." He told her then about Kemal and what to do. The T in the sand, like a child's game.

She went first out of the door. He noticed that her back was very straight and that her hair fell away below her shoulders. He stayed, looking beyond a newspaper until he was sure she was not followed. It was a game, surely it was that, arama tarama, search and seize, arama tarama—the beginning of a song . . .

He had not asked her who her family was or where she lived when she was not with him or at the Univer-

sity. Facts he did not know could not be beaten out of
him.

When Lale walked out of the door of the kahve they
had known each other exactly three weeks.

There was nothing to do but make his way home to
hide, to wait, as a boat finds a cove until the storm
passes. Now he had only one battle left. It was not to
forget his bright future.

The evening call to prayer was spreading from minaret to minaret in the darkness, mapping the space of
the town as faint as wind. He did not know how long
he sat watching, so long that, as too often before in the
six endless weeks, it was as if the mountain herself
were using his eyes to watch the seedling lights below.

He feared sinking into that dark state of seeing that
had no end. Behind the hollow eyes that were his windows, behind Horst's false statue below, through the
façade of the cave, deep within the empty eyes of the
stone woman behind Timur in the cavern, deep, deep
into the black corridors, there were others blindly staring, behind them others, deep, unending, within the living mountain where he could sink forever, no bedrock.
He could see the soles of his father's clean feet as he
bobbed his forehead to the prayer rug, see his blind
unquestioning trust, his dirty hidden heart. Such dark
dream mist repulsed him. He made himself recite in a
whisper the parts of the body, the bones, the glands,
the muscles, the diseases of the trachea.

In the valley below, the discotheques had begun
their nightly pulse beat, mingled with the humming of
Japanese transistors. He caught the sound of the
nearest, in the old burned-out Greek villa at the foot of
the mountain, but no music—only, from so far away,
the insistent beat, and the tiny fuzzy light word, EN-
DYMION, winking on and off. He got down from the
window, thinking he would try to sleep, caught the
beat in his body, and began to dance in the moonlight.
He danced until he was tired at last, and then lay down
on his tomb, and tried, beyond the urgent rhythm of
his twenty-two-year-old muscles, to recall the necessary
future that kept eluding him.

He built a hospital from the treasures in the corner of the cave. He dammed the water of the deep cleft mountain stream that now wasted away into the sea in springtime, turning it brown with topsoil from the denuded hills. At least, he tried. But the vision kept fading, duller than his night passion, until he finally slept. Nothing moved now in the cave but his heart, his steady breathing. Only the hollow eyes of the goddess stared out into the moonlight.

It was midnight.

Vines grew over the walls of the office of the Chief of Police. They crossed the ceiling. They burgeoned in the corners, pyramids of glossy leaves. The leaves moved as the breeze fingered the prisms of the hanging lamp. Sometimes the Chief of Police could see them growing when he sat making himself timeless, and he thought of Dionysus and the sailors, but not often.

Mostly he thought of the Kurd country. Exiled to the alien coast of western Turkey, he had been homesick for twenty-eight years. He was a man made sad by circumstances. Within himself there was often great joy, unshared. It was simple for him. He had deeply loved his wife. She had died. No one else had ever replaced her. She had left no child with her face. He was telling all this to the young judge as they sat drinking raki. The judge had heard it before. They were old friends, comfortable together.

"It is not true," the Chief of Police was saying, "that a happily married man will marry again quickly when he is widowed. That is only one who loves marriage itself, not the woman."

The judge, who was married to a schoolteacher who he honestly had not thought about for five or six years, nodded, full of understanding. He leaned back in his leather chair, easy after the watchful afternoon. He was tired. What he had come for he still had not put into words, even to himself, and it was drawing near the

time to say it and he had a friend to say it to. He
tasted the relief of the moment, approaching it from
the side.

"That is why you came here?" He prodded the Chief
of Police with the question.

"Yes. In the mountains I thought only of her. Here,
at the sea, sometimes I can look at all this and
forget . . ."

"How is it . . . ?"

"My jail is empty," the Chief of Police said proudly.
"The jail of a good policeman is empty."

"There should be more like you."

"Oh, it is the time. The time makes jobs for bad
men to do. The Captain of the Gendarmes now . . ."
The Chief's pause was eloquent.

"He has made trouble for you?" They both knew the
answer.

"He wants me to give him jurisdiction . . . no, work
with him. He is obsessed. There are terrorists under his
bed. A dangerous man." He offered the judge a cigarette.

"It is hard for an honest man to know when to compromise and when to resign."

"Survive and wait. Things change."

They had nearly touched the point. They both
veered away from it. Down below on the quay they
could hear the late boats returning from Yazada, and
the sound of singing.

The Chief of Police began to sing, "I left my love in
the mountains and went to war. Only a fool would do
that. Now at night I watch the stars . . ."

They both enjoyed the song. The Chief had a beautiful voice.

"Dürüst Osman invited me to lunch. He wants a favor. If I do not go along they will start the rumor that
I am corrupt." When he finally got to the point, the
judge stated it quite simply. They were both completely
calm. The judge pulled his nose.

These two men, and their ancestors, had been facing
such facts through a thousand years of pressures. They
were as much a part of life as the camel shit one
avoided in the street.

The Chief of Police began to tell a story. He paused for the silence to give him the right dramatic pace for it.

"Last September, after the tourists had all gone, and the storks, there was a man. He owned a small meyhane—only four tables—beer and wine and good börek his wife made. It was beside one of Dürüst Osman's gardens. It was a favorite garden with lemons that produce all year. The old man likes the green lemons with his rakı. They have many such gardens, as you know. Dürüst Osman wanted to tear down the meyhane and put a deep well and irrigation pump there so he would not have to sacrifice any of his trees. The meyhane was this man's life. It had belonged to his father and his father's father. He would not sell. No one said a word to put pressure on him.

"Dürüst Osman owns the warehouse and the trucking company. His son Huseyin owns the boat that takes the garden produce and the fish to the Izmir market. Huseyin is also the müdür, the mayor. All of the villagers use his boat, all the fishermen with small boats. Not a word was said, mind you. But for two weeks the trucks were out of order, the warehouse was empty, the boat went into dry dock for some much needed repairs. There was no sugar, no tea, no rice, no oil at the bakals. The fish stank in the dock. The vegetables rotted. After two weeks the man who owned the meyhane came and offered to sell it to the family. Since the offer came from him they bought it at a good price. There was no law broken, nothing said. The oil, the rice, the sugar came back to the bakals. The trucks were fixed. The boat came out of dry dock. All this to get a convenient water pump placed near the road so it would not disturb the trees."

The Chief of Police poured more clear raki into their glasses and added water very slowly. He liked to watch the rakı grow opaque. He began to spread taramasalata on a piece of bread.

"Last winter a fisherman refused to give half his catch in return for permission to fish off their land. One of the private guards shot him. He said he was trespassing on the shore, but his boat was found at sea with his body slumped over his catch. It was outside the town so I could do nothing. The Captain of the Gendarmes is in more than their pay. He is in their bed. It is like being a spider web of steel."

He handed the bread to the judge.

"What have they asked you to do?"

"They want me to help them get permission to build a tourist hotel in the cove at Yazada."

"That is protected coast."

"There is no law for sharks." The new judge could not yet tell even his friend how gently, with what friendly concern Huseyin had informed him that he had heard a totally unfounded rumor from the American official who had sat across from him at lunch that he was in the pay of unfriendly powers. Huseyin whispered that he had of course stopped the rumor at once.

The judge's back had gone cold. It was not only himself who did not want to go to prison. He had no right to expose his wife to a prison sentence, even though he did not like her very much. He knew as soon as he got home he would have to burn his treasure, the Little Lenin Library. Allah, how could he be in the pay of a foreign power when he couldn't even afford three pairs of socks, with his widowed mother and two aunts to keep on his pay . . .

"Which stick are they holding over you?" the Chief of Police finally asked, although such directness was against both his manners and his nature. "There are four. They can accuse you of smuggling gold, drugs, guns, and antiquities." He ticked them off on his fingers. "They lay these rumors as a louse lays nits in your hair."

"Worse."

"Politics?"

They were silent for a long time.

"Aman Allah," the Chief of Police finally said. "They really want their hotel."

When the urgent knock came at the door neither had said another word for ten minutes.

Basil screamed over the voices of David's bar that he couldn't stand it for another minute. He finally shepherded his little flock out into the street. The electric music had been soft in the bar, but in the street the loudspeakers clashed in a continuous war of noise. The floodlit castle towers rose high above them in the black sky. The crowds flowed against them.

"Why does the crowd seem always to be walking the other way?" Ariadne said to Miranda, who was clinging to her arm for fear of being left behind. She turned to David, to keep Miranda from giving one of her long logical, sociological-psychological answers. Miranda gave it anyway, but no one heard her. They were passing through a barrier of singing students; behind them a taxi herded the crowd against the house walls of the narrow street with its incessant piercing horn. Lights spilled over their faces.

They had reached the point in the night where they clung together, wedded to intimacy, the next bar, the next step, each afraid of betraying the others by parting from them. They were no longer going, they were simply going on. Now that the bars and the discotheques were too crowded with students they were going on through the tunnel of street and bodies to drink more of the night on the terrace of Ariadne's house, but only Basil knew this.

Behind them Horst was trying to get away, only for a little while, without being noticed. He felt vaguely disloyal, but he knew that health was important. He leaned down, his lips breathed as sweetly as he intended on the tourist girl's ear.

"No one knows who carved it," he was whispering, "don't you think that the artist as a personality is a passing capitalist phenomenon?"

"I don't know," she whispered back, "you'll have to ask my friend. That's her bag."

Horst's lips moved two centimeters forward and touched her lovely stupid ear. He sighed.

"It's funny," she said. "I could have bet money you were from California."

He guided her away from the crowd and up a rock lane where the houses had been built touching close as a protection against pirates.

Miranda had picked up a young Ceramian flute player, who was being ignored, saddened, and drowned out by the loud American music that poured out of the doors of the bars. While her head was dealing in abstractions to inform Ariadne, her secret hand, almost unnoticed even by herself, was feeling at his crotch. The flute player did not like it. He thought of the young girls he could not afford while she made his trousers tighter and tighter. He was afraid he would spurt into her impatient hands and foul his new jeans. Oh well, she paid. Everyone knew that.

"Now this is something you just can't catch with a camera," Trader said, as the taxi caught up with them and flattened them against the wall, but no one heard him.

David, drawn by some urgency in Ariadne's face, had left his bar to Taner and his brother on a night when the money rolled across the counter, enough to pay for rent, bribes, and supplies for weeks ahead. She had her way of calling him, without saying a word, and this unspoken request he clung to, knowing she called to him, David, and not some function he served. He spent so many nights listening, with his acquired bartender's tact and necessity, to the demands to take seriously, if only for a drunken evening, the parodies of constancy, parodies of affection, quick, flashing parodies of hate, the intimacies and tears of last night, or last year, the names of old lovers or old enemies who had passed through Ceramos.

For most of the year he honored, compassionately, their disguises, the clean hands of businessmen posing as sailors, the anti-Semitic Jews from the Levant masked for protection as émigré aristocrats from defunct regimes. He understood the sad translation of their pride, their questing hopeless hope, although he carried his own Semitic blood with grace, scorning their fear.

He watched the shamed homosexuals, naked in their hidden signals, flirting with women. Something in the Ceramian air, the country sophistication of the people, he recognized and learned. They took the disguises of the strangers for granted and did not strip them, out of good manners, good business, and a kind indifference.

So he had learned to let alone the old, pretending to be richer than they were, and the young, pretending to be poorer. The only self-protection he indulged in was to forget their names, and remember, if at all, only the categories of their sorrows.

But once in a while, one too preoccupied, too tired, too unashamed to hide or be forgotten came to him as he sat at his still point in the corner of the bar, and then, as on this night, this year, and in this street, he chose them for his friends, as he had Horst and Ariadne, for the time being. He kept that warning of time in his blood, immune to disappointment.

He had traveled so far. The journey had begun in the black hold of the boat, hidden with his mother, huddled among the filth of refugees sick in the winter sea, from Holland to England. From there, as extra-legal as a cur, he had wandered through the postwar cities, alone, until he was cast up on the shores of Ceramos, a Jewish Odysseus seeking an illusion to sustain him.

Something in him refused to go on. Why? He had adopted Ceramos as one would adopt a mother, in time of need and change. Why did he step ashore on such a pier to find himself at home—not better, not happier, but more at home than in all the other landings? He didn't know. He only knew that it had happened to him.

David understood, he thought, more than the others where he was in this street, this little lost city. For four thousand years Ceramos had been a city of refugees as most ports are, of people in flight. To him that slow flight, the perpetual glance over the shoulder, the quick illusive consolations of passing security, was the secret that he shared with them. Under all the surfaces, cares, individual isolated luxuries of sorrow or joy, there were to him three kinds of men: the conquerors, the residue of the conquered, and those who fled. In the word fled he saw and joined the streaming ones, lodged always, if they stopped at all, as leaves caught for a pause against the shores of world-old flood waters, knowing that there was nothing safe, nothing, not a chair, not a glass, not a roof, a house, a street, a law, a friend.

Sometimes he caught a glimpse of something in himself that was drawn to Ariadne so deeply that, had he not been so without illusion, he would have called it love. For the first time since those short years when he had been allowed to be a child, she made him feel young.

He guided her now, reading in her preoccupation a need to get out of the narrow street to where it opened again onto the great curve of the eastern harbor to sea-lap and the night. One night, some night, he would tell her, no, ask her what it was, but the night had not come. There were always the others, pressing close, no privacy, no way.

Ariadne was worried about Lisa. She was watching herself being worried, and it offended her. She was too tired. She had done it too often. Lisa was not the first dangerous child who had come to her to be mothered, asking for and rejecting at the same time her patient, wordless preoccupation.

Ariadne saw herself forced into a mission. There, in the mission street, she, missionary to the fly-by-nights, lost mother, followed the unhappy lost children of the American rich. She felt, without freezing it into words of cold charity, that she was a part of some force that owed them something. They, with their wary eyes, closed in and self-entranced, the last neglected products of an age, with their Abercrombie knapsacks, torn jeans, and credit cards, were the ones not allowed by the world to be sad, and this, to her, was a kind of starvation.

They had what the world wanted. The unknown man, Arizelos, had asked the oracle of Zeus what to do for a goodly possession of property. Three thousand years later his descendant on the Ceramian quay wanted a tape recorder. So she saw the lost children laden with the dreams of others, followed by whispers, "you have," "you ought to be happy." She saw herself, worried and wandering, a Demeter of the cafés, seeking them.

In such moods, Basil was furious with her, her soft American innocent face, Huckleberry Finn's aunt, Billy the Kid's mother, running through whole summers after them to heal their bloody knees that were her own. He saw the preoccupation as a danger, that she would break the circle again, wander home, leave him stranded.

"We will go to Ariadne's," he announced. "The poor darling's in one of her velvet fits." He pushed Miranda away and grabbed Ariadne's shoulder. "Oh darling I am so sorry. What can we do?" Ariadne caught a sense of panic from his insistent fingers, as a child clutches, afraid of the dark.

She wanted to pull away. "You're making too much of it. I'm only tired."

"In our day, dearie, it was called angst."

She let herself be led. "Where is Lisa?" She tried to be casual, ashamed that she was afraid of offending him into the cruelty that lurked at the edge of his voice.

"My dear, sex. Have you forgotten?" Sometimes it made Basil sad to have to nip Ariadne into line, herd the flock, bite at their heels. He glanced back at Miranda and Trader, who had been thrown together by the maneuvering of the crowd, and saw that they were still following doggedly. He sighed.

The evening had been a long tangled maneuver of arrangements. He was relieved when one of the sailors

from the quay whispered to Monkey, and he had got
up without a word so quickly that his chair had fallen,
and followed him.

Oh well, Monkey was always jumping away on one
of his secret Ceramian errands. It was just as well.
Basil didn't feel too happy when Ceramians joined
them. It broke up the intimacy of his family. Horst and
David spoke Turkish with them, which Basil in ten
years had not learned. It was all right about the flute
player. He was totally silent, and Basil liked his music.

On the whole, the evening wasn't a total disaster, all
things weighed together. The barriers were high and
safe. He was even managing not to look up at the
castle, and as he had the thought, he did, stood stock
still, rapt, until Ariadne pulled him along.

Instead of anger or hurt, Ariadne had
long since learned to protect herself by changing the
direction of her pity. Naked and aware, made to listen
and powerless to speak back, watcher of wrecks, she
found herself concerned with Basil, answering his cry,
demand, insistence. He was, to her, a man to whom
nothing had happened, having nothing a man his age
should have, not the welcome calm of fatigue after long
work, no children, no garnered harvest of a mind, no
long-lasting love or brave act behind him.

She saw him patching a past for himself out of other
people's rage, memory's beggar, using his chance en-
counters with fame, his passing moments with the rich.
He stood perpetually on a dark periphery. At least, to
her, something, however catastrophic, had happened.
She wondered if it were this shared glimpse of the pit
that made her sometimes see herself and David as
watching the others across a river with a broken
bridge.

Because she had loved before, and, as a woman who
has been pregnant knows when she is pregnant again,
recognized it, tenuous and faintly alight, between herself and David, she longed to nurture and feed it. She
knew that Basil was aware enough to see it, too, but as

a destructive threat to his magic circle. Love has no power; Basil lived on power, no matter in what shreds he found it. He had to lead them; his limp soul filled like a sail with their attentions and concerns.

She clung to her own periphery of the light, afraid as he was, although she did not know it, to leave the thin precarious glow of time-passing intimacy for the darkness she knew so well. She did not fear the darkness. It was too familiar. She only dreaded it.

It was so late. The moon rode high and white, and she was tired almost to death of lingering, ashamed of too easy despair. All noises, sex, laughter, repetitions, the jokes said over and over, the farts treated as bombs, the minor itches as fatal diseases, she could hear it all as children crying in the marketplace, "We have piped for you and you have not danced."

"We'll light a fire," she said. "It's not too late to light a fire outside." Children, old children, come, we'll have a treat, and another, and another. We'll have fun and nobody will die.

Miranda was pleased. Her brave face thrust forward against some old adversary she had forgotten, she didn't see the street at all. It was only a way to get to the next place, the next experience.

She had almost forgotten the flute player. Miranda had been in more cities than the Wandering Jew, but unlike him, she fled not from, but to. If her habits were dirty, her urge was innocent and driven. She wanted, once, to taste Paradise, just once—to lick it from her fingers. She sought it at the bars, among the fishermen, in the hospitable islands. Her questing hands clutched at it, whether genital or artifact.

Her colonialism was that of sensation. Like a new crusader, her time in most cities had lasted a Biblical forty days, her plunder was beads from Morocco hung over the sea-stained mirror in what she called her stateroom, a jumple of embroidered shirts thrown dirty into the corner, a copy of an ancient vase from Crete with one handle broken, full of cigarette butts, many

Aphrodite shells brought up as offerings by Trader when he dived, now gone pale and lifeless in their exile from the sea, guidebooks, ashtrays, menus, a tinseled crucifix from Spain, and two plastic containers that had once held penicillin for the souvenir of gonorrhoea she had picked up on Ibiza, which now held salt and pepper. She had told Trader it was cystitis.

Trader had long since learned at what time in Miranda's evening he should shut up. He had made it a whole philosophy of his body. Intent on enjoying the night, the crowds, the moon, he strolled apart, his thin, now nearly vacant face lifted, the lights etching the grooves of age, sun, and denied sorrow down his face.

He had acquired to cover that sorrow, not an occupation with anything, but a vague wandering attention. He had shed as an old coat the responses left over from his meticulous days of pleasing a different world, though some still stuck, as Hercules' coat, sunk deep within his skin. When he used them, unthinking, Miranda's glance censored him.

On the whole he felt that there were compensations that he sometimes mistook as decisions. At least, he loved his boat, loved her buck and tremble in the sea, loved her voices, her caprices, her need for constant care. Though he felt it disloyal in himself, he loved the noise her engine made at sea, where, at the wheel, he could not hear a word of what Miranda said, for though his love for her, her beauty, her body, clung within his brain, his spine, his heart, he sometimes needed rest.

The meticulous habits of his accounting days, the precise timing of the commuting train, the satisfying foursquare in-tray, out-tray of his desk, the neat columns of figures, had been shed, or replaced rather, by the boat. Except for the cabin where Miranda had cast her being so messily, though he had been taught to think of it as freely, the boat was as meticulously clean as his work had been.

Where once he had fed on the reactions of clients, superiors, and the Bureau of Internal Revenue, now he lived on casual notice, a flower from a little girl, smiles from the men when he passed the cafés; he felt he had been accepted by them. People are the same, he thought wisely and slowly to himself, all over the world.

Now he walked through a corridor of kindness, following the nice people who had befriended them. He had enjoyed the festival, the parade, the day, the night, certain in himself that his camera angles were good, his exposures correct.

If he ever showed homesickness, or lingering doubt, Miranda seemed to smell it in him and it made her angry. She showed her anger in long, tense explanations of what they were doing. He understood, but he was awash sometimes in poignancy when in order to get a traveler's check he had to unwrap the nightgown he had given her on the last Christmas they had spent in Plainfield.

At last, after the buying of the boat in England, the sail through the canals, the months in the Mediterranean when she disappeared for hours at a time saying she needed to be alone after the confinement of the boat, and came back like a beaten bedraggled pup, she seemed to have reached some pause in her mysterious urgency. Such pauses gave him time for the contentment that always waited to claim him, happy with what he had among these new and shining people.

He caught the eye of a man in uniform. His neatness pleased Trader, his finely trimmed mustache, his erect carriage. Trader smiled and called out "Merhaba," one of the few Ceramian words he knew. He thought it meant "hello"; actually it had once meant "I am not armed." The Captain of the Gendarmes smiled back and nodded. Trader was glad to share his happiness.

The Captain of the Gendarmes was in exile, too. He was from the Black Sea. He hated Ceramos. He was sick with fury at the Chief of Police,

who seemed to move with his eyes half closed through
the bayram, allowing it all to happen. He was poisoned
by the impotence of having no power within the borders of the town to reap the fine harvest he saw passing, furious that his dedication was wasted on a few
country villages and a stretch of coast where nothing
ever happened. At the moment that Trader saw him,
he was bathing himself in righteous hate, his back stiff
with it. It made a rictus of his mouth which he was
turning into a smile. He was, at that moment, dreaming
himself, armed and well mounted, seeking some enemy
he was not bothering to name, through the wild mountain passes, the wind across his face like a knife.

The inane grin of the gavur slammed the Captain
back into Ceramos and the Chief of Police who
laughed at him and called him Napoleon, and, once in
front of foreign women, Hitler. The Captain knew how
to wait. He waited now, and could smile again at the
foreign fool who passed him. He could see the horns,
put on him by the foreign slut, his wife, who slept with
the fishermen but refused to sleep with any officials;
she said she didn't like their politics. He garlanded the
horns with donkey shit, garlic, and that plant called
priest's balls. Trader, pleased, gestured vaguely, having
no words, sharing the moon with him.

The Captain stood there strong, serene with hate,
hate of the foreigners, their exposed soft flesh, their ir-
religious ease. He could smell the sweet hashish, the
hot sex, the smuggling, the need for purge. He was
sure, watching them, that these arrogant rich students
with their western ways were riddled with hidden anarchists. He had no need, as the Chief of Police had tried
to do for him with that condescending patience that
disgusted him, to define the word.

Anarchist was as good a name as any for the enemy.
A man knew his enemy in his stomach muscles, not his
mind. Why, when he already knew them, did a man
have to learn the thousand names of evil?

He would never have admitted that what had fed his
fury was that he had not been invited to have lunch at
Dürüst Osman's house as his rank demanded. Even
Huseyin, his friend, had betrayed him. They had spent

so much time and talk together through the long nights
of winter boredom. Once, out of their mutual winter
loneliness, both so misunderstood and hated by the
filthy Ceramians, he had shared ecstasy with him. It
was, of course, an accident.

He could feel it now, the remembered urgency that
began with manly wrestling so fierce that there was
blood, and ended in massive orgasm. He remembered
its beauty, the hot hard pure muscles, the peace afterwards, the blood on their fine bodies. As the memory
came back to heal him, he forgave Huseyin the slight
about the lunch. He knew that he must have some plan
that was not his to know yet, maybe to get rid of the
Chief of Police. His spirits rose.

The crowd had thinned. Ariadne paused
and looked out over the water. She could recognize the
dark shape of Munci's boat moving toward the distant
bobbing lights of the cluster of boats in the summer island cove—one pause, unnoticed, one half-formed wish
that she were with him sailing in the night.

She had been too far away to catch more than a few
words, "Yazada . . . Huseyin . . ." and something
about a boat, when the sailor who had run into David's
bar had leaned down and whispered to Munci. He had
gotten up so quickly that his chair had fallen, had not
looked back or said a word. He had simply disappeared after the sailor. The chair had fallen. A chair
falls, a glass breaks, boredom is punctuated by such
sounds, and after that—a sense that things have
changed.

She shivered, heard David say, "What's the matter?"
Or she thought he did.

"I'm cold, and tired, all of a sudden," she said, surprised, and watched the night sea.

She knew Munci's sudden decisions to put out from
land like that, away from all their voices. Sometimes he
took her with him and they would glide through the
moon on the water and fragment it, not saying a word,
letting the shore babble flow out of them, cleaned by

the night. Munci's element was sea and air and an occupied silence. Gracefully he shared it with her while the others, left behind, were certain that they were making love.

"My dear, you *need* someone like Monkey," Basil had said, as if Munci were a lonely woman's servant. Then, vaguely aware that what she should have felt was anger, she saw instead, and it weakened her with the familiar compassion, that the old man had never had a friend he had not used.

They turned up the hill away from the bayram crowds, concentrated in the narrow streets along the quays. In the streets beyond the waterfront the town was asleep, ageless and peaceful, inured to the noise which grew fainter, only the pulse beat of the music left. Their shadows climbed the stones of the steep narrow street, white under the moon.

It was two o'clock. The distant now darkened quay, with only a rim of street lights left, lay in a circle below them. The long reflections of the harbor lights were still lines in the dark water. The light from the terrace fireplace brushed their faces. Even Basil's voice was quiet as he told Miranda and Trader the difference between a baronet, a baron, and a knight.

All evening, caught like a fever from the smell of sperm and wine in the kahves, the wandering casual sex of the young, Ariadne had suffered her own body on her own Naxos age. She could feel her thighs widen with longing. She thought she had escaped it, but when Horst had come back after his meeting, he had brought it with him, the easy body English of one satisfied and unthinking. He leaned against the wall, watching the fire, loose and peaceful.

She knew her tomorrow. Sometimes she would be touched, as tonight, beyond her protective benignity, the one who did it inadvertently never knowing the flaying she suffered, such brutal recognition of her aloneness that she would have to shut herself away, almost from the light itself, until her skin grew back.

She would wander, she knew, dim and distracted, in a timeless darkness as her mind lifted out of her night's sleep through levels of old brutalities. Finally the irony, the self-recognition would cover her and she could once again face the others with that light courtship they expected of her. Her nerves, revolted by the demands of her illusions, banked up to crisis, and then painfully shed the load of falseness.

All this would be, of course, in secret. For days afterwards she would wear the blue beads, virgin-colored, against the evil eye. She knew that there was nothing to be pitied and avoided more in a woman of her age than the misunderstanding of gestures that were, to them, a part of their mildest language of play.

She thought of lust and love, the difference so clear to her at that moment, watching Horst, and knowing that David had moved close beside her. Lust, she told herself, has a thousand reasons, love only one. It is its own reason. She thought behind the act to its reasons, behind the flesh to its use. She knew that it was lust, not love, that was blind. She, who would be alone when they left, once again washing glasses because she hated getting up in the morning to a dirty kitchen, rejected lust, its substitute for thought, its entertainment, its fear of love, the calculated geometry of sin.

David, who had fallen into watching her almost as a habit, thought she must have been so beautiful—he saw her as she had been, but he knew that the blurred softness of youth in her that he wanted to touch was now only the kindness of the firelight.

"Please tell," he was not asking but offering to listen.

"I can't," she whispered back, under Basil's insistent party voice.

How could she tell him about all the reasons she saw acted out every day, the worry, the loneliness, the demand for power, the frustrated ambition, and even as Basil's voice was demanding now, the awful need to find the center of a safe circle of his own making? All this she saw now, alive with it herself and ashamed, answered by sex, sex as lock, sex as key, sex as money, sex as safety, all lusts, using the flesh, and, oh, one time, diminishing all else, love, its responsibility, its wisdom, its light and burden.

"Aristocrats are the only true democrats." Basil had got to that point in his evening and his voice rolled on like a homosexual *Reader's Digest*. Soon, thank God, he would go past snobbery into abstraction, Basil on marriage, Basil on art, Basil on some perverted version of Know Thyself, and it would be, at last, time for him to leave. Miranda and Trader sat at his feet, as unsophisticated as turnips, basking in his attention.

Ariadne wanted to tell David what Blake meant when he wrote, "We are put on earth a little space that we may learn to bear the beams of love." She knew now. Tomorrow she would have forgotten again. Her mind lightened, threw away the weight of her vision.

What she had seen as profound, she suddenly glimpsed as trivial and shallow, the lives ahead of them all so fated by their present, so habitual, that she realized that she had been reading in them more than was there in order to—what? Forgive them? She was totally alone. As most reformers, she was a lover of potential, not people.

"What is there about us? We are all afraid to go to bed," she said instead.

David thought, she has the eyes of a woman to whom something totally unjust has been done. He touched her arm as if he were trying to hear through his hand what she could not say. Basil saw the hand on her arm and his voice faltered.

She was ashamed of the vanity that made her wonder if her arm muscles felt too soft, old and repulsive. She moved her arm, shied from the touch. David turned away from her, hurt.

"They are not worth her easy suffering," he told himself. "She has wasted her heart and now it is impotent. She would rather yearn than act. She is American, after all." He found it easy, at last, to dismiss her and watch his own night, relieved as the fulfillment of what he had expected all along.

Basil's voice speeded up again.

The flute player wondered what they were all talking about. He had caught a few words he knew, but they made no sense. He wondered when Miranda was going to stop listening to the old man who was always putting his hands on the town boys, and let him fuck her. He would rather have fucked the other one, the lady. He had never had a lady, a hanimefendi.

Oh well, Miranda would do. He liked her dog face. Her legs were good, strong from the sea. He could see her wading out of the water, not in the tight pants she was too old to wear, but in a fine skirt with flowers on it, raised up so he could see the black triangle of her foreign hair, exciting, forbidden. Ceramian women shaved it as obscene. He knew she would be hot and quick. Foreign women were. So many of their hands had played over him that sometimes he felt like one of the embroidered velvets in the Pazar. He began to play again to draw her attention, a haunting minor trill, then the beginning of a tune.

The music silenced even Basil for a little while. He dreamed of Simon, waiting in his dark house, a terrible shadow, adored and untouchable.

In the distance Ariadne saw a small crowd gathered on the eastern quay. Another boat was putting out into the bay. She knew them all, the ones there in the night, still playing, still waiting, knew herself as one of them. She watched the boat move slowly beyond the outer harbor, its fishing searchlight sliding over the dark water.

Lisa and Huseyin were furiously making love on the roof of the Endemon Pension. Huseyin had convinced her that it was the safest and most secret place in Ceramos. Lisa was in love with Mehmet the Conqueror. Her body bruised from the concrete under the thin blanket, and from the weight of his body. She thought, having taken Comp. Myth. One, "If he takes me again I will give birth to Gilgamesh, even though I'm on the pill."

One of Huseyin's sailors waited in the hall on the floor below. He had known where to find Huseyin. He knew by the diminishing sighs, the slowing rhythm, that Huseyin would be finished soon. He went on waiting. He was afraid of Huseyin, afraid to interrupt him to tell him that one of his boats had sunk off Yazada, the summer island.

II

The Second Sacrifice

Frank Proctor heard it. That's all. It came from about a foot above the floor, in the corner of his room. It was that that had waked him. "Frink Frank Frink, your sneakers stink."

Very important sentiment, important enough to wake a man at dawn . . . profound, must remember it. He answered, "Right. I'm not frank, I am frink, and I sneak, and I stink." His eyes opened. There was a spider staring at him. "Jesus, come *on*, Proctor, guilt at five o'clock in the morning?" He turned his back on the spider. It was still nearly dark in the room. The pillow was hard. His head hurt.

There's always some bastard at the corner of the school yard, all your goddamn life . . .

Who had said it, no, chanted it, an evil little boy soprano wail? All he remembered was that it was in the third grade in Antonia, Pennsylvania. Red hair? The bastard probably hadn't amounted to a hill of beans. After all he, Frank Proctor, was the only one of them smart enough to get into an eastern college. The little red-headed bastard didn't have a name.

Frank peed in the sink and then ran the water as quietly as he could. He staggered out onto his hotel balcony wishing he hadn't forgotten to go to the PX in Izmir and stock up on Alka-Seltzer. After all, he'd known what to expect.

He leaned on the balcony. The weight of the world was on his shoulders, as his grandmother would have said, and he didn't know why. The first light was rising from the sea.

He could hear the electric whir of a loudspeaker from the direction of Salmakis kahve. The recording of

the accusing stricken whine of the dawn call to prayer
from the dark, hidden minaret flung birds into the sky.
He felt intrusive, leaning there on his hotel balcony
watching the still water. The double image of the castle
was beginning to form and the faint outline of the sub-
merged ancient harbor was traced by sea light.

By habit he kept a neural watch for movement,
shifts of shadow on the gray hill against gray rock. He
watched for movement, not color. Color was deceptive.
What he was trained to see were flicks of the pattern
against the natural mass. The gray rocks could move
and slink. The bushes killed.

He was in a silent war against the leaves and the air.
Leaves could turn counter to wind flow and when you
shot the bush burned, or sprouted an arm, a leg, the
bush bled, the bush screamed. He went on watching. It
was the dogs of Ceramos, not men, skulking along the
stone walls around the shipyard. In a second of sleep
Frank saw the war, the war against the leaves and the
air, the war that made him go pale, and kept him on
his dignity not to hit the floor and try to dig through it
at the sound of a tire blowing.

He knew then what it really was that had whispered
him awake at five o'clock in the morning. It was ever-
present, ever-denied body fear.

He shivered and told himself it was the cold of
dawn. He wanted to wake up, wanted to sleep. Instead
he succumbed to the floating deception of the town
coming into light so quietly it might have been the way
it was three thousand years ago, or when he first saw it
only three years ago, discovered it, rather, when it was
unknown and kindly, before they knew who he was
and whom he had to court.

He had come to Ceramos first as a friend. It was his
hidden home from home. The easy walking around the
harbor, the nobody nowhereing in peace and quiet, a
cup of tea, a little rakı, diving as a pure act of respon-
sible affection with a friend; he had for a while been
taken at the value of his face.

He was not then, as he was now, doing his duty,
standing on the balcony of the newest hotel, paid for
by speculative money from Ankara, behind that a little

AID, a little Ford money. Still the bastards wanted more, more hotels, more AID, more Ford money. Frank sighed. Away across the sea channel under the shadow of Yazada, he could see the circle of lights on the night-fishing boats growing dim in the first dawn. He wondered why they fished in a circle and made a note to check. He took pride in learning local custom. Why couldn't they stay like that, innocent fishermen, in untouched circles, undefiled, fishing at night, making early morning love to their wives, and a perpetual place for him, Frank Proctor, to rest from his labors.

He could make out all along the seafront roofs the shapes of people still asleep, mummies of cloth on their low, dirt-packed roofs, children of nomads and sailors instinctively seeking the stars as a ceiling for their dreams. He saw a man roll away from the pile of clothes that was his wife, straighten himself, stand for a minute as Frank was standing, looking out to sea. The man disappeared out of sight down a ladder, stood in the corner of his courtyard with the contemplative air of a man having the slow, long piss of waking, and then moved toward his donkey which was calling its slow strangled in-and-out haw. The man went to the well in the yard. Frank could hear the bucket hitting the stone sides of the well as he drew it up. He could see the black mouth, at ground level, without the huge protecting walls of the well on his grandmother's farm. He saw it as part of the deep passion for danger and accident, the thoughtless flirtation with death that permeated the town.

The weightless town touched the sea, and he was part of it for one of those moments they never really allowed. No matter what their manners he sensed that all the doors slammed in his face without sound. Self-pity—he'd seen it often enough around the petulant mouths of the men who had been there longer, were older, their naiveté turned to softness. Something plummeted down inside of his body, warning that he too would be like them in time. No, dry mouth, heart-sinking light-bodied hangover, that was what was the matter.

The heavy lunch, its parodies of seraglio whispers,

oh, he knew about that. He'd seen it often enough, the
color, the flowers, the cologne, the shaded balcony
where they watched the parade unseen, Monkey's
mother trying to put the evil eye on him. The whole
day of the new Ceramos he hadn't known before, and
the night that followed plagued him.

The awful dinner at the ancient Han, when he'd had
to pass his old friends; they were cold, they nodded,
that's all. Only Monkey had exchanged with him the
double kiss of friendship. Even so, he knew that Monkey knew his double kiss had changed to double cross.

Later in the night, he was certain. When he had
wandered into David's bar, Monkey had gotten up
from his table so quickly that he had knocked over his
chair. He had run past Frank in the doorway and pretended not to see him. Frank had flattened himself
against the door to let him and his sailor pass. Frank
was hurt, but he told himself he understood.

After all, Monkey had watched him earlier at dinner, sitting apart from them all at Dürüst Osman's
table in the newly decorated inn where the camel well
was filled in with stones, and surrounded by subdued
green plants instead of the old riot of geraniums and
fuchsia. The Istanbul and Ankara women, told to be
nice to him, had sat in their embroidered caftans from
Paris and spoken banalities perfectly in three languages, changing languages as they changed partners.
He had felt ashamed there of his training at following
orders. There he was, doing his duty, cultivating and
influencing the power elite who were busy cultivating
and influencing him. The importance of all that at five
o'clock in the morning was as dry as his mouth.

Why the hell the overcivilized Osmanli bastards
made him feel as if he still painted his ass blue and
lived in a tree was something he could not figure out.
Only twice during the day and the long evening had
any hint of the matter that had brought him to
Ceramos shown itself. Instead, they spoke cosmically
of the nature of reality while they drank rakı, still mull-
ing over questions that Heraclitus had posed beside
the same slow sea.

Turgut Bey, the Istanbul businessman known best

for having made his fortune running guns to the Middle East, but who also shipped drugs to Europe nestled in figs from Izmir, still called Smyrna figs because of the western market, and who was rumored to have started two African revolts in the copper mining country, spoke slowly and in perfect French about twentieth-century angst, and the crisis in values since the deaths of such great men as Churchill and de Gaulle.

Once, though, he had turned, taking for granted that Frank understood little or no Turkish, and had answered Dürüst Osman, Huseyin's father, who had muttered to him that it was time to reach the matter of the hotel because he wanted to go home.

"Yüzdük yüzdük kuyruğuna geldik," Turgut Bey had said, grinning into his raki glass. Angst and Churchill forgotten, he had stripped down to the old country philosophy of the nomads, have patience, move slowly, skin the beast carefully until you come to the tail.

It was the second time that the tourist hotel had been mentioned. It was as if the wily old bastard knew in his fat jowls that Frank had prepared carefully to register his objection to the hotel. He had waited all evening to confess that his report to AID would have to be negative.

It was, Frank and all the rest of his colleagues knew, a scandal, another hotel when the town of Ceramos was already moving inevitably toward a cholera epidemic by overfilling the town every summer when the water supply was not sufficient for the indigenous population. Frank smiled at the agha's tomb that was faintly white in the dawn, and edited himself.

Hints of official language amused his five o'clock self, standing there in his capacity as Frank Proctor, with no cover except his pajama pants.

"You see, it is most important to us to industrialize so that we can take the place among the modern nations," Turgut Bey had explained to him in English, still not mentioning the hotel. Frank was an economic expert and he knew it. After all, the consular service was a stopgap. He had been trained for the economics cone in the State Department.

He did not say, "So you can make a quick killing in the tourist business and then abandon the town." He said instead, "Your workingmen certainly have the capacity and intelligence," then, feeling it was time, carefully vague, "I would hate to see you lose your . . ." Too vague; he couldn't find a word to finish.

"Soul?" Turgut Bey veered safely into the cosmos again, and laughed so joyfully that his face bobbed up and down. "You Americans are the only people left besides the Germans . . ." The soul was not what Frank had meant and they both knew it, but he let it pass. It was no time to speak on the subject of a reservoir.

Among the raki, the jewels, and the noisy silk of the caftans, it was time to be likeable. He had been likeable all evening. He had a face like Stephen Crane, intelligent and silent. He had been intelligent and silent. He remained intelligent and silent, parrying the passes of a fifty-year-old woman, smooth as a pear, listening through her moaning about only being able to go to Europe once a year to what Turgut Bey was saying so passionately in Turkish to Huseyin.

He was speaking of his daughter whom he had brought with him to Ceramos. He was arranging for a bride price with far easier directness than he used to make a half-million-dollar match between AID and a hotel. The daughter was beautiful, she was serene. Oh no, she could not join them at dinner, Turgut Bey explained. The company was far too worldly. No, he certainly did not approve, he said in answer to a murmured question. The University was, he told Huseyin, a passing phase.

"It is better if you meet for the first time tomorrow in my hotel to make your offer. You will bring your father, of course."

Frank saw a plain girl with a fine body who would end up, not like the lady beside him who had to sing for her supper, but like Huseyin's mother, fat and unmoved as the hill she resembled. Their voices dropped beyond his hearing and he knew they were talking business, a sophisticated version of bride price.

But when Turgut Bey remembered his duty and spoke to Frank again in English, he offered him the use of his house in Istanbul, his boat on the Sea of Marmora, and his new Chevrolet Impala. He did not, though, mention a daughter.

Frank remembered thinking that Turgut Bey was like the Sultan's opium pill covered with several layers of gilt, gilt of western ways, sophistication, hospitality, bargaining, thinner and thinner until the gilt was gone and he came to the core, the main line, the hard kick, the eyes of an enemy. He had rolled to sleep seeing Turgut Bey's pasty face and the black hard pills of his eyes.

In the five o'clock morning twilight Frank knew he would fail. He even knew the emptiness, the relief of failure, the "this is the way it is" that would come with the full light of morning after the absurdity of the dawn. It was growing lighter, as if the light lifted from the water to the air, light enough by now to see the great brown stain of sweet water that flowed out to sea unchecked from the green, flower-decked foothills, water that would be needed later by the tourist-wrecked whorehouse the town would turn into in the dry desert of summer. In keeping with his cover as an AID adviser, he had, too soon he felt, approached the reservoir question at lunch.

"Ah, you do not understand the Will of God," Dürüst Osman had said.

Frank had long since found his unspoken answer for that. "A God who eats off the holding plants must be a big black billy goat." God was taboo for a diplomat. He was unaware, having been born to a Republican mother in western Pennsylvania, that he was thinking what his hosts at lunch would have called Communist thoughts.

He thought of the advice of his superior in Izmir who had said to him, "Don't get too involved, Frank." He saw the man, one of so many with that vast protective innocence so akin to a depraved indifference.

He began, leaning on the balcony, to write one of

the letters to the *Washington Post* that he was always
nearly writing but never put down on paper. It was a
favorite one. It comforted him.

"Sirs, do you realize that most of the men of the age
to be in decisive positions today in the government are
products of security checks made in the days of Joe
McCarthy, when if you could read and write, you were
suspect? . . ." The rest of the letter faded out of his
mind. He wished his knuckles were white with anger
on the iron railing of the balcony. He wanted to be
sickened by his own impotence to do something about
it all, but he no longer was. He was only tired and
hung over.

He went back into his room to try to read himself to
sleep again. On the chair that he had pushed up to his
bed to make a table were the books he thought he
ought to read in order to prepare himself in case he
ever got transferred to Paris. He picked up the notebook that lay beside them, the notebook that contained
his third self, neither his cover nor his career, not
touching either, the sane compartment of survival, the
one who questioned, and fell in love.

"It can be done," he wrote. "But it never is," he
added. He picked up Proust and trudged dutifully
through two pages, laid it aside for Eric Ambler, and
drifted off to sleep again. He dreamed that the whole
anti-Turkish opium lobby in the Senate was being paid
by the Mafia to keep the illegal supply running. He
could see poppies in the dream, strapped to big black
billy goats.

He woke to full sun, having forgotten the dream and
why he had written the note. He felt his morning urgency for a woman, refused manfully to masturbate,
and went instead through the third level of the Cana-
dian Air Force exercises. The drip-dry shirt he had
washed the night before was dry, his trousers smooth
and well creased. He wondered, as he dressed, how to
translate Brooks Brothers into Turkish, not Brooks
Brothers, but the concept of Brooks Brothers. He
shaved carefully around his mustache, combed the
dark hair that touched his collar. Nobody in Ceramos
knew he looked like Stephen Crane. Oh hell, he told

himself, half the men around the tea kahve looked like Stephen Crane.

It was not yet seven o'clock when Frank Proctor, with his disheveled, rejected memories neatly covered, combed, cleaned, and pressed, walked along the quay to find his breakfast, anonymous to all but himself. Far away, a dynamite blast sent high a section of the ancient wall of the city that was in the way of the new six-lane highway. He did not notice. He was conscious of spring flowers, warmth, and girls, the steady stream of men going past him toward the docks, the past of Ceramos that lingered in the early morning, the mountain withdrawn from the town, aloof and gray with mist.

He was already disciplining himself to touch and taste every minute of his rare day off. He could feel his mind shifting the weight of facts, logical, pertinent, cross-referenced, the lists, lists for everyone, the loyal, the suspect, the rich. He had, he was proud of that, made a grid of perception, hindsight and forecast of the district. He had nothing to reproach himself with. He had had his conference with the Captain of the Gendarmes, whom he didn't like very much. He had made his contacts with most of the ubiquitous group, the community leaders, the landowners, the manufacturers, the more malleable and influential media. He had been efficient. Sometimes he fell into amusement at how many more straight solid facts he knew about the country than most of the people in it, especially the young, his third-self friends, myopic with a naive desire for change. He loved them, as one loves simplicity and children and the clean sea and birds, on his days off. The sun blessed him and the day spread out before him, so long as he avoided his contacts. He promised himself that.

Sir Basil de Montfort, the English Torquopolier of the Knights Hospitalers, had walked home through the silent streets at five o'clock in the morning, wishing, as usual, that he were somewhere else. When he had opened his own door at last, and reached for kitty to fondle her, he had done it with a sigh. He had laid his armor of lies aside with his clothes in the dawn moonlight, reviewing the night and waiting for the sun.

At three, Ariadne had really been quite rude and they had gone and sat on Trader's charming boat. Basil loved boats. He had told Trader and Miranda about being aboard the Cowes Class yacht belonging to the ex-king Alphonso of Spain with Lady Margaret Hall. He had described the mahogany fittings, the carved order of the Golden Fleece on the head door, her lines, the lines of a sea virgin.

He had neglected to mention that she lay, no longer seaworthy, by a frail catwalk in a North Sea port under an empty sky, for rent as a houseboat, and that his sister had hired it for the most boring week's holiday he had ever spent. There had been nothing but ragged clouds, jellyfish and oil spill, salt water in the tea, perpetual television, and his sister with one of her mysterious attacks, all accusing eyes and frozen back.

If he had not told that, or that Lady Margaret Hall was an Oxford college, it was because he was an artist. Sometimes, Basil thought, he was tired of his stories. There had not been a new one in so long. He had to retailor them as times changed like the clothes of a vain spinster on a fixed pension. He needed either new people or new stories.

As the night stretched on, especially sitting on the deck of the *Miranda* in the moonlight, he had seen Trader and Miranda grow in charm. If they had been a plague to his nerves before, Trader had healed it by asking him to tour the islands with them. Trader had been really quite delicate about it. "Miranda will be so proud to have you as a guide." She wasn't there at that point to ask. She and the flute player had walked so slowly behind them that it was nearly an hour before she came aboard.

When she did come aboard—Basil said "aboard" aloud to the cat, liking it—she curled up like a little girl, more silent and peaceful than she had been all evening. Later, Basil had peed over the side, exposed

like a Ceramian sailor, while at distant Yazada the
little lights rocked.

When the sun was high enough to defeat the
shadows that could turn without warning into mon-
strous errors of vision, Basil began to get ready for
bed. He had trained himself to sleep in the morning.
He had no place on earth in that awful busy
brightness. His veins showed, his lies, his rib cage, his
unshadowed defeat. He faced that, too, as he examined
his underpants to see if they would do for another day.

He looked around his room, the only one furnished
in his three-roomed house that huddled behind the
quay. It was little different from all the rooms he had
been through in the years in London, the dreary procession of evictions, evasions, brown wallpaper, and
dirt, where dust-covered milk bottles were piled in the
corners, and marg had lain half out of its paper. There
was the old bread—what was it? how strange to forget—oh, Allinsons, Heals Mod bread he called it. His
sister had brought it for him. She said it kept his bowels open. There were the postwar brown paper boxes
with his notes, the volumes of notes.

They were still piled in the corner, gritty with sand
blown by the last storm, their edges old and dead gray.
He did not like to think how long it had been since
they had been opened, all that fragmented gossip of a
perfect medieval world. He was, he really was, it was
not a lie, a medievalist. He had, and that was not a lie
either, been brilliant at Oxford. It simply took time, all
of it, time and silence, and, because he made it a rule
never to lie to himself, a crossing of the room to the
boxes as long and fraught with peril as the crossing of
the wide ocean.

The bottles, too, had piled up again, water bottles
from Salmakis fountain, old bread from the bakery,
and marg half out of its paper, melting in the morning
heat.

Basil could feel the old boredom of despair sink
down through his body. His fingers tightened on the
cat's fur and she poured off his lap. He told himself
sternly that he had survived before and that he would
survive again. The mood began to lift. After all, he was

at the source. He had to remind himself of that too often lately. He remembered how important it was, how
hard to persuade his sister that the one thing on earth
he needed was to follow the hints he had unearthed to
the world of Islam. She had softened at that. She had
always wanted to travel.

He was used to her balking. He could hear her
whine in her letters, her checks smaller and fewer,
blast her, rabbity references to publishing as if it were
the easiest thing in the world. He had to keep on reminding her of the fact, and it was a fact, that he was
the brilliant one in the family, and that her periods of
impatience tarnished him. She spoke in her not mute
enough innocence as if one finished a life's work instead of moving along it as a path.

He was following some grail of buried fact that
would redeem the drift of his years and give it, in ret-
rospect, the direction that he sometimes sensed.

He wondered if Miranda could take shorthand.
Women like that often could. He saw himself spinning
by his voice, polishing and sculpting the mean little
facts God had given him to work with. After all, what
was an artist but, in his way, a liar, a more seer? He
liked that.

He leaned down slowly to inspect the water bottles
to make himself tea before he faced sleep. There was
no water. He paused just beyond the window to watch
the safe morning come, back against the curtain so that
no one could see him until he was rested and ready to
be seen. A plant without water was dead in the win-
dowsill, one of Ariadne's little gifts, poor dear. He
smiled.

Dear Miranda, naive but really sensitive, had loved
his stories, especially the judicious one about the fountain which he told so well. As he reviewed it, judging it
in his mind, he was pleased. He had mapped with it an
absolutely delightful voyage.

It started in Ceramos, at the center, the fountain, the
font, he had explicated, that was it, unfolded, like a living leaf, a story.

"You see," he said to the cat, who was mewing
faintly for food, "Ceramos is the perfect example of

what Archilochos meant when he said that the fox has a thousand tricks, the hedgehog one. They did not conquer. They never built great monuments.

"St. Paul did not stop here. The Crusaders built bigger castles at other places. But it had, and still has, as towns have their own atmosphere"—he remembered a mysterious lowering of his voice, a pause, he had done it well—"humor, my dears, a straight-faced, subtle humor. They are, you must remember, descended from mountaineers and sailors. As a point of local pride they never keep the first promise. They do, however, keep unfailingly the third. For the first, it is too comic to think of people waiting, women to be made love to, boats to be built, while delicately the hands that lift the two-handled Ceramian cups they still drink from control the waiting hope with long fine tenuous reins of evasion. Which brings me to their one addition of culture, the tavern. They invented it. I will show you tomorrow." Basil had been glad that Horst had gone home. Horst, well, tended to diminish Basil's fancies.

"You have sat there, not knowing. The Salmakis kahve by the mosque is the oldest tavern in the world." He waited for that to sink in. Americans, he knew, loved the word old.

"Give me your glass," Trader had said, reminded of himself as host. "You can't fly on one wing."

"They were also the first advertisers—oh God sleep is coming too soon—the first advertisers. They started stories that the water of Salmakis fountain, mixed with wine, made you strong, virile, and as potent as a bull. Since so many sailors were coming by then to Ceramos, other cities around the great bay spread the story that the water made you impotent, homosexual, or syphilitic.

"I am afraid of sleep. Layers of legend, still layers of legend around the fountain. Ionians, or was it Dorians, oh God what matter, they built the twin temples to Aphrodite and Hermes, and said that the Hermaphrodite was born in the water. Salmakis, that nymph, fell in love with him when he was drinking there and drew him into the—oh God, oh God—still drink there and as your habits and your tastes dictate you can still draw virility, impotence, it can make you a raving queen like me or, with women like Miranda wandering about, it can give you syphilis."

He hadn't said that, he was sure he hadn't. He had sung for future suppers as sweetly as an angel. He was slipping nearer and nearer to sleep, the terror of it. He dared not sit down. He had to stay away from his bed. It was no use.

She, Basil, the darling one, lay against the wall beside the window, panting with desire, delicious girl. She knew who was coming. He was beginning to intrude into the daylight at last, even the light was no longer the protection it had been for so long. Virginity of her illusions stripped, madness her only sanity, she, deity of the young, the crass, the unprotected, she with all the hysterical wall of answers stripped away against the rape of the light, the scream of I DON'T KNOW. What is happening to me? Wonder? She had not wondered in so many years, and now wonder, awful wonder was thrusting itself out of the night and coming toward her in the morning sun, that naked dream, hint of the whirling of something awful beyond the certainty of her eyes. She, the raper, rapier and the raped, lay there, wall tilted horizontal. Don't come. Don't come I pray thee, prithee. Stay in the night.

It was no use. The dream she had lived with so long was seeping into the light, forming. She could see him, still as vague as a hint at the corner of her eyes, but forming, and he spoke.

"Help me. Basil, why don't you help me?" Simon the Crusader had the voice of the Geordie boy in London, Geordie boy's face and the vestments of the Order of St. John of Jerusalem. He came from the English tower of the castle in the harbor, forgotten there out of all the brown boxes, all one coming toward her, sweet Basil, it was a joke. "I won't hurt you." It was the one, the Crusader he had followed all the way to Ceramos, run away from to follow, not knowing.

"I haven't anything," she cried out, loudly enough to make Melek Hanım, Munci's mother, look up at the window as she walked past. She cut the air in front of her with her hand, gesture of killing. "Always boys," she muttered. She hated hearing such evil when it crossed her path when she was going to pray.

"I only want to get home." Simon came nearer, armored, the cross of St. George brackish on his filthy once-white cassock. They were in the English tower. Basil de Montfort, Turquopolier of the garrison, could feel its wall, with the incised dragon behind his hands. "I can't stop it."

"They're after me. Please hide me. I done nothing." Why were the London police after the last Crusader? Why? No why in the dreams, only reality. Fact came closer. "Oh Christ," Sir Basil begged, "don't let me feel your touch." She begged him. She could feel the air move as he walked toward her, begging, no flesh yet. He had picked up one of the dirty milk bottles from Salmakis fountain.

When the soldiers of Suleiman burst in and caught him, disarmed him of the bottle, Basil ejaculated weakly and sobbed because her new dress was stained. She was made to watch while they tied him to the wooden cross in front of the castle chapel, naked and ashamed, and brought the girls, real, and incised of time passing, one reality of vision in a flower-colored veil, and then the next, a parade. He could hear the Janissaries' march. They giggled as they flicked the poor boy's exposed penis with their tiny pink tongues, torturing with promise, and he prayed, the last Crusader, stripped of all, cross and cassock, while the officers of Suleiman's army stood and laughed at the gavur. Then one girl, sorry for him, stayed long enough to relieve him of the hour on hour of torture, and he sighed.

They were on the floor of Basil's digs in London, the ones in Brewer Street, oh Christ, the Geordie boy he loved and had been so good to betrayed him there and sighed, oh, oh, oh, like a prayer while she relieved him and Basil stood over them, screaming, "You little bastard, you can't do that in my house!"

"A perilous thing," he recited the rule of the Order of St. John quite calmly, he thought, "is the company of the female, for the old devil has lured many through the company of women from the straight path to Paradise. We believe it to be a danger to all religion to regard too long a woman's face. None of you, therefore, should presume to kiss any female: whether a widow, child, mother, sister, aunt, or any other. The Knights of Jesus Christ, for this reason, must eschew by all means that kissing of women by which men have so frequently put it in jeopardy that they should ever live and rest, in purity of conscience and surety of life, before the face of God forever."

"Are you quite bloody finished you bloody old tart?" Simon rolled away from the little whore and picked up the milk bottle.

Basil screamed, "Don't!"

Melek Hanım, below, sitting cross-legged under the tamarisk tree of her choice, spat and muttered, "Allah belâsını versin." After her curse she felt more at peace and ready to begin her prayer.

Basil fell onto his bed and sobbed himself to true sleep. The twenty-year-old scar from the milk bottle was livid in the morning sun, his face stained with dirty tears like a child.

Melek Hanım watched the sea. Her lips moved in prayer, making no sound except within her head, rhythm of Arabic without meaning to her except that it was the language of the call to God.

She knew that if she kept on intoning she would forget the old germ, Basil, and the times of evil for Ceramos, at least for a little while. She knew the summer sounds of evil, how they grew and grew like the cry she had just heard, cry of the babe for the tit. No one could sleep at night by midsummer as the invasion grew, and the cry roared through the quays, as if the bayram went on without stopping, and all innocence and gentleness were drowned, and the doors were shut to any stranger except for money, such a terrible sin, a Christian sin. It was not for nothing that it was said that to the fool every day is a bayram.

The young lions, the aslanlar, turned into stray tom cats, taking money from foreign women—it made Lady

Melek mourn all summer until her family hardly spoke to her. She prayed then only to exist until the face of Ceramos went through its autumn change, and the laws of hospitality and kindness would begin again, and they would live the winter peace the summer had earned them, but even in the winter the strangers left their marks, and instead of the old days of talk before the fire, they sat silent now before the television, or played the tape recorder. There were not even Turkish words for these boxes they had sold their souls for.

Money. She spat, her prayer forgotten. As if money could stop anything—tidal wave or earthquake or the black times when the men rampaged like wild goats. She sat like a stone, remembering. It did not bother her to remember. It brought no tears, or even a slight heart heave, nothing. It hardened her. She was sixteen again and it was night on the island. The night had a word, *enosis*. The Greeks had come to the village, those same men who had been friends of her father, her brothers, and had eaten in their house while she watched from behind the shutters. When they shot her father and raped her and her mother they had the faces of strangers. There was not even hate. That was the strange thing, it was as if they were doing what was expected of them, a duty.

The house had burned as fiercely as if it were only a pile of waste wood, shots of light piercing the night. Her brothers had come down from the hills and found her. She remembered the boat cutting through the fierce sea. She had never been off the island, but now she was shifted like a bag of grain—a population shift they called it. Applied to her it had been a dumping on an alien shore with nothing but what she stood in, still sore from the rape, with her soul numb from what she had seen, her face filthy under her veil, and the tight marks of a man's fingers still on her jaw.

It was not, nor had ever been, a nightmare. No conjured dream could match the reality of man. So time for her, and family, and growing older in her own courtyard in Ceramos, and finally learning to speak a new language, and the hard work of her fine husband, had built up again the barriers of safety. She did not trust them. They were, to her, as frail as politics, or greed, or summer lightning. Men were naive to think that the whore money of summer could protect them; better the sea, the old and terrible dependable sea.

Why, she could not even walk to the garden without some half-naked stranger taking her picture as if she were an animal caught in slow flight.

She sat close to the water, cross-legged on the ground in her shalvar. The wide trousers fell around her, a pool of tiny flowers. She drew her striped shawl around her chin, and tucked it closer, by habit, not knowing she did it. She thought, smiling, poor Munci is ashamed of his shame that my head is covered and my feet are bare. She looked up at the mountain to tell the time. Remote and gray below its sun-haloed crest, it still shadowed the eastern end of the town and made the wide sea valley between its sea cliff and Yazada the dark gray of sea dawn. It was seven o'clock.

Munci belonged, that one, to the sea, her wily sea child.

"Mother," he had told her when he was only twelve years old, "what you know as the sea is only the surface. It is a blue ceiling, and from under it you can see it waving like a silk scarf. Billowing. You see there?" He had held her hand, urgent to tell her, and he had pointed to the mountain and then to Yazada island in the distance. "I saw it today, Mother. Where the land seems to end there it does not end, it keeps on sloping down and down, an underwater sea cliff that flows into a sea valley. Fish hide in caves just like the caves on the mountain, and you can see the octopus look at you from his home with a wise eye like a quiet man. There are fans of lace, and pink flowers that hide from you if they see you, flowers that know you are coming. You float, oh, glide like when you have a dream and the air welcomes your slow flying. In the sea you fly slowly like that among the fish."

He had never talked so much to her and she knew that he had found a home he had never quite known before, and that she had lost him in the moment that he had found his own soul, down there below the silken ceiling of the sea. "In the sea valley," he was saying, "there is sand and grass, and the shells of clams stand up in the grass like tombstones, only alive, and they shine in the sea light all purple and blue pearl. You can see them breathing, but so slow, slower than we breathe. We are nervous. You have to wait to see them breathe, slow down your eyes. Oh Mother, we are nervous. You know the little lady fish, streaked with bright green? As you go deeper—only it never seems deeper because you do not measure how deep or how far as on the land, it is just there—the fish get bigger. You know it is farther from the sea ceiling because it is the home of the big fish." He dropped her hand and spread his little arms wide. "Big. Bigger than I can stretch. In the middle of the valley, fifty meters down . . ."

"You went fifty meters?" She had interrupted.

He laughed. "I ran away, down there. Anyway that is only the measure of land people." He had been contemptuous, already a man. "There is a little hill, like that one." He had turned her around toward the conical hill west of the town. "It rises from the sea valley, like that, only instead of the temple floor and the agha's tomb, and the goats, there are pieces of amphorae, and plates, and there is the arm of a man, sticking out of the top all covered with sea life where animals have built the hill up higher with their homes. Inside the amphorae, the octopi and sometimes the moray eels make their houses.

"Can you fly down a cliff except in a dream? No. Not all your prayers can do it. But there you can, down a cliff where there are caves with orange and yellow sponges that make their own light, and purple starfish that glitter, and Mother, the red starfish are pure red. Oh Mother," he said sadly, "you only see them dead. The color of their life fades out up here."

The sadness was gone as quickly as it came. She smiled. He was still, at least in moments, a little April boy.

"When you look up the cliffs they are like the castle walls and the sea ceiling curls around their towers. The light comes up from below you, from the sea floor, all shining blue. Mother, Yazada is not an island. It is a

mountain, a sister mountain to Annadağ. They meet in
a valley under the sea. There," he was suddenly all
mischief, "the fish have green blood. When you cut
your hand on a rock, your blood is bright green." Then
she had not known what to believe and what not to.

But there was something there, a closed world, and
he had gone to it and never was at home on land
again. He, troubled by landfall, sought that sea film,
sea surface, whatever it was to him. Once he was below it he was a thousand miles away from her, and
only prayer could dive after him to keep him safe. She
knew he was down there now, diving somewhere. She
had heard them come in the night, and the sound,
heavy and familiar, of the steel tanks being moved
across the floor. She had spoken to no one since. She
had awakened at six o'clock to an empty house, and,
as she always did when the men were out, she came to
her tree beside the water to aim her prayers down fifty
meters, farther than the height of the minarets.

If she did not know the sea, her bone knowledge
was of its cost. She had married among the sponge
divers, and, mashallah, was not one of the ones who
had been widowed by it. Oh yes, little Munci that day
had told her about the sea's color and seduction and
light, but, already a man keeping the sea's secret, he
had not spoken then or ever of its cost.

She was left, cast ashore by what she did know
about the bad times when the men had to dive too often in one day for the sponges because the sponge
market had fallen. Some who went out then as young
and arrogant lions were brought back moaning in the
night, their youth stolen, their limbs bent like old men
by the weight of the sea.

She had always when she was younger known when
the men were going to dive. They turned their backs
on the women and there was no warm love, no turning
to their bodies, no demand for the relief between their
thighs. It was as if they feared the sea would know
when they had been unfaithful on the night before they
sank into her, and would twist them with the bends for
jealousy. Or worse, and she had seen that often, too,
they would be brought up, their faces knocking against

the windows of the great helmets they wore in those
days, dead. She had prayed so often over the red dead,
and the blue dead that the sea had stained with the
color of its killing.

"I fear it," she had said that day to Munci.

"What you fear," he had laughed at her, "is only a
film as fine as a veil. It is no more deep than the sky
you walk in is deep under the stars. It is only the way
you see it. Look at it, Mother. Look at it breathe."

She had thought ever after of the sea swell as a great
alien breath and the water as a live thing, a rival.

Up above her Basil had rolled onto his back and begun to snore. She could hear the struggling of his
breath as he played at his nightmare, his spoiled gavur
nightmare. Far in the distance she thought she could
recognize the shape of Munci's boat returning. She got
up slowly to go to make breakfast. She knew how exhausted he would be after diving. Sometimes the men
put their heads down and slept among the plates.
When he dived with the sea torch before dawn, sometimes he would bring back a fish as big as himself. She
had to prepare the caldron with a bed of bright vegetables to cook the fish. Later she would spend the morning helping to stamp the black skin from the sponges
with her feet. She could already feel the day grow hot
on her shoulders.

Under the shadow of the cliffs of
Yazada the little kayıks lay in a semicircle in the water,
so close that the sailors could jump from one deck to
another. Munci's father sat on the low cabin roof,
smoking quietly. The kayık bobbed gently as one of the
sailors landed and stood poised, his toes clutching the
gunwales.

"Efendim," he whispered, "efendim."

Munci's father did not look up. "It is not time," he
said. They all waited for the lifting of the old man's
hand from Munci's shoulder.

The wet and sobbing girls had been taken from the

shallow water and wrapped in blankets. They sat watching too, their crying long since stopped. Two of the boys had left with the two recovered bodies of their friends after Munci's underwater torch had carved its bright column through the infinite black water to find their faces, floating among the still fish. Three were down below, five hours after the overloaded boat had tipped under the singing, swaying students.

On Huseyin's tirandil, one of several larger boats that formed an outer semicircle in the deeper water, Turgut Bey sat staring down through the carved railings at the little boats, and beyond them at the wide deep circle of black water where his daughter was. He was drained of everything but waiting, blank, except to rouse himself from time to time to send the sailor from boat to boat to see when Munci would dive again. It was clammy cold, and under the shadow of the mountain there was only light, no color yet, no deception of beauty, just the gray rock showing through the shallow water of the cove below them, and within the circle of the boats and the cliff, black water.

"It is not time," Munci's father told the sailor again. "It is only an hour since he went forty meters. He has made four dives in four hours. Now he must wait until light."

The father had spoken. No one contradicted him. Munci reached up and his father put his cigarette between his fingers, neither of them noticing that Munci had never smoked in his father's presence before, not in all his thirty years.

On the tirandil, the message aroused Turgut Bey from his stupor. "But it is light." He could feel his will push against that of the other father, and knew he had no right to lose his temper. He had taken in through his muffled shock in the night that the diver had to rest between dives. At first he had balked. "Where are the other divers?"

"But there is only one sea torch. Munci does the night diving."

In the face of so many facts, for once so huge and unmovable around him, that he could not manipulate, Turgut Bey sat on in the cold patience of shock. It had been a question of light before, but now, with the dawn, and the sun like a halo on the great mountain across the channel, they had made a new excuse.

"Efendim, it is not yet light under the water. There it is still night."

Along the shore beyond the cliff, where it widened into a field, dawn-colored with black poppies and stark white daisies, Turgut Bey could see the perfect land where the hotel would rise. He could see it as if it already existed, pure white, with a balcony for every room, facing the sea, if only the young fool would listen.

Why they so often had to go through the soft needle's eye of some young American fool who looked like every other young American fool whenever there was a new enterprise, he did not know—blank-faced, boneless, badly tailored, bad-mannered, provincial budalalar, imbeciles. He longed for the old days of the British and the French. Most of the Americans did not even bother to learn the language, and they treated men of culture, ruined before they began, as you treat children, careful to explain the obvious.

Oh well, two eyes see one sword edge. At least they had little chance to go beyond the barriers of the educated, the businessmen, and the landowners who could keep control of things. He thought then of the new, dangerous exceptions to that, the misguided young and their evil leaders. He thought of his own daughter, his flower, how she had been ruined and depraved by the education he could not stop her having—an intelligent girl. Allah deliver a man from an intelligent daughter!

The old, habitual prayer was a foul thing that made his stomach melt. His prayer had indeed been answered. Allah had delivered him from an intelligent girl. She lay somewhere down there under the black water. He began to cry again, and his mind jumped and trembled. That hole will make a good pool for diving and swimming. We will make a wall around it. The water that surrounds it is only two meters deep— less. A man can stand in it. It will cost 40,000 Turkish lire, 100,000 lire, 140,000 lire, he recited a litany. The people who are not staying at the hotel will have to pay . . . and for docking . . . such thoughts could not save him. They were like dream flashes. He went on crying, seeing her as a little girl. She would have outgrown her revolt and been a good daughter. She would have married a good man like Huseyin. He knew it.

He began to see her as she would have been, later, except for this accident. He resolved to remember her as she would have been. He knew she would want that. How far back did the accident that had taken her go? Where had he made his mistake with her? If she had not been with the students, if she had not refused to come to dinner, if she had not been led astray, she would not be there lying somewhere deep below him under the darkness. Neither he nor Huseyin, who had come up behind him and put his arm around the older man's shoulders, mirroring Munci's father, thought of the overloaded boat.

Not a boat moved, no wind, no motion in the dawn. The mirror reflections were still. The men stared at the water or at the mountains, as men do when they wait, all apart from each other.

Kemal noticed that. He was doing it, too. Behind him on the afterdeck of Munci's boat there was something he didn't want to look at, a bundle wrapped in a sail, leaking water on the deck. Its feet stuck out wearing new handmade sandals.

Kemal had long since crawled out from where he had hidden among the fishing nets. He stared at the black hole in the water and willed himself not to look behind him. Even if his father beat him and then made him pray for staying away all night and keeping his mother from sleeping, he knew he had to come, to be Timur's eyes. He looked up into the distance to where Timur's mountain rose, so mist-gray and remote in the morning that it seemed as far away and uncaring as the moon, so beautiful that it made its smaller sister mountain in the sea, Yazada, look like the backbone of a mule tethered under water.

Timur had told him about the black hole, and how it

took a million years for it to be there. Eons, he called the time. Kemal wondered at how long it took to make an accident—eons or a second. He didn't know. Timur had told him about how the earth grew. He told him how slowly it cast up its mountains out of the sea, how once the fishes had swum around the top of the great mountain, how on the shores of Yazada the rock had been thrown up, sometimes slowly, sometimes by the earth's anger, the earthquake. Timur said no—he said the earth could not get angry like a man. There were things even Timur did not know.

The rocks rose in waves, layer on layer. Timur said that Yazada was hollow, too, like the mother mountain; its caves ran all the way below the sea floor, fathoms under. He showed him the cave ceilings under the shallow water, an undersea shelf so smooth in places that it was like a manmade floor, buckled by earth heaves.

Timur had told him many reasons, too many, but not enough. Now the men around him had reasons of their own. He tried to plait them all together into an answer of his own. He had heard an old man murmur in the night, like a prayer, when the first body was brought up in Munci's arms, that Allah took whom he wished to take.

Then, as the waiting stretched and covered them all so that he felt as if he would not want to breathe for fear of disturbing it, he heard the sailors blaming Huseyin for the overloaded boat. All the reasons were too much and not enough. They had forgotten the hole itself, how it was made, how it had waited for the strangers.

He remembered it well, because it was the day before his circumcision, when he was eight, and he was nervous about that. They had heard the earth roar and shake in the night. It had rattled the windows and put out the oil lamp, and his mother's wedding pitcher had jumped off the shelf and clanged on the floor. In the morning it looked as if nothing had happened. The sea was as calm as it was this morning.

But there, beside the shore of Yazada, the sea surge and earth tremor had caused the ceiling of one of the underwater caves to give way. They had rowed up to its edge where the boats waited now, and there in a circle, bound on one side by the cliff and on the other by the old sea floor, the sea hole had fallen in one minute of one night, deep blue in the pale inshore water in daylight, but in the night invisible in the black sea surface.

He knew what had happened as if it had happened to him. In his mind, he could hear himself singing with the students. They sang, swaying the boat in rhythm. One of the boys was playing the saz. He could feel it with his fingers in the dawn.

He could feel the boat tip over, the bottom under his feet, the fright, the water to his shoulders. He waded to the rickety quay. He counted noses, a still voice in all the hysteria of the night, the realization that five of them were missing, the stretch of minutes while they waited; they called names into the dark. Some of the boys went back into the water. He dived with them. There was only black water, and nothing, nothing but cold and fear.

Then he was one of the five, seeking foothold in the black hole. He sank with them into the blackness, the surprise, the panic, the flailing, then slower and slower they sank among the eels and the octopi, spread-eagled, over twenty fathoms falling.

She was not there. She was not anywhere but in his mind in the night when he smuggled himself aboard Munci's boat, and came with them to find her. He had tried, jumping from boat to boat. They said there was a girl still down there, but it could not be Lale. It was the daughter of that fat old man, the derebey, and that could not be the girl Kemal had followed, being Timur's eyes.

In a single release of light the sun edged above the great mountain and turned its slopes to gold. It stained the poppies red and the daisies bright yellow in the field at Yazada. The black hole turned blue as an evil eye. Munci leaned over the side to clean his face mask and adjust it on his face. Kemal always liked that part. Munci held his arms out for the tanks. Kemal watched the black man with the glass face and the black tube like a snake in his mouth tip backwards into the water, his huge black fish-fin feet comic in the spray. He was proud of him, Timur's friend, his dost, his ağabey. He knew that if he needed help for Timur it was to Munci he would go. Then he knew that it was hopeless. There was no way to tell him. Munci teased him too, but he was not unkind like the others.

        Ariadne floated between night dreams and the day. She wanted to think of it as her creative time—not that she made anything then, just lay under her grandmother's quilt. She simply wanted to exist for a while, fashioning thoughts for herself. She saw them as thoughts of dew and steel, ephemeral and lasting.

For a little while, as the seven o'clock sun touched the far corner of her room, she was really in Ceramos; she saw it again as on the first day she had seen it, luminous with possibility.

She knew that if she moved a muscle, she would begin to float toward her real waking through the fat, sad debris of old despairs, self-derisions, old scenes got wrong in dreams, detritus left over from the night. In that flotsam of sleep there were voices she didn't want to hear anymore, and places she no longer remembered as they had been.

Sometimes when the sun touched the inner corner of the window ledge, and threw the latticed shadows of the shutters on the floor, they were like prison bars. She would still be struggling so within the past, left over and made grotesque by sleep, that for a while she wouldn't know where she was, after three years. Sometimes, the better times, the images were blotted out by waking and only the tears were left on her face to remind her of where she might have been in the night.

So she lay still, hoping for repose, a state which she glimpsed sometimes as a growing maternal sluggishness, the peace past despair.

But that hope was already being pierced by the voices of the neighbor women gathering in the street below, as they did every morning, a dawn chorus of old birds. She tried not to hear them, not yet. There was something she wanted to know, some kind of justice, and she was willing to wait for it alone in her bed poised in the touch of sun which now reached her face, above the blue harbor of Ceramos.

She knew that her memory had been blocked by a scar. She had gone down once in defeat, before an act so central that what came from it twittered and slipped away, and what came after it was so colored by it that there was no chronology, only the central wound, with all her subsequent acts splayed out from it. She wished it had more style, an importance of its own as an event, but it didn't. It had been, God help her, too domestic, too dim for tragedy, neither as well made nor as original as her pride would have chosen. All the same, it had brought her down as far as despair.

She realized sometimes that she had been silly, that was part of the crime. She saw her marriage resolve itself into mile after mile of wool forming into needlework before her eyes, all that native wild Virginia flora spread on pillows through familiar houses. She saw pot on pot on pot, for flowers, for nuts, for fruit in fruit colors, and one absolutely dear one her friends had all loved, designed to hold potpourri. She gave it filled, and with her own recipe on a little tag.

"What was wrong? What was wrong with all of that?" She didn't know she had begun to whisper. "It wasn't an important activity, but I didn't hurt anybody. I spread pleasure, minor pleasure to be sure, but dammit, nice things, thoughtful things." And then she said aloud, "Oh Roger, why didn't you let us have children?" and had to laugh there all alone, because this time she called him up, he came all comic from the dream she had forgotten, standing stark naked under one of the twin maples on the lawn in Fairfax County, and she could smell again, she always did, the scent of damp, new-cut Virginia grass.

He was wearing Argyle socks and nothing else, but

that had been later, she was sure, in what had really happened and not the dream, all telescoped by her half-dead desire.

"*They* paid attention to me anyway," she said and sounded, even to herself, like a child. "You hated that too." She was trying to remember what he really looked like. "You said they only gathered around me to work in the afternoons because crafts were in and the country club was out that summer. It was mean to say, but it was true. They treated me like one of themselves. Oh God, I really thought that at the time. I was caught up in the fashion for the young."

Lying in bed, and seeing the old smokehouse, and the potter's wheel she'd left behind, she saw the red water flying off it, the wet clay a whirling center. She could feel more than see something form and grow within the vortex of that mass alive within her cupped hands, reflecting some perfect thing forming in her center, her tandem. She had studied Zen. She could feel all through her body the dreamy sensuous pleasure of the clay's wetness, growing upwards in the circle of her deceptively strong intelligent fingers which seemed no part of her as they worked on their own. She drifted under waking for a second until the voices of the women below the window jarred her back, and she brought with her the end of something, a fragment, and thought before she thought, "I must tell Roger . . . it was all that icy honesty the young impose on you . . . why, I would watch a boy's long hair fall forward as he bent his head and think, you couldn't bear it, honesty I mean. But not many people can at any age. Anyway, I knew I was letting them say too much of whatever it was, as we all did then—you see I was afraid if I didn't they would leave. They opened wounds they had no inkling of, and I offered them as gifts they hadn't asked for. I remember one of them told me once I looked like St. Sebastian, St. Sebastian! and reached out and took my hair in his hands, but if I'd touched his . . ."

She had driven them into Washington when they asked her to, because they paid attention to her. She didn't like thinking that. "Who would?" she defended herself against the thought. "Oh God, why did my only brush with martyrdom have to be such a parody? I suffer as much as if it were real. There I was, Joan of Arc from the suburbs; my car was full of the sons of old friends and government officials. I was excited that day. I felt brave; the smell of Mace, not too near, intimations of violence just out of sight. One of the boys cut his head and was sick in the car.

"Poor Roger. Poor old Roger. Why did we go there? I should have known how they'd treat you, and you minded so. I watched you adjusting yourself to a world I'd grown up in . . . Roger the outlander, although no one said it. They said instead how bright you were, which was just as bad. Damn them, they could have helped, but you know how stupid they were. I saw you take too much time to learn to beat them at a game not worth a man's spirit."

The voice from the minaret near the quay called "Dikkat, dikkat" for the seven-thirty bus to Istanbul. It was so faint, so far away she could hardly hear it. She fell into paths, roads, the aircraft, the trains, the busses that moved her along that path of inevitability. The past, she dreamed, always seems inevitable. It had to happen that way. But it didn't. They didn't need to go to Washington. It was her own fault, all her fault.

She had wanted to guide him out of a place that demanded less of him than he could give, and punished him for giving more. What is a woman for? She wanted to break the suspension of potential he lived in that diminished him, that constantly reminded him of things other men were allowed to forget, a man in a student's world, the trials of strength that didn't need to be, all those innocent loose sensualities.

"The vocation you chose wouldn't let you grow up," she told that resident who would not leave her mind for long. "Was that why you wouldn't let us have children? Did you want one place where you wouldn't be reminded?"

She could see him in their bedroom mirror, trusting her to watch him draw in his diaphragm twenty times. She could see his face setting itself for one of those self-expanding hints of little adventures consciously arranged. She understood. Understood. Stood under the weight of them. Anger welled up from the memory and she clenched her teeth and hands, then, feeling the tension, did the Yoga dead man asana until she was quiet again.

It had been a relief at first to go to Washington. It was more than a compliment. Roger was honored by it. He took on honors gracefully. It was a talent of his. She was astonished that she knew so little of what he did, looking back. Who wanted a historian whose period was Persia in the sixteen hundreds?

But they hadn't escaped the young, and that was her fault. All at once she saw the boys again, the potting shed, herself freed for afternoons at least from that preoccupation with Roger he had always taken for granted.

She saw herself as glowing from the kiln, after the closeness of them. It was that he envied. She had not known it before. She had not. In Cambridge she had looked older than Roger. In Fairfax County she looked younger. The new little habits, her hair, her nails—he had seen them day by day, and had said nothing, banking up his resentment. Her anger of a few minutes before she saw growing in him, as unknown to himself as his had been to her. Inside his skin, failed, flawed, it had been worse, as it was, she was sure, with a man.

It had struck, as everything did sooner or later, his man's unstaunched ambition. Roger's ambition had for so long been a thing to be cared for, fed, ever growing, never satisfied. She saw him doing everything else to assuage it except the thing he wanted and could never name, not knowing what it was. She felt him naked and revealed, as in her own body, and it hinted of a private, unnamed tragedy. He had envied and acted on the wrong thing in her. Little and silly as they were to him, she had made things of her own, hints of the lineaments, Blake called them, of at least some desire satisfied. She must have maddened him so often, that daily calm of satisfaction rubbing across his ragged hope.

She saw a man trapped and beating against the prison of his ambition while she, like the parody of in Weimar, went on cutting bread and butter—made pots with the children, did needlework, baked bread, made yogurt, grew flowers, and turned the pages, without much attention, of those conceptual books that women read who are not sleeping very well—Martin Buber's *I and Thou*, excerpts from Kierkegaard, Emerson's essays. How selfish she had been! The books had rested always on her bedside table, her retreat from his breathing, beside an ashtray of rose medallion he had given her, while she waited for something she knew was never going to happen.

But it did. My God, Roger, it did and I know when, the day, the hour even. I do miss our kitchen. It was the first kitchen I ever had that was the way I wanted it. I heard your car door slam and I glanced up at the clock.

What was I doing? Oh, putting vegetables into the best bowl I ever made, not looking but gazing; how important small things are. Against the blue, a true cobalt for once, so hard to get, the sliced carrots, the cucumbers, those tiny red tomatoes were no more alive than its color. I could still, when I held it, feel it being born into my hands. I didn't see you come into the kitchen. I just heard the screen door whisper behind you. That's when you said, "They're not coming," and you sounded like you were announcing the end of the world.

I looked at you then, and . . . you know I really thought somebody had died and you were going to break it to me, as people do. You jerked open the refrigerator door and got out ice, and I knew it was a quarrel and not bad news.

I hadn't told you I'd asked other people—my people, you called them. I went to the telephone in that wide, dark, dog-run hall. Oh God, it was a lovely, quiet old house. I thought I'd be there forever. Jamie Stewart was petulant, being put off like that, but then he always was petulant about something. I was sorry about it. I knew any little thing could start him off again.

When I came back you were gone. I saw you through the window, standing in the garden as you are in the dream, only you had your clothes on. I think I remember . . . every time I kill you you are standing in just that place. It was as if you were waiting for the darkness to hide your face. We sat without saying a word until the light from the kitchen window cut across the lawn and the lightning bugs were little darting stars. You got up three times to fill your glass—not mine. Mine had long since been drained. I could feel it dry and warm in my hand. I was afraid to put it down and I didn't know why.

So I sat there on the lawn in what I called my dark and sacred wood. I never told you that. You would have laughed. So would Basil. I always loved it at the first dark—my small-town lawn with maple trees and the lovely deep scent of the grass that I had ordered cut one day early because people were coming for drinks.

I can still hear you saying, "I resigned," and I still want to turn those words back into your mouth. Why? You didn't have to. No one told you to. You could have ridden it out. You could have defended me. You had been waiting all banked up with resentment I didn't know about for something to jog you into retreat.

You made my sacred wood into a small area of terror and cold. "Did you hear me? I resigned," you said and you didn't need to say it again. You knew that. The word *resigned* was active, not passive, not resignation in any Christian sense . . .

Your fury was as sudden as if you had already told me the beginning instead of just the end of it. How did you say it? "The boys, dear, were a mistake," or is that the way Basil would say it? Sometimes I get your voices mixed. You told me we had been investigated, but that was no surprise. I know your words were cold and abstract and cube-like, like the ice I could hear in your glass.

Oh God, we were judged in those days by evil-minded men, and we were part of it. We hardly even questioned it, except as a luxury once in a while. You said another thing you didn't have to say; you told me for the hundredth time that academics were mistrusted, playing a little bit at academic freedom as you did

sometimes. You told me the drive to the demonstration
had been reported, and normally, you said, it wouldn't
matter but you were—what was it?—working in a very
sensitive area. God, what language! What you said
then, I'm remembering right no matter what you say.
"It's all known," you said. "Every day's conversation
over that damned kiln reported to his goddamned gen-
teel government daddy by one of those little middle-
class bastards posing as revolutionaries. They were all
the children of your smart friends. Jesus, I knew they'd
finally get to me." You were raving, Roger, you were
using your social hatred like a knife. I honestly didn't
know what you were talking about, national security or
your jealousy of a few half-stoned kids.

Anger still rose throat-high as she lay in bed in
Ceramos wishing she were free enough of memory to
get up. She never knew anymore whether it was all a
perversion of memory, the truth, or a dream. That was
the trouble. She couldn't be sure. She only knew it held
her there.

"I will go back," she thought he had said, "to Harvard." He sounded tragic and she wanted to giggle. He
had said *I*, not *we*. That was it, the moment under the
maple trees, the depths of darkness touched by acid-
green electric leaves over their heads.

You had already decided to leave me. There wasn't
even another woman. Fear? No, something worse.
Sometimes I suspect that you were bored, and that you
felt guilty about it. You felt, somehow, unsafe. You
were using one small act of mine to excuse yourself.
What I didn't know was that you brought your corruption with you. I thought it was part of what we were
running away from. You had been weakened for too
long by too small a safety, and it never entered your
mind to do anything but save yourself and give yourself
redeeming reasons for it. The pattern I had seen in a
hundred mild little faculty betrayals was traced there in
our own garden, and I was the one who had to be betrayed for safety's sake and I don't think by then you
even knew it. You had been so trained in what you
called the politics of circumlocution. You just left me
to it instinctively, without considering for a minute that

you had any other choice. You even left me to pack everything up. Oh dear, Roger, your sadness was so dim, finally, when for years you had shone for me like a light.

Had she guided him into the kitchen after that like a drunk, hurt boy? Had they sat down together and had some supper? By the time he had finished a bottle of Old Crow, his resignation had nothing to do with her at all. He was General Gavin. He was Sidney Carton and Eugene McCarthy. He got younger and younger, the boy who stood on the burning deck. He was sick on the kitchen floor. He said that even a turtle had a soul. He said it was an act of conscience, an act of national conscience. He had believed that firmly of himself ever since; he was a hero at Harvard. Later he fell asleep naked in his Argyle socks on the sofa from Altman's.

In the morning he left. He said it would look better if he left right away, and when he went out to the car he was crying and he kept his head down.

Between the act on the dark lawn, the I, and the knowledge of the I which came later, there had been that time she looked back on with the most embarrassment, the time of her awful blue-green courage. She was very fair about Roger. She understood. It had been a habit for so long, hard to break. She understood all through those months at the Georgetown shop, surrounded, as for a safety of her own, with needlework and ceramics. She saw herself as the brave victim of the gentle, sensitive academic mind that had destroyed her. She told herself that she was relieved to be out of it, that community like an old monastery, with too few saints and too many sissies, men whose will had failed, all gentle, so gentle, and scholarly women who fought old aggressive battles Ariadne could not name.

Then there was the phrase of her sorrow when she sought out novels written by academic wives and held them up as mirrors to herself. She saw Roger then as a victim too, sapped of courage and toughness by the occupational hazards of his job. She was unaware that she had caught it too. That awareness came later. She saw it as a disease, the preoccupation with small hurts, the ambition in miniature, the anger diminished into malice.

She convinced herself in turn that she had been the one to act, but she carried, unknown, her longing for the small acceptance of the others, whoever they were. Knowing later that she had been infected didn't help. She still stayed up too late at night, washing glasses.

Then, one morning in the Georgetown apartment, as on this morning, she woke with something between her and the day. It was the knowledge of that I, not safe in her head, but in her gut, the ice of its inevitability, its no way back. That was a year later, Thanksgiving, the beginning of Advent.

She heard a voice. It was a woman's voice. It said clearly, "In order to find light you must go where it is dark." Her grandmother would have said it was the voice of Jesus, but she heard it as the voice of a woman.

All of her muscles of courage melted. She saw, flickering against the pretty silk curtains, a hint that the apartment was on fire, but it was cold as ice. The fire threw shadows of women as tall as the ceiling, thousands of them, an army. They whispered, not even whispers; they were breezes and shadows at the edge of her eyes. She remembered making herself get up, all surrounded by the cold fire, and put on her dressing gown, tie its belt slowly and carefully, and go to the telephone. She canceled every date in her date book. She called the shop and said carefully that she had to quit for religious reasons, to honor Advent. She made a long order to the health food store and told them to leave it outside her door.

Then, very deliberately (she remembered how slow all the decisions were) she went back to bed and stayed there for a month. Once in a while the telephone rang, and she roused herself out of the bog of sleep that lasted eighteen hours a day and answered it as if she were just on her way out.

Once you called, Roger, and, after all our living together, you didn't hear anything wrong. You had misplaced an insurance policy, and all the time we talked, the shadow women watched. They were suspended against the ceiling. I lived on Bircher Muesli, Tiger's Milk, raisins, nuts, and therapeutic vitamins. I found myself at one with the thousands of shadow caryatids that flowed in waves about me. I wanted to apologize to them for something I didn't bother to name.

Sometimes I was all the women in all the apartments in cities, behind locked doors, gin-laden or religious or unwanted.

I made my bed carefully every day and got back into it and watched the soap operas if it was light outside and the family shows if it was dark. There was only light and dark, no time. I found myself in the television too, perpetually pregnant, perpetually abandoned, perpetually accused of ring around the collar. I cried about that. I hadn't known I was guilty of that. In old magazines the cleaning woman had left in my kitchen, in the Mother of God when I turned on the Mass on Sunday, I saw myself. I became universal and nameless, in my pretty blue-green room with the materials at hand.

You see, I had not known, before that Advent, how deeply in love with you I was. You had, within me, become young again. I had seen you husked of courage, God knows, but I was left pregnant with a braver man to love. You left me the man you wanted to be. He was as far from you as I am far from home.

At the end of the darkness, three days before Christmas, I walked into my kitchen and picked up the blue bowl. I saw it in my hands, and I saw it on the floor, smashed. Now I remember looking at the fragments on the dirty floor, but I was holding it in my hands. I saw that part of what I had been doing was helping you destroy me, as I had helped you in everything else. I held the bowl high.

I noted the sun slant, and thought it was morning. I dialed for the time, and set my clock. It was four o'clock in the afternoon. I noticed the rat's nest of my hair and the baby sour smell of my body. I drew a bath and weighed myself. In four weeks I had gained thirty pounds.

The sun reached deep into the room. Below her the neighbor women had begun their first quarrel. It was time to get up. Ariadne was as tired from the recall as if it had been the real thing, not an obsessive repetition. She put her feet to the floor, disappointed.

Recall was supposed to be therapeutic, a mental bath; abreaction, liberation by revival, the psyche's deep confession. The assumption underlying the practice of abreaction was that—wait now—forgotten or repressed ideas—was it ideas or pictures?—were, what was the word, *besetzt* by a charge of emotional energy or libido, and that the process of abreaction discharged this energy from the . . . something . . . body? System? That's what it was. A system.

"I must not do it right," she said aloud, worried.

She lifted her body from the bed. She felt as heavy as she had felt that December day, even though she had lost the thirty pounds again. It had taken three years. She still found lists sometimes—an envelope from the Greek-American shipping line marked, feta cheese, 100 calories, 5 olives, 26 calories; an American Express Company receipt; white wine, 100 calories, one glass a day. She thought of the self-occupation as a kind of blessing. It had, except for rifts of despair, protected her.

She looked around the same bedroom where she had seen the great caryatids built of smoke ascending against the ceiling. She had carried that room with her, a continuity of safety and taste, from Virginia to Georgetown, to Majorca, to Greece, and now to the Turkish coast. She placed her "pretties," as her grandmother had called them, always in the same places.

The rose medallion ashtray that Roger had given her sat beside the books and the lamp on her bedside table. The quilt her grandmother had made had fallen to the floor. Needlework pillows, a blue-glass vase, the same blue-green silk curtains, the always white walls—all were the same.

The dark blue wall charts that covered the wall opposite her bed were new; she had "taken up" astronomy for a while because the stars were so demandingly bright over the Aegean. Her bulletin board was an old habit; its reminders, in heavy black Magic Markers, had evolved as she read, or thought, or traveled on. Roger had called them her intellectual's "Jesus Saves." Most of them were faded, dead from being unread.

Only the size of the room and the view outside the window had changed, as objects of sight change and leave the sense within at whatever peace or torment or old scenes it carries, the same, always the same at the eye's core.

She thought that this designed sameness she carried with her for safety was individual and conscious, not realizing that her habits were as primal as a Bedouin woman's, who sets up her permanencies every night, or that her belongings, her endearments, were of the kind a woman carries slung over her shoulder to run before war or nature.

She stood in front of her window, breathed deeply, and moved slowly through her morning "hymn to the sun" four times.

The sun had touched Yazada in the distance and she knew by that that it was eight o'clock. She could see a faint circle of fishing boats, and it made Munci intrude on her cleansed mind. She knew then why he hadn't taken her with him. He was fishing with his own people in a closed circle of little boats. She felt left out and was ashamed of that.

The stairs were rickety and she tiptoed down them and across the courtyard to her kitchen, trying to keep from waking little Lisa, unofficial goddaughter, Jamie Stewart's child from Culpepper County, Virginia, who was sleeping in the storeroom at the corner of the terrace that she had made into a pretty guestroom. She thought, Lisa, like the curtains and the rose medallion, has followed me here.

As she made her coffee, she thought of the sheep on the boat's prow, and the ribbon of blood. She thought of sacrifice and its demands and felt a little happier.

Now it was her pleasure time, coffee in bed, and

peace and a little reading. She gave herself this every morning. She pulled the quilt over her feet and looked for places to repair.

"The only thing I don't remember is that Christmas," she complained to a place in the quilt where the stitching had come loose. "That's funny. You usually do. Holidays I mean. I remember every single one, especially the ones in Virginia. We were too civilized to make much of it and Roger is agnostic. But that one . . . you would have thought. I must have been alone still. I wouldn't have dared let my mother see me unhappy."

She found her needle and thread and began to match her grandmother's crow's-foot stitches. But as soon as it was over, I moved. I promised myself I would start the new year someplace else, any place Roger and I had never been together. I bought an annuity that gave me one hundred dollars a month. That, with Roger's two hundred dollars' alimony, I instructed the Chase Manhattan Bank to send me each month, wherever I was.

Now he was married again, a woman twenty years younger than he was, with a master's degree in what she called Lit, one of those deceptively safe little faculty wives with a will of steel. Ariadne knew that when he thought about her at all, it was with a mild mixture of kindness, indifference, and hope that she would marry again. She knew he could use the two hundred dollars. She could see him, drawing on his Argyle socks, and not allowing himself to say, "I wish to Jesus she would marry again."

"Those goddamned Argyle socks," she said aloud and set her cup down so hard that coffee spilled on Emerson's essays and she had to run for a cloth.

The morning felt good in Frank Proctor's body. By eight-thirty he had already made two of the self-promised visits to his friends. He had ordered trousers from Hassan, the tailor, and drunk tea with him while he watched his twelve-year-old apprentice iron seams with the ancient tailor's box-iron filled with coals, and wanted them to change nothing ever. He had had his feet measured by Aydin for sandals, while he listened to old Beatles songs on the tape recorder. He had bought cigarettes named for the City of Samsun, where the ten thousand had shouted THALASSA, pleasantly aware of the fact.

He had been received with the warm politeness, that mirror of friendship, affection's gesture, that he knew was cultural. He had written guidelines for new people pointing it out. The narrow street opened to him like a private home, the early sun stretched and healed him. Dirty Dervish, in the door of the bakal, scratched under his arms to wake himself, and called "Hoshgeldin." It was all exactly right, the beginning of the kind of day in Ceramos that he had promised himself as soon as his work was finished. He looked back on the day before with some derision, the heavy pretentious lunch, the long parade, the too expensive dinner with its false hospitality and its carrier wave of watchfulness and money. They had, in the morning light, those men, the naiveté of vultures. He had totally forgotten his uneasy dawn.

He knew he ought to be noticing the sweep of the castle against the sky, the dogshit in the gutter, at least the bougainvillea, being in the sea south, unaware that it did not bloom until June. Someone had taught him, or he had read, or something, that it was the mark of a good eye, an open mind to notice. He simply felt good. He bought a Paris *Herald* and wandered toward Salmakis kahve.

The awning of leafy branches was still fresh. The sun filtered through its edges where the branch ends ran free. Under the thick roof, it cast its own green shade onto the tables set around the door, the doorstep made of half a marble column, the hunched backs of men already playing tavla and drinking tea. Frank sat where he could see Salmakis fountain.

On the low cliff behind it a fig tree hovered, protecting the water. Its large flat leaves rippled with reflected light. No time had disturbed the pool; the marble pebbles, the flecks of fool's gold still washed down its floor from deep within the hill behind it. On the marble wall inside the fountain a perpetual line of old men marched across the rock, now little more than rock visions carved by the water. Their faint pert beards were cracked. The votive cups they held up toward the cleft overflowed with fine rock moss. A marble ledge ran round the outside of the pool. On the café side, Murat, the owner, had set broken sea-encrusted amphorae of geraniums and sea orchids. On the mosque side, a low trough had been carved from the rock; from a small lion's mouth of brass, water ran into it to wash the hands and feet of a few old men making their ablutions before they went to pray. In the center of the fountain ledge, nearest the sea, one of the sailors was filling a plastic jar to take to his boat.

Beyond the damp green smell and shadow the white mosque shone in the new sun, its bowl of a roof glistening so that Frank had to turn his eyes away. Its delicate minaret was etched in light. There was an almost imperceptible movement of men from fountain to mosque, and then to the kahve tables.

Frank couldn't catch Murat's attention. He was staring out across the quay at a line of fishing boats, new painted for the season, their red flags with the crescent and the star lifting in the morning breeze. Frank ignored an American Impala parked on the quay, and stared with Murat beyond it.

The boats were sailing toward their mooring after the night's fishing. It made Frank feel safe that it was all the same, year after year. He was pleased that he had sensed it again so quickly, the timelessness of attendance in the shade. They were all waiting. They had been waiting for years, for centuries for something unnamed, something, Frank was sure, that was to come from the sea. He set the *Herald* aside to read later, when Murat was ready to bring his tea, as happy in his own native slowness and patience, just like the others, as if he were dancing with them. He was dedicated, at that moment, to the preservation of Ceramos.

He had seen the other towns along the coast already lost to creeping convenience, AID advice, wide highways, the Euro Club chalets, the articles in fashion magazines that brought the rich, but not yet Ceramos, not, at least, at eight-thirty on a kind, uneventful spring morning. Far away he heard the faint boom of dynamite for the new road. A tiny blossom of yellow dust rose beyond the hill houses and lingered in the air. A cat's paw of sea breeze was troubling the fountain's surface. Troubling. Frank couldn't remember where the word came from. Someone had troubled the waters.

A few old men were drifting out of the mosque. They leaned down slowly to put on their shoes, and moved with habit faces like the bas-reliefs of the marble ancients toward the kahve. Behind them a group of young men came out into the sun, looking around them, registering the demand to be noticed there. They were the young politicos of the Emir party. A few men came out alone. There were always a few, Frank noticed, who came out alone from any church, with still, devout faces. He wished fleetingly that he could be one of them.

Huseyin and the Captain of the Gendarmes stood together in the mosque doorway. Frank saw that Huseyin's face was streaked with red, as if he had been crying, or someone had slapped him, and that the Captain had his arm around him, supporting him. Frank hoped the Captain wouldn't notice him, not on his day off.

It was Saturday, not the right day for public prayer. Frank had not heard the müezzin cry. The loudspeakers at the top of the minaret were silent. Frank remembered that the Friday sermon usually boomed out over the end of the town while a steady stream of blasphemous comment went on below among the young men in the kahve. It was the first clue he had that something was the matter.

A sailor on Huseyin's tirandil was tying a rope to a bollard on the quay in front of him. The polished railings on its elegant fat stern were shining with new varnish. Beside it Monkey was backing his small boat into its mooring. On deck, his father held in his arms a broken old man. Frank recognized Turgut Bey, stripped of Paris and London and money, his face blank of any intelligence at all. No one was speaking.

Men were gathering around the quay where the boat was slowly nosing in. He saw that Monkey was still in his black wet suit. Everyone seemed to have his back to Frank, except the two old men.

"They pass us by as if we were not real when something like this happens. As long as I have been here. I have had a friend die and not been told until I saw the funeral pass." The European proprietor of the Artemis bar had sat down beside Frank. He had tried to get a handle on him at one point. He had thought a bar owner might be useful in Ceramos, especially one who was shaky about his license, a semilegal foreigner. Frank thought he might be able to use a friend with some clout. David was clean. He had looked that up, no contacts with the left outside of his business, and Jesus, even commies had to drink once in a while.

There were his contacts with some of the expatriates, most of whom had fairly seamy but totally unimportant fringe records. Frank had a real contempt for them. He couldn't stand emotion without intelligence. His instinct had told him, though, not to try to make the contact. He had a fairly sure feeling that if he moved any closer than the width of the bar, the man would not even be annoyed. He would laugh and the laughter would be public. Just as a matter of business, he knew better than to trust him.

"What's going on?" he asked David. It wasn't that he was prejudiced. He'd never been prejudiced. He'd always been attracted to Jewish girls. He just didn't know why he felt so careful and exposed in front of him.

"There were five students drowned last night at Yazada."

"I didn't know." Frank felt impotent. Death made a man feel impotent. Even with that one sentence David had made him feel guilty and dumb.

"How would you know? They turn their backs when there's trouble. It's pride. They brought two of them in about four this morning. The other three . . . they must have found them." David wasn't looking at him.

Even at Yale Frank had learned to be wary. They were so damned intelligent. "Don't use them. They're all pinkos," he had been advised once by one of those old men he had always despised. Frank was ashamed of himself. He tried to pull himself out of the isolation of his shame and get interested in what was happening. The Captain was supporting Huseyin over to the crowd around the boat.

"What's the matter with Huseyin?"

"It was his boat that overturned. He is probably mourning the paint work." David picked up Frank's *Herald* and seemed to scan it. "I wouldn't stare if I were you. They might resent it. The boat, of course, was overloaded. That man would fuck his mother for five kurush."

"Why are you whispering?" Frank was suddenly annoyed at the man, at his playing at secrecy. Even in disaster, that salty Ceramian malice always shocked him. Americans and Europeans picked it up when they had been there too long. Bartender descreet, that's what the man was. They never get drunk, Jews. They let you get drunk. That wasn't prejudice, nothing to do with that. It was a known fact. He wondered what David was really doing in Ceramos.

David rattled the paper to cover his voice. "Huseyin is müdür, mayor." He explained what Frank already knew. "They say he cried in his mother's womb. God knows it's his only qualification, outside of owning the place. I don't want my dog poisoned, my license revoked, hash planted in my bar, or my kitchen declared unsanitary."

"What kitchen?" That nice German archeologist had come up and was standing behind them.

"The one in the toilet."

"What is happening, oh my God!" Horst sat down without speaking to Frank. He couldn't help but wonder why.

A bundle wrapped in a sea-stained sail was being eased into the arms of the men on the quay. They handled it awkwardly, as if it were heavier than it looked. Frank tried to watch a dragonfly playing on the surface of the fountain. When he had to glance at the boat again, a second bundle was being passed over the stern. As many hands as could reach him helped Tur-

gut Bey ashore. He pulled away from them and fell
across one of the bundles, sobbing. Someone pulled
him away. His hands were still clutching the sail. As he
was pulled to his feet, it came up with him.

The girl rolled out of it onto the pavement. Her face
was washed completely calm, there were black sockets
where her eyes had been. Her head was slightly turned.
Water poured from her mouth, her clothes, her hair.
Frank felt the tea come back into his mouth, sour. He
wanted somebody to wipe her nose. Her wet hair
splayed over the pavement. Her face was light blue,
her opened mouth blue-black. On her blue fingers, her
nails were bright red shells of European polish. Monkey jumped ashore and tore the sail from Turgut Bey's
hands. He covered her face again, and walked off alone
down the quay.

Turgut Bey looked up then and saw Frank. "You!"
he screamed. "If there was a hotel there is lifeguards
like the hotels in Miami Beach in Florida. This would
not happen." Because he had screamed in English,
none of the men around him understood or cared what
he said. He had shouted at a foreigner to relieve his
feelings. Grief made a man deli, mad. That was reason
enough.

Frank was stunned. He didn't know what he had
done. He knew that if you hurt a Turk's feelings you
became not only yourself, but the British, the French,
and the Suez Canal. He had put that in his briefing for
new people too. It was a premise for protecting yourself in the Middle East. He corrected himself—Asia
Minor, Little Asia, Byzantium, the Ottoman Empire.
Turks, he reminded himself, were *not*. It was not, in
official policy, what they were, but what they were not
you had to define.

No abstract thought helped him. Everybody was
looking at him. He prayed not to be sick. His hands
were doing a dance of their own on the table. He put
them in his lap and held them together. "Jesus, what
the hell did I do?" he whispered, and the nice guy,
David, held his hand on his shoulder, and said, "Please
. . ." He was a nice guy. Frank felt he had been wrong
about him.

Turgut Bey was helped into the front seat of the Impala. It took too long to put the wet bundle in the back seat. Sailors carried the other bundle along the quay, followed by the crowd of men. No one but Frank, David, and Horst were left in the kahve. Even Murat had followed the men.

The quay was as silent as if nothing had happened. The boats rocked a little in the wind. The pavement was wet with the shapes of the two bundles.

"Jesus," Frank said again. He was still trying to stop his hands shaking. "I wanted to dive today with Monkey," he said, not knowing why it came into his mind, and feeling once more selfish and shamed.

David looked up from the paper. "Munci will have made at least five dives between two o'clock when he left my bar and this morning." He wanted to comfort the raw man, but didn't know quite how.

Horst knew how and did it, sternly. "You must not mind what the man said. They are very emotional."

"It's OK." Frank didn't want to look at them.

"What hotel?" David asked.

"They want to build a hotel on Yazada. I don't know. That's all I know," Frank stumbled.

"But they cannot do that for two reasons." Horst was as passionate as Horst could be early in the morning. "Together with the fact it is government-protected land, it is also historically most important. You see, the second-millennium trade route was running between Yazada and the mainland. There is even a movement in the Ministry of Education to stop tourist diving there. Of course the Ministry of Tourism was fighting it . . ."

Frank knew about that. They hadn't had to spend money on the Ministry of Education. Those guys were really dedicated. Instead they had sent expert after expert, every archeologist they could find who wanted a grant in the Aegean. The government had backed a lot of good advice. None of the people sitting half asleep in Ceramos seemed to realize or give a damn about the strategic importance of the coast. His mind was wandering again. He supposed it was the shock of what he

now saw as an insult, an incident. He wondered if he
ought to report it.

"They will build the hotel and they will stop the
diving if they wish. All it needs is to butter enough
bread."

"Palms," Frank corrected David, wanting to laugh.

"They are crazy," Horst said. "There is not even
any water on the island. They are like little children."

"Ah well, what do you expect of a place where two
of their heroes are Attila the Hun and Genghis Khan.
They are the most malicious people in the world and
yet they will never betray a friend," David said.

Frank was aware that they had fallen into the foreigners' laments, to comfort him, and he was grateful.

Out of politeness he added, "When Mehmet the
Conqueror entered Constantinople he carried a rose in
his hand."

"Rose and sword, that's good. That's very good."
Horst weighed the words. "I am enjoying an enigma."

In the distance beyond Frank's shoulder David was
watching the tiny figure of Turgut Bey being eased out
of the Impala in front of his hotel. "Nothing is enigmat-
ic here," he said, "it is only unknown. It is a paradox.
I too . . . paradox. I love them and I hate them."

"He quotes himself sometimes," Horst laughed.

"I have not said that before."

"There is always a first time." They had left Frank
out. They were performing for him. They want to
impress me, he thought. You have to watch for things
like that. It made him embarrassed again, to think like
that.

"How old are they," he interrupted, "the old men in
the fountain?"

"This is very interesting." Horst was pleased to be
asked. "As you no doubt know," he settled back, "the
first mention of the fountain is in Greek. There are
Karian texts but they have not yet been deciphered.
Some words only are known. I would say that the carving is later than the fountain rim. You see those same
beards in the Acropolis Museum—sixth century, what
you would call Dorian for lack of a better term."

"You can't get a straight fact out of this man," David explained.

"I do not wish to mislead him," Horst said. "Now shut up. Notice the spade-like shapes of the beards."

Frank got up and went over to lean into the fountain. Horst followed him. "There is something, though, innately Ceramian about them. The sense of humor," he said seriously. Horst leaned over the marble rim. His fingers touched faint traces of figures. "You will notice the tiny boys peeping from behind the old men's robes. They are peeing into the water. The first putti. You even find this motive of the imps on their stelae, tombstones," he explained. "There the dead are grinning. You see," he was wandering back to the table, "the temper of the city was never solemn. Even the temple friezes that were discovered here of the war between what you call the Greeks and the Amazons show this. They are later, and more serious, of course. I would say there is more ironic wit and less bald humor. By that time they had been conquered several times. It tends to modify a culture."

David looked up at Horst, too surprised to speak or laugh.

"The temple friezes have distinctly sexual overtones—the war of the sexes. They can be studied as the old Indian kundalini sculptures are studied. They are more belligerent of course—a *war* of the sexes. Later," he waved away two thousand years, "the Romans . . . the Byzantines . . . needless to say the Moslems, much of this quality was lost."

"Who won?" David asked him.

"What?"

"The war between the sexes."

"Oh, the men, of course."

David went on reading the editorial page.

"Of course they won. Look at the splendid phallus." Horst laughed and pointed at the delicate minaret. "That mosque was built on the foundations of a mother temple, an early Artemision. It was later dedicated to Aphrodite. Now a woman isn't allowed inside it."

"Horst," David said, "why don't you go dig up something?"

"No use." Horst didn't move. He explained to Frank, "I have not the permission yet for the student diggers. I cannot use the local work force except to move rocks and debris. They are not trained, you understand. Even they will not go to the dig today. Every disaster means a holiday. None of the men will come to work before noon if then. At least these ones who have drowned are foreigners from Istanbul. If they were relatives . . ."

"You really are a shit, Horst."

"I am only speaking practically."

"Can you believe this?" David said to Frank. "I have seen him cry over the body of a woman dead over two thousand years."

"Who is that American?" Horst asked David when Frank had made an excuse to leave. He wanted to catch up with Monkey, say something nice to him, show him he was thinking about what he had had to do. He wanted to call him Munci, make a special point of that.

"Oh, he is the local CIA man, he uses AID for a C-O-V-E-R." David looked after him. "You guys," he smiled, "your only real emotion is embarrassment. You are very dangerous then."

"Not me," Horst corrected him. "I am a deeply emotional man. I suffer."

"My ass," David said.

When Frank Proctor reached the end of the quay, Monkey, Munci, was nowhere to be found, and he really didn't want to ask which way he had gone.

Brave acts set a man apart. Munci was aware of this. He always had been. He walked through an isolated corridor of his own up the quay between knots of watchful men, naked to their mixture of admiration and envy. It made him shy, and shyness made him swagger.

He had always felt alien for a while when he came

back through the sea ceiling. He, knowing the silent
depth of sea fall better than any land fall, had always
stepped back onto the quay with a twinge of anxiety he
didn't bother to question. What he had seen in the
night and the morning he carried like a weight to put
down when he could. He had no place to go. He
strutted on.

Like all physically heroic men, Munci was occupied
with his own body. He knew that this was mistaken often for vanity by those who did not know themselves as
machines, as he did. But it was not vanity. It was a fas-
cination with the muscular possibilities, the speed, the
care, how far it could be pushed, as with a racing motorcycle. He was proud, and a little afraid, of what he
had asked of it. In eight hours he had made five forty-
meter dives. The decompressions of the later dives had
nearly made him panic, but he had fought it down,
hanging to the cliff, holding the last bodies in his arms,
their eyes opened, watching him surprised through the
film of their death.

He knew his mother would be waiting for him and
he feared the demands of her service. She would child
him and weaken him and make him ashamed to show
the weakness. He walked on, still not knowing where
he would go.

It had always been expected of him that he do brave
acts, as it was expected of Bombok Ibrahim that he
would empty the cess pits at three o'clock in the morning and throw the waste into the sea or onto the
gardens, or of Huseyin that he would cheat his own
mother, or of Horst that, Christian-like, he would taste
and devour women. If there was a wall to be climbed,
Munci had climbed it, a cat down a well, Munci had
brought it up, a fight to be stopped, he had walked between the men. Any man would be proud of such a
place in his world.

He had always taken women in the same way, as
public challenges. When the gavur women came to
Ceramos, he was the first to have one. It was almost
his duty. He was, after all, the erkek adam, the leader
of men. As they expected him to, he carried the news
to the others of what the foreigners were like, pale and

hairy as they were. "They are good," he reported. "They talk a lot, and they move, and enjoy it like a man. Very active. They wait for the man to make the first move, though. It is very demanding, but it is very interesting."

He won fights, prizes, envy, mostly because he never questioned the fact that it was expected of him. Even before he was born, the expectations had begun, when his mother had named him Munci, the deliverer. He had been appointed to his service in the town that he sometimes saw as a single spider web of nerves with many bodies, all with their own functions. Part of it he had inherited from his cousin Dorsun, who had been shot fishing too near the derebey's shore. At least that was the excuse, the real reason was that Dorsun was bashi bosh, a free speaker, a danger.

Munci's own successor had long been chosen, his friend Timur. He was nine years younger than Munci, and he had trained the boy as his brother until he took it into his head to go away. "You cannot save the world; it is too evil," Munci had told him, disappointed to lose him to something he couldn't fight, the boy's own head. Timur had looked within, and no man could go with him there. He had made his brain his own sea, choosing his service for himself.

Munci didn't know why Timur had come into his tired mind. He only wished he had been there to dive with him. He would have taken no one else.

Foreigners never understood this halter of service to one's place. They wanted to be everything at once, inside themselves, their bodies and minds their own cities, isolated, alone. He felt sorry for them. That, he thought as the sunlight touched his face and warmed it, was the first thing he had learned about them, and it had drawn him to them. Under the sea he was his own city too, alone, and as he saw them, struggling on the land in the loneliness they carried, his recognition went out to them—almost.

He also knew, very early, a second thing about them. He had been hurt into knowing it. They went away, voices faded, letters faded, then stopped. This fact alone made it dangerous, more dangerous than sea depth, to take them seriously. Inoculated painfully, he could enjoy them, and play at what he had once been fooled into seeking as the warm understanding he had looked for all his life, isolated by his function as they were by being so far from homes he felt they had never really had. So he played at horizons he had learned not to want, and hopes he no longer had. It had been an agonizing education for him. He had once believed in them. Now it was a pipe dream, a pleasure. He let himself be rescued by them from things he neither wanted to leave anymore nor feared. But even though their understanding was false, it was there, and he had grown used to it.

He decided to go to Ariadne's house, or rather something had decided for him. He realized that he had walked past his own turning. Time was spatial, as it had been in his shock and deep fatigue for the last stretch of the night. He had walked, without seeing himself do it, the length of the seafront. He thought of animals and time. He, like a donkey, had been there, then not there, now here. It was the way it had been with him between dives. Time had not passed. It had been a space in which he lay, cradled in his father's arms, and he had taken his father's comforting for granted.

It was the first time he could ever remember that his father had put his arm around him as a man, a friend, instead of lifting it to hit him as his son. He had never smoked a cigarette in his father's presence, but all through the night he remembered his father doing what a friend would do, lighting them and passing them to him as he lay like a wet exhausted fish, not moving until time for the next dive.

He saw now that it was his sonship the old man had punished and hated and not the man within the son, as he was within the wet suit. Kraal Mehmet, Mehmet the Conqueror, the old king, had sat there all night, hunched over his foot, crippled sideways by the bends, he who had taken his revenge on the sea for twisting him by harvesting a fortune in sponges. He had thrown Munci into the sea as a diver when Munci was twelve years old, son to sea, hating both. But in that night there had been love between them, and Munci remembered taking it for granted as if he had always expected it.

Munci was suddenly so stunned by that, so alone, so exhausted, that he knew he was going to cry. He couldn't let his own people see him that way. All he could think was, "I can't cry in the street." He needed a friend, maybe a woman. He didn't know yet.

He turned up the hill toward Ariadne's gate, held together by the wet suit, dim-minded and unutterably cold, a cold brought from the sea and the bodies, smelling of their fish death. The smell clung to his nostrils, smell of the same water he had loved but it was suddenly filthy, streaming out after its invasion of the girl's flaccid body, terrible parody of a body satisfied. He could not get rid of the smell of her wet leather handbag, the silly thing she still clutched in her hand when he brought her up, and she got heavier and heavier as if she were growing enormous in his arms as they flowed up nearer and nearer the sea ceiling. When he pushed her through into the air she was as heavy as a stone statue. The first thing he heard when he surfaced was her father's shriek.

No one must see the tears that were coming faster behind his eyes. He would die of shame. At such a time a man must have a woman. There was no choice. His weary mind drifted toward the thought of Ariadne's strong western hands. He liked to watch her as she let them, on their own, mold clay on her wheel in the walled garden as she talked, not looking at what they were doing. Like the sea fingers of the octopus, they had their own eyes. He walked on toward her hands; she was what he needed, a woman, but a woman who was a friend—not a fuck, that was easy, but a friend who would let him cry.

The women perched cross-legged row above row on the rock steps up to Ariadne's gate. They had watched Munci walking toward them, quiet for once with excitement at the prospect of being told at last what had happened. Not a white coifed head moved. Only their eyes were lively, watching.

They had already turned hope into expectation that

he would come, since they knew as surely as how many teeth age had taken from each other's mouths that Munci came to Ariadne either when no other woman was available, or in time of trouble. It accounted for their easy polite amusement at her which she took as friendliness.

Some of them were sure what he came for, even though the men said it was not true. Others said the men were right, but even they were not sure. Since the idea that a man would spend more than ten minutes with a woman alone in her house for any other reason than to loosen her belt was outside their mind span, even the ones who defended her were more tolerant than convinced.

Gül, as usual, was the first to break the silence. "Hey hey, didn't I tell you, sisters? After a night like that a man needs a woman." Her wet red eyes were tiny with pleasure and sun.

The oldest, Fatma, argued with her. She had always tried to stop Gül's malice, even when she was a child. Now she chomped her bare gums and spoke, "Not that one. I have told you. He goes as a friend to her . . ."

This made Gül angry, as it always had. "She is a widow without children. What other good is she? The tired animal goes to the nearest water."

"My husband when he came from the sea would take me on the floor in his wet clothes," their neighbor Hatije dreamed aloud.

"The blind take what they can reach," Gül giggled.

No one paid any attention. Gül was eighty-three, Hatije eighty. Fatma scratched herself through her shalvar.

"No man would touch you," Hatije spat. Gül had not married. She was very ugly and she had the temper of a small dog. No one had paid her bride price. Also she had been damaged by being raped when she was thirteen. It had been almost the only thing that had happened to her, alone, and she had never stopped talking about it.

"Six men . . ." she began to yell.

Their bird screeches rose in the sun.

Ariadne had shaken the last rug from her living room. She hung it over the terrace wall in the sun. She wished vaguely, knowing that it would not happen, that the women would be quiet. They argued as regularly as the clock striking nine each morning. They always had. She didn't want them to wake Lisa. She wanted to move instead through her morning habits, alone.

She was still webbed by her waking dream and it made her move slowly. As if she were in some black contentment with the pain, she put off being taken out of it into the unknown day. She tried to stand still and appreciate the sea. It was empty. She tried to feel that, its horror vacui, something, anything to bring her quietly into the present.

Yazada in the distance lay still asleep. She saw that the boats were gone. Fear and loss clogged her. There were things to do, each thing after the one before, breakfast, the cleaning of the fireplace. She turned away from the unsafety of the sea and went back into the house. She stood in the doorway, forgetting why she had come in.

The sun had reached past the petit-point pillows, fingered across the now bare floor, and touched the blue bowl on the coffee table with a miracle of live color. It made her smile. She picked it up to dust it. She stood dreaming its shaping in her hands. Whenever she held it there was always the feeling that whatever it was she was seeking she had brought it with her. She remembered that she had dreamed again of breaking it. It made her shiver, and she wondered who was walking over her grave.

Outside on the rocks the women were watching Munci come nearer.

"How terrible he looks," Fatma groaned.

"He will be ill, I know it," Hatije told them.

Gül laughed. "That family can afford it. He walks
like a rich man."

"Why shouldn't he?" Fatma defended him. "It is not
because he is rich, but because he is a man. Gül, you
are always jealous. Do you think it is because his father is rich that he did not cry at his circumcision? Timur did not either and his father is poor."

They all knew this. There was not a man under
eighty in the town of Ceramos who did not pass
through this moment of judgment from them all of his
life, from the moment when he, at eight or nine years
old, had stood before the hodja as the holy razor came
nearer to make a man of him. Not a cry or a sound
was ever forgotten. No act of courage later, or of cow-
ardice, made them forget the moment until the grave
hid him.

"Sihirli Timur! What does he have to do with it?"
Gül tried to taunt Fatma into anger. She had never
succeeded, but she still tried.

"He was not always bewitched. It is not a madness
anyway. He is ambitious. He wants to be rich," Fatma
argued.

"Like Huseyin."

"Not like Huseyin. Sihirli Timur dreams of great
things."

Hatije finally remembered something that could
make her laugh. "What about Huseyin's circumcision?
He bellowed like a calf."

"They would not invite us." Gül was bitter. "We
stood outside the wall."

Fatma laughed. "Do you remember at the election
when they told us he cried in his mother's womb?"

Hatije giggled, but Gül was still annoyed at the old
hurt. "It was not true. I remember. They said it to get
him elected. His political enemies said he came out of
his mother's ass-hole. When a man-child cries in his
mother's womb he will be müdür or kaymakam." Gül
told them slowly what they had always known for a
fact.

"Not a girl-child, though." Hatije saw her chance to
draw Gül on.

"No, that is bad," Gül explained. "She will be a

shrew and no one will marry her." When Gül heard
what she had been trapped into saying, she turned and
hid her face in her shawl.

"Gül, did you cry in your mother's womb?" Hatije
jeered.

Munci, coming closer, heard them all laughing and
was afraid they would see through his eyes to his unfall-
en tears.

"Munci, what happened?" Fatma wrapped her arm
around the calf of his leg to hold him. "Tell us. Were
there ten of them?"

"No. Only five." He tried to pull his leg away without being disrespectful to his grandmother's sister-in-
law's sister.

"Who?"

"They were strangers," he said, and thought, I have
held them all in my arms and I have not yet put them
down.

"What strangers?"

"From Istanbul . . ."

"Oh, Istanbul," someone spat. "Hippistudents," all
one word.

"They are anarchist. The government at Ankara is
going to have them all killed, anyway," Gül said. "The
hodja told me."

Fatma still watched his face, missing nothing. "Aye,
Munci, what a terrible thing for you. Health to your
head, poor boy," Fatma groaned.

Munci had succeeded in freeing himself. He knocked
on Ariadne's gate.

"She is there, Munci," one of the women called behind him. "Usually she has gone to the Pazar, but not
this morning."

Someone laughed. "There was noise there late into
the night. Maybe she is still sleeping."

"No. There is a man there." Gül giggled like a
young girl. "She talked and talked this morning early."

"Did you hear his voice?" Munci turned and smiled,
teasing her. Gül admitted she had not.

"We heard the stairs creak. Only one person."
Fatma slapped at her and missed her.

It was a formal argument about Ariadne that had

gone on ever since the women had gathered to listen
and be entertained under her window in the early sun.
They had been doing it for three years. Ariadne's voice
sometimes whispered, sometimes spoke aloud in half a
conversation. She spoke English always, so they decided the unseen man was a gaˇur. The men, who
liked Ariadne, had been defending her for almost as
long. "Did you hear his voice?" was what they always
asked.

The women had to admit they had not, only hers,
but they usually added, "Often in the living room there
is a man's voice."

"There is no place in the living room to make love.
Not with comfort," the men told them.

Both Munci and the women knew they were playing
at rumor, but there was a politeness and a pleasure in
it that they honored in each other. Everyone in
Ceramos knew that the foreign lady often talked to
herself in the morning like a haunted woman. There
were many stories about why she did this; the favorite
one was that she had killed a man in America and so
had to leave. Why else would such a lady leave all
those washing machines and tape recorders and Fords
to live in Ceramos where there was nothing? There was
even a favorite reason for all this among those who
liked her. The man she shot had been her husband. He
had brought a younger woman to live in her house.
First they had poisoned her dog. Was that not always
the first warning that they meant to get rid of her?
Then they had locked her in an upstairs room and had
spent her money. Those who tolerated no foreigners
said that it was not her husband but her lover she had
killed. All American women were whores. Everyone
knew that.

Ariadne heard the second sharp knock
on the gate and it annoyed her. She had not finished
her morning and she hated to be disturbed. She put
down the blue bowl carefully and went across the terrace to unlock the gate. First she picked up the full

water bucket from under the garden tap to show that she was too busy to talk much.

The sun reflection of the water she was carrying swam on her face. It was all Munci could see. It made him feel sick.

"Get a towel. A thick one," he ordered. He walked past her into the house. She heard the stairs creak. She knew that something was wrong. He had never gone up the stairs before.

When she got to the top of the stairs, he was trying to unzip the wet suit. "I cannot do it. My fingers." He was annoyed. She ran to help him.

When he was naked he threw himself face down on the bed. His hard back was sea-blue and covered with goose pimples. She began to rub, first with the towel and then with her bare hands, as hard as she could. There was not a word. She kept on, finally straddling his body as if she were giving him artificial respiration. Gradually his sun-dark skin reddened, and he stopped shivering. She went on until her arms were exhausted, the rhythm of her movement making the bed groan. Then she covered him with the quilt and tucked it close around him. He had not moved or spoken. She got up to tiptoe out of the room so he could sleep.

"You do not read this book. There is dust on it." His voice came from behind her.

She turned around. He had turned on his back and pulled the quilt tight around him. He was pointing at *I and Thou*, reading the dust. She did not care why it made her so happy to have him notice it. She was aware of sunlight.

"Come here. I am cold. Stay close to me." He was nearly asleep.

She sat down beside him. "What happened?"

Tears were running down both sides of his face. She saw that he was too tired to notice that he was crying. They melted out, like sea water pouring from his eyes.

"How can I tell you?" he asked himself. "How can I make you see?"

"Try." She put her palm against his forehead, worried.

"You know the sea hole at Yazada?"

The Second Sacrifice

The Second Sacrifice

The Second Sacrifice

"I have snorkeled over it." She saw the sun shafts around her pierce in straight lines through the water and meet in a dark point on the sea floor forty meters below. She saw the sea hole falling in a circular cliff all around her, and below her, the lady fish flick lazy blue and green and purple. Down the walls the gardens of pink flowers became shy animals as her shadow passed over them, folding away to hide in the rock, leaving the frail white sea fans and the stark red starfish sprawling. Looking down the long shaft with the sea ceiling billowing around her was like looking into a door she had not entered, promise of light and peace. She had thought it would be dark below her, but it had its own pure blue light—no fear, no loss. She swam free of words, deflecting the sun with her body into a geometry of light.

"From midnight when I left you until now I have been bringing four bodies out of the sea hole."

She knew better than to say a word, no words under water.

"It was black. Black. Did you know that black is heavier than light, even to swim through? They are telling me I do not tell about the sea. I tell, but they do not listen. I tell all the time. How do you tell silence, how noisy it is in your ears? And black. How do you tell black?" Munci was crying. "All you can see is your own body." He tried to hitch himself up on his elbow, but he failed and sank back into the half sleep. "The phosphorescence clings to your body and reflects the moon. It is a million of tiny algae looking for food. My hands glowed, and my arms. I went down and down. They had sunk. The fish were still. The beam of the underwater torch freezes them. How do you say it?"

"Hypnotize."

"Yes. That. In the light beam. It does not deflect. It cuts a very clean tunnel through the black. The fish are pinned by it. They cannot move."

He had shaken the quilt loose and was shivering again. She tucked it close around him without knowing she did it.

"The first boy. Maybe two meters down. His eyes glittered in the light. Trance. Just like the fish. Stared.

He was lying on a ledge on his back. He watch me come down to him. I thought he is alive and I knew he is not. He was glowing like my arm."

"Shimmering," she was seeing.

"The algae and his eyes reflect the moonlight. I put my arms around him. The boats had turned their fishing lights on around the hole to guide me. I could see them up there in a ring. There is a word."

"Halo . . ."

"No," he laughed, "that is like angels. Don't be silly. A circle I meant. I brought him up through them. Then I went to find the second boy, although my father did not wish me to go so quickly," he said proudly. "It was a longer dive. I found him at maybe twenty meters. His back was to the light. He had been washed against the cliff, spread out like a starfish. I had to pry his fingers loose. I think he had tried to climb the cliff. Everybody hates me because I learn to speak English first and I make the first money from the tourism." He was crying again.

"Tell me later. Sleep now." She tried to get up but he clutched her hand.

"No. I tell you now or I will not ever. You know that. My father made me go down two meters to decompress after the second dive until my air was gone. We knew it was too late for any of them to be alive. I had already used two tanks of air, and he made me rest long after they were filled again. We did not know then how many more there were. It was hard to find out how many are in the boats. They keep calling each other's names and crying back and forth between the boats through the night. No one would leave. Finally we know that there are three more missing."

He was quiet and his eyes were closed. The tears, which had not troubled his hard factual voice, had dried. She thought he was asleep until she tried to pull her hand away.

"I dived once more in the dark, maybe six o'clock. There is a current below thirty meters that comes from under Yazada mountain. Ribbons of sweet water. It had carried him under a ledge and curled him up like a little baby. I knew I would hurry for the others. I had to. A moray eel was already feeding on his hand."

Slow voice, gentle morning, Munci was whispering, not knowing, and then his voice was strong again. "I went down again, and I could find nothing. But I knew they were there. I could see them in the blackness, waiting for me. I could not find them. My own bubbles began to get in my way, and I knew—very much good sense at the time—down there in the dark I knew that if I gave my bottle and respirator to the sea, it would be easier to find them. It was my death telling me that, you see. I nearly did it, but I had, you know, a little tiny land voice left in my head. It said, you fool, you are having narcosis. Go up. I was laughing when I came through the ceiling. My father told me. He would not allow me to go down again until there was enough light. Maybe I went to sleep. I don't remember. She gave me helva to eat. And cigarettes."

Ariadne wondered who "she" was, and then realized that Munci had made the commonest mistake in English. Turkish had no sex in the third person. Munci was talking still about his father. No sex in the third person. One did this or that. Ariadne wanted to make more of the fact than was there to keep the power of his demand. She wanted to experience it with him; wanted to transform the habits she called peace into the sea surge he brought. It hurt. He was talking about his father. It would, in another language, have been a fascinating psychological mistake, she thought, clinging to the thought.

He clutched at her arm to wake her. "There was no sun yet. You understand. You see that? Even at eight o'clock, it is still in the mountain's shadow. Twilight water, only blue and green like the deeper sea, all the way to the surface. But I could see all around me. Allah, it was so peaceful that for a minute I forgot why I was there. The fish were feeding and they did not care I was there. I started down very peaceful. Away down below me I saw her hair. At first I thought it was seaweed. The current from the mountain was combing it."

In the water space where he had taken her Ariadne

waited for him to open his eyes, but he did not. He spoke from the blind silence of the dive. "I went down."

She saw him tip and turn, let out air, swim toward the floor, a sea-goal is always up not down, up to the floor; she followed him.

"They are both there in front of me. The boy had grabbed her ankles in a panic and he had borne her down. He was half lodged under the rock. Locked them there. She was standing swaying and nodding to me from the mouth of the cave. She would have been looking straight at me but she had no eyes. The eels had found them, and her lips. I stand on the sand floor facing her. I cut the eels away with my knife. I am afraid of them. They are fierce if you do not kill them right away, but they are busy and I kill them one by one. Their blood make a cloud of bright green around our heads.

"She was nodding to me in the current. She nods no—oh to you yes, head nodding, your yes, Turkish no. She was holding her handbag like some girl waiting for a bus, her face streaked with fine waving green ribbons. I tried to free the boy to bring them both up together, but he was lodged too tight. He is still there. I pried his fingers from her ankles. She weighed nothing. By the time I got her through the sea ceiling she was as heavy as stone."

"Do you know who she was?" Ariadne had fallen, without knowing it, into stroking his hair back from his forehead.

"Her name was Lale. It means flower."

"I know. A tulip."

Munci began to retch. She lifted his head. He was only dribbling. She wished he wouldn't. It was ugly. She felt that he was ruining something. What it was she didn't know.

"Nothing comes up. I need food."

"I will get you some. Dry crackers." She started to pull away, relieved, as when a sick person sleeps at last and their tentacles of pain and need fall away.

The retching had waked Munci from his half-sleep and he wondered how much he had told her. He could

remember so little already. He could not let go her
wrist. He wanted to give his soul away. It burdened
him. The sun made a circle around her blond head,
like the boat lights. He had never in his life taken
down a woman's hair. He could feel a surprising current of good desire making him hard under the quilt
and was proud that the energy was in him. He wanted
to feel life and be warmed by another pulse and blood.
Red, red blood making her woman's face pink. His fingers pulled at the pins and her hair slid down over her
shoulders in two snake-like braids. He unbraided them
carefully and shook them out to make a live tent over
her shoulders and breasts. What he had done made
him afraid, but the dead girl was alive. He thrust his
hand inside the stupid man's shirt she wore and felt her
heart pounding under her breast. He longed to force
from her the strength he sought.

Never in her life had Ariadne been needed without a
name, or wanted without reasons or words, as under a
sea ceiling. She slid down beside him. One pants leg
hiked up, but she didn't dare move to pull it down. He
waited for her to bring him toward her. He was exhausted and awed before the woman. There had only
been girls before, like spearing a fish. He had forgotten
how to make love to a foreign woman. He waited.

She waited for him to touch her, to turn, to do anything but lie there, hardly breathing. She was afraid she
had mistaken what he wanted, afraid to make a move
for fear he would be replused by her desire. Then she
whispered, "Oh my God, Lisa . . . will we wake her
up?"

"Shut up," he said. He had heard her say Lale. "Oh,
why did you say that?" Manhood was worm. He
nestled into her side and cried instead. Her flesh had
become as dead as the girl's.

Ariadne, all alive and wondering, let him lie still.
She was on the edge of something. She knew she had
done something wrong, been too old, failed him. Then
she caught a memory, Attila the Hun, a Turkish film.
She saw the men, lying like that after battle, and she
saw the women, houris, mounting them and turning
them. She saw herself and David and Horst and Basil,

discussing, discussing, late into the night, sex and culture, culture and sex. She recast in a panic for Horst's voice, "The woman, you must remember, is the seducer in the eastern cultures. It is her role. At first, you understand, the westerner thinks she is, now shall I say, overbold . . ." and she heard David laugh.

She felt awkward, turning to do what Munci expected. She was conscious of her knees and elbows.

Munci was fast asleep among the petit-point cushions. She covered him with the quilt her grandmother had made, then eased herself off the bed, pulled down her pants leg, and went to the mirror to put up her hair.

"This," she said in her mind, "is the way it is." The words seemed to her both profound and casual. They made her feel carefree. It was a new heady feeling, almost silly.

The people of the sea kingdom believe that if you lean over the water or look into a mirror and do not see your face you know at last that you are dead. Ariadne let herself sense the girl, bowing beside her in the currents of sunlight, but in the mirror she was alone and remembered being pretty. She still saw that, thinking she could see herself, but it was only her reversed image, and that dim with time. She liked a faint new remembered color. Happiness and the eyesight of her age and habits softened the concise edge of her vision. The lines, the hauntings seen by the young were hidden from her, and she smoothed a cheek of thirty years before, wondering at its soft glow. She lifted her elbows high and began, more lovingly than in a long time, to dress her hair.

Dear friend, her dost, her Munci stirred deep in sleep, and the fact that he was there at all comforted her into facing what it was. She had been fooled, no, in the truth of the morning she had fooled herself. What she—here David intruded and she wondered if this was what he already knew—what she had thought of as discovery in Ceramos had been only a false choice between illusion and despair, and under it, comforting if not joyful, as a floor, a sense of there being no use in going any farther.

What she had looked for for four years, not knowing it, was the one quality that Roger did not have. It was courage. She saw him husked of it, she was left with it, the quality itself, to love, like a coat cast off and left in her hands. She shivered, as Munci had, from the cold.

What she had searched for was deeper than courage; it was what a man was. She had run seeking, through skies and porches, and great empty halls and lawns of dreams. There she had found boys and clowns, the intelligent, the wounded, and the silly. She had listened for it from drunks, and old men, and the aloof with their faces turned aside, searched and listened as far as this alien shore, with a strange simple man asleep in her bed, and the voice of Peter Abelard in her head, and he said, "God knows that at times I, too, fell into such despair that I proposed to myself to go off and live the life of a Christian among the enemies of Christ."

"I am making too much of this as usual," she said, not hearing her voice until Munci stirred again.

She looked out of the window to read the time in the smoke signal from her neighbor's chimney. Fatma always lit her fire at ten o'clock to start cooking the bulgur for her great-grandson's dinner. Over the rock and mud chimney, whitewashed almost smooth, the wind tugged at the smoke. She put a scarf over her head. She pulled the curtains against the sun so that Munci could go on sleeping. In the deep green shadows they cast, the room was so dark that she had to touch the night-blue wall to keep from stumbling. The constellations on her star charts showed white pinpoints in the new darkness. She tiptoed down the stairs and into the kitchen. She needed bread and vegetables and cheese for Munci and for Lisa. Lisa was still asleep. There was not a sound from her little room across the garden terrace.

Ariadne let herself out of her gate, ready by instinct to placate the bird women and draw forth their rewarding morning smiles. She was so used to seeing them that she missed them when she saw that the street was empty. Only her neighbor, old Fatma, knelt in her rock cave room with her rump in the air toward

her, blowing the smoke up from her three crossed
sticks in the white fireplace. Cave room, old woman,
same gesture; she thought of six thousand timeless
years of habit in that place. She called, "Günaydın,"
but Fatma did not hear her.

When the foreign woman had disap-
peared, without, mashallah, throwing her shadow over
the new fire, Fatma bunched her left fist, passed the
fingers of her right hand over it, and clicked her wrist.
It was the worst insult she knew, so bad that she would
not have not done it where anyone could see her. She
turned toward the low door and sent the gesture after
the pig-eater.

Fatma was not only furious, she was hurt and
ashamed. She had defended her as her neighbor against
the tongues of her own kin that clacked at both ends,
and she had been wrong. The woman had listened,
grinning, while she sat there bowing her head with
shame under the pig-eater's window, to Munci's voice
in her bedroom and the telltale rhythmic creaking of
the bed.

Lisa's body felt *wonderful*. She knew she
was awake again when she saw the room shadows, real
ones, and lost the dream. She was left only with the
question to her father, echoing, if you can see that why
can't you see this, please Daddy, and the dream place
where the question made sense already lost by waking.
All morning she had been drifting, dipping into sleep,
into strong visceral dreams that made her body ache as
she rose again, time after time, to the morning in the
dim shade of the alien room, that strange place that
until she waked fully weighted her with homesickness
for something that in the daylight she didn't even like.

She had, she remembered, been composing a letter
to her father. She could hear it in snatches, song-like,
at a level just above the plea that came out of deeper

sleep—only snatches. She sank below it, and rose above it. All she could catch of the letter through these lacunae, dark spaces, rifts, was, "Dearest Daddy, my own dear Daddy Onion"—Little Onion, Daddy Onion they were to each other and everybody knew it—"I am so happy." That word she censored at once by springing fully awake and aware of some kind of funny danger.

Her body was in the way, rosy and sore, spread-eagled as if the morning itself lay on her sweet and heavy. It was already hot, and she felt too naked to let her daddy into her waking mind. She fumbled for the rumpled sheet and covered herself. A spray of clothes, prayer beads, money, and writing paper fell to the floor. She nestled down again into the voice of the letter.

"Oh dearest Daddy, this time not even you would be worried about me. I have . . ." In deference to her beloved daddy, the shock he might feel, she found the word *beau*. "I have a new beau, oh Daddy, please, please Daddy, don't let anything bad happen this time oh please . . ." Prayer and placation mingled with the sensuousness of one tiny tear forming. "Please God Daddy don't let him know I am rich." But she knew in one icy second that he would and that he would ruin it, reach out the feared-as-God hand of his power and speak the wrong words and shrivel her soul yet again.

This time sleep was dark. She dreamed of his indifferent interference. It made her whimper again into wakefulness, awake enough to hear Munci come into the garden, and then his voice. She knew he had come to seek her out, why else would he come? It contented her and made her stretch and sigh, even though he was too late. She sank into blank sleep again. When she woke, really woke, the sun had spread over the end of her cot and she knew it must be at least ten o'clock. When she heard Ariadne pause for a second to listen at her door, interfering, they all did that, she lay holding her breath so that the old woman, as Huseyin called her, would go away.

Now, fully awake, she was ready to do what she had to. She let herself giggle now that Ariadne was gone, and picked her letter pad up from where it had fallen onto the floor.

How she wanted to begin and how she knew she would begin were two entirely different kettles of fish. She let herself play the first beginning out of her mind, "Dear keeper of the checkbook, keeper of the keys, you old bastard, chum chum, easy pal, FLOP, father." She sucked her pen. She scratched her head with it. She concentrated on her stomach. She found a cigarette in her macramé bag, lit it, and watched the smoke float in the square of sun.

She let herself see him, there in her mind's eye, as always, in the morning, heard his voice, "Lisa, get up Lisa!" He was at his most lonely in the morning, and his voice called through the door of wherever she had escaped to in the night, petulant, rich, insistent Virginia voice calling, "Lisa get up," overlaying her sleep with the demand that she follow him, but he never never touched her. They had always shaken hands, since she was five and he had suddenly clawed her arms from around his neck.

He was sensible in patches, dressed correctly at all times, even to the age of his clothes, the old tweed hacking jacket, the whipcord britches, the stained canvas of his New Market boots. Even wrecked as he was, seamed, sun-brown and habit red, he was still handsome. The childish petulance of old safe money that he thought of as strong-mindedness lined his cheeks and made his pretty eyes droop, and she told the vision of him that this time at least he was wrong.

This time she knew that Huseyin was not after her money, not like the others, that long line of them. (Her father had always been right. He could smell it.) Huseyin believes in me, by myself. She remembered this, not allowing herself to touch the rest of her memory of the night, there being no place for such magnificence when she had to concentrate. Even that memory was delicious, more delicious because of the surprise she had planned to reward him for accepting her, just as she was. But always intrusive, her own voice said, you're at it again, running the game, mixing money with desire, clinching the matter.

"Oh God," she prayed easily, "don't let me do that again."

"It is not," she answered her own prayer, "like that at all."

"Oh shit," and dismissing both herself and God, she picked up the writing pad and began her letter.

"Dear—no—dearest Jamie." Even if she thought of him as Daddy, she had not been allowed to call him anything but Jamie since she could remember. She had to be light, light was the touch he cared for, Jamie did, and she couldn't let herself forget it, not if she wanted his yes instead of his no.

"This is the most interesting place I have been to in all my travels. I like staying with Ariadne. She is so understanding of my needs." She laughed aloud, liking the clean line of strategy. If there was anything Jamie feared it was her needs. "She has a lovely, TINY house. Her lifestyle is interesting and relating to her is easier than I thought it would be. If I were in her way she would not let me know it. You know how sweet she is."

Lisa tacked easily through his prejudices. "The sailing is good, although there are quick squalls from a wind called the meltem." She bit the end of her pen. "The harbor is snug. There are berths in the inner harbor for large yachts." She saw him seeing Star Class yachts on a safe rich silver sea.

"I have met some interesting people. You would really relate to them. You would be surprised at how civilized they are even though they come from the Middle East. After all they have had eight hundred years of empire behind them." She let Huseyin's voice guide her. "Some people who come here see them as barbarians and that is silly of course, and they are into a lifestyle that people find . . ." She had trouble spelling *offensive,* so she substituted *funny,* still unsatisfied. "I am the one who feels like a barbarian. I wish I had taken your advice and learned more languages instead of so much art. They can carry on conversations in three languages at once. One family you would like especially. They are the richest . . ." She smiled and struck out the word. Jamie hated it. ". . . most influential people here, and they have been very kind to me. They have offered to take me . . ." She laughed aloud and stopped, writing and laughing, "Oh Jesus I don't want to do this I don't want to have to do this. Why do I always have to do this?" She had written it down, and, the page ruined, she threw it on the floor, disgusted. It made her feel better, purer.

She picked it up again. She knew what she had to do. "One has to be extremely careful here." Now the words flowed fast, the writing larger, easier. "Foreigners make really bad mistakes. I am worried about Ariadne. She is so innocent. She is into a lot of stuff that I don't think she understands. She is hospitable to the point of naif . . ." She marked out the line. "She wouldn't know if some of the people she lets in here even brought drugs."

There, she'd said it. She had lit the fuse and she knew it would burn through the rest of the letter. Jamie wouldn't touch an aspirin. She went on easily. "The experiment of living on a hundred dollars a month, so long as I stay with Ariadne of course, is working. You were absolutely right to insist on my doing it. Being poor is an interesting and valuable experience. I will save up and buy nothing so that I can entertain the family who have shown me such kindness." Her square finishing-school writing marched across the page. "I am surprised at how little we know of the situation here." She twiddled her hair, and inspected it in the sun. She sighed. "All right. Eat a little shit," she told herself aloud. "You have to do it to get what you need. You've had enough training."

"You have been right about so many things." She wrote quickly, end in view. "So many people are not ready for democracy. They have to be cared for." She could hear his voice saying it, his voice in the mornings, never drunk, never sober, his intelligent pouting voice, benevolent autocracy he said. She had learned at last what he meant, in one night under the Aegean stars, and she had to admit had been as thrilled as if Haroun-el-Rashid had whispered in her ear. Everything, she was sure, had fallen into place as she had fallen onto the roof of the Endemon Pension. She wanted to lie back and let Huseyin take her mind again, all the same, mind and body, but she put it off until she finished the letter.

"You wanted to know about investment here." She loved the word *invest*. Once she had looked it up in Jamie's dictionary—*invest*. She almost said it aloud but she thought she heard a door close and was afraid it was Ariadne, coming back from whatever stupid errand she used to get through her dull mornings, and she didn't want to be bothered with her yet. To invest, to clothe, to dress, to cover, and finally, to adorn; she wrote, "The coast is opening up here, and money is flowing in . . ." Oh the flow of it all, all together, the night threatened to come back to her sweetly sex-sore body.

"The most interesting investment is a projected new hotel. The government is interested in it and so is AID, so it will not be a fly-by-night speculation." She saw a shooting star over Huseyin's shoulder. "It will be," she copied down for the letter Huseyin's words, "a new Riviera."

"And I," she told herself, letting the letter pad fall again to the floor, "will be its Brigitte Bardot." She found her torn Winnie the Pooh under her pillow. She curled up on her side, put her thumb in her mouth and thought she would sleep again. Later she would reread the letter in the light of full day, and in the light of Jamie's language and Jamie's ideas, and before she slept she made the vow that she had made before, that when Jamie died she would never bother to lie again.

Ariadne swung her canvas carry-all against her leg. She strolled as slowly as she dared, with all she had to do, through the pastless sunny morning that touched her face with a cool breeze and fingered at her scarf. There had been death, abstract to her, now there was life, as abstract, unpersoned. Ariadne had never been pregnant, but she had a pleasing taste of the condition; she was sure it would feel like this, ecstatic and nameless. She knew she was overreacting to the stimulus. How often that had been explored down long verbal paths of recognition. She didn't care, for once. For half an hour, she congratulated herself, she had been treated as a woman instead of as a problem or a solution, and she liked it, liked the long-forgotten revived awkwardness that made her smile with her oldest self, the girl-child. In the galaxy within her brainscape she saw a point of stillness, new, and a little frightening to understand. She had been used to "knowing" more, now she "knew" less. She saw that she had, out of a necessity that didn't exist, crushed her fool-self; she had been down, but not out, and now she was rising to haunt her old body.

She was surprised at her lack of empathy with what had happened in the night. She could not thrust away a new morning for that—a morning of sunlight and color, color that was so pure and bright it seemed to invade her head, color of geraniums, poppies, the great shalvar trousers of the women, sprigged with blossoms, and the piercing white of their sun-bleached cowls as they strolled at the same pace as herself, all the way as far as she could see up the long street that led to the Pazar. To ignore such a morning for unwitnessed tragedy seemed presumptuous.

She was passing the kahve where the fishermen sat. She knew she ought out of respect for their ways to walk past with her eyes lowered, as the other women did, but she was too happy and, after three years, she knew most of the men sitting there, counted them her friends, knew their names, their inevitable nicknames, their histories, including the all-important question of how they had behaved at their circumcisions. She smiled a good morning, and went on.

Behind her the answering smiles erupted into laughter. She realized that she had passed through, and interrupted for exchanged smiles of politeness, some man's morning joke of his own, and she marveled at their always polite recognition that seemed to open a door of kindness. If only we could be like that, she thought, not bothering to define who "we" was. If she had turned she would have seen Kemal's father lift his hand and wave a circle of his thumb and forefinger in

the air behind her. It was the sign of the whore. But
even if she had seen it she would have recognized it
only as the underwater sign for all's well, and agreed.

She strolled on toward Basil's house beside the shop
of Dirty Dervish, sensing in the swing of herself alive
that at least for a little while she was slim and young
and well. She was surprised when Basil ran out of his
door. It was far too early. He was wearing his new
white canvas jeans, and a striped French matelot's shirt
she did not know, and his old captain's cap. He
grasped her arm.

"My dear, I'm late. I'm in despair about it. I'm
cruising from Friday to Monday with those charming
people." Basil never said weekend; it was the first time,
though, that she had heard him say cruise seriously.
"In a tearing hurry . . . too ghastly . . . rather sweet,
aren't they?" He spun away from her and down the
street.

"No. No, they're not . . ." she called after him. She
watched him run away. She knew he had found new
people to fall in love with for a little while, and was
moving on. She could feel the worry about him, and
the gadfly of his fascinated prying interest in her, lift
away from her. She was so relieved she laughed aloud
at the retreating small, skinny body with its angry
muscles maneuvering around the village women, all
their heavy, solid bodies so much alike.

"She is laughing at us. They all do." Dirty Dervish
muttered from the door of his shop. "Ayran. Ayran,"
he called to the street. Nobody turned to listen. He
didn't expect them to. It just made him feel better.

Ariadne could feel in her body the daily movement
of the street. It seemed to flow through her. She
wanted to touch it, hold it, mold it, talk to one of
them, see her separate existence reflected in a native
eye. Like a prayer answered she saw little Kemal hunkered in a doorway, so beautifully unthinking, doing
nothing so gracefully that she wanted to share it. She
knelt in front of him and touched him lovingly on the
knees.

"Kemal." She made her voice smile, and waited until

the familiar tremor of recognition had passed. "Günaydın, Hel-lo."

His eyes said good morning, and brightened, watching her.

"Hele, hele!" Ariadne Hanım was saying again. The repetition, the demand that she knew he couldn't answer, "Tell me the truth," was beginning to embarrass him. He wished for once that she would have something else to say.

He looked away from her mouth, over her shoulder. His knees jerked away from her hands, he was up and away, leaving her squatting on the pavement. She watched him weave through the crowd, running toward the mountain.

She got up slowly and looked along the crowd, trying to find what had frightened him. She saw four village women crossing the square, one behind the other, ponderous as geese. The last of them was Kemal's mother, slow and dignified, almost imperceptibly turning her head to the left and to the right, searching the crowd. She stopped, close to Ariadne. They kissed each other on both cheeks, wordless and familiar, and, still holding each other, looked off down the street after the boy, as a single worried mother, occupied with responsibility and the morning. How like their names they became. Ariadne sensed this, still leaning her cheek against Meral's, smooth and warm with sun and young blood.

Meral, the roe deer, mixture of creature and woman, astride the past and present, hung prayer rags in the branches of the saint's tree near her village and never went abroad without an evil eye to protect her. Yet she would sit on Ariadne's terrace to read the Istanbul newspaper and ask questions where her husband could not find her, and she talked about her five years in the village school as if she had spent a short time in heaven. Unused intelligence made her face sad. Her smile seldom rose as far as her doe eyes. That part of her, the hidden part, had Ariadne as a secret friend, and her older son, Timur, as a secret pride, but she seldom spoke of him, even to Ariadne.

She reminded Ariadne of Mary, from the Bible pic-

tures of her childhood, the white kerchief, the down-
cast eyes, who kept all these things and pondered them
in her heart. She could see Mary with such a slim
brown face, such roe deer eyes, and strong, lithe, used
arms.

The Pazar, at ten o'clock, was no longer crowded.
The still life and roundness of it, the great flat basket-
woven trays piled high with peppers and tomatoes,
oranges and lemons, the barrels of lentils and bulgur,
lay open to the incisive sun that made knife-cut
shadows across the street. Village women hunkered behind white cloths spread on the pavement with bundles
of herbs and garlic and mountain grasses lying for sale
in neat rows. It was all so still.

The street, the color, poised for Ariadne in air. She
could feel herself floating slowly through the Pazar, all
the way to the palm grove in front of the municipal
building that had once been the sight of the pre-Greek
royal palace. She turned to begin to choose and bar-
gain. It was then, in the distance under the trees, that
she saw, clearly, her husband Roger, leaning his head
forward from his tall slim body, air of blondness about
him, languid among the festoons of donkey straps that
hung from the lobed stumps of the palm fronds. She
saw in that instant and so far away, with her vague
sight, the way his hair grew on his neck where she had
touched it so often, the small-boy haircut under her
fingers, as if her sight had become a telescope.

How young he looks, the thought came with the
vision. It was only for a second, but it left her
breathless and pale. It was only the American CIA
man, what was his name? Frank. Frank something.
"How alike they all look, the tall tentative men." She
clung to the words, ashamed of feeling faint.

D avid leaned against the front of the
bakery and rested from the sun, thinking slowly of how
much food he would need for the night, the bayram
over and the tourists already surging back over the
mountains. He saw her there, stopped still, oblivious,

and saw the obscene gesture from an adolescent boy
behind her back as she paused, not hearing the burst of
laughter. He ran up to her and took her bag from her
arm.

"What happened?"

"Nothing." She wasn't lying. "Nothing really." She
sounded surprised. She moved, for him, uncivilized, exposed, naked, with the funny misplaced dignity of a
brave child. He was afraid of her. He had seen such re-
leases before in her. They made her naive while they
lasted, and people sensed it and treated her more
harshly than she could understand or more gently than
she had earned. His dislike of what she called these
moments of balance made his fingers tighten on her
arm.

He guided her into the pastry shop and sat her
down.

"Now," he took her hands, "what's happened? You
look stoned. Come on. Focus on me. David."

It made her laugh. She said what she had been trying to put into words all through her morning of wandering in fields of conception. "First," she said it
carefully, "to have . . . oh . . . all the things that
people yearn about . . . but *not* to know it . . . is
youth."

He waited for her, her habit of wisdom, to be over,
waited for the familiar American abstract flow to cease.

"To know but to cease to have," she was very serious, "oh, not only sex, but life too, taken-for-granted
life, all unhusbanded, fields of it, is something of what
age is . . ."

He went on waiting patiently for her to tell him what
had happened.

"But, oh David, the moments of balance, to have
and to know, for a second, at the same time!"

"Has someone been making love to you?" he asked,
trying to steer her to the point.

"No," she smiled. "Nobody. You see, life . . ."

He squeezed her hands. "Shut up. Do not use these
words, life, love, or eternity, God, or not the word
paranoia. Just . . . tell . . . me . . . what . . . happened."

"Munci turned up at the house."

He dropped her hands. "Is that what he did? Everyone is looking for him. He is OK? Did you know what to do?"

"He's asleep." David had already gone to the counter to pay for their untouched tea.

"Ariadne you are an idiot." David went ahead of her out into the street. "Is he warm?" he called back.

"Yes of course." She ran after him.

"If only he had told me," David said. She could hardly hear him; she was trying to keep up. "I would have dived with him. No one should have to do that alone."

"He's asleep," she called to him again, afraid he hadn't heard. All of her euphoria had switched to guilt. She saw through David's concern for Munci that not for one minute of the morning had she seen him as separate, isolated beyond her feelings and her dreams.

"He needs a pair of jeans." She had finally caught up with David. "He was wearing his wet suit."

"I'll get a pair of mine, and a sweater. Go to the kahve. I will meet you there."

"Don't wake him," she called after him, troubled.

He had disappeared toward his house, still carrying her shopping bag.

Basil, newborn yachtsman, was fuming at a corner table of Salmakis kahve. Trader and Miranda sat close to him in the pretty green shade, happy and cowed. Trader was leaning forward, still listening to something Basil had finished saying. Miranda looked up and smiled at Ariadne. A net of leaf shadow softened her face.

"We can't find the beastly harbor master," Trader fussed at Ariadne. "They're never around when you need them."

"You don't know what's happened, do you, Basil?" Ariadne's newfound responsibility made her stand tall over the table.

"Oh," he waved her to a seat, "sit down for God's

sake. There's always some excuse for their inefficiency. It's too nerve-wracking." Trader and Miranda took up his annoyance and glared with him down the quay.

"What do you think of F. Scott Fitzgerald?" Miranda asked once to break the nervous silence.

"Oh Christ not now," Basil told her, but kindly. He turned to Ariadne. "We must go before noon," he said. "The wind you know." He had just found out this Aegean fact.

"Where are you going?" Ariadne felt she ought to ask.

"We were going to Patmos, a Christian pilgrimage. But it's north, against the afternoon wind. Now it's simply too, too late," he mourned.

"But it was, after all, a pretty awful thing," Miranda said, meaning to ask for more facts from Ariadne, but Basil shut her up again.

"Oh, my dear, not to feel so badly. They don't really value life as we do. That's a Christian complex, not a Moslem one."

Miranda, suddenly tired, didn't bother to answer.

So nothing was said at all until David appeared with the jeans and handed them to Ariadne.

"Darling, aren't you a bit wide in the beam for those? These American women," he turned to his new friends, "two pairs of jeans and a social security check . . . geriatric teenagers." Then, remembering that they too were American, he patted Miranda's bare leg. "You, my dear, are not one of them. The international demands of sailing. It brings out the wiry boy in a woman. Oh why don't they finish today's crisis so we can get our papers signed?"

Kemal stopped running at the ruined gate. He climbed over the hill of fallen stones. Down below him the sun was beginning to brush the little mountain valley. In the distance he saw the boys from the village driving goats along a narrow path to new pasture. He jumped down before one of them could see him, and ran low along the stream, up the steps cut into the rocks, around the black boulders. He had to get to Timur. He didn't know how. There was no way to camouflage the entrance to the inner caves once he was inside. He ran on, sobs and lack of breath catching at his throat.

It was no use. As he looked from behind the last boulder he saw Horst, sitting alone at the false cave entrance, staring down the mountain. He had a notebook on his knee. He was staring, then writing, then staring. Kemal had seen him doing this so often, listening to the air, then answering on paper. He knew it would go on for a long time.

It was nearly noon. He saw no other movement around the dig. The men had not come. He knew that Timur would be safe, at least for a little while, from hearing the news as they talked. He slithered down the deep-cut bank of the stream, crept under one of the overhanging rocks into the shade, and, not knowing that he was exhausted from his watching in the night, nestled in the deep grass under the stone shelter and went instantly to sleep.

Something was bothering Horst, troubling his mind, and he hated it. Was it the white sun, the delay, the debilitating intrusion of events on his concentration? There was so little time. But that too, that urgency, was only a mood and he knew it. It was an inner fight against the delay, the inevitable delay. He glimpsed in his mind the busy concentration of the year before, the discoveries, the intensity in the sun. He put the vision away. He suddenly wanted to tear and rip at time.

He was fighting, too, in waves, an almost uncontrollable wish to sleep, as a man sated with emotion would sleep. He remembered wanting to sleep like that after his mother's funeral. Yet what was she to him, that girl lying on the quay? It was her position, the position of all the girls who had fallen into the covering innocence of sleep beside him, girls without names, stupidity and longing and angular desire brushed from their faces.

"I am certain," he began to write to keep himself awake, "that there were several highly evolved Middle Eastern and European cultures which predated the second millennium B.C. I do not believe"—he knew he would have to prove all of this; he would find the proof somehow, the safety and clarity of proof—"that the religious practices grew up as separate manifestations of human questioning and spirit (and fear?). The sacred caves, the mother-son marriages, all touch the primal Oedipal scene. That is true as far as it goes. However," the pen went faster, talking again to the man, "it does not go far enough in the systaltic-diastaltic change. It was first the son who was killed, NOT THE FATHER, son as warrior (trace to modern war), as king, as consort—the intrusive father who kills the young to stay alive is ALWAYS the sign of the end of an age."

He put down the notebook and stretched out on the grass. He knew, for a second, that the royal son, the sacrificed king, had a golden body like his own, lithe, spare, and wisely used. There were no shadows on his notebook. The sun was straight over him, flattening the distant sea, leaching out all color, making the sky white, dulling the steps of meadow below him, and lifting the great round rocks in his swimming vision as if they had no weight.

"Noon, to the ancient cultures, was a recognized time of madness." He reached for his notebook, wrote the words, and then dropped the book on the grass again and sprang up as if he were trying to throw himself forward out of his mood.

He made himself walk over to the edge of the grass shelf to look along the path that tumbled down deep between the boulders. There was no one coming. It was so still he could hear the spring water from the stream flowing from within the mountain, and the loud beat of his own pulse in rhythm with the heat waves.

He wandered toward the sigh of the water along the tiny goat path that narrowed to cliff drop on one side. There the gorge cut the mountain from its foothills, hill behind hill. He could make out the snake road that had led through the northern pass from the plains of Anatolia since eons before the time of Alexander.

He knew, standing there on the path, that his hair was shining. Alexander had stood like that, and the great Genghis Khan. Up to the right of him were the caved-in stone circles of ten-thousand-year-old hill settlements, the beehive shapes, the tumbled rocks.

Near them a small huddle of white houses, Eskiköy, Kemal's village, had grown on top of the ruins of what had been, when Ceramos was only its port, a holy city, huddled under the mountain that it served.

He had walked so often in the room-sized ruins behind the village, filled with grass where the few cows grazed in the evenings. He had measured the ancient rock-carved courtyards, still used by the villagers, the waist-high tapered columns, the tiny doorways, the outdoor ovens set into the courtyard walls. The patterns of rugs woven by the women were still the same as wall paintings eight thousand years old, their stripes of darkness reflecting the women's dark time of the month. But all these were only clues, these and the name, Eskiköy, the village of the old men, the ancients.

One day, Horst knew, he would take the excrescence of the village away and find the holy city. To do it to Ceramos was only a dream. The land was far too valuable—but this village, worth nothing—it was possible. Eskiköy, all white, shone above him in the noon sun, a barrier to his pure past, Kemal's village, shrunk until it was as mute as he was, idiot boy, idiot village.

He turned away, disgusted, and looked down toward the valley where the great seven-mile ruins of the old wall of Ceramos were like a fragmented drawn line. He had once measured it, a great curve, over the foothills and through the valleys. He could see the outlying tangerine groves and gardens of the town, still nestled inside its no longer protecting semicircle. Beyond the fallen sacred gate, twin half-fallen watch towers looked down still on the old road to Anatolia, high tombs of squared tufa.

There had stood the watchers from the new city of Ceramos, who had protected themselves from their own mountain pasts, and left themselves naively exposed to the marauders from the sea. For another thousand years, time stretched, time shrunk, hardly in the noon sun a measure of anything, they shut themselves away from the mountains, made the past their fear and their enemy, and opened themselves to marriage with the sea.

Horst felt in himself that long pause in the sea light of safety, then the darkness of Christian invasion and defeat. He found their castle that crowned the harbor a small thing from where he stood. It was to him a medieval parody of the great ancient wall, a copy of the thick battlements, high towers, the castellated structure, the dry moat, built by barbaric invaders who knew no past but the cross.

There ten thousand people had huddled in their own shit and brutal safety, and now the tourists came and saw in it some fiction of Crusaders. He turned away and, as if he had ordered it to prove a point, he heard over him the whine of the noon jet from Istanbul to Beirut. Down along the distant sea lane of the Argo and the wise Phoenicians the little diesel boats plowed their white furrows.

Horst wished he thought he saw the nomad horsemen with their banners lined up across the opposite hills, black against the light, but he did not, and could not conjure up the fear of Genghis, Timur the Lame, and the Turks, come to eat cattle they had not bred, and tear down what they had not built, dishonor the tame with the discipline of their hard thighs. He only saw below him, under a shadow of an outthrust rock by the stream, the huddled figure of a sleeping boy, and knew it was Kemal. The once high, holy, and powerful Tartars sank for him into an idiot boy alone, the mighty finally conquered. He remembered all that was left, the tilt of Kemal's eyes.

He went back to pick up his notebook again, thinking still of the horsemen. He could feel the surge of them in his noon blood, the contained wildness of their games, the pure skill of them, life lived at the edge of its awareness, strength, and muscle.

He made himself write. "Make preparations for the following to be ready to go when the permission comes. More lodging than last year. Use some of the grant for another jeep. Do not neglect the protein.

Steady supply of eggs and daily inspected meat. This year the water from Salmakis must be kept in cave site four. Get the rubble out of it. Someone has been sleeping there this winter. Probably hunters."

He could feel, as he wrote, the defeat of the horsemen in his own body, the victory of mind and grace. "INTELLIGENCE," he wrote, and doodled a circle around the word.

"Put a barrier to keep out visitors. Talk to Murat. PERMISSION," he wrote. "ENDYMION, ANCHISES, ADONIS, OSIRIS, AXION." He could map the Aegean with their names. He added, "Map the Aegean. Frontispiece. The Chalcolithic Aegean."

The goddess came always to the sleepers or to the dead, her path a gambol of wolves and lions and panthers. There were no mysteries. That was only her hypnosis. There was only the perpetual unknown, a darkness before and after that could and would succumb to mind light. He saw the blackness of her triumph in the caves succumbing to the first faint light of man-fire, mysteries of fear dissolved into understandable forms of rock, water-carved, where men had sensed their own shapes, then helped them to be born, releasing their mirror images, larger of course and simpler, with the rubbing of flints, making their own mothers out of the raw material of fear and rock and size remembered from their own child eyes, the safety of legs towering over them.

Horst reached again for the notebook. "I think it unwise to seek for Ceramos as an ideal city in any given era," he wrote. He got up, stretched himself, and began again to search the narrow path among the rocks.

Timur watched and waited, confused by the silence. He had read the time by the shortening of the mountain shadows, and when, at the time he expected them, the men had not come, he had lain back a while to doze, and, half mindless, scratch his itching beard. The absence of the daily familiar voices of the men disturbed him. He looked forward to their voices,

sometimes as near as across a café table, sometimes so
far away that he had to put his ear to a place he had
found near the tunnel entrance to hear them at all. By
some tricks of sound carried through the hidden corridors of rock, they seemed nearer often when they
were farther away.

Timur knew this, and his movements in daylight
were spare. He knew that the mountain could carry the
sound of a cough, a dropped pencil, a rustled paper,
like a broadcast. He had long since trained his bladder
and his bowels to work before they came, again when
they spread out like birds along the cliff side of the
little verge below to eat their lunch and listen to the tin
voice of the news on Horst's transistor. As he listened,
too, above them, it was the high point of Timur's day.
He perched inside a windowed eye, wishing he could
smoke, but feeling as near the men he had known all
his life as if he were with them, part of their grumbling
and their stories which he had grown up on. He knew
through them all news, all rumor that their minds and
their gossip could encompass. It lacked something. It
always had. He missed Istanbul, its crowded streets, its
nervous pulse, as only a transplanted country man can
miss the city.

He yawned and scratched again and wandered to the
window. Below him only the German, Horst, stood
watching the mountain path. He respected Horst, although he found him naive in his love affair with the
dead. He would have liked to talk with him. Sometimes
he caught in Horst's voice the same loneliness among
the uncomprehending that he felt himself, and he
longed to answer, to argue, to enjoy him when a remark that showed the distance between Horst and the
men fell flat among them, unanswered.

It was obvious at last to Timur that he had miscal-
culated the day by one. It should have been Saturday
but it was Sunday. He resented having lost half the privacy of his Sunday by his mistake. He struck another
X on the fragmented plaster wall to correct his calen-
dar, and stretched his arms as high as he could to wake
himself up.

The dim green daylight was almost over. It was

nearly time for the sun to make its bright afternoon journey across the floor. Even with Horst below, so long as he stayed on the grass verge, he knew he could speak softly. That was why he saved his English conversation to study on Sundays. It was a far far cry from the English he had learned to read in the medical library. That, slowly, he could do, but this, this daily speech defeated him. He sighed and began. It took so much time. Well, he had that, time as a treasure, stretching before and after him, a gulf of hidden time.

"Good evening, Mista Butler," he said to the stalagmite goddess, "it is nice to meet you. Who is your wife, Missus Butler; he is well?" He took his hand from the page. He was tangled again in the pronouns and the gender, and he said, with more anger than he meant, "How is your she wife? How how how is your bombok shit she wife?"

"I hope you sleep well." He found it a rude language, harsh and direct, like they were sometimes, not meaning to be. It had lost, he thought, its animals and its politeness. It was neither soft nor peaceful—too many k's, *OK* and *Kill*, and yet, as if their mouths carried their mistrust, they did not open them but let the language slide out, muttered and foreshortened.

The time in it was urgent. That was the first thing he noticed, as when the el, the foreign soldiers from the bases, shortened chokteshe kürederim, a sweet sound ending when the thanks was over, into choktesh. He had tried to find the ways of politeness in it. How do you thank a man's hands for work, or wish his eyes would always shine to congratulate him for births, and all good events? He wondered what they said to the grieving and the troubled. He had tried to find the phrases in the dictionary. All he had found was "I hope you sleep well." He said it again to the goddess, tried to keep from scratching his beard, and yawned. He flipped to the next page.

"Which way to the airport, Mista Butler?" he asked the goddess.

"Turn right at the corner," he answered.

"Do you like fruit, Mista Butler?"

"Yes. I like oranges and apples. I like apples more

than oranges," he said carefully, with only one peep at the page.

"How many apples in one dozen?" he asked, and, remembering a lesson in English from an American sailor, he added, "I do not give a shit how many apples in one dozen, thank you, Mista Butler," and threw the book on his bed. "Why do I have to go through apples and airports to get to men?" he asked the book and threw himself down beside it and yawned.

Down below he heard a voice. "Yok, efendim." He froze like a hiding fox. The men had come. The men had come. It was not Sunday after all. He tiptoed to the wall and scratched out the X.

It was a jumble of words . . . a boat, twenty in one boat, that Bombok Huseyin, a murderer of his own fiancée, and Lale—Lale, a student someone said, another, No. She was respectable, Turgut Bey's daughter. Well, anyway, she is dead now. Munci brought her up. Four bodies. There are still three. No, four. They had begun to argue.

I must move slowly, was his first thought when he heard it. I am not sure. There are other Lales. He knew he had to get to Munci somehow. *Observe*, he clung to it as a spar. I am cold. In shock, details stand out. False calm, very bright, edged . . . this window. I had not noticed so clearly that it is carved from within the room. The adze marks show this. There are two ways they could have entered, the old men. From the false tomb? No, this is older. From the corridor behind the statue, within the mountain? Why is Horst laughing? The men say there were ten drowned at Yazada. He says only five, that they always exaggerate. It could not be Lale, only her name. The fiancée of Huseyin? They are making a story. Her father is Turgut Bey? How old is this carving? Why do I feel nothing? Munci brought them up. He will know. I must get to Munci. This is something Kemal cannot tell me. It must be very cold. I could kill them. Munir is saying that the girl students are whores and they were making umum in the boat and it turned over with them. Why do people talk about disaster in terms of where they were? Who cares if Munir was drinking coffee when he was

called to the boat? He drinks too much coffee. It is bad
for him. They are making their excuses for being late. I
must find Munci.

He moved slowly away from the window and began
to check a small bundle of equipment that he had
prepared for an emergency. He had known that at any
time the hidden entrance could be discovered, and that
he would have to get out through the corridor behind
the stalagmite goddess.

Slowly, as if the muscles of his thought were frozen,
he checked what he knew of the mountain. He had
worked it out as well as he could, as well as any man
can map the unknown from what he knows.

Across the mountain pass from his village, there was
a cave mouth where a stream ran out from deep within
the mountain. It was the cave of the women. Men
never went to it. He and Kemal had broken the first taboo he ever broke by following the women there on
their secret errands. They had done it because they
were hungry. When the women brought fruit and
bulgur to the cave mouth, he and Kemal had eaten it.
Then, they had hidden until the women came back and
chittered together over the empty plates, sure that the
ecel perileri, those fairies who knew the hour of their
deaths, had eaten the food. They had watched and listened, he trying not to laugh, Kemal with eyes as
round as the empty plates. Some of the women came
after their wedding nights, some after childbirth, to
leave blooded rags within the entrance, although the
hodja frowned on such things.

By the time he was fifteen, Timur had explored for
half a kilometer inside the cavern mouth. No one else
had the courage to take a tallowed torch and search
within the mountain. He had crawled upstream,
through a long low tunnel of the stream bed, black
stone with scars of white quartz that glittered in the
torch light.

He knew he was not the first to go there. Men had
been there. At the steep places there were steps carved
in the pitch black walls.

Once his torch had dropped into the stream, and he
had crouched in the pitch dark, afraid to try to stand

for fear he would hit his head on the tunnel ceiling.
The thousand whispers of the water in the dark began
to whisper his name, "Ti-mur, Ti-mur . . ." He felt the
blackness, total jet, heavy against his eyes and his skin,
as if he were not just blind, but had no eyes. He had
had to feel his way downstream, through the water
path, until he saw a faint faint easing of the darkness.
He crawled toward it as it turned to the tiny mouth of
the cavern in the distance, and he had, he remembered,
been half sorry to see it after the darkness and did not
know why.

But he had gone back, called there over and over,
had gone up the low corridor as far as he could, to
where he was cut off from the unknown by a veil of
water that seemed to carry its own haunted light. He
promised himself that one day he would plunge
through it. Finally, secretly, he had found the nerve to
do it. He had made a leather pouch, had wrapped
candles and matches in plastic. All the night before he
had stayed awake. He told himself that it was excitement, but he knew later that it was fear, fear crouched
in his chest, of what he was going to do.

He still could relive that day, fifteen and more
scared than he had ever been in his life, reaching that
veil of water, putting out his torch and feeling in the
blackness for a dry place to leave it. Gradually his eyes
got used to the faint light of the waterfall itself. He
plunged through it, found no foothold, sank in freezing
water, and was swimming, swimming in black air,
black water. He had sensed vast space above him, with
the blackness moving, as air moves. He swam to his
own right, felt rock. His fingers scuttered across flat
stone until he found a rock handle to pull himself up
out of the water. He sat waiting in the black space until his hands were dry. He had never been so cold.

The space was taking on a faint removal of
darkness. High to the left, and far away, he could just
see the wall of water he had passed through. The
smudge of—not light—but lightened darkness came
from a faint star so far above him that he had to
measure the fall of space with his ears, not his eyes. He
thought he knew what it was, the old spring hole

beside the deserted Byzantine church high on the mountain opposite his village.

He tried to measure a right-angle triangle in his mind, its base the long corridor he had come from, its long side the slope of the mountain up to the chapel. He calculated that he was half a kilometer inside the mountain. The word *kilometer,* the measuring by right-angle triangle calmed his mind. His hands had dried. He unfastened his bundle and lit a candle.

The ice-covered wall glittered behind him, but when he touched it it was dry rock, white, opaque. Angles of quartz caught the candle flame and gave it back to him. He leaned over the water, a vast lake stretching out beyond the circle of light, so still that the reflection of the candle did not move. Around him the tiny light sphere from the flame was swallowed up in blackness.

He began to move beyond his own awe around the lake edge, at first on his knees, afraid to stand, to expose himself to space. Gradually he realized that he was crawling on a smooth path that wound around giant pillars of stone, their bodies glittering white. Out of the blackness great icicles hung down, huge folds of stone curtain, long straight gashes of glistening crystal in the black stone walls. He found more manmade steps carved in the rocks where the path rose up, so that he could look down on the lake from so far above it that it was disappearing out of his small periphery of light. In a few more steps the lake disappeared. He could hear water ahead of him, a small fine treble of sound.

At the end of the path he found a little rill of water running out of a black cavern, already almost too small for his fifteen-year-old body. The manmade steps disappeared into it. It was as far as he had gone then, but he had promised himself that someday he would know the mountain like his hand.

Then he had turned to go back, and turned into a pillar of stone himself with fear of what he saw. A huge ghost was forming in the distance where the waterfall had been. Light radiated from it until he could see the whole end of the vault. It reached higher than he had dreamed in his puny measuring. He had

no idea how long he stood there, watching the wall of
light creep around the cavern walls. There never was
before or after in him such still terror. He made himself look up. Far far above the ghost the spring opening was shining like the evening star, showering the
waterfall with bright gold. It was the noon sun, pouring
straight down the lines of water. Gradually it began to
fade. He pulled himself into movement again and felt
his way forward, crawling around the giants that
guarded the lake. He found he could not stand yet; his
body was frozen from his wet clothes.

At the end of the lake where the waterfall still
spread an afterglow of the light beam, he saw shining
at the bottom of the pool it made an Aladdin's
treasure, a floor of coins, a gold Christian cross, an old
green adze of bronze, some crystal-covered branches
that could have once been bones, piles of silver and
gold and green bronze, here and there on top, a
twenty-five-kurush piece with a profile of Atatürk. Although he was, at fifteen, a scoffer at the women, he
did not touch the treasure, though he put out of his
conscious mind that it was the hoard of the ecel perileri who knew the hour of his death.

That was the cavern he would have to
find again to get out of the mountain. How far away it
was from his cave hideout he could not know; he only
knew he had to do it. Standing in the cave room where
he had hidden for so long, hearing the men's voices below him in the sun, Timur realized that he had frozen
again, this time in the protective memory of his fear, as
a man pinches himself in one place to keep the pain
someplace else from being intolerable. He made himself move, inspect the packet of candles and a supply
of folded newspapers wrapped in layers of plastic. He
put the cache of matches and the American lighter that
Kemal had brought him with the rest, and tried to seal
the packet against damp.

The lighter made a smile flick across his mouth. Kemal was standing in front of him. "Did you steal it?"

he asked him. He heard the click of Kemal's tongue, the toss of his head, saying no, offended. Kemal acted out his watching of the drunk American soldier. He had not stolen or begged. He had just watched until the soldier handed him the lighter to get rid of him. Timur flicked it to see if it still worked, and put it back into the packet. He tied the packet around his neck with a thong, then put around his head the goatskin band he had made to hold a candle like a miner's light over his eyes so that the light would not blind him and he could use both hands. He put on a vest he had made of goatskin, then took it off again, afraid it would get sodden with water and weigh him down. He put it on again, remembering the coldness of the caves, annoyed with himself that his mind was wandering after all his preparation. He was conscious of himself moving carefully, one step at a time, slow with urgency.

Far behind the goddess in the niche, he had listened to the breathing of the mountain on night after night, sometimes weak in the calm weather, sometimes almost screaming as storms hit the hidden tunnels. He knew that he would follow the water flow, move slowly, take time.

He could no longer hear the men's voices. He turned to read the sun. Nearly three o'clock. He looked for the last time around his cave room, at the goddess, the carvings, his books, the skeleton. He knew he could come back for his books, and even hide there again after he had found Munci; but he knew, too, he would not hide there. He thought of Atatürk. A man who goes to prison once is a donkey. A man who lets himself go twice is a son of a donkey.

Slowly, slowly, he forced himself around the goddess into the dark corridor behind her, and lit his first candle. It filled the body-smooth corridor sides with light. A dry level floor stretched ahead of him. He blew out the candle and walked along it in the dark. Far ahead he heard a whisper of water that at first was wind. He saw faint light. He walked until he could see beyond the corridor a round opening, door size. He stepped out of it. High above him, to his right, light brushed the walls from a cleft on the mountain's surface. Across his feet a small stream moved slowly, very slowly, as he stooped and read the flow rate with his hand. Its floor was soft mud. It disappeared to the left under a low curved mouth into the dark. He turned left, felt the mud under his bare feet that would have to be as sensitive as hands, as directional as eyes. He saved his light. He had brought fifteen hours of candle-light. He had no idea how long he would be in the mountain.

He lay on his back, and wriggled himself slowly down like a snake through the mud. He guided himself with one hand against the ceiling, less than his forearm's length from his body. He went on until the black was heavy against his eyes, his skin, his hair. He used his back and the skin of his feet to guide him, sensing the downward slope. His body had grown vast, filling the tube. He could hear the loud boom of the mountain, and realized that it was his own heartbeat against the stone. There was no time, only the tube, stretching on and on, blind.

The ceiling lifted gradually. He could no longer touch it. His feet felt a wall of rock. The tunnel was jammed. He stayed animal still until he could hear, be-yond his heart, the beat of water falling somewhere to his left, a free flow through a space near his feet. It was only when he freed the lighter, and a candle from the bag around his neck, that he found that he had moved with his eyes shut tight against the darkness, in some effort to control it. He saw the film of light first through his closed eyelids. He opened his eyes slowly. He could judge how long he had been in the dark by the sting of the candlelight against his exposed eyes.

He was lying in the waterfloor of a smooth tunnel a little more than a meter high. He moved his head enough to see that the vein of water had turned and was disappearing downward through a body-size hole in the tunnel side. He was still for a minute, consider-ing the way to move his body. Slowly he turned over and thrust his feet through the water into the space be-yond the hole. He inched backward until only his trunk and one hand kept him from falling. He twisted until he could hold the candle out into space. He saw a waterfall drop of two meters that disappeared into a water gash so narrow it was like a mouth of rock. It made a whirring noise. To the right of it the candle-light hinted at a dry stone floor at the edge of what he hoped was a cave room.

He did not dare stop and think. He blew out the candle and let himself fall, trying to throw himself as far to the right as he could, into blackness.

III

Flower Storm

Dürüst Osman, owner of more of Ceramos than any other man, sat in his walled garden alone. At five o'clock every day the garden was his kingdom. No one dared come into it unless he commanded it with a slight nod of his head. A little dapple of sun through the clusters of the wisteria warmed his scalp and made him feel wise, calm, and happy. To Dürüst Osman it was a deliberate exercise. To be happy on a day of disaster was, to him, a triumph. He had learned it, and the training contained a contempt for the unhappy and the weak who drowned themselves in waterfalls of passion and events.

Dürüst Osman knew better. He had learned to love himself, the five o'clock garden, the smell of a lemon from the best of his groves as he leaned forward and sliced it. He lifted half of it to just the right distance from his nose, warm and—not sour—a light green sweetness, the right sun, the right choice of fruit, the right time to pick it. In the street, stone quiet, sun sleep quiet after the noise and bustle of the parade that had bored him so and upset the day before, the tamarisk feathers sighed in the imbat, the afternoon breeze from the sea. It rose so faithfully that he could tell the time by it in spring, as the gold of the afternoon mountain side was to him a great clock face.

Dürüst Osman sat with the glass and saucer of lemon tea in his hand, not remembering having squeezed the lemon. These tiny lapses of memory annoyed him. Carefully, he let his mind clear, paused as if he were going to read the future in the glass, and allowed the scent to touch his nostrils where early in the morning he had so carefully plucked out three snow-

179

white hairs. He smiled, sighed, so still. He had long since adjusted his English cloth trousers, and smoothed down the subtle embroidery of his open shirt to just the way he wanted it.

Beyond the roofs the minaret near the Pazar was the white of sun-drenched brass. It measured his gold mountain behind it like a giant yardstick. Unlike the Prophet, he wanted neither to go to the mountain nor for her to come to him. At five in the afternoon he wanted everything to stay, poised, in the right place.

Everything was, for once, in its right place, and its right color at the right time. The lemon tea was nearly cool enough to drink. Lemon oil blended with the scent of rose geranium, wisteria, the delicate new leaves, the breathing darkness of the spring earth, and the blue sea breeze. Dürüst Osman let the reins of power go slack in his soul, and sweetness come, and night. There was space between his thoughts as between notes of music.

His fat wife Hatije, so justly named—she, too, had brought money—did not even dare look through the shutters when he had his time of rest. "I will not be spied on, Hatije Hanım," he had told her with the politeness of steel.

As for Huseyin, he was too busy dealing in the Pazar like a Greek. Dürüst Osman frowned, and his own frown bothered him. He did not wish to think about Huseyin. He felt the flesh of his own slim body between his fingers; no, not slim, young men were slim. Dürüst Osman was thin, like strong wire, like Munci and Timur would be when they were sixty-five, well, seventy. Even alone, he did not care for this truth.

Huseyin would be fat like his mother, with fat fingers in rings, and a fat neck, and scheming eyes. He would be like Turgut Bey, dissolved in fat grief, not like him, a beautiful strong old man, contemptuous of tears; not even old really. He could still make love to his mistress in Izmir as regularly as the imbat blew.

Dürüst Osman was having a time of not liking Huseyin, the way he had slobbered over the girl he didn't know because he had lost a good bride price, holding on to Turgut Bey with the perfume of the young gavur girl, the one with the unlucky red hair,

still clinging to him. Dürüst Osman banished Huseyin
from his mind. It was time to drink his tea, and be
calm, and enjoy the sad pleasure of a little loneliness.

To arrive at the deliberate peace of such an afternoon and such a fine wire body at his time of life had
taken, as it always did, a day of habits his family knew
better than to interrupt.

As usual, ignoring the men clustered around the
quay, waiting for the boats to come back with the load
of disaster they would feed on all day, Dürüst Osman
had ridden out at dawn, his small Arab mare treading
the blank street delicately. His feet were secure and
handsomely shod in boots that felt like an outer skin in
the Seljuk stirrups of the fine old saddle that was supposed to have been in his family of derebeys for two
hundred years.

He had bought it in the covered Pazar in Istanbul in
1919. Or at least he had chosen it. It had, of course,
been paid for by his friend, the military attaché from
the German Embassy. Ibne. Catamite. Kept boy. He
smiled at the words. When you have been dumped
ashore from Crete, your family lost, and all because
you called God by one name rather than another of the
ninety-nine, looking for food like a stray handsome
little Istanbul cat, you are lucky ...

He let himself be, again, just for a little while, that
small boy in the fish market, looking for his cousin
Mehmet Ali where there were a thousand Mehmet
Alis. The night had come, and he thought he would die
of the cold. There he was, without passion, just quietly,
logically considering suicide at eleven years old because
he was so tired. Ah yes, at such a time to be chosen, to
be let into a house, ibne or catamite, Allah Allah, you
are lucky to have such eyes and such a mouth. When
at eleven years old, my friend, he told himself, you
have considered suicide so calmly, that part of you
stays calm and unsurprised, for you have seen the bald
black ass of God with his back turned.

When the attaché had left him at the disastrous end
of the First World War, going away rigid with unshed
tears, he had given him the saddle, the books, the collection of rugs, the jewelry. He said it was the least he

could do. He had gone to Germany still thinking he
was rich enough to make such gestures. Dürüst Osman
thought of him very little; once he heard that he was
teaching in a boy's school in Germany and that he was
growing fat. He could see him with an ever slimmer,
ever younger line of ibnes, as beautiful as doves, as he
grew fatter, older and fatter. Dürüst Osman thought it
an irony of that God of the midnight street, that terrible teacher, that everyone close to him should run to
fat when he hated it so.

At least, at sixteen, he had learned the manners of
an Osmanli and had taken their name as more suitable
than his own. He had also learned three languages and
a hard muscular training in disgust, especially for the
Osmanli he imitated. During the occupation they
cringed and fawned on everything, on the French, on
the English lords of Istanbul.

One day in 1920, he had ridden out of Istanbul,
through Bursa, along the empty brown plains of Anatolia. He had never before been farther into Asia than
the coast of the Sea of Marmara. It was a terrible
country, dry, poor and spacious at the same time, and
he, for a little while, fell in love with it. He rode
through summer dust and winter snow, past millennia
of houses and tombs, broken by time and poverty,
through Anatolia to that new world and that new man,
Mustafa Kemal Atatürk, the Gazi, the hero who had,
he knew, felt the same midnight wind of God across
his face like the flick of a whip.

After such training and such a war, what could follow that was not luxury? It was easy—after all, he was
a soldier of the Gazi—to "buy" deserted Greek lands
along the coast. It was fair exchange, he thought, when
he bothered to consider it, for his own family lands
stolen in Crete. It was all part of a conscious plan, as
in the riding out at dawn, his mind cleansed by the new
light. He had seen the young American that morning,
the one who had been at lunch the day before, leaning
over his balcony, staring out at the dawn-dark water as
he rode along the quay to meet the sun. That man is
ambitious and does not know it, he told himself,
amused at his feeling of fellowship, but he did not call

out to him. He only watched, approving, his calculated silence.

So he had ridden by as he always did, riding to wash the ibne, the catamite of dreams and the night, strip himself to what he had at last become in the clarity of the dawn, seventy years old, an agha, a derebey, who had the sense to fashion his lies with all the fine tailoring of rumor used correctly, controlled, without one fat ounce of self-delusion or apology. But he carried within him to keep him warm the still shivering urchin who had seen the back-side of God, not even a God of wrath, that was naive, but of the indifference of a midnight street with garbage tossing in the wind, and cold, how cold. He had hidden the boy within himself, his own ibne, secret and cared for within the old and feared man. Hey hey, he told his little urchin self, here is your lemon, picked for you this morning, canım. He began to sip the tea.

The taste, as he had planned it would, brought back the morning's ride through the tangerine groves, past the pulsing of the fine new German water pump that fed his favorite grove, the smell of his own special lemons in the sun, past the women who covered their mouths and nodded to him, their agha. On and on, up the mountain pass on the camel track so old that their soft feet had worn deep hollows in the rocks, he turned away from the last village above him on the cliff. Eskiköy, standing on ruins older than Ceramos, where the dogs did not dare to bark at his horse.

He rode up the opposite side of the pass, up the mountain itself to the white bones of the ruined Byzantine chapel where once monks from the land he owned had worshiped, to the apex of silence. Each morning he dismounted there, and threw a twenty-five-kurush coin into the old disused spring hole, not for luck or prayer, but to hear nothing, the sound of pure nihilism as it disappeared into the deep black silence of the bottomless well.

There was another reason for this gesture. He did not like to call it ritual. That was a womanish word. Dürüst Osman had a contempt as deep as the well for money. He liked to remind himself of the time when twenty-five kurush would have kept him alive, and he had none, nothing between himself and the ibne, the catamite.

In the four years in Istanbul within that house and garden he had never once had a coin to call his own— a freedom coin. From eleven to fifteen years old he had not gone outside the garden to play for one day. He had had then everything he wanted, everything but that one thing, that freedom. It had given him at sixty-five, no, now that he was thinking the truth, seventy, a hatred of the rich and of himself as a rich man that filled him with a kind of power that the frightened, born rich could not have, the rich like Huseyin, with all his greed.

Then, too, when he threw the twenty-five-kurush coin back into God's black hole where some residue of faith told him that it came from, he leaned down through the fringe of ferns around its rim. He could feel the cold breath of his God, but never never could hear what he longed to hear, the coin hit the bottom so that he would know at last for a certainty that God was not infinite.

Now, in his walled garden, it was time to speak a little to someone else. He watched the street through the iron gate of the garden. The tea was gone. An hour had passed. He had not been conscious of that, so he knew that the hour had been timeless, pure, and perfect contemplation without urgency.

Beyond the latticed window of the kitchen, the little maid, Zephyr, watched his head jerk up. He had been asleep for a long time. It was her duty to watch for the old head to jerk like that as a signal to prepare the rakı, the ice, just so, a few olives, some white cheese, slices of cucumber.

There were so many habits to keep in her mind, not only the ritual times, but they were all easy. It was like looking after her own grandmother. They seemed to measure their days, the old, like that, leaving no time for surprise. Maybe it was to keep the fear of their dying away. She didn't know. It was like living with wrinkled people from another land always, a land where hopes were turned around and flew backward into the past.

The old man there, she had to be careful with the past hopes that he lived, how he had been an Osmanli, a young agha in Istanbul, when everyone knew that like so many he came from Crete in the old days, and shined shoes, and starved like a street dog, and how he had been ibne to an old man. But she honored the dream he lived out of politeness, and the fear that came of his ownership of her days, as the villagers did when he rode by in the mornings. He was old, and he was rich, and they knew too well how his anger, his changes of mind, could harm the rhythm of their lives. So she honored his pretenses. Hey hey, it did no harm. She had only to choose carefully who she laughed with, and when, about it all.

She knew he would watch the street, now that he had waked, and demand his due of conversation from anyone he could lure into the garden. Sometimes she felt sorry for him when no one came by. He seemed so lonely, and then his temper would be bad and he would make her mistress cry. Not that she cared about that, dripping or dry, she was the same pile of flesh to Zephyr. But she would pass on the hurt and that would make her homesick, and the homesickness was bad when she stayed awake alone, remembering the breathing of her family around her in the dark.

She saw Dürüst Osman rouse himself. How slow he was. How he floundered to his feet, the toothless old camel. He leaned on the gate. She heard him call "Hoshgeldin" to someone in the street. It was the young American he had caught, the one she had served at lunch the day before. He had a sneaky way of spitting olive seeds into his hand as if he were ashamed of them. She was pleased. He had netted a young man to talk to, and everyone knew he liked that. It would make him happy, and his happiness would shine even on Hatije Hanım, and make life easier for Zephyr until she finished her duties at midnight, and went to bed on her mat in the shed at the corner of the garden. She would lie there, letting the moonlight touch her, and dreaming of her marriage two years away, when she

would be fourteen. Already in her chest in the corner
she had a fine pile of linen, embroidered in the afternoons when her mistress was asleep.

Men, she thought as she watched them cross the
garden together, they thought themselves the pool of
the day but they only stirred it from time to time, like
wind or thrown pebbles. "Hoshbulduk," she heard the
young American say, one of those words they all
learned. She had already lifted the tray to carry it out
when she saw Dürüst Osman's hand go up, and his old
dry sticks of fingers wiggling to call her.

F rank was pleased. The day had drifted
past him as he had hoped it would, even without
diving. He had lain in the sun on the wide stone breakwater of the outer harbor, and watched the boats turn
from black dots in the distance, to white sails, to heaving decks as they broached the inner harbor. He had
lain there until the shadow of the castle covered him.

Now, at evening, he too wanted company, this kind,
civilized and quiet. When the shadowy child set down
the tray between him and Dürüst Osman without a
sound, beautiful and chaste, both the child and the
tray, he wished he could find such a tray to send back
to his mother.

There the old man sat, slowly slicing a lemon with
his own hands, not letting the little girl do it. He liked
that, too, the way such men did those small duties for
themselves as an art, two thousand years of simple, elegant gesture. They reflected a power, taken so for
granted that there was no shame in the importance of
small details, of simple things, the way the old man,
Osman, an Osmanli to his long fingers, poured the
water from the silver pitcher as a chalice into the
glasses slowly, slowly all of it, even the sea breeze
slowly through the wisteria vine, hypnotic.

They watched together as the water turned the clear
raki the color of moonstones. As Dürüst Osman sat
down again, Frank saw with a shock that his fingers

were pattering at his thighs as his grandfather's had before he died, as if they were picking at his bones.

Dürüst Osman took Frank as for granted as if he had ordered him, a right, slightly exotic dish to amuse him for a little while. He could see that he was little different from the rest of the raw-faced boys that America produced like Fords. They had no waists, but even so he was tall enough, wiry and handsome and young. It made Dürüst Osman feel wise and very glad of having kept off the softness of age from his body. He let his fingers feel his thighs again to reassure himself that it was so, pleased with the hard muscles he touched. He settled back to talk, but first was pleased to be silent and gain control by watching the young man twist in the stillness, flounder a little for words, with no manners or phrases to fall back on.

It was good to have a stranger there, too, he could tell old stories that he liked to hear again, and for once, he decided this quickly, some of the truth. The thought amused him. There was nothing about him this young man could not find out anyway. Allah knew how much he paid Huseyin for information. Yes, he sighed, content, he would play with some judicious truth, as keen a weapon as judicious rumor.

"My lemons," he began. "Now, shimdi, smell him." He handed him one of the yellow-green halves. "You will not find better lemons in the world. One of these a day and never a laxative. Never." He laughed at all weakness, including laxatives.

Frank dutifully smelled the lemon and wondered if he would ever have the poise to talk to a stranger about laxatives. That was one of the intangible strengths that took a thousand years to build.

"Evenings like this remind me of my days with the Gazi," Dürüst Osman began delicately.

Frank thought, why is he trying to fool me? An Osmanli with the Gazi. Well, there were some—a few. He had read every book he could find in translation about the Turkish war of independence. He had come to his new post far better prepared than the others, and he was proud of that.

"At twenty years old," Dürüst Osman told him as if

he were reading his mind, and slightly bored with what he read, "I was not an Osmanli or anything else but a Turk. I was born of the Gazi. I tell you. You cannot know. You are full of Greek propaganda. Why, it was a miracle, I tell you. Since five hundred years in the time of Suleiman, you call the Magnificent, there was not such a time."

Frank put the lemon down carefully and took a drink of rakı.

"Eat. You must eat after every sip." Dürüst Osman spread a piece of bread with white cheese and handed it to him.

It was a ritual enough and more, Frank saw, pleased. He will be a fine host. He will tell me how to drink rakı, and about the Gazi, and what we don't understand about Turkey, and then I will find out why he invited me into the garden. He seemed uninterested yesterday in the building of the hotel. He hardly said a word all through lunch. Maybe, Frank's spirits rose, he is in favor of a reservoir. Anyway, it pleased him to spend the hour between exercise and sleep and sun and the self-expected pursuit of girls to listen to the old man talk about the Gazi. It seemed right for the time, not like Turgut Bey with his operating, his fat, and, Frank had to admit it after the embarrassment of the morning, his self-centered grief. This man before him was a gentleman and, well, a little more to be trusted, wherever such men were found.

As a caprice, it amused Dürüst Osman to surprise Frank with some colder truths than he knew. He knew he wouldn't believe most of them. The judicious rumors had been too carefully planted. That was the trouble. Even when he told the truth no one believed him.

"I was cast ashore," he began, "when the exchange of populations happened between Crete and Turkey. I worked from eleven years old. The streets. I slept in the street. I see you don't believe me." They both laughed. Dürüst Osman's mind wandered back to the night wind.

"After 1918 it was terrible. England and France and Greece were going to carve us up like a karpuz, a

melon. We did not exist as men. When I heard about
the Gazi, I stole a horse from a German Embassy attaché and rode to Anatolia. Here, try the cheese. It
comes from one of my villages. You cannot believe.
Every place people were hungry. Ankara was a little
village then called Angora, all mud. There for the first
time I saw Mustafa Kemal. He was not Atatürk then.
He was called that later. Mustafa Kemal . . ." he let
the words fall gently, following them with a pause for
reverence. "There was a town of mud, and so much
talk, twenty-four hours at a time."

He was amused at the way it sounded among the
leaf shadows. He thought, watching himself talk and
posture a little, "I will let this young man think I am a
garrulous old fool, then I will plant his mind like a
garden."

"Do you know what he had to do?" He forgot the
posturing and leaned forward. "Do you know the awful
mountain of the past we had to move? These people
had been on their knees for a thousand years. To sit
was regarded as the only respectable posture of a man,
and the behinds, the po pos, had grown fat. We had to
take away the fat, and we cannot let it come back.
Now, shimdi, sons selâmed, you know, knelt, before
their fathers, and wives before their husbands, and the
country man before the city man, and the people before their agha, and all of us with our noses and our
foreheads to the ground before the Padishah, the sultan, and even more before the Caliph, how would you
call that? The descendant of the Prophet, ah, you
know, like the Pope is the descendant of Christus. But
how can that be? Your Christus had no wife. Maybe a
little umum . . . ?" His wrist flipped back and forth.

"Uh, I am a Protestant," Frank explained.

Dürüst Osman was no longer interested.

"Our task was literally to teach the people and our-
selves to stand . . . up . . . on . . . our . . . feet." His
fist pounded the table and made the glasses dance.
"We had to go from your Henry the Eighth to your
Franklin Delano Roosevelt in two, three years!

"Do you know what the worst sin was in the days of
the Caliphate? Bidat! Innovation. Anything new.

Mustafa Kemal took that sin, that bidat, and he committed it into a new world. The holy law, the sheriat, that had covered everything, what you did in the morning, what hand you held your cock to piss with, your business, the way you sat, the way you knelt, the way you ate, everything. Ah, you look at us to find out what you were once, my boy. Our last Sultan was only fifty years ago. I have seen him. Your Henry the Eighth was—what?—five hundred? How can you understand what we did? You take too much for granted. In my own lifetime, in 1923, I have heard the guns fired all over Turkey for the death of the Caliphate."

Carefully, Dürüst Osman sliced one of his precious lemons, smelled it, judged it, and handed half of it to Frank.

"Even the scent of it is like the perfume. We sell some to make a sweet lemon oil, very expensive. You call us a young country. You are right. One of the youngest. Many thousands years." Dürüst Osman laughed, making a fine shower of lemon juice.

His laughter woke Hatije Hanım. She turned a little in her bed and thought to call Zephyr, but she knew she could not while Dürüst Osman was still in the garden. She dozed again, waiting for the time when Zephyr could come and get her out of bed.

Frank was hardly listening. He had heard it all, the voice, the pressure of it, before such a place as Turkey had been a part of his mind. He was with his own grandfather who had fought in the last Indian war. He was being diminished to a small boy again and he didn't mind it, for a little while. He watched the narrow fine skull of Dürüst Osman, the deep eyes that had not filmed, the color of his skin, color of brown, burnt, country wisdom. It amused and pleased him that all of the centuries of breeding he saw there should make a naive gesture of lying about his past, almost a gesture of honoring both Frank's and his country's youth. Frank thought it fine and thoughtful, a thousand years of deep country politeness.

Behind Frank, the mountain had gone dark against the evening sky. The wind was rising. It tossed the tamarisk fronds. It caught a glass and threw it on the table. It grabbed at Dürüst Osman's shirt and he sat up, poised between laughter and anger, honed by the wind.

"Could these young men you see now have ridden with the Gazi? With their transistors and their pretty shirts." He could see Huseyin's soft flanks, the sky showing under his seat when he made him ride. "Was it to produce such sons that we rode with the Gazi? Let me tell you this. How shall I say . . . ? You should know this language." This stung Frank. He was perfectly capable of carrying on a pure conversation in State Department Turkish, so long as too many idioms were not used, but no one would let him.

"Oh, they are clever enough," the old man was saying. "They care for nothing but money money money." He swept his arm in a great circle, one of their gestures that Frank did not know. The wind was whipping the shadows into nervous flicks of darkness along the walls and across their faces. "Vay kâfir! Very foreign. That is how we say clever." This Frank had not heard. He made a mental note. "The young . . . they live and think like Greeks."

Hatije Hanım tried to get out of bed. She couldn't get her feet to the floor. Allah, when will they stop? Mutter mutter mutter. She needed Zephyr badly to get her to the bathroom. She cursed her fat, remembering how beautiful she had been, and comforted herself that she had the only bidet in Ceramos.

Frank said nothing still. He thought it better that the old man see him as stupid.

"In those days, the new days," the old man was back with the Gazi, "we read. We read everything. We were making a new country." Dürüst Osman dropped into sadness. He watched a shadow brush back and forth across the rakı bottle. "Mustafa Kemal died—our father Atatürk, that means father of Turkey. He became, for the first time," he allowed himself to smile, "what every single person who wanted to use him wanted him to be. He left us stunned, as a father's death stuns his children. Time stopped, I think. Do you not have the feeling here that time stopped with his death? You have a legend, I think, that the clocks stop

when a man dies, and dogs mourn themselves to death.
Here the clocks stopped and the dogs died. It was like
that. Maharet had been our watchword. Skill. We
wanted to learn." Anger fluttered in his voice. "And
you. You come here. You pour money all over us. You
make a big tractor factory." His English was slipping,
with rakı and excitement. "A peasant with one tractor,
she have no field large enough to turn him in, she
wants a good hand plow to hitch her oxen, or her wife.
You try in the conquering of us with the tractor and
the highway. Aye, will you never know us?" Frank was
embarrassed. He thought the old man was going to cry.

Dürüst Osman felt a tug of delight in his bones. He
was setting the scene for what he had decided to do.
Not that he cared very much, but it would make peace
in his house and that was important to him. He was
tired of the incessant talk. He knew, if the young man
did not yet, that he was going to persuade him to
recommend the building of the hotel, get it settled, out
of his mind and his house. The idea pleased him. He
saw all the agonizing, the discussion that bored him so,
channeled in some direction away from him. The evening vines were beginning to release their scent. The
pink clouds were long tendrils across the sky, combed
by the wind.

"You try," he said, his English intact again, "to conquer so naively. I am sorry for you."

"We only . . ." Frank hoped he would let him
speak, but Dürüst Osman waved his hand, as he did at
his own table, for the boy to be quiet. In the silence he
demanded they both heard a stick beating frantically
on the upstairs floor. The old man grinned.

"Zephyr!" he called.

"Efendim?" she said. His voice had caught her on
the stairs. She ran to the door.

"Some more cucumbers. Very thin. Very cold."

Zephyr disappeared. The stick rapped again.

"Conquering. That is for boys. It does not last. You
have to do it again and again. We know. We had eight
hundred years of that conquering."

Six hundred. Five hundred if you count the nineteenth-century concessions made to France and Ger-

many. England . . . At least Frank could let his mind answer, even if the old man would not let him speak.

"There is a prophecy in Turkey," Dürüst Osman said. "It is very old. It is about a Sultan, a Padishah." He leaned back in the correct way to tell a story. "He will conquer the realm of the gavur. He will take the Red Apple and capture it. If after seven years the sword of the gavur does not come forth, he will keep the land of the Red Apple for twelve years. He will build and plant and move his people there. But after twelve years the place of the Red Apple will rise and put him to flight. To capture the Red Apple and rule there! What an illusion! We found it out. You cannot buy or promise or kill enough. The Red Apple has been many things to us. It was thought to be the orb of Justinian in Istanbul. We conquered that. Or it was the jewel in the hand of the Virgin in Sancta Sophia. We turned it into a mosque. Then it was the sun hitting the spires of Vienna. Then this. Then that. Always illusive. Always the next thing. To conquer. *Aman Allah!*"

He jumped up. "A man cannot even conquer in his own house." He went to the door and called, "Hatije Hanım! Olmaz! You will please stop that pounding," he added in English in deference to his guest, although she did not understand a word. There was dead silence. "Thank you very much." He sat down again slowly.

"So now it is your turn to seek the Red Apple. You plant what? Tractors that only landowners like myself can use, roads that only the rich can travel through a country that is poor to cities that do not matter so much here. Then there are the tanks and the planes and the guns and the Coca-Cola and the Ford trucks. You try to construct out of all of these a nice bourgeoisie, dependable and sly. Ugh! Je les déteste. Une nouvelle bourgeoisie—quelle pomme rouge! Vay kırmısı elmayı!" His face showed despair lightly. "You may earn the politeness of my people, but the Red Apple of their souls you will not have."

Frank was disappointed. He had hoped to escape the safe circular talk of the soul.

Dürüst Osman pointed his finger at Frank. "Do you know what will defeat you? It is sad. Some of us, not

me of course, will go down with you. The good minds
of the country? No. The young ones? No. They do not
know how." He tapped the ends of his fingers at the
words. "Oil," he said sadly. "Tungsten. Bauxite. Tin.
Copper. These will defeat you." He smiled. "But Turkey? Smyrna figs! Mmm. Hey hey . . . we still export
our figs from Izmir as Smyrna figs. Those damned
Greeks have, how do you say that, washed your
heads."

"Look, sir." Frank leaned forward to stop the spate.
It was time. He prided himself on his timing. Bad timing, he had told himself many times with some profun-
dity, was pissing against the wind. The old man was
pulling him into facts and legend and prejudice, inter-
twining them like a thick rope around everything he had
wanted to say and he had to cut the rope of it all.
"Sir?"

Dürüst Osman watched his fine smooth dumb young
face grow intense. It simply annoyed him, all that
power behind such a face. It made him strip down to
another layer of what he liked to think of as the truth.

"What no one has learned"—there was an edge to
his voice that he used with his agents on the telephone—"what you young have not learned is how to
use your power. You must *use* it." The boy in the midnight street banged on the table with the old man's
hand. "They amuse me. I hear the young ones talk
about the peasants as if poverty and prejudice and the
stone wall of bidat were something to fall in love with.
They go to the villages from their university and they
sit and talk in the kahve and they think they are in
heaven and they are not. They are in hell. Hell," he
said, quiet again, "is having no money. They will not
change from this. Aye. There was after the revolution
of 1960, only a little revolution, you know, there was
free press in Turkey for the first time in our whole history. Only for ten years. It was very dangerous. The
young read everything and it gave them diarrhea of
the mouth. We had to stop it. Our people are used to
the despots, the arama tarama, the search and seize, the
sheriat."

He had forgotten the war of independence, the Gazi,

and the beautiful sin of bidat. "You see, despotism in
the daily life is good for the soul. It forces the mind
upward toward God. There is no place else for it to go.
This is why I back the Emir party. It will bring order.
Is not order what you want in what you are pleasing to
call the young countries? Young!" He laughed again.

Hatije Hanım and Zephyr were changing the wet
clothes on her great slow body. The laughter from below foretold a peaceful evening. They smiled at each
other to hear it.

Frank was all too familiar with the drowning sense
that he was up against facts without future, unable to
breathe or speak in the face of all the fathers—what
was and is and ever shall be. He wanted words and
had none. He was aware that much was being kept
from him. He was, once again, being charmed into the
myth of inevitability, the foxy father manifesto of
despair. He was also enjoying himself. The ground was
known.

"They . . . the young socialists. Aye, if I were
young again, how I could lead them . . ." Dürüst Osman dreamed, and sighed, and filled both of their
glasses. "And now," he asked—it pleased him to be
direct in a rude gavur way—"why are you here?"

"Sir. What is your opinion of the water supply in
Ceramos?"

Dürüst Osman laughed so widely that the back teeth
of his fine German plate showed. "You do not have an
opinion about a water supply. It is there or it is not
there. It is the will of God. There is water in the
months of ilkbahar, you even call it the springtime. I
like that. Then it goes." He shrugged.

"But you also say, what is fated will happen. More
positive. Why couldn't a reservoir be fated?" Frank
was uncomfortable. He made the point as casually as
he could. After all, religion and diplomacy . . .

"Because," Dürüst Osman said gently, "I will not allow it. My fields have water. My villages have water."

"What about Ceramos in the summer?" Frank sat
forward. He nearly upset his glass, but he caught it in
time. The movement confused him.

"It is the will of God," Dürüst Osman told him
again.

"I thought you said *you* wouldn't allow it. Why?"
Frank forgot that he should not be too direct. He was
wiping rakı from his trousers.

"God has put me into the position of making this
decision," Dürüst Osman explained carefully. "Let me
tell you something. You build, we will say, a reservoir
. . . hmmm? Fine American reservoir. Catch the
water, hmmm? Oh how fine. Make the lake. Protect
the topsoil, hmmm? But Frank, canım . . . By the
way, your very name means foreigner to them."

He waved toward the mountaintop, now hidden in
black cloud, now clear in the racing wind. "But what
have you done? You have flooded Mehmet's fields, and
Ali's, and poor Murat who has no other because his
selfish father got ten children on his mother and the
land was divided and divided and divided again. These
little fields are their life. You give them money. What
is that to them? Can they buy more land? So, they look
over the fine lake which will bring water to the naked
women and the gavurs and the yachts that come to
Ceramos, and the anarchist students who drink too
much rakı and do not honor their fathers.

"Now, one night, although Mehmet and Ali have not
spoken to each other since many years when Mehmet's
ram got loose and serviced Ali's yew, and he saw it
with his own eyes, but Ali called Mehmet a liar and
said it was his own ram and would not give him a lamb
although there were twins and Mehmet was his cousin
and his favorite ağabey—one night Mehmet and Ali
and Murat get together and forget all that, and they
bring their brothers and they take the dynamite they
use for fishing when the Gendarmes are not watching,
and Aman Allah, the next morning there is no reservoir and the streets of Ceramos are flooded, and when
the Gendarmes come to the villages, no one knows
anything, and the Gendarmes leave and they say the
peasants are stupid, look at their stupid faces . . ."

Frank was as engulfed as the streets of Ceramos that
no one had flooded yet except in Dürüst Osman's
mind. It occurred to him that Pontius Pilate, that tired

civil servant, had asked, "What is truth?" after a long day in the Middle East.

"Canım, do not despair," Dürüst Osman smiled. "Do not be so impatient. Look at it this way. If there is a fine hotel here, then many people will come. They will buy the houses in the villages. You will pull out the stupid peasants and plant your new bourgeoisie, and they will have the bathrooms your soul yearns to God for, and it will be a fine city and you will have your reservoir in time, and that, canım, is progress western ways is it not?"

Or was it in the morning that Pilate asked the question? Anyway it should have been the afternoon.

Dürüst Osman poured more rakı for them, very slowly, murmuring to himself, not so that Frank could hear what he was saying, but so he could not speak and interrupt. Then, when he turned to give Frank his glass, his voice rose.

"Now, to be practical. There are difficulties, but they are small. The new young judge and the Chief of Police do not put their fingers in the honey. Hmm? We have had trouble with them before. How do they do it on their salaries, hey hey? Maybe a few roubles, who knows. But we can maybe jump maybe skip over them. I have many dayılar, uncles in Ankara." He shrugged his shoulders. "Who does not? When a public servant makes perhaps one, two hundred dollars a month what do you expect? We go to the Ministry of Tourism, environment, something like that, and we show them how sensible all of this is. Oh, antiquities, maybe antiquities?" He rubbed the tips of his fingers together. "No problem. There are many tracks to the well. We have a fine new hotel, and everybody flush their bombok the way you like it." He leaned back and began to giggle, then wiped the corners of his eyes. "One day you come to visit us. My house is yours and we go to see the new reservoir."

Frank felt that it was wise to catch his laughter. The sound was muted by the rising wind. The garrulous old fool was drunk. He could see that. How could such old men think they could manipulate the world? Suddenly he was aware that the old man was quite silent and that his own laughter sounded silly and false in his ears.

"I will make a lot of money, of course," Dürüst Osman said, as if he were no longer bothering to persuade, but simply to tell the facts of life. "I do not care about this. I do not want my home disturbed by not being in control of all this, you understand? Fill your bucket before the well runs dry."

Dürüst Osman, just to be polite, kept himself from yawning. How easy the young man had been. It was beginning to be boring. He could smell the cooking from the kitchen. "Canim sıkılıyor," he muttered, not realizing that he had spoken aloud. He looked up and saw that the young man had understood him. "Ah, you speak good Turkish. I am bored, yes, we say, my soul is being squeezed by all of this noise and greed."

His quiet time was nearly over and he wanted the young man to leave, but first there were other things to put into his mind. Impatience made his voice brisker than he knew. He gave orders. "Now, shimdi, this is very serious, what I have to say. We are sitting on a border here. A NATO border." He liked the magic word Nato, nato, neta, all shipshape—an almost uncontrollable desire to giggle again. "How do we know who these many divers are who come here? I do not understand why the government has allowed it for so long . . . our defenses, you understand?"

Frank did understand, and he didn't like it. He could see circumstances closing in on his yearly holiday. There was so much about the Middle East that was an unavoidable nuisance. He thought of his friend Munci, and the sponge divers. The old man had a point. He could see himself, under the black shadow of a boat of the Sixth Fleet, a plastic bomb. Why not? His mind began to plan in spite of himself. He remembered the long report about disturbance of the second-millennium trade routes, an archeological reason, very sound. He wondered what the diving was like in Antalya on the south coast. He wondered how soon he could politely leave the garden.

Dürüst Osman decided not to plant anything more in the young man's mind. It had bothered him, annoyed him rather, for some time, that diving had become so popular. Every time one of his export boats put in to some deserted cove there was some boat, Munci or another, with the divers, the foreigners who could find his sunken exports waiting to be picked up. He knew that if he went into the subject of the poppy-growing, how much he approved of the ban, they could talk too long. Also he made too much on what he liked to call the free export of opium, and it made him so happy to think of it that he was afraid the happiness would shine in his face and give him away. He let a shadow of sadness come instead. It was easy. He thought of Munci, how much money he owed for his boat. He liked Munci. He wished he were his son instead of Huseyin. Munci would be thin like him, thin and wary, erkek adam, they were both that, leaders of men. There was lamb for dinner, cooked on a bed of lettuce. He could smell the mint.

"Please, you will stay for dinner?" he said, getting up.

Frank took the hint. "No, I must go. You have been very kind . . ." The wind had begun to whip the blossoms into a shower. They walked through them to the gate.

Dürüst Osman looked up at the sky. "It is the storm of the flowers," he said. "Always at this time of the year." Wisteria blossoms stuck to his hair and made him look like an old satyr.

The wind tugged at Frank's shirt as he walked along the deserted quay. He was grinning to himself. He had enjoyed the old man, his manners, his confidence, his naiveté. He was no fool, but he had, Frank decided, a stupid heart. He liked thinking that. It cut from his mind whatever influence the old man might have had, cleaned it as the wind was cleaning the quay. Intelligence, age, and selfishness together make one brutal virtue. He tried to set the phrase in his mind for his notebook. The wind made his eyes water, and the few lights along the quay quaked when he looked at them. Not the failure, but the gradual shrinking of his mission to Ceramos came to him as a sadness. He thought for a minute that he might resign, live on what money he could pick up teaching, find one of the little houses perched above him, and write. He had always wanted to do that when he could.

The coming storm had sucked the sea back from the quay and bared the flat mud shore. It lay naked under the wind. Abandoned tendrils of seaweed, gray-bearded, half-submerged tin cans, broken bottles, an old sea-eaten keel, the great flat stones of the ancient harbor jutted out through the mud. The small boats had been pulled onto the quay. Through the windows of the local cheap restaurants he could see shadows of old seamen through the cooking vapors that fogged the glass. They watched the sea and waited for the storm to hit.

The wind fell, paused, then blew again, picked up an old gallon tin and sent it dancing and clattering along the pavement. A boy ran from a shop to rescue it. Frank watched him chase it down the street. They save everything, he thought. He tried to stop to watch the crew of a newly painted tirandil batten down the loosening sails, but the wind pushed him on. When he got to David's bar, the wind flung the door open ahead of him and he had to lean his body against it to close it.

After the noise outside, which he had hardly noticed, the silence of the bar was pure, a relief. There was only the bartender, and one old sailor, a bit of flotsam like the tin cans in the mud, who told stories for the tourists to cadge drinks. There was no one else to talk to.

"It is the storm of the flowers . . ." the old man told him.

"Where is David?" Frank asked the bartender.

"He is coming," the bartender said. It was one of the few English phrases that David had taught him.

Frank tried to think of his name. It was important to remember names.

"Güven," he almost shouted, "nasilsiniz?"

Frank was pleased to speak some bar Turkish. They moved toward each other and leaned together over the bar.

Munci was caught on the rock ledge. He could not move. He glimpsed vague star clusters at the water's surface far away. Weeds moved through the nearly night-blue water. It was not night or day, a suspension of blue-green light and in the distance, the stars or animals reflecting the moon. Somehow he had lost his tanks. He made himself very still. Beyond the surface of his fear inside his own darkness, he knew there was a quietness that would sustain his body against moving too quickly upward and bursting his lungs. He could not understand what had happened to his tanks. Somewhere there was the sound of banging, far away through the dark water. He knew what it was, rock against rock tumbled forever at the seashore. He judged the water distance by the sound, and faint voices, and knew that he was near a quay or a boat. He looked around for the last body. Something was tangled over and around him, holding him. He was sweating.

The shutter went on nagging. He was awake. He thought he was awake, then knew he was. The star clusters settled on the wall opposite him, Ariadne's star charts and the blue-green of her curtains, filtering the late evening sun. Down below him in the garden he could vaguely hear voices, hers and David's, Horst's—was it Horst?—the girl whose name he could not remember. He was conscious of his nakedness and wondered if he had made love to Ariadne. He could not remember. He hoped not. He valued her as a friend, not as a lover.

In the garden Ariadne was trying to keep the others quiet. It made David smile. "You are in your natural element," he told her.

"You are mothering. Gözün aydın—may your eyes always shine."

"It's just that he needs sleep," she told him, but she looked up at the window. "He was so upset."

Lisa had copied her letter, and edited it, and then sent it on to her father before she could change her mind. She was trying to remember exactly what she had said. There was a solemn atmosphere of quiet crisis in the garden. It made her feel patient and kind. She sipped at her wine and watched her pretty feet, and wondered how soon she could get away.

Ariadne was sure of . . . something. Her mind flickered. What it was had gone. She had not felt so useful in a long time.

"So the old man, the father, he left?" Horst asked David. "I was on the mountain."

"Oh yes," David told them all. "My God, they just drove away in the big Impala, with the girl's body in the back seat. Thirteen hours to Istanbul with the girl's body in the back seat. They took the boys to Izmir in a truck. Someone said their families will come to get them there . . ."

Munci remembered. He read the wind strength in the banging of the shutter. He jumped out of bed. David's jeans fell on the floor.

I wonder. No. I know what he will be like, Ariadne prepared silently her own gentleness for his waking. She could feel his sad peace with her, his new trust, as tangible as if she held it in her hands like the blue bowl. She had long since prepared the fruit, the food he would want when he came down to them, new from his sleep. We are like people in a waiting room, she thought. The alien wind was ripping at the pale new fronds of the grapevine; it was creaking the long trellis that would later be a roof of leaves over them. They sat huddled in the only corner of the garden that was not torn by the wind.

"David, you bastard, your pants are too big," Munci called from the upstairs window. "I need one belt."

Ariadne jumped up.

"No. David, you come." Munci watched them, grinning. "I am embarrassed."

David was already explaining as he ran up the stairs, taking off his belt. "Why didn't you call me? I would have dived with you. I will go when you go back."

Munci was examining the sea from the window. "We cannot go now. Look." He pulled David to the window. Ariadne waited for him to look down and felt her body react a little. She saw Munci point toward the island, and heard him say, "You see there are caves. When the storm breaks they will be flooded. He is lying just at the cave mouth under the sea at the bottom of the blue hole. The water from the cave will free him. It will do our work for us. Jesus Almighty the wind! I must get to my boat."

Ariadne heard them running down the rickety stairs.

"Don't you want any food?" she called as Munci passed her.

"I must get to my boat. There will be such a storm. The flower storm." He stopped long enough to wave to her over his shoulder. "Thank you for the bed. Now I feel very strong."

He was gone, with David and Horst after him. Ariadne could hear their footsteps running down the stone path under the wind's roar. It was to be for her an evening like any other. She knew she would fight the wind after a while through the streets to David's bar. She was ashamed of her hunger to be part of the crisis.

The two women sat on under the nearly nude grape arbor as the darkness came almost unnoticed, leaving the food untouched, waiting for the wind to die a little, with nothing to say to each other.

All day Meral had waited for Kemal to come home. She had not spoken a word, not for many hours. There were so many things beating to get out of her mouth but no one to say them to. She had cooked the supper and given it to her old man, but there was still not a word. He hadn't even turned on the transistor. He had just sat, cross-legged, and stared at the storm through the glass window that Timur had put in for them, while she put the big brass tray down be-

tween them, the best bride gift she had brought, and
had spread the white cloth over it.

That had given her pleasure. She was proud of the
white cloth. She had woven it herself, and she liked the
feel of it in her hands. It got softer with the years. All
through the supper she had been afraid he would
speak. "Allah give me silence," she begged while they
dipped into the yogurt and the pekmez, and she listened to the rhythm of his mouth chewing on the
börek, and the bulgur fell on his chin.

Aman Allah, what could she do? Kemal was like a
fox. He had fought his way out even when he was
born, already stubborn. The other women had had to
toss her in a blanket for a long time to help him come,
and when he did, and was rubbed with salt and
blessed, the first thing she saw of him through the veil
of pain was his red face and his little fists clenched as
if he were already fighting the world. How was it you
loved the little wild one so much? The charm of his bewitched silence? She didn't know when the büyü, the
curse, had been put on him, nor if she had done anything to bring it, or if anyone else had done it, though
for a long time she had suspected Aysha because she
had no children and was bitter.

Kemal hadn't always been silent. When he was little
he cried like the others, and he spoke his first words at
the right time. She could remember him chirping
among the animals out on the stones of the courtyard.
He played with the yellow bitch dog they had then.
Then, one night, the old man had come home and
found the bitch. Oh, it was cold that night. Kemal had
crawled onto his mattress and the bitch had nestled
down beside him. It was her fault. She hadn't seen the
dog come in, but the old man had found it and kicked
it out as any man would, only one kick and the dog
. . . what was its name? What had he called it? Kek
Kek, a baby sound left over though he was already
three years old. The rest of them called her Kaba Saba,
she was such a common cringing ugly little thing.
Maybe he was trying to say that.

She had heard the dog yelp and land on the stones
outside, and there was not a sound in the dark room

except the old man taking off his shoes and the rustle of his straw mattress. In the morning Kemal had run out first and found Kek Kek dead, and the blood that had come out of her mouth frozen on the stones. Now, it could not have been that, only a dog, but she could not remember if he spoke after that. Anyway it was about that time. He didn't cry when the dog was killed, but he hid on its pallet under the shed and wouldn't come out. He just stopped saying a word.

She had teased him and beaten him, her little wild animal, to bring out the words, but they never came. It was the will of God, she supposed. They had done everything they could for him—herself, the old man, Timur most of all—but the words never came, never a sound. He spoke only with his eyes and with his hands. Sometimes he would nestle up to her, oh not for years, but when he was still little, and she would croon to him like a song, "Hele hele, tell me, tell me the truth," and sometimes to her shame he got on her nerves and she would take him by the shoulders and shake and shake and scream "Hele hele" at him, but he only cried the silent tears down his face, and whatever truth she demanded of him, the why of his silence, stayed locked inside.

They had taken him to the hodja many times, and once to a healing hearth. They had gone inland, up into the plains for thirty kilometers. She could still be there for a minute, riding in the dolmush along the bumpy road. She was scared. It was the first time in her life she had gone over the mountains. But no prayers and no charms had made the words come.

The prayer rags tied to the branches of the saint's tree above her whipped in the high wind. She had had to push against it to climb up to the knoll and sit down under it beside the saint's grave. She didn't know who the saint was. No one did. They had long forgotten. But she tied her prayer to the tree and the wind almost tore the rag from her hands. She sat down to watch along the mountain path. Her neighbors knew she came here when Kemal was wandering, and no one bothered her. The women never teased him like the men did. They were good. They pulled their own chil-

dren off when they taunted him. She pulled at her kerchief and tucked it tighter around her face. She asked
the saint to bring the boy back before the rain came.
At least he could do that.

She examined her feet. They asked her to. They
hurt. Her whole body hurt, as it had done lately in the
evening. At dawn she had gone to the bahche to weed
the vegetables, and had watered and fed the donkey
and the cow. She had gathered grass in the ruins for
the börek. She had walked to the Pazar afterwards
with her neighbors, and had had a visit with her sister
from her own village three kilometers away. She had
washed the clothes, and gone to the mountain for
wood. She had cleaned her house and cooked the food
for the day. She could not understand why she was so
tired. Why, she had been a lion for work, but now . . .
she thought it was because she was fatter than she had
been.

How many years since she had been led up that path
from her own village, frightened as the fawn she was
named for? She was thirteen. She could read, even the
newspapers, until her mother-in-law caught her doing it
and beat her with a stick and said they were for the
men. Allah, how frightened she had been, but not of
her old man, only of the parents. When his father and
mother were alive he had been like a lamb in the
house, and for all those years she had served her
mother-in-law like a servant. The old woman was lazy,
Allah, she was lazy. She had not moved a muscle after
she got a daughter-in-law.

Then there was the boy-child Timur. She could still
feel him coming out of her body when she was tired,
the women pulling and heaving at her, and when it was
a boy, the moment of elation that went all through her
like light, better than any feeling she had ever had,
even when her old man gave her love in the dark. Every morning before she started to carry Timur, her
mother-in-law had questioned her, "Did he umum you?
If he did not it is your fault. Are you with a child yet?
Are you?"

You would think a fine boy like Timur would have
shut them up. He was so brave, and such a man, even

when he was little. All that reading of books after her
old man had gone to sleep, the only burs from the village to go to the secondary school and then to the University in Istanbul. You would think that was enough.
But no. Nothing satisfied the old ones. Timur had
worked harder than all the rest, as if he were making
up to them for being so different. She didn't dare show
her pride and bring him bad luck, and bring their malice down on him.

A lamb in the house, a man in the fields and on the
sea, and in the bed a lion, that had been her old man,
mashallah. But then his father had died, and he died
cursing. You could feel the house roar with it for two
days as he was dragged fighting into whatever Gehenna
was prepared for him, the old devil. Why she hadn't
dared stay in the house with him alone after he was
old. All his life finally went into his staff like an old
furious donkey. What a way to die. They could hear
him masturbating and cursing as if he were trying to
flog himself back into life again.

Then the change had come to her dear old man. He
seemed to put on his father's skin like a cloak when he
inherited his fields. He started giving orders in his father's voice and making the house tremble. She had
wanted so often to tell Timur and Kemal what he had
been like to her, the shyness that made a man gentle
before a woman, but she could not. They were men
and you did not tell such things to men.

The wind tore off a prayer from the tree and slapped
it against her face. It was an old one, tattered by winter
and rain, faded by age and summer. It looked like a
piece of Aysha's old shalvar, those trousers she had
worn until they were more patch than trouser, a puzzle
and a history where she could trace her past. Well,
prayer had not helped her, that Aysha, she had a
mouth like a snake hole and when she spoke little
snakes poured out, so many she could not even spread
a rumor anymore. No one believed her.

Far down the mountain path she could see a man
fighting his way toward Ceramos through the sea wind
that was roaring up the narrow pass. It was her old
man. She felt sorry for him, all bent like that, and now

going down to Munci's boat to keep it from wrecking
on the shore in the wind. Hey hey, what a fool he was.
You would think it was his own boat and not Munci's.
She knew how it hurt his pride to work for Munci as
his sailor when it had been Timur that Munci had
trained before he had gone off and left them all to be a
fine agha and make a lot of money. He had explained
that the money would take a long time, many books,
many years.

"I can see no sense in it," she spoke aloud to the
saint. "Allah make me understand." All those years
and he will marry some hanımefendi, some city lady
who will smoke before his father and show her bottom
and not give me the years of peace I have earned as a
good daughter-in-law should and I have the right to
expect. Hayat böyle! Why—her plea came all the way
from her swollen feet—could he not be like the others?

And yet, as she prayed, or muttered to herself, she
knew she didn't want him to be, and another picture
came to her, a picture with cushions and she was in a
city with her feet up and she could read all the newspapers she wanted to, and go to the cinema without
asking a soul.

Having said her prayers she sat, blank as a stone,
staring down the path to see if Kemal would come.
The sun made a last fine line of light at the horizon
around the piled up banks of storm cloud. She sat until
the sky darkened and the moon ran like a wild thing
tossed among the racing clouds, showing the earth
light, then dark, casting her shadow, descendant of the
Tartars, who went on waiting.

There was no time. There was
blackness, candlelight, and space, measured far away
by the growing scream and whistle of the wind, by the
nearer whispers, by the rhythmic tremble of the mountain and his heart. Years of dripping water, seconds of
flicked pebbles, echoed as they fell. Timur's feet were
warm and wet. He knew it was blood, but he could feel

nothing but the warmth on his cold skin. His body was deadened with chill.

He had gone downwards through spacious corridors of time, walked through caverns, squeezed through tunnels, always downwards, had knelt and slipped and fallen. He had flogged himself into movement through vast felt space, through confines as close as his body. Sometime during the movement, directed as an animal by the water flow, he knew his face was wet with tears that felt hot and salty in his mouth, but he knew he could not stop for the luxury of mourning, and he made himself forget it and concentrate on the survival lodged in his seeking, grasping fingers.

Once he found himself praying aloud to Allah to guide him to his mother. He was aware that someone had been there before him, but he tried to cast such hopes aside for fear they were illusion. From time to time, during the gradual and endless descent, he had felt what could have been steps, carved by men in the blindness of the corridors of fanged rock. He had learned to feel for them, judge with his fingers and wait until he was sure they were there, then let his feet find, in an ecstasy of care, the footholds that seemed to have been made for him.

The pounding wouldn't stop—the rhythmic, endless pounding, tap-tap clock-beat pounding—he had to stop it, stop whatever spirit angel djinn was pounding his head through his body to the stone wall behind him, making panic rise until he yelled once "Dur. Stop," and the dur dur dur of his echo became part of the ruthless unceasing sound.

He lit a precious candle and sat for a minute in its light, until his heart and mind were still inside him and he cursed himself for a fool. The light made a round glow around him in a vast space of black. He fastened it to his forehead band and crawled, then got up and walked, conscious of the blackness closing in behind the light circle.

He searched the boulder-strewn floor. Now the pounding was strong, now dim. He was playing a game with it as if it were a live thing, only it was not a game. He knew it was water, water somewhere, and he had been

lost for so long in the dry caverns that he had to find it.
Finally he found it, one drop of water falling, forever
pounding on a pool of ice, but warm ice, ice made of
flow stone. As he leaned over it, it showed him faintly
the glow of the candle and his own face. It was a
strange face, caked with mud, wet beard, wet hair, and
his eyes with the pupils pinpointed. He sat back. Now
that he knew what it was, the pounding lessened. It was
time to think again. He had read the beginning of panic
in his own eyes and in the short breathing he heard, as
if it were someone else's, someone very close beside
him.

Measure, calculate, plan, and remember. He clung
to his own sanity for measurement, such a little rod in
the black space, and forced himself to track back
through his own memory.

First there had been the long mud tunnel; then he
remembered jumping onto the dry floor. That had been
the first grotto, pile on pile of calcite, five-meter-long
tendrils of stalactite as frail as lace. But dry, the omi-
nous dryness told him that the water had long since—
how long? years or eons, who could know—deserted
the cavern, formed and forgotten it and sought, by its
law, the mouth-size sink he had seen to carry it downward, always downward. He had wandered through
rooms of the abandoned system, trapped in dryness.
Then, behind a fall of rocks, he had found a squeeze
the size of his body, and heard and could feel with his
hand a movement of the air that meant that somewhere
below there was flowing water again. He had forced
himself downward through the squeeze until a force of
water caught him in the dark.

He remembered the steep corridor made by the
water flow, and being tumbled along it, trying to stop
himself falling, clinging, letting himself be carried
through the dark, clinging again to a projecting rock,
but most of it was smooth, smooth and fast, carrying
him down until, in the blackness, he struck a large
boulder and crawled behind it above the thrashing
water to rest. The roof was higher, how much he could
not tell. The water roared. He finally lit another
candle. The roar was where he had come from, down

the waterfall, and he knew he was bruised but could feel nothing. Where there had been limestone, and once he had remembered sandstone, now all around him there was black basalt, limed with white, and great frozen folds of white shields and curtains hung from the ceiling.

He tried to remember step by step, after that, but the memory faded. He had been lost twice in dry systems. Once he had fallen and hit his head. Once he had found before him a long gentle stream with a sandy floor to walk on.

He set his candle down on a flat rock and got to his feet. He stooped in its lovely light and gathered a handful of glittering stones. He threw one as far ahead of him in the darkness as he could throw, counted and heard it hit, not wall but floor. He turned a half turn and heard a pebble hit the floor again. He turned another half turn. At the count of three he heard the third pebble reverberate against a wall, and ping against something that sounded like a chime. He picked up the candle and walked slowly toward the direction of the sound that still echoed in his head. He had to keep it there, concentrate. There were so many whispers, the roaring of water, the brush of space itself moving. Black had a sound, the soughing of the mountain. Once he had heard music, the distant moan of a flute. He called out before he could stop himself.

He had calculated correctly. The wall ahead of him, its white flow of rock curtain, rose high into the darkness. He touched it. It was the chime, a low sweet sound. He set his back against the wall and lit one of the precious newspapers, making himself look around the walls instead of being drawn to staring at its flame and blinding himself. He could see as the flames lit higher and higher for their minute of life that the ceiling was too far away for the light to reach. He was in a cavern at least fifty meters high. Out of the black space huge sentinels of stalactites hung and glistened. He was on a wide shelf, halfway up the cavern wall. He kicked the burning newspaper over the edge. It fell and fell and went out.

"I have dived that far through the water," he told

himself for reassurance, and did not know he had spoken aloud until the last word was thrown back to him through space, "Daldım daldım dım dım dım."

He shut the echo out, and searched again for the water flow, keeping to the wall, searched with his eyes, his hands, his feet. The candlelight caught frail flows of rock, pink with iron, licked over crystal, and made the huge white towers jump and move. When his feet found wet mud at last, the beginning of water, the candle was low enough to burn his hand. By its length he had been an hour in the cavern searching the walls.

Candle four. He put the stump in his package carefully. It was his only way to calculate the time, but it was false. He knew that. Four hours of light, but how many hours of darkness he could only guess as he remembered slithering like a snake through black mud tunnels, his cheek against the mud, the ceiling brushing his chest.

He found the water exit, a low tunnel, and in the distance the familiar call of water. He had learned to listen with new ears. It was loud, and seemed to be near. Out in the air it would have been the sound of a high waterfall, but in the cave's reflected sound he had learned better than to judge its height. He let himself slide toward it.

Instead of rock floor he touched and sank in water, slow moving, then slower, then still. He felt for the bank, and huddled on a ledge until his hands were dry enough to unlock the precious bundle of light. When he was finally able to make a candle light, he saw disappearing in front of him a long easy corridor, sand-colored walls six feet high, and a ceiling of tiny needle-like shining drops, reflected in the water. Just as he lifted the candle to blow it out, he saw mirrored in the water the red print of a hand, like the hand prints of sacrificial blood on the boats when they were launched into the sea. At first he thought it was on the stream bed, and then, when he swung the candle and it moved, he realized that it was on the wall behind him. He turned and looked at it, afraid to touch it. He knew it was blood, dry, he could see, but still red. Someone, a woman, the hand was small, had passed through the water tunnel within the hour.

Panic and relief fought in his stomach. He made himself touch the hand print. A smudge of red powder came off on his finger. The hand had been there, not hours, but eons, a labyrinthine track mark. For the first time he let himself know that the steps behind him had really been man and not water carved, and he let his mind go beyond the next step, the next tunnel, the next mud shoot, the next vast room, to the manmade steps he remembered having found as a boy.

It made him move with greater care, for fear the hope-surge would warm him into carelessness, but he allowed himself the luxury of candlelight through the long corridor ahead. This time the roof did not close down on him. Instead the walls narrowed and curved as water had surged once, through a great mountain vein of sandstone. The floor was smooth, the walls sleek, but narrower and narrower, a cleft out of candle-sight above him and so close to his body that he had to go sideways, and the candle made the corridor walls day-bright.

He stood at the topless door of a room. Beside him on the wall he saw a second red hand. In front of him a clear wide path of ice stretched, ice but warm, sending up a shimmer into the light, a highway of crystal. The stream fell beside it, a long ribbon of water, disappearing into blackness. He walked along the path. How many meters thick it was, whether it could hold him he had no idea. He only knew that he had seen the hand again, and that it had come from beyond the crystal road.

There were no walls. There was wind, blowing up from under him, the untrustworthy sound that could have been a murmur of voices somewhere below. He walked toward it. His feet felt the edge of space. He lit a newspaper and dropped it into the chasm, saw it go down and light, as it went, a great round tube. He was standing on a natural bridge over a space so deep that the paper went out in the dark long before it reached any floor. His body was too shocked for more than a twinge of fear of a never-ending fall through black

space. He refused it, turned, and paced himself along
the glittering guide of the bridge, until he found a wall
ahead of him and a red hand. He lost and found and
lost again the spoor of the water, the track of time.
There was only movement, himself vast in the tunnels,
then ant-like in the caverns, finding, losing, finding
again the marks of the red hands.

Once, at the bottom of a long climb, he fell and
went blank. When he came alive again his body was in
water, his head resting against a smooth rock. He
fumbled for the bundle of light and found it dry, protected by the rock against the swift water. His head
hurt, and his body was trembling so that he had to lie
and rest before he could light another candle. Perhaps
he went to sleep. He did not know.

He lit the fifth candle.

The stone he had rested on glistened as the bridge
had in the light—flow stone covering something that
lay there in a fetal curl of sleep or panic. The fall that
had knocked him unconscious had killed the small
being. He could see bone of its arm nestled against the
skull inside the crystal caul that covered it. He felt
close to it and sorrow for them both. He realized then
that it had not fallen as he had. The pose of the bones
was not accidental, but a curled body of despair and final submission to loss, as when a man drowning is supposed to stop trying and welcome the sleep of water.

He could see the pelvic girdle of a young girl, but so
small. He wondered if she had been a sacrifice left
walled there by the darkness, if her sin were one of the
two timeless ones of sex or difference, if she had been
honored by being a gift to the goddess. He got up,
made himself quiet, and walked on until he found another red hand.

He remembered nothing more, until he was kneeling
beside a half-eaten kid. It still stank, its putrescence
flooded him with hope. He could not remember ever
having felt so joyful in his life. The animal had been
dragged in from outside not many days before, only the
time it took it to stink.

He had ten candles left, and he cursed himself for a
second at being so overcareful of his light. Now he

walked in light, then crawled with a candle stuck in his head band. The channel was narrower and narrower, the water a slow mud flow, a squeeze ahead of him that he was afraid was too small for his body. He thrust the candle through it and saw the familiar tunnel of his own old explorations. He remembered that it had once been too small for him to get through. He did not think. He simply, slowly, forced himself through it, felt his ribs tight against the rock, his shoulders jammed, squeezed back and tried again, this time with his arms above his head, breathed out, remembered to do that.

He was lying beside the water of his own black lake in his own great chamber. His body was racked, his arms pulled in their sockets. He made himself get up and find the old niches where he had left candle stumps so long ago. They were still there but they had long since become too damp to light. He flung them down and put the last of his candles in the niches, lit them one after another until the cavern was a fantasy of light, light shining on the water, on the great stalactites of the vaulted ceiling, on the giant pillars of stone, light spinning and glistening. He took off his clothes and washed himself in the lake.

It was only when he was washed clean of his long climb, and let himself play under the waterfall where the coins in the sacrificial pool glittered under him, that the reason for it all came back to him, hit again, and he knew that Lale had left the red hand marks, and that it was Lale who was asleep in the egg of flow stone. He did not question the thought. He only knew that it was true as things are true in dreams, without question.

Time returned when he looked up and saw the pale star of light from the well beside the Byzantine chapel. It was pale moonlight appearing and disappearing so that he knew that there was a high wind out in the sky. Bombok, you need money out there to survive, he told the faint star, and laughed. His feet were standing in it. He went under water and brought up handfuls of it and laid it on the bank, green and gold and silver in the candle light. He examined it, and dived again. He brought up a hundred lira in twenty-five-kurush pieces, not much, but the gold and the green bronze had the heads of emperors and gods. He would have to find a way to sell them. Munci would know. He knew everything. It was strange how the modern coins looked most like the ancient bronze ones, the cheap alloy turned green so quickly. He put on his clothes, gathered the coins in the plastic pouch.

The mouth of the cave was filled with flashes of moonlight, as light as day after the blackness of the caves. His skin felt hot from the night air, and he realized how cold he had been. Something moved at the cave mouth's corner. He flattened himself against the wall and waited for the moon to ride out from behind the clouds again. It was Kemal. He saw his face, but for a pause his body would not move out to him, as if Kemal were the door of certainty to all his sorrows, and he dared not walk away from the safety of the darkness. The boy sat there so patient, so blank with loneliness that Timur could not make him wait any longer.

Kemal had not stopped watching the cave mouth for so long that it had become part of his eyes. He saw a flick of movement and ran toward it. He threw himself at Timur. Timur could feel his tears, warm against his cold chest.

"So it is true," he whispered.

He could feel Kemal's head nod yes, back and forth across his chest, yes, yes, yes. Timur felt no surprise. He had known all the time that she was dead, but he had put away his certainty as too heavy to carry with him in the caves. It was time to take it up again.

"Now, listen." He pulled Kemal away and squatted in front of him. "Stay here until the moon is straight over your head. You understand?"

Kemal nodded. He wondered why Timur did not cry. It must be right not to. He wiped his face on his sleeve.

"I will go to Munci. No. It is not dangerous. It is dark. I have a beard. No one will know me. They will think I am a hippie from Ankara or Istanbul who is going to his boat."

Kemal ran behind a boulder. He came back dragging

a large sack, and put it at Timur's feet. He opened it.
It was all of his papers, even the newspapers he had
slept on, his notes, his books, and the skull of the
young king. Kemal clutched at his arm and pointed at
it, then held up eight fingers, for the eight bones in the
human head. Timur remembered telling him that.

In the shafts of moonlight Kemal acted his climbing
into the tomb after the men had gone. His eyes
widened with surprise. Then he showed his understanding. Timur had disappeared deep into the mountain
like a snake. There was only one other door to the
mountain. He showed how he had gathered the papers,
very carefully, and had thrown them down the passage.
He covered the secret entrance again, very carefully.

Timur hoisted the sack on his shoulder.

"Remember you stay here. How long?"

Kemal pointed straight up at the sky.

"You must not come to Munci's house. It is too dangerous if you change your habits too quickly. You understand? Just behave as if nothing has happened."

Kemal nodded, so disappointed that his lip began to
tremble again.

"Listen, canım, he will come and find you when it is
safe," Timur had to tell him. "Now, you wash yourself
before you go to our mother. And tell her . . ." He
could see his mother, her feet, her swollen feet, edema.
"Tell her nothing," he finally said.

It was dark again and when the moon rode out, Timur was gone.

Ariadne and Lisa fought the wind, mak-
ing too much of a joke of it as they struggled for their
separate reasons together like best friends along the
quay. The wind tore words out of their mouths so that
they heard each other's shouts in fragments. It was already nine o'clock.

After the bayram and with the storm, the streets
were nearly deserted. They passed the sailors, batten-
ing down their boats. Ariadne saw Munci and tried to
call to him, but the wind grabbed at the sound. He did

not hear her. Somewhere above them a loosened sheet
of tin tolled against the wall of a house. They passed
vague shapes of men behind the steamed windows of
the kahves where no women ever went. The narrow
street of David's bar was a wind tunnel.

Inside, David's bar was soft, still, and warm. Oil
lamps in their multicolored shades cast prisms of red
and blue that swam in the wind tears in Ariadne's eyes.
She wondered why she had come, but then she did at
this moment almost every evening. She went to David
and touched his hand.

"When the great Padishah Canını Mehmet was
sworn into the Janissaries as an honorary private he
drank a toast to the Red Apple. You see, I equate this,
oh Christ I've picked up so much American language
. . . equate, well, in my theory, with the Christian
Holy Grail, the ever-receding symbol, the never found
. . ." Basil's voice commanded one end of the room
nearest the door as usual so that he would miss no one
coming in. Miranda was leaning forward, drinking
words and vodka.

Trader was head to head at the bar with the young
American Ariadne had seen in the Pazar. He was
rumored to be CIA, but then, who was not? She
couldn't remember his name.

David turned and smiled at her when she touched
his hand.

"It's so quiet after last night, mashallah," he told
her, and turned his head away, listening and not listening to the two men.

Ariadne felt herself slipping into the boredom and
the waiting. At one end of the bar a group of Turkish
boys looked sad to her in their tight jeans and pretty
shirts. At the last table of the long narrow room, away
from the others, a group from a yacht sat saying nothing.

"I don't understand. You mean like red like communist?" Miranda yelled.

"Don't be so fucking stupid, darling," Basil told her.

Miranda was delighted. "Oh, there's Ariadne." She
looked around, secure and surprised, having seen her
come in. "Do we want her to join us?"

"Why not?" Basil said.

Trader thought he ought to say, "I'll trouble you not to speak that way in front of my wife," but he didn't. He said it silently to his glass. He was half hearing what the nice young foreign service officer was saying. He shook his head at the glass. It was hard to be in the know, in the language and in the know. It's no PTA meeting, I'll tell the world, he thought at the glass. Here it was Easter Saturday and people talking like that. "I'll bet nobody in this damned place knows it's Easter Saturday," he said, but not aloud of course.

"Did any of you guys know it was Easter Saturday?" he suddenly heard himself tell the whole room. His voice eddied against the walls and died down.

Frank could feel those embarrassed-as-hell tremors that religion and confessions always gave him, as if the man had flipped into drunkenness, or just stood there and dropped his pants. He looked beyond Trader through the silence he had caused. All over the room people were beginning to talk again as if they hadn't heard. He could tell which one of the crummy crew was his wife, the one talking to the old English faggot. She was the only one who glared directly at the man.

He couldn't remember the name of the hangdog-looking woman sitting down the bar, but he knew the type. They showed their loneliness and their age-freckled arms. They dragged into the consulate, loaded down with souvenirs and trouble of their own making, trying too late to get home, and not knowing anymore quite where it was. Their checks never arrived on time. They got involved with foreign politics or men. They were polite and undemanding drifting nuisances. There she was, all naked-faced and ready for trouble, sitting too near the boys.

The girl beside her looked nice, though, as if she'd been to a good school. Frank thought he would let himself gradually be noticed even if it meant opening himself up to demands from the older woman. He saw them all in triplicate and sighed. The liberal Henri Bendel cut of the girl's jeans over her cute little ass made him homesick. Her hair gleamed of money.

He raised his voice a little, being interesting to Trader.

"What I meant was, I have a theory . . ." He focused his fine mind on Trader's wet eyes. "It is our innocence. I've figured it out. Huckleberry Finn is an old river bum, still thinking he is young."

Trader thought the nice young man was talking about him. He didn't know what he had done to be insulted. He had only said it was Easter.

Frank considered the cut of the pants on the bar stool and spoke to that kind of taste. "After Henry James the innocence began to . . . uh . . . fester." She still didn't look around. "Everybody thinks we are trying to manipulate the world. Not guilty. We are Not Guilty. We have gone from innocence to stupidity without an intervening period of guile." Frank was pleased with that. He promised himself to remember it for his notebook.

Ariadne could feel the wind on her back when the door opened. It blew Huseyin in out of the night. He slipped quickly onto the stool beside Lisa.

Huseyin in one glance had seen everyone in the room. He huddled down a little, trying to stay out of Frank's view. He didn't want to have to talk to him after his father had told him the work was done. If he was going to have to speak English he had other uses for it. He touched Lisa's pants and she grinned at her glass.

David, behind the bar, could tell the time by the conversations. The two Americans were at the abstract stage. The rich young Dutch group in the corner had gotten to their sad soul drink, bored to death with each other. One of the Turkish boys was trying to find a record. He knew what it would be. *Oh mommi mommi* rose and drifted over the room.

"You've read Stephen Spender's *Decline of the West.*" The drunk American CIA man had grabbed old Trader by the arm. "It's all there. I read it in college."

David thought, "Allah, they never stop working even when they are drunk." He moved to the end of the bar to stop the bastard probing at the old man's mind with his left-wing hints. "Please, my drink." He took their glasses. He went blank on their names.

"My mother," Frank, that was his name, told him carefully, "she thinks I'm out here spreading democracy with her money. You wouldn't know. Jesus, the pressures . . ."

"My grandmother thought I was the Messiah." David poured their drinks.

Trader looked up at him. "Oh, I'm sorry. I didn't know you were Jewish. You don't look . . ." He stopped. That was one of the things Miranda told him not to say. David had already turned away. Maybe he hadn't heard. He saw him take a coin out of the cash register and drop it into a glass jar. It was half full. The clink made Ariadne look at David and smile. Trader thought she had a sweet smile. It made him feel sorry for her.

Someone opened the door gently. Ariadne was too polite, with Trader staring at her, to turn around to see who it was. It closed again. One of those stillnesses filled the room, all the talk snuffed out. She realized that the beating of the storm wind on the roofs and funneled streets of the town had stopped. It surprised her. She had become used to its background, a cosmic quarrel that was making the conversation around her so diminished and querulous that she could divorce herself from it without seeming, in her perpetual fear of rudeness, to be aloof. She did, then, look around at the door. Lisa and Huseyin had gone.

"No," she said, without knowing it. It made David lean toward her.

"What are you on about?"

"Bombok Huseyin. How could she?"

"I told you you ought to get rid of her."

"You don't do that." She was vague and troubled.

"I am very very bored," one of the Dutch boys from the yacht announced in English.

Someone giggled.

"You will please do me the honor to shut up. I do not know your name."

At the cessation of the wind, Munci's
boat rose, poised, and began to turn in the dark water,
little dancing turns instead of the series of dangerous
plunges that had lifted her and flung her down as the
sea swells raced and crashed into spray over the quay.

Munci looked at his watch, wiped the water from its
face, and turned his wrist toward the harbor lights.

"Three hours," he said, satisfied. It was ten o'clock.
Sert Orhan mumbled, "It was not the flower storm
then," and squinted his salt wet eyes at the sea.

"Bekle. Wait." Munci read the sky to see if it was a
true calm or one of those storm pauses that crouched,
gathered energy, and hit again with greater force. The
moon was riding slowly among the black rags of
clouds. "Will you sleep aboard, uncle? I am very tired
after last night. If it starts to blow again I will come."

Timur's father disappeared into the little cabin without saying a word.

In the night's pause, alone on the quay, Munci felt
happy about small things, because his chest was wet
and clean, and his muscles were tired, and he didn't
have to speak. He groped his way along the pitch-dark
alley that led to his house, his bare feet finding their
own way through the familiar piles of stones and up
the steps to his gate. He had closed it after him carefully to keep the animals out of his garden, and was
halfway up his pebbled walk when he heard a whisper,
"Ağabey?"

He didn't turn. He walked on to his door and
fumbled with his key at the lock. He could feel someone behind him.

"It is Orhan Selim." The whisper came from near
his shoulder.

"I know that, mashallah." How could he not know
it? A man sensed his friend beyond lighted streets and
time, and the name, he had given him that himself as a
joke when Timur worked on his boat and spent his
nights under the tilly lamp studying until Munci called
out, "Olmaz, stop! You are drawing the bugs."

He said then, "You are like the poet Nazim Hikmet whose living was made for him by himself as a journalist and he called himself then Orhan Selim." He couldn't stop the boy from grasping at everything. After that he read all the poems he could find of Nazim Hikmet. That was in 1963, before his poetry was banned again. He did the same with Munci's captain's manuals, just because they were there, under the tilly lamps always drawing the bugs.

Munci's heart was pounding with relief, but he did not turn his head. He held open the door of his pitch-black room until he felt the form of the other one pass him, then locked it after him, and turned on the light. They stood under the naked bulb in its lobster basket. Munci saw his friend behind the dirty face, the tangled long hair, the wiry beard, the torn clothes streaked with dried mud. He held out his arms.

"Allah Allah, my emaciated, my deprived, my poor child, Orhan Selim!" Munci kissed Timur on both cheeks. "You are very dirty, you stupid boy."

Timur looked almost sullen under the naked light. It hurt his eyes.

"I will make some coffee. You need food," Munci began to fuss. Gradually calmer, and then as casually as if they had been together all the time, Timur lounged on the low yatak that was built against the wall, and ran his eyes and then his hands over the woven cover, familiar for so many years, that Munci's mother had made.

He was letting his body become part of it again, the navigation charts on the walls, the empty fireplace where Munci had put the conch shells they had brought up when he was a boy and made his first dives. They had hung the live animals like black wet penises to the boat's gunwales to die and drop their lovely birth-pink shells. Now the shells were dead, too, memory's color, so pale that only a dry hint of their sea life was left. He did not know he was asleep until he woke to find Munci leaning over him with the coffee, and heard him say, "Afiyet olsun, may it do you good."

What Timur had come for flooded back into his

mind. He noticed that the flow was without grief, and he understood that. Grief had already passed, or rather he had passed grief, where it was, back there in the cave. He told himself that he had done his mourning in the silence and the dark. He remembered the passage as a long struggle with grief, as Jacob with the angel, and he thought he had won. All that was left was to find out the facts.

"Where have you been?" Munci asked the man who had become strange to him, slouched there sick with exhaustion. He felt shy and slightly formal with him.

"I was in the cave."

Munci waited.

"I was in the cave for six weeks," Timur began. He told about the hitch-hiking. They both concentrated on the importance of the route. "I came through Muğla. I came to my village and hid up behind the old wall until it was night."

He brought the village back, the tapping on the window, the pride in Kemal's care, the cave-room. Munci thought, all this time he has kept secrets from me.

The story was over. Timur had brought himself at last to Munci's room, to the coffee, the white cheese, the bread and olives, the glass of rakı that Munci poured for them both, the peace. He was struggling to keep himself awake. He did not tell Munci what he was running from and Munci did not ask.

"You should have come before. I am your friend," was all that Munci said about it. There was no need for Timur to say, "I didn't want to compromise you, until something I could not face alone brought me here."

Instead he said, "What was the name of the girl you brought up this morning? Who is her father?"

"Lale. Turgut Bey." The room was blank and cold. The filaments of shadow from the lobster pot crisscrossed their faces.

Timur pushed the food aside and let himself fall among the dirty plates, his head in his arms, his shoulders shaking. Munci held him until the crying had diminished from man's grief to child's helpless loss, had passed, had cleansed his dear friend, his little brother whose life had been so hard, and the courage of his poverty so great, his Orhan Selim.

Timur's head had come up. "Give me a cigarette, please." He lay back on the couch and held out his hand.

Munci put a cigarette in it and lit it for him. "Now," he said, "we must decide what to do."

He thought for a long time while Timur's smoke curled around the lobster pot. Finally he was ready to speak.

"Tomorrow if the wind has died, I must dive again. There is one boy left there. He is lodged . . ." He saw Timur's eyes and stopped. "I must dive. In the afternoon we will have the imbat, inchallah, a good following wind. Maybe six hours will take us to Gökova. I always have a reason to go there. I take the supplies to my uncle and I bring back wood before the tourists come. You remember his little tea kahve in the cove where the pine trees come down to the water? We have made many dives there for sponges. Now you remember—built out over the water. It belongs to my father's uncle. Something happened between them—oh, a long time ago before I was born—and he is ninety and no longer cares, but my father does and he does not speak to him or go there. The old man owes me many debts for favors and I have never asked him one. Now, why do you want him to hide you?"

"Have I killed a man?" Timur asked the lobster basket.

"No, he is ninety. He will take that for granted. You are a man. I think you are on the run for smuggling. He respects that more. He was a smuggler for many years until he got too old. Let's see. Your father came from Crete. That is easy, so many on this coast are Cretan Turks. That is bad. He would ask you about people. No. Your father went from Crete to Marmaris and then he went to Istanbul. You were born there. You know Istanbul, its streets, its people, and he does not. But you spent many years working on the Bosphorus. You will have to make up many stories. He likes to talk. You will be his television. You will stay being Orhan. Sheytanî Orhan, Orhan the Devil, they called you on the Bosphorus." He laughed. "The old man will like that.

"I think your father from Crete was Orhan too, so you will not make a mistake, using your real father's name. Oh, there is a problem with your real father. If he comes with me as a sailor he will know you. What will I do? He is getting old and he has some arthritis in his joints. I will replace him on the boat with my nephew. It is time he went to sea. He is nearly four-teen. Now, I must not hurt your father's feelings or his pride."

Munci sensed that Timur was going to speak and he held up his hand. "Wait. Let me think. I can't put him in charge of the boat's papers. He does not read. I will tell him there is too much work for me in getting sup-plies for the diving charters. This he can do, of course. I will raise his pay. That will show him that the job is very important, and I will give him my plastic jacket from France with SCUBA PRO on the back. He has wanted that for a long time."

The stretched hours of waiting and of wine had exhausted Ariadne and left her mind blank. She had watched all evening for Munci to come into David's bar, listening to the wind rise and die and rise again, expectant in the silences after the dancing of shutters out in the dark. She knew he would be looking for her and she did not want to disappoint him. But the time had moved, stopped, and moved again toward the moment when the bar grew quieter and it was time to close. The remnants had grown physically close, waited in a spindrift outside the door as David bent to lock it.

They stumbled a little, taking each other's arms, random intimates, along the deserted waterfront under the sparse line of lights toward the yacht liman where the new Dutch yacht lay, ebony-black against the bright stars, defined by its riding lights.

The moon had gone down. Above the breathing mast the stars circled, not flat, but depth on depth in a depth of sky. Ariadne leaned back among the deck cushions, hypnotized by them. She hardly noticed when the Dutch boy sat down beside her. He seemed, then, gentle. His body moved closer, undemanding, almost shy. She trusted the closeness. It reminded her of Munci, the subtle strength of European friendship. It seemed, to her, a connection running among them, strangers or not, as a connection ran between her eyes and the stars. She felt a part of a link, a necessity in it all.

In the dark, he whispered, "I watch you all evening. I think you will understand something."

Basil, who could not have seen them in the dark, heard him and laughed, or he may have been laughing at something in Miranda's incessant voice which Ariadne had long since shut out. She could not see where the others were. They were black shapes on a strange deck.

"I will tell you . . ." The boy's voice lowered after the laugh. She had been wrong about him. The petulance she had noticed in the bar was gone. "I lost my virginity to my mother's friend when I was only fifteen. She was a German Gräfin, very beautiful, like you. This happens in Europe you know. I believe it does not happen in your country which is an unmitigated shame for boys. The rawness they must face. Now my experience was a thing so gemütlich that it marks me with a sweet wound. I am drawn to older women. Girls cannot comfort me."

She had not known what to answer and so was silent. The moment died. After it, a space of stars whirling and darkness, she was suspended in a fatigue which she thought of as a kind of peace. She could have been asleep. She wondered where David was, and if Munci was asleep, too. She knew he was. With the tendril of awareness she had felt between them all evening, no matter where he was, she had caught herself in visions of him bending over ropes on the boat, watching the sea, stopping at the tea kahve by habit with his sailors, his mind on her, drawing her. She, honored by that, was happy. Now the tendril had been cut, and she was sure it had been cut by his falling into his so-needed sleep. She blessed his sleep, feeling the warmth of his body beside her on the deck, not touching her, only there.

She was jarred by the Dutch boy jumping up. She had forgotten him. "We will have some movies," he called out. "I am bored."

They were in the cabin. He had pulled a small screen down from the frame above the rear window. It was close and warm in the cabin. Ariadne could smell polished wood, polished brass, and the scent of jasmine oil and cooking and Turkish cigarettes. They lounged against each other, watching the blank screen. In the moment of belief before the film began, she was one with the rest, a child among children.

The light in the projector went on. They stared at the glowing silver square of the screen. She heard the projector whir in the room, the only noise.

Technicolor bodies, as sun colored and healthy as the flesh of television commercials, filled the screen.

"Good shot," she heard someone mutter.

At first, without her glasses, she could see only patches of color. A girl's face stared at her then, red lips, wide eyes, heavy lashes, a face smoothed of reaction. The large lips spread into a smile for something beyond her shoulder, but the eyes were dead. The eye of the camera slid down for her over mountains of breasts. Hands pushed them, kneading, as if they were clay, or dough, worked to mold the nipples erect. The face sank behind a horizon of body fragments, the geometric triangle of legs, close-up of the red split mouth that pulsed within its fringe of hair, fingers exploring and opening it professionally as the men in the Pazar opened and presented melons. A wet red baton had its own eyes. It wandered toward the fruit, then paused. She could not understand at first if it was real. It thrust, a thing of its own, urgent and impersonal, thrust, buried itself, withdrew, and thrust again, juxtaposition of a knife in fruit, teeth biting, knife, teeth, the red hole moving, the red baton growing. The screen was filled with grinding torsos, heads not seen; there were no heads. A second baton thrust at the cleft between the white buttocks. She could see the mark of a bikini tan. Another thrust into the painted hole of the mouth. There were no eyes, no tendrils, no connections, except for the rhythm and thrust of things, things in rhythm with things. There was no person near her in the cabin. There were only things growing toward each other, mindless and eyeless. She felt, as if it were not a part of her, a growth in her own body, neither human nor close, only an isolated and demanding spasm of bodily discontent.

"It's very interesting," she heard Miranda say. Her voice was shrill.

"But hardly . . ." Basil's voice was following Ariadne. She did not hear the words. She had stumbled down the gangplank in the dark. No one had sensed her going. She had fallen and skinned her knee. Memories of old banged knees made her a little girl running from the corner of the school yard where they were whispering ugly things.

There was not a soul on the quay, no connection with the indifferent stars. She wandered almost blindly toward home, toward something, somewhere, someone alive. There was nothing. Nothing stirred. The storm had died. The tamarisk trees were dead calm under the acid-green fog lights. The floodlights of the castle had been turned out. It was a dark mound under the moon.

She heard behind her someone running and she was possessed with fear. She hid in the alley of a narrow street until the pounding of the feet had disappeared and the town was silent again.

Whoever it was had roused the feral dog packs that roamed the streets at night. She had forgotten to pick up rocks to fend them off. She was cold. She knew that wherever he was, asleep or not, Munci needed her. She could feel the pull, faint at first, then strong, as life coming back, the connection of a friend in need and troubled. She came out of the alley and began to run, faster and faster, away from the barking, the hounding, the cold abstraction of the filmed bodies, forgetting that the dogs would hear her and veer toward the sound in their perpetual night quest. She could hear their barking fill the street behind her and slap against the walls. She ran faster. She was Jezebel chased by dogs. She was filthy with the excrement of entertainment and coldness and fear.

She made herself climb a low garden wall and hide behind it. There were night-scented flowers and she was crouched, breaking them. The dogs found and bayed behind the wall. She waited until their dangerous mindless interest swung toward another quarry, a cat, and the flow of dogs and baying diminished and finally disappeared up toward the mountain.

"It is Easter Sunday, and I have not talked to an Episcopalian in years." She almost said that and was surprised. She climbed back over the wall.

Munci's house was dark. Then she saw and took heart at the chink of light that showed at the corner of a thick curtain drawn across his window. She found the poise to help her stand quietly, and stop panting before she knocked.

It was a long time before he answered. When he did, he opened the door only long enough to let himself out and close it behind him.

After the light of the room it was so dark that Munci could not see but only sense someone standing near him. He could hear the breathing of someone who had been running, but was now so silent that he thought it might be Kemal.

"It's Ariadne." The voice was nearly a whisper.

"What do you want?" He realized that it was rude to say that. He tried to temper it. "Are you all right?"

"Yes. And you, I thought when I saw your light . . ."

This made him smile in the dark. He could smell wine and crushed flowers.

"I thought you might . . ."

He had to get rid of her. "I would ask you in, but . . ." He could not think of anything to say. He thought quickly of an excuse that was the mildest he knew, one that anyone would understand. "I have a woman here."

He could hear her footsteps going away on the gravel path, so light he was not sure at first if he really heard them.

"Ariadne?" he whispered, then said aloud, "Ariadne?"

She was gone.

David, who had run after her when he saw her leave the boat, searched the routes to her house, but could not find her. Once he heard the baying of dogs in the distance, but they disappeared out of the town before he could catch up with them. He kept going back to pound at her gate, but there was no answer. Finally he went home to bed.

IV
Vines

A second-class country road runs through Jamie Stewart's Virginia farm. It cuts three hundred acres of meadow and woodland away from the other seven hundred acres. It is, and has always been, a constant resentment, one that feeds him every morning with some kind of strength that he enjoys without knowing it.

He forgets, until his often annoying daughter, Lisa, reminds him when she wants to get on his nerves, that he bought the three hundred acres across the road in 1967 for two reasons. There are birds on the edge of the woods, two and sometimes three coveys. There was a rumor that the land was going to be sold to neighbors that he, although he was liberal in many of his views, felt would be undesirable. Jamie didn't, as he put it, want to be hemmed in.

By the time he crossed the country road on a mid-May morning in 1972, Jamie Stewart had already walked three and a half miles; first, the long farm road up to his western border, where a barbed-wire fence was hidden in the underbrush that separated his land from the woodlands that he had not succeeded in buying; then across the west field where his Angus heifers grazed deep in May grass; down through the hollow by the bridle path he had cut himself to the creek that wound in and out of his property; and up across the borders of the two huge fields where his wheat was moving in bright waves of new green; along the low ridge where the topsoil was thin and the land lay in a perpetual fallow.

Usually he rode, but lately he hadn't felt very well, and so he walked instead. But he covered it, one way

235

or another, every morning. Although he thought he knew and loved every blade of grass, every stone, every mushroom growing near the old storm-wrenched tree roots, he hadn't really seen it in years. Habit had long since blinded him. He called it peace. He passed the seasons, passed the small changes, passed nests from eggs to nestlings and abandonment, musing, as he liked to think of it, and noticed nothing much. It was just that he had to do it, or the day was wrong. He had to. The exercise was a spar he clung to, depended on to tell himself something of the kind of man he was.

"I am the kind of farmer who knows his land like his own hand." He said that, and thought it, and knew, really knew, viscerally, the value of the thousand acres of farm land seventy miles from Washington as if he had inherited the knowledge in his genes.

"We can go to concerts in Washington," Carry had said when they bought it in 1950, and she stood there, still smiling then, big with Lisa, while they picked the right rise of land to build their Virginia colonial house. They never had gone to the concerts, but, as she said, it was good to know they could.

It was, for a while, an idyll, a damned idyll, an idyll that cost him more than one bucket of clams. That old thought made him stumble as he got to the north side of the country road, and he fell against the fence. His father's silver-headed cane flew out of his hand, and he had to clutch the whitewashed rail to keep from falling.

The steers, already earmarked with their tin tags for market, peered at him through the fence. One of them, a small one, managed to get his face through the fence, and nudge at him. "Get away you son of a bitch." Jamie clapped it across the nose, and then, as he watched it careen across the field, was sorry. That wasn't the way he treated animals. It made him feel lonely and foolish to be made a fool of in front of a herd of steers.

It took him some time to climb the gate and ease himself down among the cattle. He moved slowly, to keep them from running off weight at sixty cents a pound. When the cattle had started grazing again, he walked through them, across the meadow ankle-deep in blue-green grass, lespedeza, and daisies. It was the time for the wild yellow iris, which he made himself remember to call flags. If he had listened, he could have heard the creek, pulling away to his left, but he didn't. There rose in him, instead, the feeling that he waited for every morning, the feeling of being master of all he surveyed—and much, he had to admit, that he didn't, lodged in the Bank of Virginia, in ITT, in municipal bonds, with his broker, and some in an unfortunate investment in a nuclear-driven car that had been on paper for too many years.

He climbed the hill slowly, and stood at last—not even panting, he told himself, pleased—on the high granite outcrop that dominated the northeast corner of his land. Behind him lay the faint brush of the Blue Ridge, or the morning clouds, he was never sure which. Before and below lay his land. He could see the brick house, old brick, two whole damned farmhouses torn down to build it, and the white barn, all miniature. He thought of Monopoly, the complex from there was so small, so owned.

Monopoly made him think of children, then of Lisa, then of her letter, crunched deep in the pocket of his Norfolk jacket, made in Savile Row in 1961. He could hear it among the other papers, a feed bill he meant to question, his application for his farm subsidy—that was important, the more fallow land, the more coveys, the more government money, the more tax loss, his mind soared into the saving of it. All of this, including the letter, he meant to deal with at noon, when he set aside exactly one hour for his desk work, when the sun was too hot, and the maids had finished making their incessant small noise in the house, and there was a peaceful lull while he waited for his lunch, which was set on the table at exactly one o'clock. He prided himself on the times when he used his whole day efficiently, without succumbing to a pre-lunch drink.

But at nine o'clock he had to keep his mind clear for what he was deciding as he looked down on the fields mapped in front of him—the rotation of pasture for the heifers, the choice of what fields he wanted to leave uncropped for fall and winter, which to allot to the already fattening steers that would be slaughtered in late September, which to leave for the nurturing of the coveys of quail where he would, when the chicks were old enough, work his dogs. He told himself that the men he saw in the distance, cutting the first hay so far off that the cutter made a faint chuck chuck like a bird, could tell the time, dependably, by his figure standing there on the hill against the sky.

The sound was answered by the fainter call of a bobwhite, and he let himself sit down, not because he was tired, but because he felt peaceful, and he tried to map where the coveys were feeding by the calls, back and forth, carried by the slight breeze.

Lisa was impinging on his mind, and he put her aside for the moment, but it was harder, too hard, to get rid of his wife, his Carry. She seemed to walk there, right up the hill into his mind, and he let her stay, morning grief, as much of a timed habit, although he did not recognize it, as the rest of his habit-ridden day. He thought of this meeting with her as ritual, as near a religious observance as he ever allowed himself.

He took for granted, as did his acquaintances flung like a web over the east of America, from Nantucket to Georgetown, around the country with himself as center, that he was still, after ten years, poised—not sunk, he would never use the shameful word sunk about himself—in grief over the loss of Carry. He could feel it within, a blank cold stone of loss as if she had been wrenched physically out of his center by death.

He would not dwell on her last months, the receding stranger locked in what she had had to face; that was obscene and unfair to her memory. No, he let her come to him at her most beautiful, swaying, imperious and selfish. He smiled at that, as selfish as a jewel with its own isolated facets of light, a lost treasure. He used her high incisive voice to pierce him with advice from time to time, more than he ever had when she was there in life, and he let himself, proud of his honesty, blame her for what he saw as desertion. Annoyance banked sometimes so high—as it was doing now, brought on by the thought of Lisa's letter, which he knew would call for some decision—that it threatened to overwhelm him as he sat on the rock; the weight of it brought a few tears that the breeze dried.

It was this experience that he called grief. If he hated the weight of it, he also found it useful. It kept away the women, and there were legions of them, who wanted to marry and comfort him. And why not—he had said that to Lisa—I am still a handsome healthy man, intelligent, interesting, and God knows, rich. I am, he told the Carry in his mind, a natural bachelor, you always knew that and you liked it.

He glanced at his watch, although he didn't need to, being a country man, and got up. It was time for the next phase of his day. What was it? His mind went so blank he stood shivering. All he could remember during the pause was, I must not drink until six o'clock, and the cry, Carry why did you desert me to cope with all this?

"All this" was, as the grandfather clock in the hall chimed noon, the now very dirty unopened letter from Lisa. He put off going into his study by examining the clock as it chimed, liking the soft glow of the wood, feeling the carving with the palm of his hand where he had more feeling. As a little bit of vanity he let himself tell friends, close ones of course, from time to time, that he had outbid the White House for it.

He finally sat down at the George Washington desk and took the letter out of his pocket. It lay, with tobacco crumbs clinging to it, like a time bomb to destroy his day. It was not that he didn't adore his daughter. He did, absolutely adored her, everybody said so. He didn't really like her very much, though. There was, after all, for a civilized man, a difference. Leaving the letter unopened, he got up and went to the decanter. Once in a while he let himself drink a glass of Château Haut-Brion at noon. It was healthier than white wine. It had more iron in it. He rolled it around the glass, liking the fine ruby film.

He sat down again in front of the letter. "Dammit, TeeTee," he said aloud, using her baby name, "look

what you've done. You've made me break down and
take a drink."

Finally, as the fifteen-minute chime came from the
hall, he put down the glass, picked up the gold pa-
perknife, stabbed at the dirty envelope, and slit it open.

"I knew it wouldn't last," he said aloud when he had
read it.

B eyond the closed door, Lewis tiptoed
away when he heard the voice, and took the hot dish
from the dining-room table. He was setting it back in
the oven when the bell rang. He took his time to walk
back through the conservatory, the dining room,
through the wide hall, and open the study door. "You
call me, Mr. Jamie?" His voice was suitably surprised.

"Lewis, put off lunch until I tell you. I have some
work to do."

Lewis felt sorry for him, as he did sometimes, seeing
him like that, crumpled clothes, crumpled room he
wouldn't let any of them touch. He said it disturbed his
papers, his system. What the system was, Lewis had
never found out. It looked like a junkroom of piled
magazines, newspapers, old bills, catalogues. He bet
there were a thousand catalogues, catalogues for
stamps, for rocks, for those men's hunting clothes he
ordered, guns, wines, painting auctions, antiques, a
huge pile of junk. There were never many letters. The
farm manager intercepted them when he could, and
when Mr. Jamie did get hold of one or two, it was
Lewis's job to get them out of his pocket and pass
them on to the manager. Sometimes they got lost in the
study and there was trouble with the government and
the cattle buyers when they did. Lewis wished Mr.
Jamie would let him shave him in the mornings. His
face was cut and there were patches of old stubble he
always missed. He'd fallen again; that old coat had new
mud on it. He wished Miss Lisa would come on home
from wherever she was this time, although he couldn't
blame her for staying away. When she was home it was
worse, the house was electric with argument. There

was nothing to do, he saw, but to leave him there talking to himself.

"Yes, Mr. Jamie," he said, and closed the door softly.

Jamie read the letter again. This time it made him smile. He read carefully between the lines. So the phase of living on a hundred dollars a month was over. He wondered who the man was. All that unmitigated crap, he liked the phrase and used it often, about the fine family of some wop dago she'd picked up. He knew it was there to reassure him, and reassurance from Lisa always meant she wanted money.

"You were right . . ." he read again. If she had written that she wanted a lot. Well, he sighed, at least it wasn't another genius. All through the late sixties she had gone in for neglected revolutionary geniuses. Jamie hated the word. He had tried, in the beginning, to explain his views quietly, calmly. He despised geniuses. It was as simple as that. He liked to write a little himself, and one winter he had done some quite good paintings after the hunting season had bogged down in heavy snow. He had painted every one of his hunting dogs and his favorite horse, so he knew, as he told her, what he was talking about. Talent, he told her, trying to train her to recognize such things, was acceptable. Genius was not. It went too far. It was bad manners. Nice people didn't have it. It was, in a word, trashy, too much dilemma, not enough explanation. You could see—he told her but she wouldn't listen—the butcher in Shakespeare, and the drunkard's background in Beethoven.

But she hadn't listened to him since they lost Carry.

The wine glass was empty. He got up and filled it again and brought the decanter over to his desk.

At least it wasn't art again, but property. Property he could understand.

The fuse about Ariadne fizzled, went out as he took another sip of wine, lit again as he concentrated. That damned fool woman. He'd always felt a bit sorry for her, and he thought of it as affection. No money, all that brave décor, a house too small and too near Washington. It smelled of clever ways to make ends meet. She deserved better than that. He was glad when she got rid of that awful husband of hers. He remembered pointing all that out to TeeTee. He could hear himself again.

"You see what happens when you marry a clever nobody?" A nobody professor he despised, self-important, tied up with a bunch of Washington clever nobodies he despised more. He never had them in the house—oh, State Department and CIA, yes, that was different. Don't entertain civil servants or elected officials, he'd tried to teach TeeTee that. My God, that what's-his-name of Ariadne's was typical of the kind of man from some midwestern university, doing too consciously things a rich man knew were useless and unimportant.

He had learned that at his father's bony knee. J. Press gents, he called them, like that riffraff at the White House, skullduggery in the well-cut gray suits of Mafia lawyers. Ariadne's husband was the kind of man who mistook hospitality for friendship, and that was a presumption that few men understood. He'd seen that nice girl, who'd gone to school with Carry, spew out her life and pride on such a man. From what he read she was still spewing it out, forgetting who she was, and here he had made the mistake of putting that dear child TeeTee in the middle of it, hints of drugs, and God knows what.

He had to do something. He had to think. Get Lisa back? It wasn't that he didn't want her, it was simply that she didn't fit in with the way he lived when she was hanging around the farm with nothing to do. It wasn't good for her. He got down to brass tacks. He asked himself the most important question: "How much will it cost?"

He picked up the phone. He put it down again, very careful to set it straight in its cradle. He had to be very cunning with the damned phone. Sometimes it disconnected itself. A little consideration. He needed a little more consideration. He saw the sea, not the wild tearing green of the North Atlantic that he was used to, but a wine-dark sea in a vast caprice of winds. He saw islands with white houses and Cyclopean caves. He made himself feel the slip of silk that only a fine yacht can cut through the water. He could feel peace spreading out through his nerves. The sea breeze pulled at his mind. It would be fine to buy some of that. He guided his hand back to the telephone. He was aware that Lisa's letter had played him with rhythms of wishes, rhythms of fear, counterpoints touching his deepest opinions. He laughed aloud. "The little bitch," he told the crystal glass, "really knows how to do it."

Lewis in the kitchen heard the slight burr of the phone being dialed and picked up the extension to listen. It was one of his few pleasures in the empty, sad, clean house. Besides he felt it his duty. Somebody had to keep watch on things while Miss Lisa was away.

Bob MacKay had finished, as well as he ever did, the pile of decisions on his desk, and was finally ready to leave and pick up a couple of hours of tennis and then lunch when he saw the red light of a phone call on his intercom. He signaled through to his secretary. "I don't want any more calls, Sport," he told the machine.

"Sorry, but it's Mr. Stewart . . ."

Bob MacKay sighed and looked at the fine day through the Venetian blinds. He punched the extension button. "Jamie, what can I do for you?" He was conscious of not sounding impatient.

He listened for a long time. He watched the third hand of his desk clock go around twice. He leaned back in his chair and studied the magnolia tree outside his window. He had planted it there, and now it almost obscured the window. Had he been there that long, at that desk? He had a panicked sense of time slipping. He had never seen the blossoms so fat, great cones ready to burst into flat white flowers, funeral wax, Christ what had happened to all that time, while the tree grew and he did the same thing, over and over?

"Well, now," he cut in as Jamie Stewart's voice slowed. "Where did you hear about this?"

The third hand began to crawl around again.

He waited until the inevitable question came.

"Now, look, Jamie, I don't really know a hell of a lot about the Turkish coast." They both laughed. "I can tell you from this end. You can get government insurance on foreign investments. That will protect you against all the usual things, insurrection, government take-over, acts of God. But I don't know how the Turks are about controlling interests." He wondered if he ought to signal Sport to call the club and tell them he'd be late.

"Hell, I know you want control. Sure, I can see your point. You see, there are two kinds. There's portfolio investment, you know about that, less than ten percent, no no, of the voting stock. Now wait a minute. Then there's leverage investment. There you have some clout. Do you want to do it anonymously? Through a front company? I only asked. Yes, I know you do, I'm only trying to lay it all out. What's the initial stock issue? Did she tell you?"

He could hear the crumple of paper.

"Oh that's OK. I have it right here, wait a minute. That's about eight hundred thousand dollars. They're thinking big enough for that coast anyway. You'll have to spend over eighty thousand dollars to buy clout, Jamie. Hell, I can't let you spend nearly a hundred thousand dollars on some Middle Eastern fly-by-night hotel scheme we don't know a damned thing about. All that Med coast is as crazy as the Florida boom." Bob MacKay couldn't understand why he was suddenly so angry. Something that he'd forgotten, what was it? He'd been looking at the magnolia. Something had made him edgy. He couldn't think what it was. "Yeah, yeah, I know it's all for Lisa." He tried to soften his voice. "Why can't she take up painting?"

He held the telephone away from his ear for a long time. That's what he'd tried to remember, and now he was sorry. Eighteen years. Eighteen years of listening to spoiled rich bastards. He could have been a gardener if he had it to do over.

"Oh yeah, sorry Jamie, I forgot about that. OK. I'll look into it and call you back. Well, it'll have to be later this afternoon. All my contacts in Washington are out to lunch on your taxes. Now," Bob MacKay, the gardener, was as patient as he would be with a young plant, "let me have all the facts." His pencil scratched on. "What? How do you spell that? Jesus. OK. Call you back. Remember, it may take some time."

At last he put down the phone. He didn't give a damn how Jamie Stewart spent his money, but he'd done his duty. He ran out of the office before the red eye glowed again.

"Sport." He gave her the penciled notes. "Find out as much as you can about the AID, OPEC, and private investment picture in Turkey. Jamie Stewart wants to buy the Aegean. Find out how much is in his play-dough fund." Sport was writing quickly under his eye. He leaned close to her. He touched her shoulder. "And find out who our affiliate bank in Turkey is. It's through Chase Manhattan. Oh, and place a call for Lefty Leftwitch at State in Washington for three o'clock. No, Sport, he's not a red, he's a southpaw." He looked out of the open window. No one was passing in the street. He kissed her piled-up gray curls, as he had been doing since they were brown as mink. "Goodbye, Sport, don't you dare try to find me."

After the door shut behind him, Sport gave herself a few minutes to stare out of the window and sulk. In the winter, between the bird season and the first good days for golf, they were together at lunchtime. She still, after fifteen years, called it sleeping together, although they had never been together after dark since one weekend in New York and that was an accident due to his wife having the flu. Then after golf there was tennis. Sport had to admit that except for rainy days, and there were few enough of those in Fauquier County, she was as seasonal as a grouse.

She heaved the Washington telephone directory onto the desk and wrote at the head of a new piece of paper, Stewart, play-dough. She let herself giggle, and then folded her mouth for fear someone outside the window would see. At least they had their private, dear language—the play-dough fund for the money Jamie Stewart was allowed to play with, the grump fund for old Mrs. Armstruther who was always suing people. With over eight-million-dollar principals not including real property, he said they ought to be allowed to play. She began to write down telephone numbers to prepare for the afternoon.

Lefty Leftwitch was a busy man. He had a busy body. At three o'clock in the afternoon, after a lunch in which nothing had happened, and he had had to speak through an interpreter which always tired him, he had one of those pauses with nothing to do that always panicked him slightly. He was glad to hear the telephone bell signal him into action.

"It will take a little time," he was telling the telephone a few minutes later. He was smiling. He wrote down another question on his desk pad. He listened. He wrote down a name, Ariadne Schrader, with a *c*, obeying the voice he listened to. "Wait a minute. I remember her. Nice woman. Wasn't she married to some professor from Harvard? No, no. I just met him. Those guys come and go. Sure, I'll find out. No trouble at all. We'd love to. I'll have to ask Mary. She keeps the book. Can't think of anything nicer. Washington's already hot as hell. By the way, fill me in on this guy. Oh Jesus, how can you do this to me? Political money. We sent him to Laos once on a mission. He blew it. He had a nice wife. Oh? He was drunk for four months and he tried to play with some woman's foot, some princess or whatever they have there. It's a deadly insult, like touching one of our women's crotches. OK. Call you back."

Lefty Leftwitch felt happy. He rang through to the Turkish desk. He glanced at the clock, timing himself about how long the job would take. "Not back from lunch yet, Jesus, it's three-thirty. Is the head there? What conference? Oh. Is there trouble? Listen, can you help me. Some damned fool I used to know in Virginia has got hold of some scuttlebutt about some port on the Aegean coast. No, no. Not the Greek side. Your bailiwick. Right. Yeah? Right. Sure he's got clout, about eight million dollars of it, are you kidding? Call me back. Oh, that sounds great. I'll have to ask Mary though. She keeps the book."

Lefty Leftwitch had made four telephone calls by four o'clock. A short history of an obscure town in Turkey and enough of the background of one three-hundred-dollar-a-month aging expatriate lay scribbled in front of him, surrounded by stars. He had a habit of doodling.

Outside of the cool undersea green of his office, he could see the Washington Monument cut through the hot blue sky. It was one of those days in May when the breeze from the Chesapeake made Washington into a sea city, its white Greek buildings ancient in the sun. Everything was calm, even the intercoms seemed to wink their red eyes slowly, no rings to jar the peace as the day neared its end in the last hour before the streets would be a clogged exodus to the lawn mowers of Fairfax County or the cocktail parties in the little walled gardens of Georgetown.

Lefty Leftwitch sighed. He was at peace. He'd had a good afternoon. He'd found out everything he wanted.

Sport put her head around Bob MacKay's door. She could have signaled through, but she suddenly had a yearning to look at him. "It's your call," she told him.

"Thank God. I thought I was going to be here all night. Hello, Lefty? Oh good. It'll be great to see you. Bring a tennis racket, and tell Mary the pool's ready but the water is as cold as hell. Oh, and Lefty. You know the wine store. Here's what I want." He read from a list he had been preparing slowly while he waited for the call. "Right. If you can't get the Gewürztraminer, get some of the Swiss we had with you. That's it. I have an account there."

Sport, listening on the extension, got her pencil poised. The electric voice said, "My God those rich

guys are shot with luck. The place is a potential gold
mine. The land's still cheap. It's mostly owned by some
local pasha. He'll be in on the ground floor. Yeah,
that's the right name. Oh, by the way, your man can't
buy more than ten percent. Turkish law on foreign investment. No, no. I'll find out for you. Interesting
problem. But I'd invest if I were allowed to and had
some extra money, like buying into Portofino in 1950.
Yeah, it's important. We're advising AID investment.
Look, it isn't just some fly-by-night hotel. It's part of
the big picture. Look at the map sometime. The border
between Greece and Turkey runs between the islands
and the mainland. No, it's one of the few Turkish islands left. Too near the mainland. It's a favorite resort
for rich Turkish officials. We want to be there. Lot of
action. Some smuggling to watch. The Sixth Fleet
comes into that bay ever since the people threw some
of our boys in the harbor at Istanbul. We've already set
in motion an order to stop scuba diving there except
for a little afternoon splash for the tourists. It's been
wide open. God knows who's down there looking
around. We've had a lot of local scuttlebutt about it.
Some kids were drowned. No, no. Just Turks, but the
locals don't want any more dangerous sports. Bad for
the tourist trade. The archeologists are bringing some
pinprick pressure to add to that. It seems some old
trade route ran past there. Sure it's a cover reason, but
you know what all those new emerging nations are
about their antiquities. Oh by the way, there is a dossier on that woman. Something stupid. She demon-
strated against the Vietnam War too early, before it
was OK. Oh it's nothing. Gave me a chance to look
into the picture there. OK. See you next weekend.
We'll get there in time for dinner on Friday."

Sport put down the telephone and decided to take
her mother to Richmond on Saturday. She'd been nagging her to go for weeks, but Sport never liked to com-
mit herself in case she was asked to work overtime.
She hadn't worked overtime for eight years, but she
kept the option open.

She heard the click of the dial from his private

phone. It made her feel sad and shut away for him to do that, but she understood. A man had to have some privacy.

      Lewis, how are you?" Bob MacKay leaned back in his chair for a good view of the magnolia. He was especially jovial with Lewis so he wouldn't feel black. After all, he kept reminding himself, Lewis was a college graduate. "Everything all right? You getting your money all right?"

Lewis sank back in the rocking chair he kept by the kitchen phone. Mr. MacKay was one of the few contacts he had that he felt he could be frank with. It was a relief to talk to him.

"Oh sure, Mr. MacKay. Everything's about the same out here," he told the silver tray on the kitchen table. He decided it didn't need polishing yet. He gently eased one shoe off his heel.

"Now Lewis, tell me. How is he?"

"Mr. MacKay, he's been drunk since last February. His skin flakes off."

"Damn." Bob MacKay was annoyed. "I've been working all afternoon on some business for him."

"I know. He called at noon. I was listening. You go on pay attention. He meant it. He always means what he says in the mornings. He don't start drinking until noon. In the morning he takes real good care of himself. Real good." Lewis said this with some pride. "He remembers, too. You go head and do what he said. It will give him something to think about."

"Is there any hope of Miss Lisa coming home?" One morning, tomorrow, the next day, the magnolia blossoms would be there outside his window, white satin. Bob MacKay was sure that if he were standing by the open window when it happened, he would be able to hear them, a quiet burst into bloom.

"No, Mr. MacKay. This ain't no place for her. I think he knows that, no matter what he says."

What would the sound be like, a burst of blossom? Swish? Pop? "Yeah, I guess you're right. Maybe he can go over there when they start to build if this thing goes through."

"Aw, Mr. MacKay, he can't go no place. I wouldn't tell anybody else this but he can't even hold his water. Soon as this one is over we're going to get him into the hospital for a while."

Bob MacKay noticed that it was just on five o'clock, time to go. "Well, Lewis, thank you. Don't know what we'd do without you. Oh, be sure and let me know you're here when you bring the bills in. I'll give you a cup of coffee."

"That's mighty nice, Mr. MacKay. I'll do that."

From the study, three rooms away across the house, he could hear the faint roar of Jamie's voice, "Lewis, you damned nigger, come on in here."

"I got to go now, Mr. MacKay, he's calling me," Lewis said politely. "You go head and do what he said. He'll remember."

Lewis hung up the phone and slowly, carefully, eased his shoe back on again. He walked slowly, stopping for a minute in the conservatory where he kept the jasmine plants and the monstera deliciosa just like Miss Caroline had left them.

He paused in the dining room at the huge dining table where the single place was still set for lunch. A spot of sun touched the crystal water glass and he picked it up to inspect it and see if it were chipped. It wasn't. The late sun had caught an edge of its etching. He took it to the window and turned it, pleased with the prism colors that flowed through it and made a patch of rainbow on the polished floor.

"Lewis, help me." The voice had lost its edge. Lewis knew it was all right to open the door. Mr. Jamie wouldn't throw anything at him, not at that stage of his calling.

"I fell down." Jamie looked up from the rug and grinned. He looked like the wreck of a little boy. "Some sonbitch pushed me."

"Sure, Mr. Jamie," Lewis laughed. It was expected.

He picked Mr. Jamie up. He'd lost so much weight he felt like a small load of dry kindling wood. Lewis lowered him gently into his favorite chair. His whipcord trousers were sopping. "We going to get you to bed, Mr. Jamie. You been doing too much. You're awful tired."

Jamie Stewart's fingers curled and clutched at Lewis's collar so he couldn't straighten up.

"Lewis," he began to whimper, "do I pay you enough?" He niggered at him, "Ain't five hundred dollars a month plenty for you to lay around in da wood pile?"

"Sure it is, Mr. Jamie. Now leave go of me and I'll carry you up." Mr. MacKay had been paying him eight hundred dollars a month for three years. "I can't stay out there for less," Lewis had told him. "Mr. MacKay, it's downright dangerous. I have to watch he don't burn the house down." But he let Mr. Jamie think it was still five hundred. That way he let Mr. Jamie feel he was more loyal. The rich were funny about money. If they got you cheap they thought you liked them better. "Sure it is," he said again, and went on trying to pry Mr. Jamie's fingers loose.

Jamie went limp and began to sob against Lewis's white jacket. "Lewis?"

"Unhhunh?" Lewis carried him across the room, dodging the mess, and easing the door open with his foot.

"Am I going to see Jesus?"

"Sure, Mr. Jamie, you will sometime." He began to move up the stairs slowly.

"How come great big niggers like you can see Jesus and I can't see Jesus?"

"You will, Mr. Jamie, you will." The stairs seemed to get steeper with the years.

"I want Jesus," Jamie Stewart sobbed.

Lewis let him cry against his shoulder for a long time after he got him into bed.

There had been another of those dawn awakenings, making his nerves ragged. Frank Proctor decided to talk to the doctor at headquarters about it, then as quickly decided against it. He disapproved of Valium. Sometimes he thought the whole American government was run on it.

Instead he decided to walk to work, almost the length of the three miles of the harbor front of Izmir. He took some pride in living in Esrefpasha, the southern slopes above the waterfront, far from the other Americans. He walked in a half-dream. The docks passed him, the customs houses, the warehouses, here and there the rotted hulk of what had been a fine building left over from the fire, the new office buildings. He was not conscious of the morning racket of the busses, the dolmushes, the calls of the drivers. One shouted "Siktir!" almost in his ear as he jumped out of the blare of a taxi horn.

The town noise was muted by the size and silence of the sea. That silence gave an air of sadness to the harbor beyond the dock area, where the traffic thinned out, and the wide fine street stretched away ahead of him in an almost imperceptible arc, still shaded by Büyük Yamanlı, the scarred mountain.

He passed the equestrian statue of Atatürk and liked the image of the latest of the Anatolian Gazis, perpetually reined in on the edge of the confining sea.

He had reached the stretch of elegant apartments with their balconies facing the water, none older than his mother, all built after the sacking and burning of Smyrna, the city of Homer, and he thought of Troy, as he usually did at this place in his walk. The new level of the city now called Izmir, risen over death as the new levels of Troy had risen, was solid, and faintly rich. There had been care, as there must have been in each new Troy, in the planting of parks and trees.

Then, as he opened the door of the reception room, it happened, as it did sometimes when he was tired, the clutch of smells and textures. He could map these same rooms all over the world of his moving, oases of leather and steel and carpeting, green and expensive. It made him homesick for his own country and it always surprised him. After the years—there had only been six of them but he thought of them as years, as an old man does—of being placed as impersonally as if a finger had pointed blindly at a turning globe of the world, in Papeete, in Japan, in Vietnam, in England, in Yale, and now in the impersonal dust and heat of Izmir, he felt it, no, not even a feeling, simply registered it as having happened again for a second, with the opening of the door.

There was the smell of the air conditioning, the green carpet, the carved eagle on the wall, the desks, the safe American ashtrays, the photograph of President Nixon, the smell of disinfectant, the steel file cabinets, the distant electonic hum of the Xerox machine, the computers, the electric typewriters, the linotype machine, the cushioned ring of telephones in rooms large enough to mute the sound.

The Turk arguing with the receptionist in Turkish was out of place, the sound of it an intrusion. He shut the door of his office to keep the feeling for a little while. He swiveled his chair around and stared unseeing at a ferry moving slowly in the distance across the huge harbor to Karshıyaka. He murmured thanks as he heard the click of a coffee cup on the desk behind him.

He had to turn around when she said, "The boss is already in. He wants you."

Frank took his coffee with him and knocked on the door of the large corner office that seemed sometimes to be like a control tower over the harbor. The door was usually left open, but he did not think of this until the old man said, "Shut the door. I have a few questions to ask you, son."

Frank's mind raced to prepare itself. These early morning conferences usually took two forms, depending on the old man's mood and the amount of gin he had drunk the night before. One was money-saving. More servant to the memos that represented his superiors in Washington, and God knew when he had been drinking, less civil to his subordinates when he was clutching one of the offending memos in his fist; he saw that every request for equipment, down to the Kleenex order, came across his desk and, by Parkinson's law, when the mood struck him, queried it. Frank prepared himself to defend a request for a ream of writing paper with the gold-embossed government seal. He had upset his coffee over the last consignment and he and the receptionist had smuggled it out and thrown it away before the old man saw it in the wastebasket. On rare and unpredictable mornings when the housekeeping mood was on him he snooped through the baskets and the shredding machine. Nothing was safe.

The other subject was to the old man a prime sin— localitis. This was also rare, but rampant with a sense of doom that blew past, dark when it happened, and blessedly forgotten when it was over. Frank kept tabs on the secretary to see if the lectures ever made their way into his conduct reports, but they never had. They were the products of the old man's moods, and, so far, forgotten as soon as they were aired.

The lectures took different, not forms, but intensities, depending on what had set him off, so that Frank, even after two years in Izmir, had trouble defining them. Sometimes a lecture was brought on by a remark as simple as telling the old man that the air conditioner didn't work because the power was off in the whole of the Kordonbuyu section of the town.

"Don't make excuses for their inefficiency . . . Localitis, it gets you when you least expect it . . ." The chair would tip back, the hands would go together as if he were praying to save Frank's soul.

Frank's favorite had started with, "They have good yogurt."

The chair had slid back so fast it hit the wall. "What's the matter with Dannon for Christ's sake? Can't you remember that when you open your big mouth in public you are a goddamned ambassador." He could conjure up whole restaurants of indifferent foreigners hanging on to every word of minor American officials. "You never know when they're going to use it. They are always after something."

Sometimes it was worse. "I have here a report that

you went to dinner at the Balikhane last night." He would have heard by eight o'clock in the morning. "I don't care if the fish is good. It's a socialist stronghold. You know that. Sitting there blabbing in their language. Hobnobbing. Why don't you see some nice Americans?"

That lecture usually happened on a morning when his dislike of the younger Americans who had been trained to speak the language made his face taut with old despair. The old man was seeing himself—Frank could read it in his eyes—redundant, retired too soon, growing big fat tasteless American tomatoes in Reston, Virginia. He had once in a weak moment admitted a liking for English and Turkish tomatoes as if it were a confession. He had been in the consular service for twenty years and he prided himself on never having spoken any of the gaggle of languages that went on outside of his office. Sometimes Frank thought he was so alienated from the country that he was still, after five years, in the "harem and opium" stage of knowledge, and then he would surprise him with subtleties filed in his mind marked Turkey. At these times the old man seemed to know everything. He paid for it without the unwise barrier, as he pointed out, of knowing not quite enough of the language.

"Even if they trust you to talk to you, you don't know what the fuck they are saying when the conversation gets important, now do you? They're *foreign*, Frank, for God's sake keep that in your mind." He never waited for an answer. "Hell, of course you don't know, when it all gets down to brass tacks. I keep trying to tell Washington that." At those times he spoke of Washington as a person, unconcerned and prejudiced, staring blindly out at a far-flung forgotten domain of martyrs like himself away beyond the sea rim. Sometimes when he talked about it, Frank could see Washington as a huge woman, a statue of liberty preoccupied, turned away.

"Goddammit," the old man said so often, "sometimes I think I might as well wrap communications in mudballs and throw them at a wall."

Frank could see them, sticking there and drying, marked Top Secret, Ignore.

But these were minor unhingings on gray-minded mornings. For much of the time Frank liked and sometimes even admired the old man, especially when he let his guard slip in the ease of his balcony over the harbor in the evening. He would rare back, reminding Frank of his own father, Ritz crackers from the PX beside him, PX gin and tonic in hand, the sound of good American ice against the glass—he said it was harder when it was made in an American refrigerator—he would wax wise, and if he seemed cynical, it was the cynicism of long fatigue, some loss of contact with home. He would so easily, and without trying, make Frank feel like a fool, but he was kind about it.

"State Department Turkish, hey, efendim?" he could laugh, unthreatened and at ease. "So what do you know? Where the best food comes from, and the right bus from Istanbul."

But at eight o'clock in the morning, it was none of these things, not localitis, not waste paper, but a letter that the old man clutched in his hand. "What the hell am I supposed to do about this?" he moaned. It was one of his mornings to be plaintive, which was rare, and when it came it made Frank feel important. It meant that the old man had at last run into something where he had to ask for information, within reason.

He waited.

"Ceramos," the old man read, "you were there. What did you find out?"

Frank had been waiting for this question for a month. He had tried to talk about it when it was fresh in his mind, but the old man had waved the subject aside, wrong day for it. Now that the right day had come, Frank prided himself that he was ready with names, circumstances, seasonal water flow. He hardly mentioned the hotel, and when he did, he colored it as fly-by-night as he could. The old man didn't move until he had finished. Then he started to laugh.

He picked up a pencil. Without looking at Frank, he began. "Question One. Who is the power elite of the town? How many times have I told you—cultivate the

damned power elite. The name of the game is *power*."
It was one of his favorite refrains.

There was no way out. Frank had to tell about the
hotel scheme, detail by detail. He finished with a last
plea. "These people own a lot of land. The son is
müdür, mayor," he said quickly. The old man had
raised an offended eyebrow at the Turkish word. "Nobody else in the town wants the hotel. If they keep on
building without an improved water supply they are
headed for a cholera epidemic."

The old man was patient, and even kind. "Frank, to
paraphrase a late president of ours, Franklin Delano
Roosevelt, they may be sons-of-bitches, but they're le-
gal sons-of-bitches. They have also wormed their way
around us." He looked lost for a second. "Washington
wants a full check. There is American money coming
into the project. How the hell these Levantines get
around us I don't know. I have to hear about them first
from Washington, for God's sake. Get me a handle on
these people."

Frank made a last try—for the good of his friends,
as he told himself later for comfort in his office. "Look,
these people are hated in Ceramos. They aren't Levantines. They're Turkish aghas . . ."

"I don't give a shit what they are. Look, I know it's
hard sometimes when overall policy contradicts our
field findings, but it happens all the time. It's part," he
said this with some reverence, "of the Game Plan.
Sometimes we can only see a part, you understand?
This is why I warn you young fellows against localitis.
It obscures the Game Plan. You're supposed to be
representing American policy, not getting yourself involved in some minor local feud.

"Now, take a pencil. Here's what I want you to find
out." He read from the letter. "Financial position of
the family, not including real estate. They could be
land poor. Have they been through to SPO? That
ought to be easy for you." He grinned. "Have they got
Ministry approval? Is the project okayed for American
investment? I don't need to remind you to keep sentiment out of this when you answer these questions. According to AID regulations, investment has to satisfy

one of three requirements." Frank felt he was being
punished by being treated like a schoolboy. "Does it
bring new techniques to the country? No. Does it contribute to exports? No. Does it contribute to the de-
veloping economy? That's your baby. Look up the
rules on yearly profit transfer, and," he referred to the
letter again, "the amount of voting stock. Have your
report in here by noon. A lot of this you can find out
from our contacts at Ish Bank. Get Güven Bey to help
you if you run into trouble. You know how they turn
suspicious when you least expect it. He's an American
employee but he's a Turk and the man there is his
dayı. Who isn't around here? Oh, and if you have to
mention water, for God's sake keep a low profile. After
the Aswan Dam, it's embarrassing. The State Department doesn't like water. Oh, one more thing," he called
and made Frank pause at the door, "there's a mention
here of diving off the coast. Show you know about it.
We've had a couple of pin-prick memos from archeologists. There's some NATO scuttlebutt about it. Just
show them you know. Protect your flank. Always protect your flank."

Back in his office, Ceramos seemed so far away. It
was resolving itself into facts, a report, diminishing into
part of the Game Plan. Maybe the old man was right.
Frank considered the sea beyond his window. Once
you cleaned him in your mind of his prejudices, the
terrorists under the bed—especially the beds of foreign
women, as he pointed out, sensing when Frank had,
well, indulged himself, as he called it—he made sense.
The anti-red wall he erected around himself every
morning when he got up, the warnings that came from
old Rostow comments from the fifties he had memo-
rized and now thought of as his own opinions, Frank
discounted all that. The old man was right about one
thing. Localitis could be a disease, a disease of the
heart and of the young. It made it damned hard to
concentrate on your job. Frank drew a memo pad
toward him and picked up the phone. He felt something of the old man's excitement at some of his field
work being noticed at last.

He put down the phone. Ceramos flooded into his

mind like a lover. It was bad, a pure attack of localitis.
Faintly behind it, he heard the cry of Turgut Bey, "If
there had been a hotel this would not have happened."
The drowned girl lay on the dock again, heavy in his
memory. He picked up the phone again. It had gone
dead. He stormed out of his office.

"Hatije!" he yelled in Turkish. "Who unplugged the
phone?"

Both the receptionist and the Turkish captain looked
up, mildly surprised at his excitement over nothing.

June pleased Dürüst Osman. He walked
slowly between the last of the storms and the dry hysteria of summer, with the imbat caressing his face. It
was still a young woman of a breeze from the sea, not
an aged nagger, nerve-wracked and dry, as it would be
later. It was his special, he would have called it delight,
but he was too mature for such an airy emotion; he felt
it rather as a sweetness on his chest, to stroll through
June, at least the beginning of it.

He was thinking of all this with some care. This
June, he had to admit, was special. For the first time
since he could remember he was pleased with Huseyin.
He had lost weight. It was no longer necessary at the
table to keep his eyes turned a little above his son's
head so as not to have to look at him. Sex, sun, and
cleverness were good for the set of a man's shoulders;
they gave Huseyin's face an intelligence that disappeared behind petulant flesh in the winter.

All had gone so well, so quickly for once, and this
gave Dürüst Osman added pleasure. He had hardly
had to manipulate at all. Only a few words had been
dropped into the constant river of attempted influence
that flowed toward Ankara. But, ah, what words! He
waxed poetic, flowers of words floating, arriving at the
quays of the official mind, almost as surprises, almost
untraceable, a few decisions made, the right thought
striking the right mind on the right morning; the deli-
cacy and chance of the game entranced him.

It had also cost so much less than he had expected.

Then, completely unexpected, and for Huseyin a triumph, first the rumor, and then the actual arrival of one hundred thousand American dollars from its mooring in some obscure corner of America—what was it called?—Virginia. Bakire. Huseyin had told him and they had laughed together, aloud, so that the old woman had lifted her face out of her food and said, "Hayır! She is no virgin, that pig-eater."

He could actually see it coming, moored for a while at the Chase Manhattan Bank, then launched toward the Ish Bank. Even the rumor of its coming had stirred paper after paper to be signed at the Ministry. Now who would have thought that one young girl, one of those summer nobodies, could summon such power with a turn of her pretty little wrist. America never ceased to surprise him.

Already the deep diving had been stopped. The second-millennium trade routes, his exports, and the Sixth Fleet were safe. The hotels were already full to overflowing. At this he laughed so freely that he woke a sleeping donkey and it joined him with a strangled hee-haw.

He could see on the shore of Yazada tiny dots of white, piles of stone for the generator plant. He liked the name for it—hasıl edici cihaz, the machine that starts it all.

He saw Huseyin walking in the distance toward him. The girl walked behind him, her eyes cast down. She carried a large portfolio in her arms. Huseyin was neither speaking to her nor looking at her. He was allowing her to follow him. That pleased and worried Dürüst Osman at the same time. It made him smile, of course, to see the girl already broken in like a colt, more Turkish than a Turkish woman. She had about her all the parody of conversion.

They parted in the distance in front of the tobacco bakal. She disappeared down the street toward the castle, and Huseyin strutted on toward him. Dürüst Osman decided to wait, turn and walk with him—not to influence, the boy was already straining at the reins with the new energy of his success too much for that but, man to man, to advise a little. Success with women, he prepared to let him know, was like any other art, the arrogance that stretched to the limit but did not break the material.

Huseyin saw his father in the distance, and for the first time in his life was slightly afraid. He had pulled it off. The hotel rose in his mind, the money flowed through his skin like sunshine. There was only one slight cloud. Lisa was beginning to bore him. It was, he told himself, a fault in his character. He liked conquest, but he grew tired of his triumph too quickly. She had, like all the other Christian women, been too easy, a plaything, but a plaything with such power that he had moments of resentment, as if it were himself and not her who had been caught, bagged, beached.

He had to keep telling himself not to let his annoyance show. The few times he had been overbrusque with her, had gone too far, he had seen in her eyes something that was not beautiful, a warning hint of cold sense, very unfeminine. For the most part, though, she remained true to form, too true, too easy. Although it had been necessary to get her away from the influence of the old woman, he had a twinge of disgust and warning at how easy it had been. If she would turn so quickly on her friend like that, she would turn on him. He had to admit that the fear added needed zest to having her draped around his neck for the summer. There was something wrong with American men that made their women too vulnerable to orders, to a training that they had never had, and that was essential, he told his father as they walked along the western rim of the long harbor street. American women took to orders like a new game.

Dürüst Osman said nothing until they had passed, and ignored, the Salmakis kahve, now full of dollars, francs, marks, escudos, with even a table of yen, drinking tea and watching the summer in Ceramos that they had bought but could not take away.

It was then that Dürüst Osman brought the conversation around to the art of the control of women. He prided himself that he guided it so subtly that Huseyin could not have felt the change of direction from his own bragging. Dürüst Osman used, delicately, the lan-

guage of flower cultivation. They leaned on the ancient
sandstone wall with its fragments of imbedded marble
that showed hints of carving, and watched the golden
grain of one of their town fields, ready for the first harvest. It took nearly an hour, neither of them conscious
of the time passing, for the seed of doubt to be planted
in Huseyin's mind.

Huseyin decided to go and find Lisa. There had
been, he admitted only to himself, a hint of that look,
he had seen it in animals, stubbornness without words.
He was worried that he might have gone too far. There
in the street by the tobacco bakal, they had faintly
brushed past a quarrel. His father watched him for a
while as he walked, fast, back along the quay. When
he was tired of watching he turned his body back to
the wall to listen to the grain sing in the imbat. He
could hear it, a June song.

Lisa sat in the grass among the last of
the spring flowers under the highest towers of the
castle keep. She felt tiny. She and Huseyin had actually
quarreled, and she couldn't believe it.

At any other time, a part of her told a part of herself, she would have been more conscious of the way
she was looking, sort of medieval in the right place.
Her hair now flowing and left to curl fell over her
slight frail shoulders and across the embroidered silk of
her caftan. The gold thread and the hair shone together in the sun as if the hair were a part of the silk
itself, left over from the design. She touched a strand
to rearrange it over her right breast, and went on
mourning. Her skirt spread around her, a pool of shot
blue-green silk that made the grass around it greener.
But she was beyond caring, even though she had
spread it when she sat down. She let the tears dry on
her cheeks and sat so still that a rabbit paused among
the castle poppies and watched her, no more afraid
than if she were one of the fallen, forgotten stones. She
was waiting, now that her storm of sorrow had passed,
for her eyes to dry so that the drawing on the board in

her lap would stop swimming, and she could work again on her drawing of an ancient marble bas-relief of a snake which had been used as a stone in the rubble wall of the tower in front of her.

She had nearly filled the book with sketches, all drawn since five special pens with a drawing board and handmade paper had been sent from Izmir by bus. Now, with the half-finished sketch in her lap, she had a surge of satisfaction. She had captured the snake, the texture of its marble, the subtle frozen writhing, the swelling of force in the formal carving that seemed to pulse through its white marble skin. There was a word she was trying to capture in the drawing—euonymus, no, that was a plant, animus, homunculus? Ouroboros. She finally remembered, going slowly through the alphabet, what the word was, the never-ending symbol, an echo from one of the ten art history classes she had taken for credit. It had meant nothing until she had arrived at that moment at the castle, the circle completed, the ouroboros, the ancient snake. She dipped a No. 2 pen in violet ink to fill in the shadows under the coils, and lift them from the paper, alive. "Find the pulse." One of her teachers had told her that. She couldn't remember which one it was. She was finding it, the snake's pulse on the tower wall, the pulse transmitted to paper.

Almost, and then it was not there. The paper was dead. She wanted to tear it and tear it again and fling the scraps over the grass. She was excited by this. I am having all the experiences of art I was taught to expect, she told herself. Even—what was it?—subjective disenchantment. That was Pratt Institute. Long hot rides on the subway with Donny.

She was hot in the afternoon sun. The damned silk caftan made her sweat, but she had to wear it. The dresses she was having made from her own sketches were not ready although they had been promised, and promised again, and she was secretly paying more for them than Huseyin had told her to.

The sketching at the castle was on his orders. She felt a moment of revolt that could have turned into sulks had she let it, but instead she said her mantra to pass the moment of despair over her art and the sweat running down her body when the part of her that jeered at herself told her she ought to be in a bikini, swimming off the outer harbor. But Huseyin had told her to work instead of sitting around as the other foreign women did, half naked, turning Ceramos into a whorehouse. He had forbidden her to wear jeans, halters, bikinis . . . and she was hot as hell.

"Oh Christ!" she said aloud and the rabbit scuttled away down one of the bolt holes, now at ground level, in the wall of the castle keep behind her. She had let her annoyance charge through her hand and had stabbed a too-large blob of ink in the shadow of the snake's coils. She kept herself calm, and sketched around it until it faded into greater darkness.

It was better than she had intended. The snake stood out in a drama of late twilight, the kind of divine accident that made a better work of art. She held it up, then let the board fall again to her lap. Her eyes were tired. She was conscious of her contact lenses. If there was in her mind a shadow like the snake's shadow, darker than she had intended, she told herself that it was her own childishness, her own old fear.

At least Huseyin was not like the others who had hurt her. He was rich. She let herself use the word baldly, naked in her mind, at last without guilt. When he had advised her to invest in the hotel it was pure business. It was the only act of trust she knew how to make, and when Jamie had finally said yes after all the hard letters, the swallowing of his advice, and the money was at last lodged in the Ish Bank ready for the contracts, she thought it would clear away any embarrassment between them.

She had to make herself forget the horrible fight in public in front of the tobacco bakal, when he had ordered her to stop following him and go to her work. "Allah allah," he had said, and it delighted her, in the middle of her anger. It opened sheikdoms of complicity; she saw him tied by her hair and trying to get away, as if they were already married. "You have the house to fix, you have your art . . ."

She had, she decided, been unfair. After all, he had

got her away from Ariadne where she had been so deeply unhappy, and had found her the lovely old house with the lattice-worked shutters still over the upper windows, where once, he told her, the women watched life from behind the grilles, the outside world crisscrossed with bars, as from bird cages.

He had seen the investment through a series of mysterious permissions that even she who had had to do so many business errands for her father could not quite follow. It would provide her with an income of her own, he had told her, magnanimous in his understanding that foreign women needed money for their sense of independence. In the same spirit, although he admitted he owned the little house, he told her that he was losing tourist money renting it to her.

All in four weeks, no, five now, she had for the first time in her life acquired a family, a beautiful strong old man for a father, a mother who stayed at home, she had to admit, too much. She sat, an enormous Buddha-like creature, and smiled at her and offered her one odd-tasting piece of candy after another.

Well, at least Huseyin knew where his mother was, not like her own. She had not heard from Carry for six months, and the last hurried scrawl, beginning "Darling . . ." had been sent from Hammamet. Now that she had an English lover she no longer signed her letters "Con Amore." Lisa had not at the time, when she was twelve, blamed her for walking out on Jamie. Any woman of spirit would have done the same thing.

Carry had only once let Lisa come and stay with her in Europe although they'd made plans over and over. Most of her mothering had been done at the Plaza. Lisa was sixteen. She would not let herself dwell on what had happened in Rome; somehow such memories did not belong in the silence and the sun and the safety of the castle wall. It was Carry's fault anyway for exposing her to men like that.

After all, Huseyin had had his tragedy too. It had seemed, he said, providence, only he had called it kismet, that marvelous word, that she should have been sent to comfort him after the dreadful loss of his fiancée. He talked about her often, as a dream, some dream of shyness, some innocence she had somehow to replace for him. She did not envy the girl whose name was a flower, but she was haunted by her shape, her grace, as if she had to learn to fit into a body of sorrow that was not her own. Even the hotel, which would rise, Huseyin actually cried when he told her that, as a monument to safety where she had died, was haunted by her. It is all very beautiful, Lisa's imp whispered, but it's costing you one hundred thousand clams. She was ashamed, caught by herself in the middle of a grin that she felt was out of place. Well, the imp had, as usual, the last word. "It's a big pot of glue, TeeTee."

She made herself recapture herself as a princess in silk below the castle keep, all virgin and protected. If she had moments of suspicion that once again she was being used, she told herself that it was only the past that was hunting her down, the paranoia of the un-loved rich, as she had yelled once at Jamie when he had accused her of being—well, the word had to come back to be exorcised—a sucker.

Someone was walking up through the ruined sally port that had been the gate to the inner bayle. The fig-ure was black against the sun, and she hoped for a minute that it was Huseyin. She prepared to smile, and forgive him. She looked up through her hair.

Ariadne, lagging a little behind the oth-ers so that their voices would not jar the calm she drew from the stones of the castle hill, saw Lisa, the enchant-ed child in silk, far from home, patient in durance she was obviously not yet finding vile, so small, so vulner-able. She looked about twelve years old in her blue-green pool of silk, pitiful in the grass below the massive walls of the keep with its towers that rose two hundred feet in the air behind her. She seemed so contented there that Ariadne hoped that the others would not see her.

But Basil had seen her, and he loped, as best he could, across the grass, with Miranda close behind him. Having finally got him with promises, that after a month had turned into threats, to bring her to the castle, Miranda was determined to miss nothing.

"Bless my soul," Basil was saying when Ariadne caught up with them, "if it isn't our Lady Hester Stanhope. Aren't you burning up in that tent, dearie? You look sweaty."

"I'm working," Lisa told him before she could stop herself.

"Let me see." He grabbed the sketchbook from her. "La! A Victoriantable book! Sweet little drawings to entertain your grandchildren. What's that? A worm? You made a teensy little blotty, oh dear, too bad. My granny made a table book, all those acres of efficient drawings. We had to look at them on Sundays. She was a Methodist and wouldn't allow us to do anything else. It was of Brighton pier and environs. It said so on the cover. In gold." He let the book flutter back into Lisa's lap, and grabbed Miranda's arm. "Come, my dear, we mustn't interrupt the artistic pursuits of ladies."

He jerked her around to face the keep. "Now that," he pointed to the highest tower, "is the French tower. The tallest of all. You see, the French got here first. And you, my pet, are going to climb it." He pulled her toward the deeply worn steps that led up to the entrance of the great hall of the keep, now a gaping cave mouth, its carved wooden doors long since rotted away.

"You're hurting my arm." Miranda tried to pull away from him.

"You asked for it, dearie, now you're getting it. Come on."

"Why are you acting so mad?"

"Angry, not mad, you barbarian. Madness is something you wouldn't understand in a million years," Ariadne heard him answer as they disappeared into the dark.

Ariadne didn't know whether to go or stay. She was lost for a second between their areas of anger. She had never seen Basil so furious. For days, like water dropping on his head, Miranda had worked on him to take her to the castle. Half an hour before, she had finally worn him down, and he had jumped up from the kahve table and said, "Come on if you're coming."

Some instinct had made Ariadne follow them, drawn by curiosity to see why he hated the place so. Something in the way he looked as they walked down the long ramp of the outer fosse made her stumble and take Trader's arm.

She was already tired of his voice, his snippets of knowledge. He was pounding at Miranda with his lecture. Far away she could hear it go on.

"No. I told you at the outer fosse. Those are not windows. They are bolt holes. See, in the shape of a cross." Some remark of hers in the darkness made him shout, "No. No. No. For the cross-bow. They were so powerful a good bowman could have shot you at the kahve from here. They were true at four hundred yards."

Lisa had looked down again at her sketchbook. She was so obviously shutting Ariadne out that it made her flutter for something to say, awkward in the silence. Ariadne had not seen Lisa since she had left her house three weeks before, except to be avoided in the street. In the last week of her stay there had been a long bout of silence, nerve-wracked and word-filled. She could still hear her own lost questions.

"What's the matter? Are you unhappy? Tell me what's the matter."

"Are you all right?" she finally said now to break the silence.

Lisa was picking at a poppy, intent on finding out what was inside.

"Yes, fine." Her voice was muffled.

"Is your house nice?" Ariadne felt a fool.

"Yes, it's fine. Come over and see it sometime," then quickly, "I'll let you know when. Sometime," she muttered at the torn poppy.

"Lisa?"

"I'm *fine*." She flung down the ruins of the flower. She stared past Ariadne at the ruins of the sally port.

"If you need me, you know where I am."

Lisa waited until she was sure Ariadne had gone before she looked up. She was sorry she had to freeze her

out like that. She had to do it. Huseyin had told her it
was dangerous to have anything to do with her. She
was a friend to smugglers, he told her. She took part in
secret orgies on foreign boats. He knew it. He had
proof. It made sense, a sort of depraved sense, all that
soft solicitude.

She had told him, or he had told her, or they had
decided together, she couldn't remember which of them
had first said it, that the old woman must be a lesbian
to carry on like that, all that hovering, all those questions. "You must move out of there," he had told her.
"You must get rid of the old woman." She hadn't actually said Ariadne was a lesbian. She wouldn't ever do
that. She had simply not argued the point. After all,
Ariadne did surround herself with all those strange
people.

She watched Ariadne's figure grow smaller as she
climbed to the entrance of the keep, and was dwarfed
for a second in it, shrunk rather, shrunk and bent. She
was getting old. All that chasing of the young. It made
Lisa shiver, hot as she was. She had tried. She was sure
that she hadn't actually said anything against her to
Huseyin, even if she had let it be said in her presence.

She couldn't draw anymore after the interruption,
couldn't work, couldn't wander about for fear of being
caught by them again. She knew Huseyin would be
furious if he found her with them. She felt trapped and
small in the grass, just sitting there waiting for him to
find her.

B asil told himself for God's love to breathe
slowly and keep his voice down, to keep the panic that
crouched in the corner of the great hall with a name but
no shape from coming nearer.

"There's nothing here. Come on, Miranda." It was
dark, too dark, like the last of the night. The vaulted
ceiling was too low for him. It rose, a vasty prison.
Basil tried to will Miranda out into the sun.

"No. Look. You can read it." He could see her, getting closer to the wall, the carved escutcheon with its

huge bird spread like a benediction over her head, over anybody's head. That's what he hated. Anybody is nobody. Parce nobis Jesu. She was tracing her fingers over the cut words. Let her not say them. Domini libera me.

"Salva nos Domine vigilantes . . ." her voice read the Latin slowly. "What does it mean?"

"I don't know. Come on."

"You *do* know. You're supposed to be a medieval scholar. What's the *matter* with you today?" Miranda had learned how to deal with him and it pleased her to show him. After all they were feeding him and keeping him in drink. She had a right. "Read it." She didn't mean for her voice to be so sharp.

Basil sighed out the words, using the translation made by the Countess of Pembroke. "Save us, oh Lord, while we are awake, and guard us while we sleep." He could see lovely strong fingers carving it, as men carve when they are imprisoned, etching time, day after day. He knew how long.

"There's more."

Serva me Domine, Basil prayed. I must get out of the dark. He could hear the swish of the vestments in the cold room, cold fingers touched the chalice. We wear no gloves here. Soft sighing of the chasuble, the clink of mail as they knelt.

"Credo . . . something. Dominu, domine, which? It's not very clear."

"It's graffiti," he was begging. "Please, Miranda, come out into the sun."

"I thought graffiti were always dirty," she laughed. Her back was turned to him.

She had found it, made by a knife chipping at the dark wall as at the wall of God. Basil sobbed without sound. Don't let her voice say it.

"Ne perdas cum impiis, Deus, animam meam: et cum viris sanguinum vitam meam: in quorum manibus iniquitates sunt: dextera eorum repleta est muneribus. That's very clear. It's modern writing. Very interesting." She turned but Basil was watching the sea through a shaft of sun beyond the far door. "Read it." Something about his shoulders made her add, "Please."

"I was left out, always left out. I came at night to find you, Simon," Basil whispered blindly to the distant sea. "I tried to knife my way to you through that wall of sorrow. De profundis clamavi ad te Domine." He did not know that he had said that aloud. At the first mass, cold dawn, always dawn; his mother made him go it's all you've got she said and don't you forget it, always to that wall, invisible between himself and the tired priest, always in the early morning, you're lucky you're Catholic bright as you are there's no one else will see you right. The priest smelled of coffee and dusty vestments. There was nun dust on the altar cloth, and he, too, knelt before that invisible wall between themselves and the Host, the dry Host, the most grievous evasive Host of Blackpool.

"Basil?" she said again and it was not his sister it was Miranda, that woman, like the rest but a stranger.

"Basil?" Miranda had heard him. Why, there were tears in his voice, and it wasn't the Latin on the wall that he was saying.

He turned and shouted at her, very fast. "Lose not my soul among the shameless, God, my life with blood-lusty men. Their left hands are empty with prejudice, their right hands full of gifts," he thought he was whispering. He had not let those words, his own translation with all the nuances he knew they would hear, pass his lips since the night in oh God was it 1947, drunk in the Marquis of Granby, and he was young and as beautiful as any of the rest.

Dylan was there and Malc and John, the talented butch butchers all dead now I must get get into the sun, and he had shouted at the wall of their backs as he had tried to pierce this wall with his knife and then there was not even laughter in the Marquis of Granby, only silence for a minute as if a record had run down and then they wound up their noise again. He could only hear their voices through their blank backs.

He didn't exist, except as a noise to stop, for that one pause, a pint mug halfway to their lips. It was his last brave act before he lost his faith, as he would lose money out of a torn pocket, where he landed among the shoes on the crowded dirty floor, betrayed. "I will

never forgive her. She made me say it." He did not
know when he told this to the stones of the base court
who she was, mother, sister, Miranda, stranger. It
didn't matter anymore.

"Why, Basil, I didn't know you were a believer.
That's absolutely fascinating." Miranda was quiet, as in
church. She felt close to him at last. She walked over
and took his arm. He was too weak to withdraw it.

He found his light voice again. "Like the Knights of
St. John, to paraphrase the historian Gibbon, I neglect
to live but am, I hope, prepared to die in the service of
Christ. To do that, I am sure you must glimpse hell.
One time the Marquis of Granby and I . . ."

Ariadne came into the doorway as they were leaving
the other side, arm in arm. Trader was setting up his
tripod before the graffiti-covered wall. "It will have to
be a very long exposure. No. Wait a minute." He felt
in his pocket. "I've still got a flash bulb. We like to
remember what we have seen. Keep a record." He
looked through the viewfinder. He read, "Sgt. Shock,
Canton, Ohio, 1970." He moved the finder slowly to
find the Latin that Basil and Miranda had been so interested in.

"What? Oh, it's Trader." Ariadne had begun to see
in the dim light at last after the bright day. The bulb
flashed on the distant stone-locked ceiling, the stained
walls, the empty gaping windows in a second of lightning, and she was blinded again in the dark, the huge
bright room reflected behind her eyes. Trader folded
his tripod, she could hear that, but she could not see
him again until his figure appeared in the far door,
running to catch up with the others.

When she came out into the sunlight of the highest
court, there was no one. She could hear no voices, only
the wind, high above the sea. It whistled and thrust at
her. She stopped and looked around her and turned
toward the stone oriel that jutted out from the wall
above the harbor, where she told herself she had sat so
often, at least she had meant to, in a stone nest of
safety and peace.

She sat down on one of the carved stone seats. Here,
she was sure, abbots had sat, if there were abbots in

the Knights of St. John. She promised herself to ask
Basil. It was an eyrie for contemplation, not for cross-
bows, or Greek fire, or boiling rock, not for defense,
but for prayer. She could trace the nearly obliterated
crucifix under the marble turban of Suleiman the Magnificent over the window.

She thought, I am tired of following the world to see
if it gets home, and she leaned her head back against
the cool stone and let herself sag down into some kind
of silence. Directly below she could see the tourists, as
small as insects, moving through the lowest base court
among the yew trees and the fragments of marble stat-
ues that had been dug up around Ceramos. It lay now
like a still dark pool away below the oriel. She could
not remember ever hearing a raised voice there.

In the near distance she could see the stone penta-
gons of the outer and inner walls, serrated for protection
against the alien land and the blank sea in the years of
watchful silence. Far away across the harbor the boats
in the shipyard were tiny dots of bright color. In the
semicircle of harbor, closed in by the harbor arms,
where once the Persians, the Greeks, the Carian pirates, the fleet of Suleiman had rocked at anchor, the
summer yachts had come to nest.

On perfect days she had seen under the water of the
inner harbor, when the sea was mirror-smooth, the
huge quadrangle of the ancient quays, and the wide
road that led to them. Now, with the wind up, they
were faint shadows. The yachts passed over them, unseeing. A toy French yacht, all white, its tricolor a
handkerchief, steered carefully through the channel between the islands, now sunk meters below the sea ceiling between Yazada and Mehtepe hill.

She had dived to them, and had seen the fallen
columns covered with sea gardens where once the
white temples had gleamed in the sun, victims of a
disaster that had not come from men or from the terrible notice of God as cataclysm. It had come slowly, a
thousand years of sea tilt until they had sunk below the
water. Now the sun found them as it found the old harbor on quiet days, dappling through meters of clear

water. Not in a night, but in the slow abandonment of time and sea, the floors of the villas had fallen.

She knew she should care more—and she was surprised that she did not—for the look in Lisa's eyes as she stared through her. Somehow she knew she had failed the child, had not hidden her boredom and fatigue, had hurt her, and she was sorry. She knew only to wait, as she was waiting now, for the others to find her, for the knock on the door, the tears, the knapsack slung down in the corner, the demands beginning again as if nothing had happened. Nothing had. Lisa had simply withdrawn without an explanation she didn't need to make. Ariadne let her eyes wander from the far distant islands, to the west, and across the northern mountains where the narrow passes led to Anatolia.

"If I only knew what road to take, I would go home," she spoke aloud to break the silence, and knew by saying it that Ceramos was slipping away from her, no longer the safe port she had found there. It was, at last, time to begin to think of going away.

What she had seen happening to others had, at last, happened to her, a veering of rumor, a change in the direction of opinion. It was as subtle and slow as the sea tilt, nameless and untraceable: it isolated her as she walked down streets where she had been happy, and no one spoke. She was left stranded among the strangers who came and stayed a little while and said how warm the people were, and how they would love to live there, and moved on. She had begun, before she realized it, to count her friends, to consider who was loyal. No change in her had started it—oh, she supposed it was when Munci had slept the day at her house, such a little thing except to her. Opinion, like the wind, had changed and left her stranded and she was too tired to fight it. She remembered being happy there as in another place.

What had begun it? She was not the only one to be changed. As the earth tremor changes, almost imperceptibly, a shoreline, the boat with the children had slowly overturned into the sea. She saw the waves of death circle out, touching all their shores. The diving had been stopped, Munci's living had gone, the unem-

ployed sponge fishermen were taking summer jobs
aboard the foreign yachts. She could hear the faint beat
of hammers, even from where she sat, where once the
blacksmiths and the machine shops had been in vaulted
Roman rooms under the outer castle wall.

The beginning of the hotel had brought new shops,
embroidery and jewelry from Istanbul, a page from
French *Vogue* on a boutique wall, the signs ENGLISH
SPOKEN, a new white, groomed city growing over the
village streets. Where men from the Ministry of Tourism showed each other progress, the government archeologists inspected the marble of the ancient city as the
medieval walls fell and released their rubble in clouds
of dust.

Across the sea, in tandem, she could see the fleet of
workmen coming back from Yazada; in the mornings,
the wind carried the sound of each day's dynamiting
for the new hotel toward her window.

She did not know that there was anyone else in the
oriel until a shoe scraped on the stone. It was the Captain of the Gendarmes. She wished she did not feel so
afraid. He was watching her, she knew, although she
could not see his eyes, only his outline standing against
the sun. Something made her get up as if she had been
caught. "Merhaba," she murmured. She tried to walk
past him. Slowly and deliberately, he took too long to
get out of her way.

She stopped behind him in the high court, afraid to
go on and tempt him to follow her, afraid to turn and
look at him. She felt his power behind her, alien and
impersonal. They let me live with them for a little
while and I have caught the fear they live with always,
and now I am alone and still have the fear. This is
what it is and I did not know it, a simple daily thing,
the fear of being noticed, of a touch on my shoulder, of
turning around too quickly. Fear is a vine without a
source that I can find to root it out. I do not know
what I am being tried for.

It seemed to her that she had been touched with this
vine of sin that had bound so many men together for
so long, for the first time in her life. She went on
slowly, elaborately casual, down the wide stairway

where generations of horses had worn their arrogant
paths.

Behind her the Captain of the Gendarmes moved to
the window and took his place to watch down over the
city. The fury at finding the foreign woman, the smuggler, the lesbian whore in his own favorite post made
his back hurt. He counted the yachts full of contraband
below him. Impotent as a saint he stood, wanting to
blow them out of the water. Down in the inner bayle
he could see the little bitch, the one who thought she
could buy anything, sitting there as if she owned the
ground, a dot of green silk as small as a flower he
could crush with his foot.

A t the top of the highest tower Miranda
clung to the wall and made herself look out over the
harbor. She could feel the two-hundred-foot drop behind her pull her toward a well of space inside the
tower where the floors had long since disappeared. She
hadn't wanted to do it, but Basil made her do it,
watching and calling from below while she crawled up
the rotten steps, clinging to the stone wall, higher and
higher.

Someone was crawling up behind her. She was
afraid to look around. Trader put his arm across her
shoulders and she clung to him and trembled with relief.

"Honey, never mind. Don't you worry. I'll get you
down," Trader whispered so Basil wouldn't hear, although he was far below and the wind was between
them.

"Boy, what a view," he said as she knew he would.
The wind tore at their hair and their clutching hands.
"But they ought to put a railing on those stairs.
They're dangerous." She didn't for the moment care
what Trader said. He had come up to get her, and he
would stand between her and that awful space when
she found nerve enough to climb down.

V
A Search for Paradise

Timur had told Kemal to behave as if nothing had happened. It was hard. Kemal didn't know how to do it, but he was learning. He watched Munci, how he remained calm and how he went on strutting down the street after Kemal had heard his father tell his mother that Munci's business was ruined because he was not allowed to take divers out from Ceramos for diving trips with a compressor aboard to fill the tanks, but had to fill the tanks on shore and dive in a little semicircle of overdived sea near the town. Most of the foreign divers had gone to the Greek islands since the ban.

The sponge divers complained in the tea kahve about the diving ban and swore they wouldn't do it and then went and sold themselves as crew for the tourist boats. Somehow, he gathered, it was all Huseyin's doing, but then they said that everything was, so he didn't pay much attention to that. Crewing a tourist boat was no job for a man, his father said. At least, now that Timur no longer needed it, Kemal could walk by the kahve tables when coins were thrown on the ground near him. He pretended he didn't hear the clank of them as they hit the pavement.

He dodged unnoticed among the July crowds on the quay. Kemal, was confused. There were the sailors, Dervish Mustafa and Crazy Mehmet, carrying vegetables, cheese, and fruit and great loads of bread and ice aboard the cuckold's boat. Munci was telling them what to do. Kemal couldn't understand why he was there. He squatted down in the spindle shade of the gas pump and watched. That skinny man, the one they called Basil, the Germ, his mother said it was a terrible

279

thing to name a man, was giving orders. He was wearing a captain's hat and Kemal knew he wasn't a captain. Munci was letting him do it and even joking with him. Kemal picked up the dirt and tried to figure out why. Munci was behaving as if nothing had happened. That was it. It had to be.

He watched until midmorning when Ariadne Hanim went up the gangplank in her tight gavur shalvar. That other one, the lady who tried to look like a boy and who slept with the sailors, was stretched out on the bulkhead in a bikini right in the harbor with her soft stomach open to the sky. He watched David Bey and Horst Bey go aboard with their canvas bags they used for the diving, but he knew they would only dive once, with tanks filled on the shore. After that they would only float along with the snorkel and once in a while dive under the surface and miss a fish. The el men could not dive, not like Munci and Timur. They only played.

Kemal had to move several times to follow the shadow around the gas pump. It got shorter and shorter until it was nearly noon. At last Munci began to act like a captain. He shouted orders to Dervish Mustafa and Crazy Mehmet, who had to push the old skinny one out of the way to cast off the ropes, and Munci at the wheel steered the foreign boat of the cuckold out into the harbor.

Kemal still could not believe what he had seen. There was Munci captaining someone else's boat, a gavur at that, while his own boat lay at anchor in mid-July when the work of the summer was at its height. His mother found him there, still staring at the opening in the outer harbor where the boat had long since disappeared. He got up slowly when he saw her standing over him and followed her toward the Pazar to carry her basket the way he had always done before anything happened. He knew it made her happy for him to behave the way Timur had told him to. He didn't have to steal anymore, and she no longer took him by the shoulders and shouted "Hele hele."

They threaded their way through the crowds, all strangers picking and chattering among the straw trays.

Kemal was astonished but he did not show it. Three
tourist busses stood in the Pazar with the people
swarming around them. He had never seen so many
people at once in his life. Every summer there were
more of them. They smelled dirty and carried their
own July heat. His mother said they were people from
the cities. But his father told her they were Christians
and Christians did not wash. They even wiped themselves with pieces of paper when they shit. Kemal
knew his father was teasing his mother when he told
her that. How could they get the paper out to put the
manure on the garden. But she laughed as if she believed him.

Out at sea, the forty-five-foot ketch built
at Tyneside in 1956, christened *Prince Charley* and
now called the *Miranda*, drove under power through
the channel between the great mountain and Yazada.
The air was sea-cool. Trader said so. He said it several
times, not knowing the almost ritual silence that even
Miranda observed without knowing why. The noise of
separate voices, separate footsteps, separate songs and
languages, the clipped call of "Dikkat dikkat" from the
minaret to announce the bus arrivals, fused into a
single roar, and then diminished to a hum, then was
lost in the sea lap and the wind, died behind it, and
disappeared. Ceramos grew smaller, an anonymous
huddle of white dots in the distance, a smudge, and, as
they passed the first headland, was gone. The sun
made the sea dance.

They passed beyond the east end of Yazada. The
boat responded smoothly to the current from the open
sea. Munci watched them all from the stern; their
heads moved closer together as they tried to talk beyond the throb of the ship's engine. To him, although
they were his friends ashore, they were diminishing as
the town had diminished. They became strangers in his
sea. He liked the feel of the new boat, the way she answered to his steering. She was narrower and faster
than the working boats he was used to, a live slim shell

that knifed through the sea. Her length, her deeper
draft made her delicate to handle. By the time Trader,
shy at being a passenger, struggled aft to take over,
now that they were out of the harbor and no longer
needed a Turkish captain, he was, to Munci, a different
man from the shore fool he had ignored.

"I like her," he put his head close to Trader's and
called out. "How she draws?"

"Unloaded, two meters," Trader called back, "but
now . . ."

The wind was rising beyond Yazada point where the
great Ceramic gulf lay before them. What Trader was
trying to say was blown away by the new wind. Munci
surrendered the wheel and ran forward to help Mustafa
and Mehmet hoist sail.

"No Greeks out." Mehmet grinned and pointed to
the small white wave tips. They ran east for two hours
before the wind, past the shore cliffs where in the distance the abandoned churches of the old anchorites
and the round breasts of the water tanks dotted the
hillsides and the narrow green fingers of bottom land
that opened out onto little sea beaches.

By four o'clock they had turned toward Hilalada
and let down the sails. Slowly, through the glass-clear
water after the dark turbulent sea, they moved over the
rock floor that seemed close enough to touch, but was
five meters below them. Munci brought the *Miranda*
about and cast anchor in the lee of the island that lay
like a sickle moon in the water, protecting their cove
from the channel wind. The true silence, after the wind
through the sails that they had experienced as silence
for so long, muted them.

"I heard something like a song." Munci was surprised that it was Ariadne who spoke first to him.

"You call it the siren's song. We call it canavar, the
wild god beast. It is the channel air." He put his hands
up. "It plays the cove air like a harp. Draws the ships
to the rocks." He turned away and called to Mustafa
and Mehmet, who had jumped ashore and were
crouched on a jutting rock, hauling the boat close while
Trader watched, worried by the deceptive clarity of the
water. "It is five meters here, all the way to the rocks.

No problem," Munci told him, and watched his new friend's face relax.

"I should not have come. The permission . . ." Horst said in the cabin from behind his wet suit.

"After all your waiting for it, what is five days?" David helped him pull the wet suit down over his body.

Basil sat alone, furious in the stern and not knowing quite why. They were all strangers and he felt trapped, after all the nagging, now that he had persuaded them to go to sea. He thought he would never get Trader to keep a promise, and, although they were not going to Rhodes when he had told him and told him they would go, at least it was the wild Ceramic bay.

It was all Miranda's fault. Most things that went wrong were. She had fallen in love with Ceramos and would not leave. Basil was exhausted, exhausted and mistrustful of them all. The boat was too small for so many people, inelegant and drab, drab, drab. Without knowing it he sat sulking on his new captain's cap. He let himself sink deeper into his anger. He hadn't bothered to watch them clamber down into the dinghy in their ridiculous black rubber suits that looked so what the children called kinky. All they had talked about was that one dive . . . one dive, as if the whole of the NATO fleet gave a damn what they did.

At first he thought it was a sea mirage, the ship with purple sails. She flew around the headland just above the water, under silent sail, boys in white aboard her, their slim legs straddling the shrouds. He heard a voice call, "Fuck, someone's already here," and the lovely sea thing turned and circled toward the mainland in the distance. Basil was ashamed that they had usurped the berth of something so beautiful, but there was no one to tell. There was only the sailor who squatted on the rock, looking like a bird of prey, seeing nothing.

Munci had said to Ariadne, "Gear up. For the one dive this is the best we can do. You go with me, the others go together."

She knew he was being kind to her, to take her

when he could have gone with the others. Now, in the
dinghy, there were no longer Trader, Horst, and David,
but three black figures set apart by what they were going to do. They were anonymous and quiet, as men are
always quiet before a dive, while Munci steered the
dinghy toward the eastern end of the island.

He touched her hand. "Ariadne, I tell you something. I must dive this time with my friend. I would be
too ashamed if a man saw me have to come up. But
you will understand."

She did not understand. She had not dived enough
and she was afraid. She did not tell him this.

"Every time I dive now I see the children. This time
when you are there it will be different. All you do is
watch my eyes. If the pupils begin to make a little
point, you will bring me up slowly as I do for you
when we dive."

"How will I know . . . ?"

"You will know." He looked at the others, the three
impersonal and formal backs, watching the water.
Miranda was leaning toward them, trying to attract
their attention. Between them the five filled tanks lay
along the dinghy's floor like bombs.

Munci turned the boat into land and cut the engine.

"Moor to the rocks," he called over the silence. "We
will dive here. David, you know the dive. Horst, you
will decide how deep you will go. Trader Bey, you can
go to fifty meters here. It is a good dive."

Not fear, not quite that, but a sense of isolation before action withdrew Ariadne from the rest.

"Here," Munci told her. He held the tank for her.
He nodded to the white rock sea floor. "You look."

You have told me all of this before, she wanted to
say from within the wet suit, within the moment before
the jump. I can hardly hear him, white water, fifteen
meters.

She watched Horst splash in, and then David. How
the suits equalize them. I would not know them. She
had not thought Trader would be so calm. She could
remember Munci pointing out, you can tell a man by
the way he dives. Watch how much he blames his
equipment, something like that.

Trader moved simply. He turned the valve, watched the meter, tested his regulator, and hoisted the tank on his back with an easy flow of movement, spare and unconcerned. Ariadne saw again, and it always surprised her, how polite they had all become, as if they were preparing for the element where politeness not only enhanced but saved lives.

She could see the black forms of Horst and David, waiting two meters below under their large umbrellas of bubbles. How slowly they breathed. I must breathe with Munci, follow him like a dancer; why has he chosen me, ah well, that is not my business, her thoughts retreated and formed themselves. My turn. Be still. She nodded to Munci that her tank was comfortable. she could no longer hear what he was saying. She adjusted the regulator in her mouth, bit on the rubber, readjusted it. He is pointing to my ears. Now we are all like Kemal, other senses heightened, speech shut off. I must think of Kemal always as underwater. She sat on the gunwale, heavy, awkward. My shoulders hurt. I feel sucked down by the weight of this steel and lead.

She fell backwards, hit a film of water and fear. Under them both, weightless, she rolled toward the sea floor. The sea ceiling breathed behind her. Yavash yavash, slowly slowly. She turned again to look for Munci. The boat was an eggshell above her in the great water, the sound of heartbeat and wave break, hiss of her bubbles surrounded her and as suddenly she was totally at peace after the fear of changing elements.

Munci, your eyes, they look sunken and haunted, dear Munci. She held out her hand and they turned, let out bubbles, and sailed together toward the sea floor, glided down, fins flicked slowly. The others had stopped ahead of them.

Is it David who has turned his head to check? Munci gave him the OK signal with his fingers. She glided beside him, propelled and silent. She was conscious of holding his hand. Now the security is running from him to me, not me to him. He is all right. He reminds me to clear my ears. His eyes have grown larger. They glow. He has broken the spell. I know it as if he

has told me. This is what he has needed, someone to
take care of to give him back his courage.

There was no height, no depth. There was only the
white floor under them, here and there a few red starfish. A lady fish flirted past her face mask. The others
had grown smaller ahead of them. Now they grew
larger again. They were waiting, kneeling on the edge
of the white rocks. Munci guided her up beside them.
She watched David.

David, you are happy here. You smile with your
eyes. How calm they all are; sweet and calm they kneel
together as if they were doing some obeisance to the
sea.

Above them the sea ceiling waved and undulated
like a banner.

I had forgotten how we speak beneath language
here in this blue world, visitors to this sea land, as
aliens might touch down on earth in heavy air from
their weightless element of space, gasping a little, calm-
ing each other, smiling with their eyes.

Munci touched her arm. He pointed to his depth
gauge.

Forty meters? One hundred and twenty feet? I can
only nod yes. I am in his element. I must not draw
back or panic. It is catching in the sea, as the smiles
are catching, and the calm breathing.

Five slow columns of bubbles rose in long columns.
Munci pointed downward.

Oh Christ no fear but awe, awe shaking my heart.

They were kneeling on the edge of a cliff, as aloft as
angels over a bright abyss. In front of them the sea was
pure splayed endless light. Straight down, only there
was no down, by turning their heads down it was
straight ahead, the cliff fell, did not fall, spread out of
sight through water so blue with depth that it glowed
toward twilight. Their heads, over the cliff edge, cut
the light into shafts too long to follow.

No down, no up, and north and south nothing, as in
a dream such considerations are beneath the dignity of
the dreamer. For once, Ariadne realized, I am not
searching for someone else's words, only my own will
do. Nothing is new in this kneeling in this place. It is

the most ancient of homecomings, astonishing familiar water fields of light. No one moves, the senses shut. There are eyes only and starfishes of white hands on the rock. Other senses flower, sea-deep memory and sense itself releasing us to each other, vibrations of sense transmitted through the beams of sea. This slow profound politeness.

David nodded to Munci, then to the others. First Trader, then Horst, then David launched themselves out into water space and followed in a line, gliding along the cliff face, growing not farther away, but smaller and smaller. Their air bubbles were delicate white ropes of lace connecting them with the far distant sky. Tiny umbrellas touched and burst on the sea ceiling as small as jellyfish.

Munci and Ariadne launched outward from the cliff face, and flowed along it. It rose slowly beside them. They sank through hierarchies of fishes, some huge, none curious. They had their own corridors, their own eyes, some stupid, some ponderous, some nervous. Ariadne wanted to touch them. They moved slowly past the cliff garden, past animals that opened like flowers, waving white Neptune's lace, sea mosses, and shell homes.

Munci guided her into a cave of color, and smiled at her child eyes. They were surrounded by the light of sea creatures, yellow and orange iridescent sponges, translucent purple starfish studded with glistening antennae as frail as hair. On the floor of the cave the skeletons of sea urchins lay, delicate cups of bone. She picked one up as a test for her nerves.

If I bring it to the sea surface without breaking it, I will have stayed as totally at peace as I am now.

She kept the shell in her palm. They turned, flicked out from the cave mouth, and now casual with curiosity she began to examine the niches and holes of the cliff, aware of the moray eels that hid inside them, but unconcerned. It was sea care, not fear, a different thing.

She knew that Munci was watching her, judging her, and she no longer cared. He signaled her to stay where she was, standing in midwater, holding on to the cliff rocks, a square meter of sea garden her whole domain. She watched him dart down, grow smaller, and she was alone.

He has trusted me not to panic. She knew this. Munci is a food hunter. That is the difference between us. She examined the urchin shell. It was pale green, etched with white patterns. She knew that when she brought it to the air it would be pink.

In a luxury of bravery, feeling so safe, she turned away from the cliff, still connected in its vertical rise with land measure, and allowed herself free suspension in the blue water, without rise or fall, shadow or direction, poised in the endless sea circle. Her nerves hummed with panic for a second at her loss of dependence on the sun and the measuring antennae of the four man-named directions. There is nothing, only my column of air bubbles rising, still obeying the law of weight. She was suspended below them, slowly revolving in blue. Full turn, the cliff was gone, full turn again faster. She saw it shadowed, farther away from her than she had meant. She flicked toward it, caught it, and looked up. Her depth gauge read a hundred and twenty feet. Far far away tiny white feathers waved above the wall where the heavy waves of the meltem were breaking over it.

Munci touched her hand. An electric shock began and died. He held up a grouper, its lips thick, its eyes perpetually insulted. A bright green string of blood trailed from its side where the spear held it. She watched it suffer the insult of its dying. Munci pointed to his watch, and they began slowly to rise up the cliff.

She looked, a last look at the infinity, not wanting to leave it, but knowing that in it, if they stayed on, a seduction of nitrogen would make them not care if they went or if they stayed. Out of the darkness below them, the others were rising into light, followed by the green tendrils of their catch. Trader held a giant flat clam. They had been all the way to the floor, the sea meadow, where the clams stood knee high in the grass.

We have been hunters, invaders all along, Ariadne could hear her own voice; it sounded surprised. It is no wonder that the sea defends itself and makes us drunk so that we want to stay forever.

They moved through their decompression time in water fields of animal flowers, now yellow, now orange, now red again. At the top of the cliff they swam across the white sea floor. Only Trader stopped for a pause to pick up one of the bright red starfish.

Above them the hollow hull of the dinghy was a shadow. Then closer, it looked to Ariadne too shallow and vulnerable to carry them. I long to stay, her eyes told Munci, it is more fearful to break through the sea ceiling and go back to weight and age and voices. Only now the sea urchin skeleton shattered in her hand.

Miranda was bored with waiting in the dinghy, watching Mustafa's back and following the air bubbles as they broke the surface. The tossing of the water, even in the lee of the end of the island, made her feel slightly sick. She saw the bubble umbrellas grow larger on the sea surface, saw them join and move together, and counted five separate ones on the dark waves, sighed with relief as one does, almost unconsciously, to see that all the divers are returning. She got up with Mustafa to help them aboard, put down the ladder while he leaned over and reached down to take aboard the first tank.

She knew that Trader would bring her a starfish and a clam shell. He always did. She helped him aboard and set the gifts aside, forgetting them.

She watched Ariadne, who looked as if she had been making love. She sat staring out over the water, watching it darken with evening as if it received the night long before the sky. Once Munci touched Ariadne's hand and they smiled at each other. Miranda told herself she would have to get over her fear of diving. In the wet suits, all their bodies looked attractive.

We have all, for a little while, been revised by the sea, I wish it lasted longer—but Ariadne did not say this. Tired beyond speaking, she let herself drift back to the dive, but it was already far away. Only her body held the memory, still floated, less weight of mind and matter.

Basil, watching for them to come back around the small headland of the cove, was delighted when he saw the silhouette of the dinghy at last. He had long since gotten over being furious at their leaving him alone. He told himself that sailors had a curious patience, like that one still squatting on the rock who had not moved a muscle since they left. The man saw them at the same time and got slowly to his feet.

Besides, he was aflame with his own plans and with vodka. Poor things, he told himself, I should not begrudge them their one deep dive, whatever that is. He didn't understand the new rules and he didn't care. He had heard Munci say, or he thought, or he hoped he had, that this was at the edge of where they were allowed to dive at all, and after that they could only swim and snorkle and not come back with that awful solidarity between them that left him out, their bodies as still and peaceful as virgins who have been deflowered without being disappointed. He liked that, seeing them that way.

By the time the dinghy moored alongside, Basil had made a bar of glasses, ice, water, meysu, vodka. He had found his new captain's cap. The first faint star was rising in an east grown lavender by the time they were ready to sit and drink like civilized people. There was, for a while, only the clink of ice, and the water lap. Basil, catching the mood, spoke little.

In the dinghy, forgotten, the starfish lay, dirty brown in its death. The clam had closed. The surface of its shell had faded to chalk, the color of dead sea wrack.

The wet suits hung drying along the boom. They ate the catch on deck after the evening had lowered into night. The light from the cabin where Mustafa was cooking faintly brushed their faces and the endless darkness made their voices soft. Miranda sat close to Munci.

"The amphorae shards we saw were Byzantine, not as important," Horst said to no one and the night.

Ariadne saw again the sea floor of broken am-

phorae, so many they mapped the surface dangers on
the sea, a vast field of them, so many frail ships, she
could see the hull of the dinghy, so many eggshells
from the waterview. She could see the tiny bones of
men littering four thousand years of sea lanes, longer;
soldiers and pirates, merchants and refugees floating in
the wake of their disasters. Those from Santorini, the
barbarians, the Crusaders, Greek and Turk, Germans
and English, and the lace ships of the Venetians
moored when the night came down and found shelter
in this cove—her mind was sleepy in the lull, in the lee
of all the human and godly storms.

Someone, it was Munci, touched her shoulder as he
had when she was underwater. "Can you hear that?"

She had not heard. There was a high hum growing
stronger that came from the black shadow of the island. "It is the snakes. At night they sing."

Horst's voice came out of the dark, "A thousand
sources for the legend of the sirens."

Miranda thought she ought to shudder.

Horst, David, Munci, and Ariadne slept on deck,
rolled in sleeping bags against the night dew, sea-
depths apart in their dreams, rocked by the water. For
a long time Ariadne was awake; from time to time she
heard a whimper, once a laugh. Someone was snoring.
How actively they were asleep; that made her smile,
and she watched the night above her where the stars
were no longer vaulted in a flat sky, but deep, sky
deep, so that infinity was brushed with light, an endless
Milky Way.

She was without thought. She had no idea when
sleep blotted out the stars. She only knew that she
turned and woke once and read the coming of morning
by the soft shield of the Pleiades sailing in the east. She
had been dreaming, but what her dreams were she
could not grasp. She only knew they were timeless and
peaceful, and there were, somewhere in them, the
shapes of sleepers like stones thrown up by the sea that
seem by accident to make a pattern on the shore.

In the first bright morning they swam to wake themselves in the night-cold water. When they got under-
way, Basil was still sleeping.

The boat was alone in the world. They slid between a haze and a glass-flat calm. There was no horizon, only a bowl of pearl sea-light, no waves, only the sound of the engine that was part of the silence. They had retreated from each other as if speech or touching were an intrusive thing.

Halfway across the gulf of Ceramos, the bowl lifted. The sky was blue. The waves trembled in the sun as if the world itself had waked out of its dream. Horst pointed to the southwest. "There, at that point, from Cnidos," he told them, "it would have taken a trireme eight hours to reach Cedrae, where Cleopatra and Anthony had their retreat."

"The fat, aging lovers," David told Miranda, knowing that she would not forgive him, and not caring.

"I wonder . . ." someone in the prow, a head masked by sunlight, called back.

Basil stuck his head out of the cabin. "I know, I can see it. The barge she sat on like a burnished throne burned on the water. The poop, whatever that is, an unfortunate word in the circumstances, was beaten gold, purple the sails, and so perfumed the winds were love-sick with them. I wish we would *get* somewhere. This heaving about in boats is extremely uncomfortable. Is there any food left?"

"It would not have been a barge," Horst said seriously while he poured Basil's coffee. "That was a river boat. Therefore I think she must have traveled by trireme, probably sixty to ninety feet, three decks of oars, two men to an oar. They would run at about four knots, seven for short distances."

Trader, at the wheel, heard snatches of their voices over the sound of the engine and the new wind. He watched Munci and the sailors raise the sails, liking their clean movements. He was used to doing it alone, but sometimes on good days when Miranda felt well, she would be as good a sailor as any man. Munci climbed aft. His bare feet were like hands along the gunwales. Far ahead the southern banks of the bay were no longer dark clouds against the sky, but separated mountains.

"We must take on sweet water," he called near

Trader's ear. "We can go into the cove and fish a little bit. Then afternoon we come out and sail to the east. I know good mooring for the night. The ladies will like it."

"What about the meltem?"

"Afternoon, to come out of any cove on this side of the bay you will have maybe twenty minutes big waves. It is normal. Very good." Munci grinned.

"We better go on toward the evening mooring now . . . she is not built for these Aegean short waves," Trader told Munci, apologizing by habit. "Your flat wide hulls . . ."

"OK, you're the boss." He could tell that Munci was disappointed, like a little boy.

"Sometime we will try her without the ladies," he promised.

Munci put his arm over the other man's shoulder. They watched the shoreline begin to turn green. "Turn her here, then. We will go along the coast."

"Aye aye." Trader set his cap and began to turn the wheel so that the little morning wind was aft, hearing nothing more but the whisper of the shrouds.

Basil had lowered himself onto the deck, protecting his bread and coffee. Ariadne and Miranda looked up from half sleep, face down in the sun, glad to see him.

He looked around in a slow circle and pronounced, "Christ, infinity is boring."

He was drawing them to him, harnessing them. They sat up. Munci swung himself from the rail up onto the bulkhead, cat-footing among the bodies.

Basil was happy with his people around him. Talk measured the silence. They began to see each other. Munci and Horst, waked from their separate voyages, began their summer sparring. David was, just for the time, too tired of their argument to listen. He dropped to the afterdeck to watch Trader, his eyes intent on the far shore. He had almost decided that Trader was more, something more than he had seemed, when Trader noticed him and grinned.

"You know, David, I don't owe anybody a damned thing. That's something for an American man to say. That's really something." He looked back beyond

David's head, following Munci's hand, that in the middle of his argument still gestured toward the starboard bow, guiding the boat closer to the shore.

"No," Munci was telling Horst over Ariadne's head. "You say we are pirates. You are the pirates. It is normal. Like us you take what you can from the sea. Make a good living. No problem. We do not stop you. We help you. Why do you stop us?"

"You do not comprehend that you are destroying valuable . . ."

"Oh shit to that. Who show you archeologists the wrecks in the first place? We, the sponge divers, since many thousand years. Hey hey, we know some you do not. We laugh at you. Outline of a hull in the sand, amphorae like old gin bottles."

"You take divers out and they steal the antiquities, together with the fact . . ."

"That is big shit. You dive, you know how hard to get an amphora out that is imbedded in two thousand years of sea rock. What you talk about? Bombok antiquities! The great gold amphora in the sea that everybody thinks to find. The Ministry in Ankara. What do they know in their offices of the sea? It is our bahche, our garden. We know when to harvest, when to leave. You are like the village men who dynamite the fish. It is you who destroy."

"What do we destroy?" Horst had stood up in his excitement. He grabbed at a stanchion as the boat rolled. "We are trying to save for you a valuable national heritage."

"You are destroying the ways of men as the dynamite destroy the fishes for a few that rise to the surface . . . you take our living from us in favor of the dead. You are one damn fools. You do what the businessmen want you to do so the tourists will stay to the big hotels and buy many things . . . What if somebody stop the men two thousand years since? Hey hey, you would not have the wrecks to take to your museums."

"You do not understand the educational—"

"I understand one big thing. My boat is in the dock in the middle of summer because it has a compressor aboard." Munci's complaint was being made to the sea.

He stared over their heads. "I know that the sponge boats are stripped of their gear to be a whorehouse for the tourists. There are many million fragments of amphorae in the sea, but if you or you . . ." He pointed to their bodies, not their faces. "If you bring one fragment up, I, Captain Munci, will go to jail for two months. Once I take out an American official from your information service, big educator, hey? He goes with his family for a little dive. He come up with one sack full of broken pots. I tell him put them back. He says to me, I am an official, I have the right, and then he brags how many things he has found and raped and bought. Who has the right? Why him?" He turned his back on them and called to Trader, "Now you run so, straight, ahead of the wind."

He turned and leaned against the mast, now looking down at their faces. "I tell you this. I am Cretan. Many thousand years this is our living. Who manned these wrecks you seek were my own brothers. I know this sea like my hand, where are the groupers and the lobsters and the broken amphorae that are their homes. I show the first archeologist the first wreck he saw. We thought he was our friend. Now I captain another man's boat and my boat lies in the dock in the middle of summer."

His back was turned to Trader so that his words were lost to him. "What's Monkey making a speech about?" he asked David, who was trailing his hand in the water.

"Oh you know, poor sod . . ." he told the water. Trader thought he hadn't heard him.

Miranda watched Munci, a tower over her, his legs strong, his genitals a wonderful mound above her head. She was faint with one of the quick desires she thought of as a surge of life.

Horst said nothing. He noticed that Munci's waist was small, his buttocks high and round like the figures on the friezes at Thera.

Far ahead the faint line of Yedi Adalar rose on the horizon. Munci swung aft.

Basil watched his nice back. "They're all so dramatic. I don't know why they complain. They're making more money than ever in their lives. I remember . . ." No one was listening, and he forgot what he was going to say. He had almost convinced himself that he had really seen the purple sails in the evening light. He could not get it out of his mind.

It was late afternoon. Everyone was asleep but Munci and his new friend Trader, who sat in the stern watching him at the wheel. "We take her among the islands. There is some creeks there that make a long series of coves, little hidden harbors. We call English Harbor now. That is where the Greeks would bring the English airmen and soldiers in the war. We would go out in the sponge boats and take them on to Ceramos. Also good smuggling coves. The ladies," he added by summer habit, "will like it there."

"What about taking on water?"

"There is one little kahve there, just a little pier in the creek. It is on the land of my uncle. They have the sweet water spring. Very good."

Timur had watched the strange boat from the time it was a dot on the horizon. He watched from behind a tree until he could make out its foreign lines, but he waited before he disappeared into the forest. There was something familiar about the figure on the prow. As the boat turned from black to white, he could see the figure lift both arms high. It was Munci's signal that he was not alone and for him to hide.

Timur walked away among the trees. The sun filtered through and dappled his bare back. He was learning each day to feel safer. It wasn't that he watched less, but that he had grown more used to watching, as an animal is watchful by its nature. He smiled, all alone in the woods, at how easily the planning had come to Munci and himself, the natural kanın kimse, the nonexistent ones.

"Become nobody," Munci had said.

Part of the disguise had been his new health. Then, too, on that night when Munci had turned him to inspect him under the light he had said, "You will now shave your beard. Where we will go the beard will be noticed. Let me see. Most of the young ones wear the mustache. You had better leave your hair long, little long. When you left you had close-cut hair and no mustache, so from a distance and especially not expecting to see you no one will bother to recognize you. Now you are white as a worm. I think we go fishing."

At dawn, when the wind was down, they had gone aboard Munci's boat. All day he had lain there under a pile of mattresses in the cabin, listening to the men walking above his head. He had recognized the steps of his father, of his cousin Mustafa, and Munci. That was all. He had listened to Munci preparing them, slowly slowly skinning the animal. He put them to work on the dinghy and on the wooden pier that was winter-broken.

"We must do all this quickly," he had told them. "It is time for the first tourists. Now I must take the boat to sea. I must go to Antalya."

No one had asked why. They never did. They were used to his going away on his own. He heard Mustafa tell his father that Munci had a woman in Antalya, and that was why he went alone. He sounded sure. He said she was married to a government official and that Munci got messages from her when her husband was going to Ankara. Timur grinned under the mattresses. They spoke with such assurance, not believing what they said, only filling in the unspoken with the art of rumor.

For two weeks Munci and Timur had fished among the islands. For days at a time they never saw another boat, except from time to time the sponge divers and the fishermen who waved as they passed them. At night they hid in the coves. By the time they came into English Harbor, Timur was stained dark brown by the sun and the wind. Where his chin had been baby pink it was burned as dark as ever, and he was rake thin. They both knew it could have been done more quickly, but they did not speak of this. Munci was letting the sea heal his chosen brother. He let him stay for hours in his numb silence. He let him talk. Only once, a few

days before they landed, Munci had placed in his head
a thought.

"Remember her as she was to you," he had said.
"The rich are not to be trusted. Finally, they go away."
It had been night when he said that and his face was
turned away from Timur. They were sitting by a drift-
wood fire, cooking a kebab of fish on green sticks. He
could still smell the fish as he remembered what Munci
had told him. "To them we are to play with." Lale was
not like that, he had told Munci and himself. "Then
think that. You are spared knowing."

It was easy to live with the old man. He had been
alone there for so long, with his rickety pier and the
tea kahve of brush that he built every spring and that
the sea took away every winter, that he did not need
for Timur to tell him much. He thought aloud, inces-
santly, instead, from the time evening came and work
was over, until he rolled himself in his old blanket and
slept.

All Munci had had to tell him was that the police
were after his friend, his little brother from the Bosphorus. Munci had told the old man it was for
smuggling. That was enough to insure his safety. The
old man had one undying hatred—the police. He had
been a smuggler for so long. For years now he had not
cared what it was, his business was his pride, whether
it was in men or goats, sheep, medicine, machinery,
hashish, gold or broken pots, for which he had some
contempt.

"One day," he told Timur over and over, "I am a
big hero, the next day a big devil. The officials are
crazy. They praise and damn for the same things."
Four times, he told him, Englishmen had come on
boats to thank him and bring him presents after the
war was over.

He had pretended to remember them out of politeness but he could not. Bana göre hava hosh. It was
all the same to him. It was his favorite phrase. He
liked the presents though, a transistor radio and two
kerosene lamps with shades, and a stove. For the rest,
it was all the same to him. He could no longer go to
sea. He didn't have a boat anymore. It had come adrift

in a storm that came up when he was too far away at his garden to save it. He didn't care. Bana göre hava hosh. Munci and the other sailors brought him what he needed.

One day they would find him dead like an animal in his garden and they would bury him. It was all the same. His mind turned with the seasons. Sometimes he almost hypnotized Timur into believing it was all the same—one thing or another thing.

Timur had put up the summer kahve roof of green branches, fixed the pier and hoed the garden the old man had planted. He had rubbed the old one's creaking joints when they foretold the bad weather. He had done all those things that inside himself he longed to do for his own old man someday when he would let him. Old Vahshi Güven could not read. He read him the same copies of old newspapers over and over again.

Sometimes, as now in the dappled sun, he forgot himself and was happy. He knew where he would meet Munci in the evening and he looked forward to it. It was when night came that he needed a friend. When old Vahshi Güven fell asleep the pain of loss he had forgotten all day would come and fill his head. He could not understand the phenomenon, how a thought, a dream, a sadness could swell his brain, darken it, make it heavy. Sometimes he found himself making notes of it, using his own pain as a problem, seeking for the source of that weight through the books he kept hidden in a hollow tree in the same sack Kemal had brought from the cave.

Ariadne looked at the still dark water, hardly lapping the boat-side. The whole of the harbor was a cave of trees after the spacious blue of the day at sea. The green manmade bower looked as though it had grown out of the water.

"Who lives here?" she asked Munci.

"My old uncle, only my uncle. They call him Wild Güven from the days of his work."

"Everybody is your uncle."

"Almost," he told her. "He came from Crete. He is very old. Old smuggler. He have been in jail many times."

They were quiet, leaning against the boat rail watching the others as the old man served tea to them. Trader had stretched his legs out across the wooden platform and was gazing up through the leaves of the roof. The old man had to step across him. Trader was talking to the sky. They could hear the bee-drone of his voice.

Horst got up, stretched himself, and walked over to the edge of the platform to gaze at the bank. David's eyes were closed. Miranda, in the shade, looked young, young and taut with boredom. Suddenly she pushed back her chair so that it fell. She ran up the shore among trees.

"Honey! Honey! Where are you going?" Trader called after her.

"Oh leave me alone," she called back.

The old man picked up the chair and set it back carefully at the table.

"Trader is a good man when he is at sea," Munci said. "I like him then and when he dives."

Trader came to the end of the rickety quay and jumped aboard. He bent his head and went down into the cabin without speaking.

"What's the matter? Where is everybody?" Basil's head rose up from the bench where he had been napping. He leaned his chin on the rail. "Is it time for a drink?" No one answered.

"Oh shit!" He climbed up and sat on the bulkhead.

Miranda walked more and more slowly. She kicked her feet like a little girl. She was almost disappointed enough to cry. She decided to look at the trees, at the path, notice objects. She had learned to do that when her consciousness was raised. She made herself begin to enjoy nature. She revolved slowly, surrounded by trees, no birds, no animals, not even a goat. The woods smelled of pine essence.

She held her palms out to the clean air and pushed away the thought of Plainfield which had come unbidden to her mind. There were a few bushes of pink flowers. She thought she ought to find out what they were. She walked slowly on, feeling sweet now inside herself. Nature was making her feel natural. She liked it. She liked thinking of it that way. She could feel the tautness going out of her face.

She tried to put the shame out of her mind, the shame of watching other people's faces when Trader bored them. It was a shame that had grown in her, so that by now when he began to talk, no matter what he said, or how the others listened, she could feel her muscles grow tight and a prayer start, "Shut him up. Shut him up. Somebody shut him up," and sometimes, "Oh God kill him."

Shame of that thought had engulfed the other shame, but now, she told herself, she was being more honest about it, and that was all-important. It wasn't that she didn't love Trader. He just drove her nuts, that's all. Drove her nuts. She could see herself all 1941, and see how she wore her hair, and hear herself saying, "Oh Mother he drives me *nuts*," and her mother, "Mildred, don't use that tone of voice with me. I won't have slang."

Slang, slang, slang. She could hear the words slanging the trees. She found herself laughing. Well, Mother I've slanged enough now, slanged men, slanged all that crap out of myself and I ought to be happy. The books say so. If you do that you are happy, slaphappy. Oh Jesus I wish I'd married somebody else. Plainfield intruded again. She tried to make a connection but she couldn't. Men? Hopeless? Why hopeless? Frank Sinatra! Oh Jesus.

Here they were with the kind of people she'd always felt she belonged with. She saw her whole life stretching out behind her, a preparation for it, sophisticated people like that stuckup Ariadne with her low your-pants-are-falling-down voice, and Basil, my God, an Englishman and a professor and he really liked her. He is in the palm of my hand. She let the trees know, and scratched her leg. There was Horst who was actu-

ally an archeologist and there he was on her boat, and
David who had the quiet way of knowing everything
about you and not telling, almost like a priest. He had
all that international knowledge and the, well,
what could she call it, the kind of patience that went
with it. She was beginning to trust her good luck
enough to enjoy it, right through her body, enjoy it
more than going the limit with men, although she did
that for the best of reasons. It was good for her, and
for a while, the attention made her forget.

Forget what? She couldn't remember what it was she
tried to forget. She had seen a cartoon like that once,
two men in the Foreign Legion. That's what she was, a
Foreign Legioneer. Anyway she really did like being
with the others more than going the limit. It made her
somehow feel the same way, peaceful. Then Trader
would talk.

"I hate him," she said aloud, and felt better. "I hate
his kindness and his voice. I hate being watched over."

She had come to the edge of the woods. In front of
her a little valley stretched, somebody's garden. It was
strange to find it miles from anywhere, surrounded by
the trees, and nestled at the foot of the mountain. One
of the creeks ran through it. She decided she would
like to put her feet in fresh sweet water and wash the
salt sea off her legs. She thought she might take off her
shirt and shorts and wash herself all over. She could
feel her skin, heavy with sea salt.

She sat down on a rock to take off her sandals. It
was so quiet. In the distance she heard the scratch
scratch of some animal in the dirt. She looked up,
scared. Munci had said there were bears and wild
boars. Her breath caught in her throat. It was a man,
hoeing, his face in profile, his back bent over the hoe.
She almost didn't dare breathe for fear he would run
away, a wild thing there.

He was the most beautiful thing she had ever seen in
her life, so beautiful that she was afraid of him. She
watched the waist, the spread of the legs in old torn
jeans. My God, she told herself, Levi's are all over the
world. It was like finding a Coke bottle lying beside a
half-buried amphora in the sea. She fell in love with his

fine shoulders, his glossy long hair, his dark slim breeding, the slow move of his back muscles as he hoed.

There was a new feeling in her and she examined it. It was a yearning, not, for the first time since she could remember, to touch him, as if touching the person could capture him. Something told her that if she tried to touch him he would disappear. No. She wanted to rescue him, lost there, ignorant and beautiful, educate him, give him hope, a horizon beyond that narrow garden in the woods, even, she went so far, put him in the movies, adopt him, take him back and open up the world to him.

Then, with that fine sensitivity that did not surprise her, beautiful things had intelligence of a different kind, she had always known that, he knew she was looking at him, and he turned his head and looked at her. She felt faint. Under his heavy black eyebrows the eyes in his sun-dark face were icy gray and they stared through her, shook her backbone. She looked away, shy of her own shyness.

"Merhaba, hanım," he said. Even the poorest peasant, she knew, had the manners of an agha.

"Merhaba," she said, and put her shoes on, fumbling with the straps. She walked away, wanting to run, into the woods again.

Timur was afraid. He had always managed to hide from the foreigners, from the boats. The old man, of course, understood that. Protecting the secrecy of his new young friend had become a passion. It made him crow to fool them all, to have the boy there to hide from them, all the interfering strangers. Timur shouldered the hoe and set off toward the mountain to wait for the dark when Munci would find him. He prayed that the gavur woman would forget him, but he knew she would not. He tried to assure himself that Munci would get them away.

Halfway up to the jutting rock where they met when the boat came, he turned and looked back. It was already late afternoon. The sails were neatly furled on the strange slim white toy boat, with its toy figures. They lounged across the bulkhead. He couldn't see the ice, the glasses, the white cheese and the olives, but he knew from reading the time by the lowered sun what they were doing and it made him feel lonely.

He heard someone laugh. It sounded faint. The breeze brought the whispered wail of the old man's flute. He smiled. He knew the old man would be drunk, and not miss him. He loved to go aboard the el boats, although he cursed them when they left. He would be their captured Turk for the evening, play for them, and drink their raki. Later he would tell stories, and let Munci translate for him.

The cove stretched for a mile out to sea. He could see it all the way to the open gulf. He watched a boat with dark sails enter the cove and sail along one of the other channels of the creek. A long thin finger of land hid it from the others. It sailed on past them and cast anchor at the near shore. Nearer, he could see that it was a great tirandil of twenty meters. He could not believe what he saw then. The boat had purple sails.

Now it was the deep blue of evening, the water black, the first faint hint of stars. The two boats lay within a quarter of a mile of each other, furled and at rest for the night. The figures on them seemed to reflect each other, doing the same slow things. Once in a while, from one boat or the other, a body would dive into the water. There was no other movement.

In the aft cabin of the *Miranda,* Miranda was arguing with Munci in an urgent half whisper.

"But I saw him," she said. She felt she had to be stern. After all, she had convinced herself, it was for the best of reasons she was making her demand.

"No. There is no one here with the old man," Munci told her again.

"I saw him."

"There is a village over the mountain. Maybe he come from there. They make their gardens where they find level ground. The creek valleys make very good soil. You see, in Turkey the only . . ."

"Shut up," Miranda said.

"I think you better not speak that way to me," Munci made himself say quietly.

"I said shut up. You forget this is our boat and you are hired out to us, and that is only because your damned government says we have to have a Turkish captain. I know the score. At sea you may be the boss, but we're in port now and we're the owners." She didn't want to be so stern. She told herself it wasn't like her, but it was important. She didn't know why. She just knew. "If we want to hire another sailor what is it to you?"

"He cannot sail. He is farmer."

"Oh. You see, you do know him. Get him. Honestly, Monkey, I don't understand you. If we want to do something for somebody, why can't we? I think you are just selfish. All Turks are. You just want our money for yourselves. Why should a fine boy like that stay out here miles from anywhere when we can give him . . ." she couldn't think what, ". . . everything."

Munci sighed. There was nothing else to do. The woman was made of iron and there was only one way to melt her. He reached for her thigh, remembering to be tender. It shocked her into silence. He moved around her, over her. "I want you very much," he said as one always said to foreign women. He watched her face melt.

"I didn't know." The stubbornness, the sullenness, had gone from her voice. She sounded thick, as if she wanted to spit or swallow and didn't dare.

"I look at you so many times . . ."

"Not here. Jesus, Monkey, not here." Her thighs were already moving. She was wet.

"I go ashore. I make an excuse. It is dark. Just down the cove is a stretch of sand with a big tree. I take a blanket. You wait a little while. Then you come. You will see my cigarette glow."

"Don't take your hand away, I'm coming, oh Jesus, I'm . . ."

He kept his mouth over hers so that no one would hear her until her body went slack under him. He had heard that she was a noisy one. "There is more, more of this . . ." he moved his mouth to whisper to her.

Miranda forgot the body in the garden.

It was easy to get away. "I want to swim," Miranda told them. Nobody paid any attention. Basil was having some long-winded argument with Horst. David and Ariadne didn't turn around. They were leaning with their elbows on the rail, watching for iridescence in the water. Trader was asleep.

Late in the night Munci heard Ariadne turn and turn again in her sleeping bag, trying to do it quietly. He knew she was awake.

He rolled over to her and showed his torch in her face, his fingers over it to mute the light for fear of shocking her. Her eyes were open. Her pupils were pinpoints, like a person who is panicked under water.

"You do not have the right to look like that," he whispered.

She didn't move.

"Ariadne."

"You made love to her."

He would have laughed but he was too polite to wake the others. "I fucked her, not make love."

"Go to sleep, Munci." She turned away from him.

"No." He held her shoulder. "What is the matter with you?"

"Why did you do that?" she asked the dark line of the trees.

"I am a little bit afraid of her. She is one innocent immoral woman. She can make trouble. Aman Allah," he sighed. "She will not even know it."

Ariadne didn't answer him. Her body was stiff under his fingers.

He was furious with her, but he had to whisper, close to her ear. "You people are too serious about sex. It is . . . oh how I can tell you . . . for many reasons. It is a pleasure, not a trial. Hey, you make me damn sick." She was still stiff, but he knew she was listening. "You think you get close to another person only through the bottom. It is the worst illusion. Use your eyes and your ears and use your heart." He shook her shoulder. He tried to see her face. She turned farther out of the dim light. "Listen," he told her back, "to fuck is easy. To make a friend is hard. There is

more love in trusting your friend in one sea dive than
in all the fucks that make a summer. You are a fool."

"But her, that woman . . ." she finally whispered.

"She want to," he said. "Big tourist. I do my job."
She had never heard him so bitter. "Love! It is your
easiest word and it means nothing. You love what stays
in you."

"Who?" She had not understood him.

"No. What. What you are left with. I don't say it
right. What they stand for."

Her shoulder had relaxed. "I cannot tell you why I
had to do what I did. But I can say you would have
told me to do it because you are Ariadne and not some
other." He kissed her hair. "Now go to sleep and don't
be such a fool, canım."

"It is different for a woman." She was trying to
apologize, excuse herself.

He laughed, so quietly she was not sure she heard.
"Hey hey, when a woman think too much about sex I
say she has not enough work to do, not like a man."

She could sense that he was gone, had rolled back
into his sleeping bag and left her awake.

They tramped resolutely among the ruins
of their fourth day. Half in the water the gaping towers
and the fragmented walls guarded the shore. They
pushed their way through mazes of thorn and oleander
to the eastern tip of the island. They could see ahead
on a hill the ruins of what had been the city of Cedrae,
where Cleopatra had made love to Anthony. Miranda
was sure she could hear snakes moving where the
plants hid the walls of the Greek agora.

Horst plowed through ahead of them. "Make noise,"
he called over his shoulder. "The snakes are more
afraid of you than you are of them."

"How does one *know*?" Basil moaned.

Horst stopped to point out the cutting of the ashlar.
"This," he told them, "is six or seven hundred B.C. But
that," he pointed to a higher wall, its windows blank

with sky, "is Byzantine. Once this city would have had four, maybe five thousand people."

He led them up a steep path where the goats had run for centuries, leaving it a narrow flattened road. He and David helped Ariadne over the tumbled stones of the city.

They stood on the highest tier of the open semicircle of the theater. Trees had pushed their way up between the marble seats in a thin grove. It was graceful and quiet after the hard walk in the sun. They could hear the sea breeze in the distance. Beyond the circle where the stage had been, there was the sea, and a mountain far across the bay, a sheer wall of dark rock, like a distant backdrop.

"You remember of course the Agamemnon where the chorus sees the signal lights that were lit from mountain top to mountain top to tell that the Trojan war was over and the king was coming home. That is what they would have done here. I think they would have been starting the play before dawn and lit the signal fires of Agamemnon on that mountain." Horst lectured on.

"What an effect! That's what you Americans would call show business." Basil sighed and scanned the distant sea. He sank down on a stone seat.

"Watch out for scorpions if you sit down," Horst warned him.

Ariadne glanced at Basil, hoping there wouldn't be a quarrel. He was in his most "you Americans" mood, his old tattered Union Jack flying, his captain's cap straight on his bald head to protect him, he said, from the ghastly sun of the afternoon.

Basil was hot and bored and absolutely furious. He was supposed to do the talking. It was what he had promised, and here was this bloody kraut, going on about dates and Dorian plinths and all that unmitigated crap. He felt redundant and it was not a feeling he welcomed. He could, he told himself, have made a better story of it. The absolute balls of saying Cleopatra may not have been there at all. What did he want for proof, her bloody ticket stub? Basil preferred legend to diggings. He felt it to be truer—truth delicate, fact a brute. How could Horst know who had once lived in a place where now there was only this overgrown sinister silence? He could have put Sappho there and made them enjoy it. He tried to remember what he could of Alcaeus, the warrior poet. He would be just right for the place.

Basil was in a great palace agleam with bronze. He threw his bright helmet hanging with horsehair on the low rafter. He unwrapped his brazen greaves. He lay his bronze sword and the shield painted with the octopus against the wall, threw his linen doublet and kilt on a pile on the stone floor. Naked he lay across the couch with the other naked warriors with their tiny waists. He lifted the bronze two-handled cup and drank sea-purple Samian wine. Slave boys in garlands of roses played their lutes and danced.

But when he did lean back on the stone seat, it hurt his bony bottom through his pants and he had to sit up again. He would have ended his lecture with Omar. They say the lion and the lizard keep the courts where tumtetumtetum drank deep. They would have liked it, listened to it, instead of wandering away from Horst's facts that were as hard as the agonizing stone.

"Now this," Basil's arm made a circle over the little island, "is Paradise. No wonder she chose it. Oh sorry." He had hit Miranda in the leg. "For God's sake sit down, or can't you?" he grinned. She inspected the stone slab carefully and then sat on the edge of it. Miranda hated ruins but she didn't dare say so. They frightened her. She wanted for it all to be over, for them to go back to the safety of the ship.

"I tell you I do not think it was her city. Wrong period. As for Paradise, is that not Biblical and therefore wrong in the context?" Horst sounded petulant; no one had been listening to him.

"Paradise, *darling*, is simply the name for a Persian pleasure garden, preferably containing a few wild beasts."

Horst turned his back on him.

"They'll throw rocks at each other next," Miranda whispered to Ariadne, and they both smiled.

"Over there," Horst said, still sulky, "beyond the

isthmus where the *Miranda* is moored, is a white beach. The *legend* is that Cleopatra had the sand brought from Africa. The villagers believe it cures the rheumatism."

At last, as one who watches the sea from a prison window, Basil saw what he had been hoping for. For three days he had dreamed of it, and now rounding the isthmus to cast anchor in the lee of the new wind, the ship with purple sails was running toward the little bay where the *Miranda* lay. As she came through the channel, all sails hoisted, Basil clutched at the nearest arm, it happened to be Miranda's, and pointed to the sea. "Oh God, look! It could be her trireme, purple sails and all!"

"That is yawl-rigged," Horst said. He was cross. "Her ship would have had one sail, velum, triangular probably, with the base attached to the broom. Therefore it was only for steering and not necessarily for the speed, you understand."

"She must have a deeper draft than the *Miranda*. See, she can't come all the way in," Trader pointed out, pleased. His voice made Miranda jump. She had forgotten he was there.

Basil watched and dreamed while the ship came about, the sails were lowered and furled, and she nestled like a sea bird on the water in the cove beyond the *Miranda*. He could see the evening as if he had already constructed it. Laughter would float over the water from the *Miranda*. He knew he could do it. It was, he told himself simply, a gift of his. I am, he confessed silently, a perfect hostess. He could see the boys in their pure white jeans, already bored with each other as all people must be at sea, see them hanging from the shrinks or shrouds or whatever the damned things were called, envious, listening to Basil the Siren, playing her audience across the dark water. He knew when it would happen—when the first stars came and the night was a deeper purple than their sails, and that sweet calm had descended to bless the water after the wind of afternoon that had in the last hour turned the enchanted blue water into fragments of white waves on a nearly black sea.

He was so happy that he began listening to Horst. After all, he told himself, I might bring the others here, and the man does know facts I could build on.

Horst only had Trader standing beside him, but since he was speaking mostly to himself, it didn't matter. He was pointing at his left palm with his right forefinger. "Here," he told Trader, "the island has sunk a little. I think the inner cove was not there at all. You remember we walked across very jagged rock, some volcanic thrust and then sunken floor just below water level. Across there," he pointed east, "there are the tombs—Carian tombs; obviously the Dorians found a Carian town here and fortified it, made the theater and the agora. It was for a while deme to a loose confederation with the city of Rhodes as the center."

"And to think," Trader said, "there's not a damned thing left. Makes you think, doesn't it?"

Horst realized who he was talking to. "Yes, Trader," he said, "it makes you think."

Ariadne climbed up to the highest tier where David sat under one of the thrusting trees and stared across the island.

"You are hardly with us, David. You've said nothing. Is anything the matter?"

"No." He let his hand lie across the back of hers. "I come once a year for the quiet. It heals something in me. I hate to hear them defile this silence with their jabber and their habits and their vodka. All year I listen, and I am good at listening. It is my job, but this time I shut them all out."

"That's why you go off alone to hunt fish."

"Unhunh. Yes. You know, I never admit this any other time, but I love this place and I love this crazy people. You never heard me say that before, did you?" He looked surprised at himself.

"No."

"And they drink and they fuck and I see my dear Munci making a whore of himself and it does not bother me. I have the sea. It is mine. And I sit among the ruins and I hear, do you believe it, the voices of the people in the rubble. This city did not sink quietly to its grave. It was destroyed. We do not even know the name of the conqueror, and I think the people moved to the mainland in what boats they had left after the killing and the fires died down. There is always," he said, "fire.

"And they did not want any more of it. So they were quiet and made their gardens and hid from the world. They had, like me, had enough. There," he smiled at her, "my dearest Ariadne, my innocent American, I have begun to talk and now you cannot stop me." He kissed her cheek, still wet from the climb. "I love you very much, and I love Horst even when he is boring the shit out of me like now. Yes, out here I even let myself love. When we get back into port," he got up and stretched his arms high, and then looked down at her, "it will be a different matter."

Miranda sat alone. Basil had walked down to Horst and was listening and asking questions. She thought it was nice of him. She let herself lie back, feeling in the sun like one of the hidden snakes. Basil had called the island a Paradise. It was not quite peopled to suit her. She watched the oleanders, that was what they were called, the pink flowers she had seen in the woods, wave and turn in the breeze that seemed to have grown stronger. She let her mind drift back, as she had done ever since, to the boy at English Harbor. She had, of course, not mentioned him again to Munci. She knew it was no use, but she had to admit she had been unfair to Munci, accusing him about being a selfish Turk about the money when it was her he had wanted.

That had surprised her. He had never shown it out of deference to Trader, she was sure of that. He seemed to like Trader. But she had taken pleasure in refusing to go with him when they cast anchor the night after that one time. The thought of the boy made her feel pure, virginal. She liked feeling that way. She rolled over in the sun. She had her own plans for the boy. She had decided what she would do, how she would make contact with him. It was a good plan and it pleased her. It had nothing to do with Munci.

The wind did not die down when the night came. It rose screaming over the mountain across the bay, whipped around the outer island and found them at their mooring. It made the boat plunge at its anchor. After the last piercing of light which turned the tower walls on the distant hill into the pink of fire reflection, the sun dived down, leaving them to the black night and the black sea. The stars wheeled above them as if the wind were stirring them. "An illusion from the turning of the boat," Trader said, and said it too many times, while he and Munci and the two sailors moved in the darkness, strengthening the mooring.

"Somebody's calling . . ." Miranda said, and her voice was small.

"No. It is the wind," Munci called as he passed behind them in the dark.

"It sounds like a woman moaning." Ariadne shivered and went below to get a sweater.

They were isolated in blackness under a depth of whirling stars.

The deck lamp was a safe light in the vast darkness. Farther out in the cove they could see the lit portholes of the yacht tossing in the air. The wind fell into sighing as if the dark itself sighed, then gathered strength and screamed again.

"I don't like this place. It's scary," Miranda called across the light to David.

"Let's tell stories," Basil said. He was desperate. He watched the yacht lights move, so far away. A hint of laughter might carry to them, it just might. He couldn't give up.

"It is my turn," David said.

"Are you going to tell a story?" Ariadne touched his arm. His muscles were stiff.

"Yes . . ."

"Once . . ." Basil began.

"Wait." David stood up and steadied himself against the rail. "It is my turn." Only his legs were in the light; his voice came from above them, out of the darkness.

"Once a year it is my turn. All the year I listen. I am the bartender to this shore as Ariadne is its nurse."

Ariadne withdrew, hurt. It had been a private irony between them, not to be thrown out into the night among strangers. Somebody laughed, once, and then stopped because no one else had.

"I listen," David's voice came down over them, "and God knows I have learned to listen well."

Horst was worried. He had seen David like this once before. He knew that he was drunk, which he seldom was. He thought he ought to stop him, but he did not know how.

"This is a love story," the voice went on above them. "Or maybe it is a love story. You will tell me afterwards. Once . . . no, no, no . . . the ruined city. I will take you there. You like ruined cities. It is winter and the river is frozen over. The center of the city is a pile of rubble in the frozen fog. You make your way through it like the underbrush of today, but there are no trees and oleander. This rubble is raw and new, and it smells sweet sometimes, but not now when I take you there because it is winter and the rubble of buildings and bodies is frozen too."

"Where are we?" Miranda forgot she was not to speak.

"We are in . . ." Here David paused. Still, after so many years, something kept him from telling the name of the city. ". . . Rotterdam," he decided.

"When the Germans came my uncle told my mother to dive, become *onderduiker*. When I hear the word for diving now I smile. In the war in Holland it meant we lived anonymous, underground. At first she argued. They were sitting at the round dining-room table under the lamp. He was a communist and she said he spread these rumors because of politics. He said, it is not rumor. The Germans have rounded up all the young Jews of Amsterdam. Later they will round up all the Jews. Jood, he said. You will be killed.

"I will believe it when I hear it on the BBC. She always said that. A thousand times I have heard her. You will go, he told her," David paused again to keep from making a mistake, "to Rotterdam. It was easier

for us. My mother was blond, and I, you see, am blond
too. When your life has once depended on the color of
your hair it is hard to take things seriously again.

"You, my uncle said to me, must learn many new
things. First . . . to keep your mouth shut. I was five
years old and he had to treat me like a grownup. He
must have realized that he looked too stern, because I
remember then that he smiled. It will be a game, a
secret game. Don't you play secret games? Like that. I
remember that.

"And then he said, you must understand, Hayim.
That was the last time I ever heard my Jewish name. I
was surprised that he would know about the games.
You understand, Hayim? You will have a new name,
like mine. David. The only other thing I remember
about that night while we were sitting at the dining-
room table was that I could see their faces in it upside
down. My mother was a good Dutch housekeeper. Oh,
and there were little books and papers on the table. I
tried to play with them and my uncle took them away
from me. I know now they were our new forged iden-
tity and ration books, and, yes, I remember my
mother's voice, I was nearly asleep. But I can't do that,
I am a trained economist, and my uncle laughed at her
for some reason I didn't see then. Later I was being
carried, yes, carried in the dark, wrapped in a blanket,
and driving at night, a big rumble, it must have been a
lorry.

"That is all—a new life. At first I hated it. It wasn't
like our nice house—two little rooms, and I slept in the
corner of the living room where my mother cooked. I
thought it was ugly, and once I said so, and she
slapped me, the only time she ever did. My mother was
a waitress in the café bar. Life became that and I almost forgot the other.

"I was David. I went to school, and my whole
memory is a child's one, the streets I walked along.
Some of the children at the school wore the yellow
star, and when that began my mother drilled me and
drilled me not to notice until all I could see were yellow stars that got dirty when the children played. What
do children do? They live their lives in streets and play

and fight. It was the same with me. And of course the children's questions. My mother told me to say we came from Haarlem and my father was dead in the war, but we hadn't. My mother was divorced and I do not remember my father until after the war. That was hard. She would punish me for lying about other things and she would make me lie about that."

David's voice had stopped. There was only the wind and the creaking of the tackle, and the waves in the dark, lapping the boat, sounds of indifference. They had swung about. The pale distant lights of the other boat were on their starboard side. There was a sound of many feet, as if of a crowd, gathering on the black shore. They felt haunted.

"What's that?" Miranda's voice was sharp with nerves.

"Only the goats," Munci called from the distant prow. "They come down to the shore at night."

"They are black. I saw them. I think this island is cursed," Basil said, and started to say something more but David's voice stopped him.

"Wait. I have not finished. I have not told you about when he came. All at once, I had a father, and life changed. He would hug me and lift me up against the gold braid of his uniform, and some of our neighbors no longer spoke to my mother in the street. He was a big, solid man. He did not say much, but every time he came he would bring my mother a little present, and some toy for me. Once a bird made of colored paper. Inside it was full of balloons and wooden things that clacked when you whirled them. He said it came from South America.

"He could not come often. He was a German sea captain, merchant navy. But I remember only those times when he was there and my mother was happy and the little room, somehow, was bigger and lighter, as rooms are when the people in them are in love with each other. The danger, there was English and then American bombing, and the grayness were farther away at those times, way beyond the windows. He brought . . . he brought something stable and kindly to us. It was all, you understand, underneath the war.

"He also brought food when he came. We needed it very much. There was famine. But I tell you something funny. My mother was in love with him, and I could hear them murmuring to each other at night beyond the shut door to her room, but she would never touch the food he brought, not one drop of it. She let me eat it though. When my uncle came he brought food, and she would eat that. She said it was Dutch.

"I remember many evenings when they were both there, my uncle who was head of the resistance in our district, and the captain, the German, and my mother, still in her waitress uniform. She always kept so clean you could hear her uniform when she moved, a bright, starchy sound. There they would sit underneath the war, the divers, all three *onderduikers* in their different ways, and they would have, believe me, a perfectly ordinary evening together. Often I went to sleep to the sound of their playing cards, and arguing a little, and laughing. They would drink a little schnapps, and I would drift off to sleep feeling safe, hidden by their voices and their big solid backs. Even the sirens would only half wake me.

"Once, though, the captain had left his cap on my mother's dresser. I can see it now. It glittered with gold braid, and it had a little black swastika on its insignia. It was very beautiful. I put it on, and was looking at myself in the mirror. I was being a sea captain, you understand. My uncle came in and saw me, and he jerked the cap from my head so hard he pulled my hair. Don't ever do that again, he said. I began to cry and he took me in his lap, the head of the resistance and he held me like a little baby and kept saying never mind, you just didn't understand, just never do that again.

"One night, it was my eighth birthday, and my uncle brought me a bicycle. I was old enough then to join the fietsers, the bikers, and go to forage for food in the country, and help clog up the roads when the German convoys came through, one of thousands of dumb Dutch fietsers who were too dumb to get out of the way when they came down the road. It wasn't a new bicycle, and I think he had stolen it, but there it sat, and it was mine, and my eyes were still on it when I

began to drift off to sleep. We had not seen the captain
for a long time. But we were used to that. He went to
sea. My mother worried so about him. It was very dangerous. The blockade was very tight. She would tell
herself maybe he went up the Rhine instead of down
into the North Sea.

"I heard a car stop outside. I was completely awake
then. Something in all of us had waited for three years,
listening at night to the few cars that were always German, and we would sigh a little when they went by. I
had heard people, Joden, pulled out of their houses
many times. Once in the apartment right over us, an
old couple who watched over me sometimes when my
mother was late. I had heard the old lady stumbling on
the stairs, and her husband saying be careful, my dear,
be careful of the stairs. Can you imagine that? Be careful of the stairs.

"We listened to the footsteps of men coming up the
stairs, and we prayed that they would go on, higher,
but they didn't. They stopped at our door. My uncle
dived through the bedroom and out of the back window onto the fire escape. My mother grabbed his dirty
plate and shoved it, food and all, under my mattress
and said, keep quiet. Keep your eyes shut! There was a
big knock on our door.

"I had to peep though when they came in. It was the
Gestapo with the groene Politie, green police we called
them. Now you think it was a big brutal Nazi like the
movies. No, it was a boy, not more than eighteen, and
he was embarrassed. Behind him were two or three
Dutch civilians, the kind who sold Joden for seven gul-
der. My mother pretended to be furious, very tough
like a waitress in a cheap café, even her language, but
from where I was I could see that one knee was jerking
and jerking under her skirt.

"What do you mean, Mijnheer van Rijn, she said,
very overpolite to one of the civilians. You know me.
Why do you come here in the night to frighten my little
boy? The sergeant kept shifting his polished boots. I'm
sorry, he told her, but we must search. Search away,
she said and sat down on the bed in front of me. What
is there to find here? The sergeant picked up my

uncle's pipe. He had left it burning on the table. Put
that down, my mother told him. It is mine. I smoke the
rats out with it. God knows there are enough in Holland and she looked very hard at old van Rijn who had
the swollen face of a drunkard.

"They went away finally. They were not going to
round us up as Jews. I think they were looking for my
uncle, and all the time he was outside on the fire escape. It was so foggy that night that when the sergeant
opened the window and looked out he could not see
him.

"Now that is my story. Did the captain inform? I
don't know. We never saw or heard from him again.
Was he dead? You know as well as I. Is it my love
story or my mother's? I know that it was the only time
in my life when I loved as one does when one trusts
the opening of a door. All the places I have been . . .
a search . . . still. I find myself scanning faces. He
would be old now. I will never know."

He had created silence. No one moved. The wind
was dying and the stars slowing down.

"I believe that he did not inform and I believe he
did." David sat down in the light. "Give me a drink,"
he said to Horst. "You know, you son of a bitch, you
look like that sergeant."

"My father was in the Schutzstaffel," Horst told him.
"You are a bastard." He poured rakı into a glass.

"Oh dear," Basil moaned to Ariadne. "This was not
the sort of evening I had in mind."

"You haven't answered my question," David said to
her. "Is it a love story?"

To answer she said, picking her words with great
care, "I understand now, David, why you call us innocent. You see, the American tragedy of people like us
is that it . . . is . . . not tragedy at all. It is some, well
. . ." she stopped, seeing herself, the sinking helix of
her years of disappointment and his, Roger's disappointment acting on disappointment. "I see it," she
said, "in myself. Pathos . . . some isolated child's hope
blown up and made cosmic." She turned her glass in
her hand. "Sexual and alcoholic thumbsucking . . .

bad habits . . . little more. Our vision is too personal, somehow."

She could hear Basil take a breath to speak.

"Shut up, Basil, don't interrupt me," she told him. "This is important. Maybe our griefs change with the fashions," remembering the waking times, the agonies of rejection she had allowed herself to suffer, "late twentieth-century personal suffering. It takes a certain income. People can die of fashions in suffering."

Then she was in the castle tower again, and the Captain of the Gendarmes watched her. "While you were telling that story, I found out that true tragedy has to have waste in it, and impersonal indifference, poverty or war or manipulated hate. We glimpse this, but we don't have the training in toughness to sustain the vision. I don't know," her voice veered away from them as she turned and looked toward the shore. "Anyway, that was what I found out. I have found it out before, and then it comes back, like tonight, and then it fades again. It gets crowded out." She turned back and her voice was stronger. "It costs too much."

"The wind has died, thank God," Munci said, coming back from his watch on the prow. "Now I can have a drink and get some sleep."

They were the first on the pure white beach. It made what the daughter-in-law had to do easier. She drew the boat up on the shore. The sand was so smooth, like tiny tiny pearls, that the boat rolled across it. The weight of the old woman was nothing. She was glad she was strong. Allah Allah, what a disgrace it would be if she were not. She carried the old woman's body over the sand, already warm to her feet. In summer, it held the sun in it through the night.

How much lighter the old woman had got with the years. She set her down carefully in the sand and dug a hole beside her. She scooped up the sand quickly, efficiently, as she prided herself she did everything, not wasting a gesture or a minute. When she had buried the old woman she sat down beside her and got out her hand spindle. She began the carding and the whirling of the spindle; the movement hypnotized time and made it stop.

"Aye," the old woman spoke. "You don't waste a minute, daughter-in-law." She sounded as though she were disappointed.

"There is too much to do." The daughter-in-law was not complaining. She was too good for that. She smiled at the old woman. The warm sand felt good through her shalvar. She adjusted the old woman's kerchief to keep the sun from her face.

"My soul is being squeezed," the old woman complained, bored.

"Never mind." The daughter-in-law wiped sweat from the old woman's eyes. "Soon it will begin."

"You are good, if you do squeeze my soul. I can already feel the pain leave my joints. Aye did you know a great valide came here to be buried in the sand? She said it was to get back her youth. Hee. Not me." She began to cry easily, enjoying it, "I am an old useless lion, good for nothing, seventy years, good for nothing."

Daughter-in-law wiped her eyes again and said nothing. The old woman was leaning her ladder against eighty years but she did not remind her of that. Let her lie about her age. Who believed her anyway?

The spindle whirled, making a spider web in the air.

"Listen," daughter-in-law said, "they are coming."

They sat high on the semicircle of beach as at a theater, watching the clear water where the white sand under it made it a translucent blue. Around the point came their entertainment, in two boats, their motors buzzing. One of them was a rubber boat, like a big mattress in the water, the other a little white dinghy with the word *Miranda* painted on the side.

"What language is that?" the old woman asked.

"I don't know," daughter-in-law told her, "some language the pig-eaters speak."

The old woman's head was still. Only her eyes were alive. She said nothing more. She was too busy watching. The time flew. From the rubber boat she saw

four young boys—ibne—the pretty boys with their
brown bodies, posing for each other, playing in the
water. They wore practically nothing. It was a disgrace.
The old woman grinned, enjoying the show. The other
boat cast anchor a little way out. She wished it were
nearer so she could see better. Two women swam
toward the beach and lay down not far from her. They
were nearly naked, too, the old whores. They were old.
She could tell that from their flapping flesh, not much
yet, but it would come. Nothing could stop it, the life
ebbing out of their arms.

One of them sat up. She seemed to be trying to
make herself smaller than she was. Maybe she was shy
at being out there without her clothes, or maybe she
was trying to be thin. The old woman didn't know and
she didn't care. The other one stretched out over the
sand, owning the space. Her feet were pointed toward
the old woman's head, and she saw that she had corns
and that her big toes were turned in, foreign feet. They
didn't go barefooted enough. Anyway, all foreign
women had ugly feet. She had seen so many from her
vantage point in the sand.

They had not seen her. The old woman couldn't
wait. She coughed, and one of them turned around.
The woman stopped herself from screaming at the old
head, planted like a cabbage in the sand. It grinned
and winked at her. "Merhaba," she called.

"Merhaba," the woman said. She didn't seem to be
able to catch her breath. She leaned down and said
something to the other one, who looked up, startled,
and then lay down again. The woman smiled, or tried
to. It was hard to smile at a head. The old woman
knew it and it always amused her.

"Chok güzel hava," the woman said, motioning
around her.

"Chok güzel hava. Nice weather." The head rolled
in the sand, and the mouth gaped in a wide pink yawn.
She grinned at the woman's back when she turned
away quickly. Güzel, güzel, it was the only word the
gavur knew, pretty, nice, lovely, everything beautiful,
everything nice. Vay apdalsı, how foolish they were.

The old woman looked beyond them, already bored.

She liked better the little drama on the beach. The old man they had brought with them had been drawn over to the boys as she knew he would be. Mashallah but he was thin enough to die, like an old rusty needle. He was cavorting around the pretty boys, trying to do what they did. One of the women, the one lying down, raised up on one elbow and called to him across the water. An insulting name, like germ, sharp, like a mistress calling her servant, but he paid no attention.

No wonder she called him that. He was like a germ, little, jumping about like that, but very very old. There was nothing much of him to sag, not even his tools, the poor little things. He was weathered, hey hey, like something left out in the rain.

Something he said made laughter bounce across the water. The woman sat up and called again.

All in all, it was a fine time for the old woman. The air was perfect, still and clear, the night's rheumatism was being warmed out of her by the sand's heat. There were deli, crazy foreigners to watch. They played like children and wasted time and made the morning pass.

VI
The Demands of August

In August a hot wind of anxiety, the sa-myeli, blew over Ceramos. It grew in the heat and dust among the arid rocks where the flowers had been. It brought with it the brown blown earth, the cracking of the cicadas, drought and rumors, malicious and dangerous.

Ariadne felt it coming and wore an iron bracelet to ward off its curse. Now, two weeks into August, it was unbearable, except when she was swimming. It made small decisions difficult and edged with anger and mistrust. Ariadne found herself having to forgive too much. She had, like the water in the town, run dry. She stayed alone on her terrace, praying for each day to pass without some small crisis brought and laid at her feet.

A dome of racket enclosed Ceramos. The *Miranda*, once the foreign queen among the fishing boats, was now dwarfed and timid, moored among the tall yachts that swung deck to deck in the dry heat of the new yacht liman. The local boats had been forced to moor side by side in the shadow of the castle.

Models from Paris posed like ships' figureheads on the walls of the castle, leaning into the wind against the sky, wrapped in heavy wools and silks that would be shown in the winter issues of the fashion magazines. In the evening, women in well-cut trousers, and caftans from a hundred ports, came ashore from the yachts and clogged the bars. Business was booming. Strangers made instant friends by the exchange of horror stories about the Turkish customs and promised to meet on Greek islands. The Customs Inspector strutted up and down the quay in his new summer suit, flashing with

327

power and happy with the best harvest of bribes that
he had ever had.

For two weeks the town had been without water.
Even Salmakis fountain had run so nearly dry for the
first time in memory that Murat charged fourteen lira
for a gallon of water. He had written the price on the
door of the kahve. Every day he changed it to a higher
price as the spring diminished to a trickle.

It had been two weeks since the voyage to the islands. They had come back to the new city. Ariadne
had noticed it first as they came into port and Trader
and Munci scanned the crowded yacht liman for a
place to moor. As they turned to back into the space
that looked to her too small for them, between two
large yachts of Panama register, Munci whispered,
"Now it is over, canım. We will go ashore and get
fucked up. Hey hey, it always happens."

She had walked up the hill with her canvas bag and
the women had turned their backs, too busy whispering
to see her. She told herself that in that dry invasion of
August she too had become only another foreigner
without a name. It would be better in the fall when the
town was its own size again and the prices went down
and the rain came.

But for now, she had to survive August, sit it out on
her terrace, or up in the foothills where she walked every day after the heat passed. Away in the distance she
could see the white dot on Yazada where the walls of
the new hotel were already rising. She had not seen
any building rise so quickly since she had been in
Ceramos. No tomorrow, no yarin, bosh ver, sorma
gech, no excuses. When Dürüst Osman ordered a thing
begun, it was begun. The walls of officialdom fell. The
money flowed. Part of that, she had heard as one of a
hundred floating rumors bobbing in and out of conversations, came from Lisa's rich father, but she did not
believe it. Jamie Stewart was a rich man, and in all but
one way a fool. That way was money.

She thought later that when the knock came at her
gate, she had expected it all summer. She told herself
from time to time what she would do.

When she saw the child standing there, her little face

no longer like a heart but swelled up like a small pink melon with tears, she hadn't the heart to do it. She simply put her arm around Lisa and guided her to a seat under the shade of the grapevines, and let her cry all huddled up until the tears ran dry. The arc of the love affair had risen and now had fallen to its end. She had seen it so often with the foreign girls, the ecstasy, the isolation in the little houses, and then the final tears that floated them inevitably to her door. This time, waiting for the girl to stop sobbing and unroll herself from the miserable little ball of her body and begin to talk, she thought, I must be careful with her. After all, this one I have known all of her pathetic neglected life.

"I am embarrassed to come here," Lisa muttered through a nose so clogged up that Ariadne handed her her handkerchief. She blew it noisily, like a little girl.

"It's been horrible. I haven't been allowed out of the house for three weeks. Huseyin hasn't even been there." It started her off again in a burst of crying. "He just kept me a prisoner. He wouldn't let me talk to anybody but the maid." Allowing for exaggeration, that would have been the pattern.

"I thought for a while you seemed happy." Ariadne felt lame. She couldn't think of anything else to say.

"I never was," Lisa was convinced. She remembered nothing but black misery. "He wouldn't let me talk to you. He said bad things about you. I told him they were untrue. I told him that."

Why do liars always look straight at you? It gives them away, Ariadne wanted to tell her. She saw at last and felt trapped by not being able to evade it any longer, the refusal of the women to say good morning, the laughter of the men in the kahves. That thing, that unnamed sea-change that she had seen happen to others, the victims of rumor, the jokes like Miranda, the gestures behind Trader's head, had happened to her and she could not believe it. She had loved Ceramos enough to be careful, to respect their prejudices, to go out of her way. The phrase sounded new to her, out of her way, a cul-de-sac of watchfulness.

"What sort of things?" She had to stop the child's bleating, which now had turned itself into a series of

minor complaints that her emphasis made sound like
eastern tortures. It was something now to do with the
little maid Huseyin had insisted on putting in the
house. "I'm sure she was a spy!"

"Stop."

Lisa looked up, wide-eyed with surprise.

"I want to know what the rumors were. You don't
realize that this is important."

Lisa twisted on the wooden seat. "Oh really nothing
serious, I promise you," she said to her sandal.

Ariadne began again, slow with controlled anger and
fear. "You know, of course, that there is a dossier on
every one of us. A rumor in the wrong ears here can set
in motion something that can end with a knock on the
door and the order to leave the country in two hours.
Of course you know it."

Lisa was intent on watching something in the sea.

Ariadne wanted to shake out of her head what she
knew.

"Anything can start it." She knew the girl knew this.
She also knew that during her sensuous and blind tourist summer of playing at love, she had not warned her,
had let the rumor, whatever it was, grow in silence.

"Well," she said, "which was it? Morals? Smuggling
antiquities or gold or drugs? Which little rumor did you
not bother to tell me so I could stop it?" It was all she
could do to keep her hands off the girl's narrow
hunched shoulders. She tried again to make her speak.
"Look here, Lisa. People like you come and go. I live
here. It is, for now, my home. I can't just . . ." It was
no use.

"Goddammit, what was said?" She found that she
had grabbed the girl's shoulder.

"I didn't listen. I said it wasn't true. I said you were
not a lesbian, honestly, and I never saw Munci sleep
here but that one time, and I never saw drugs here,
and you weren't diving for antiquities, it was to keep
your weight down . . ." This last was added in a wail.

It was strange to feel cold and ugly on such a hot
day.

Lisa had finally gotten to her bedrock of complaint.
"He made me write to Jamie and he made me tell him

to invest money in the hotel, and now I want to leave
and he says there is no way to get it back."

Ariadne walked away from her, from her innocence
and her whining and the whole destruction of her. She
leaned on the pole of the arbor and tried to find
coolness in the thick curtain of grape leaves that hung
down against her face.

"You wouldn't understand how serious it is. It's a
hundred thousand dollars," the last word was a cry,
"and everything is ruined and I've had a letter from
Carry. She wants to come here. She's heard how marvelous it is."

Ariadne looked out over her sweet city, the gem she
had polished in her mind, her paradise. She knew then
that it was finished, and that she had made too much
of it. It had reached the ears of the bored, the rich, the
tasters of cities. She could see Carry Stewart, with
whatever lover she was carrying as luggage, arriving at
the port, the new port of ancient Ceramos, a city she
did not know.

"Come," she said, "let's go for a walk. I'm tired of
this."

"It's so hot!" Lisa groaned.

"I want to show you something."

All the way up through the fields be-
yond the ancient city wall, Ariadne walked in a trance.
From time to time Lisa's prattle broke through her
silence, but she ignored it. She wanted peace, and simplicity, to get away, as she had taken to doing every afternoon since long ago in the spring when she had
walked with Kemal up to his village. She sought the
comfort of the unchanged.

Somewhere in the distance beside her Lisa had
thrown off her Thursday sorrows and was confessing to
more important hopes. "I want to find myself," she
said slowly, meaning every word. "I think I want to go
to Florence maybe or to Rome. Have you ever lived in
Florence? Most people have, haven't they? Do people

still go there? I think I'll try Europe for a while. I'll
take some painting courses and learn the language."

She was all future now, shedding Ceramos. She even
skipped along through the dry grass, now that the embarrassing part of her homecoming was over. "I can
persuade Jamie. I always can." The hundred thousand
dollars was forgotten. "I have," she added, "a little
money of my own. I can make it stretch if I'm careful.
It will do me good to . . ."

The child honestly and sincerely thinks I give a goddamn, Ariadne thought once in the blankness of her
walking. She considered that she, too, would have to
think of leaving, that she too had lived there in a kind
of untouched dream of herself as part of it all, protected and secure. She saw the child who had done what
David said she would do, brought trouble carelessly,
herself protected by money, by flight, and finally by not
caring what happened to anyone else.

Ahead of her up the slope of the last field before the
mountain gorge, she saw someone standing like a soldier on watch. She looked away for a second. When
she looked again he was sitting with his back to them
as they trudged up the steep hill along the path between the clumps of camel thorn. Closer, the heat
made the field wave and the cicadas danced in the air.
She saw that it was not a man but a stone figure. Then
the mountain field dipped and it was out of sight. They
walked through a natural amphitheater. She seemed to
be swimming in and out of awareness. She saw when
they climbed up the other side that it was only an isolated stone, one of those black-stained hunched stones
that had tumbled down from the mountain, God knew
when, when, when will I have to leave she nearly said
and then didn't know whether she had spoken or not.

"You don't care what happens to me," Lisa said,
"you aren't even listening."

"That's right, Lisa. I don't care." Ariadne could
hear at last the sound of water from the mountain
creek. They stood on its edge in a little patch of grass,
still nurtured by water mist and startlingly green after
the summer desert. Down below them the water had
carved the rocks into deep ledges where the channel

flowed. Across the gorge they could see the mouth of the cave it came from. The air was cool and sweet, the breath of the mountain.

"We can go to the cave. I do sometimes. It is cool and safe there." Why Ariadne said that she didn't know.

"No." Lisa cringed a little too much. "I'm afraid of caves. I have a Freudian phobia."

"No, you're just like any other child, afraid of the dark," Araidne told her, and went ahead of her back up the path again.

Lisa had so much to put into words that she talked on beyond Ariadne's attention as they climbed the steep camel path up toward the huddle of white buildings that were Eskiköy. Lisa simply couldn't understand Ariadne. She had changed so. Lisa hated to see it after she had practically been adopted by her. She just wasn't dependable anymore. She had come to Ariadne for comfort in her terrible trouble, and Ariadne had hardly listened. She supposed people got that way when they were older, that selfish disinterested look with the eyes glazed over like a sick dog.

Instead of letting her rest and talk about her problems a little before she had to meet Giglio in David's bar, she was instead marching her up the mountain to some deadly village like all the other deadly villages. Oh, Jesus, her feet hurt. Couldn't Ariadne see she was wearing new sandals? Her crotch was itchy and the sweat made a snake down her back. Ariadne was striding ahead like some Girl Scout leader instead of the sweet, warm person she was used to.

Maybe there was something to what Huseyin said when he called her an old lesbian and then he and that awful man, the Captain of the Gendarmes, sat together and talked in Turkish and laughed and told her, not asked her, to bring more raki. God it was a relief to talk to people like Giglio and his friend from Paris who'd been on the barricades in May '68 and told her that she was spoiled but that her ideas were right. They spoke a language she was used to. She had already decided to meet them in Florence or maybe in Paris when she got through the trouble she was in.

"Look, Lisa. It will do you good," Ariadne was interrupting her thoughts. She looked up. Ariadne had stopped in front of one of those trees with a lot of faded dirty rags tied to the branches. There was no doubt about it. Her voice had grown hard. Lisa felt like she was pounding words into her head with a cold hammer. She felt like crying again. She was very hurt. She wondered how long it would take. She had to be back in town. She simply had to. She didn't know why Ariadne had had to go all frozen and ugly. After all she had taken the trouble to warn her when she didn't have to.

The village rose beyond them, terrace on terrace, bleached in the late sun. It was a time when the women sat on the low stone balustrades between the lime-washed columns that rose head high, tapering. "Look, like the little columns at Knossos." Ariadne made Lisa look at them. "They are built the same way they have been built for centuries. I look at them, and at the simple continuity of these people, and it gives me back my sense. They are still hospitable and kind. It is in places like this you will find the old Ottoman manners, the hospitality of Islam. They have such dignity."

All along the wall the women smiled and called, "Hoshgeldiniz," as they passed by. Ariadne seemed to know most of them. She called to several of the women by name. "No evil seems to touch a place like this," she told Lisa over her shoulder.

Under the great plane tree in the center of the village, where the pump and the tea kahve were shaded by its branches, the men sat as if they had grown there, immobile, not speaking to each other. Only their eyes watched as they passed, without seeming to follow them. A woman was coming down the path toward them. She and Ariadne met and kissed in the Turkish way on both cheeks. They began to talk in slow, halting Turkish. They turned and strolled together down to the pump and sat on the bench beside it. The marble basin of the pump was carved with bulls' heads.

"I have told Meral you are my friend," Ariadne said to Lisa. "She asks why your mother let you go with a bad man. You see, they know everything, these people. I told her that you were fooled by him, that you were a foreigner and did not know better." Behind Ariadne's shoulder the woman smiled and nodded as if she understood. "They do not judge you. We are unimportant to them. This woman's son is my friend. He is the little mute boy, Kemal. She thinks it is because of the büyü, the curse, or that someone has but the evil eye on him. The ignorance here is as old and deep as that well. Look at it, Lisa. Horst says it was carved about four hundred B.C." The woman neodded and smiled again. Ariadne spoke in answer to some question. They got up, and Ariadne kissed her goodbye.

As she walked down the hill, letting Lisa follow, she said, "I go there for peace in the summer. A place where the troubles are real and money can't solve them. Meral is worried about her older son. He is in the medical school in Istanbul, but she has not heard from him in a long time. She thinks he has forgotten them because he has gone away to be educated and rich. It is the same thing with her."

She said nothing then for so long that Lisa thought she had forgotten her. Somehow though, when she did finally speak, Lisa thought she had forgiven her, but she still didn't know quite why.

"Oh, you can't help yourself, Lisa," she said. "If you need help, or a place, you know I am here."

When they got to the turning to Ariadne's street, Lisa was so late she had to shout goodbye over her shoulder, and run through the crowds all the way to David's bar.

Miranda couldn't find anybody. She had wandered around looking through half the hot afternoon. Finally when it was time for people to start going to David's bar after swimming, she saw Basil sitting with his new friends. She didn't really want to, but she stopped at his table. "Basil?" She had to speak for him to look up.

"Yes?" He didn't ask her to sit down.

She didn't know what to say. "Have you seen Trader?" She didn't mean that. The hot day was playing on her nerves. She couldn't find the flute player. She couldn't find Huseyin, who had promised her faithfully that he would see about hiring the boy at English Harbor. He had done nothing. They never did anything. Yarin, domani, mañana, tomorrow—the foreign refrain. She was fed up with it all. She thought that tomorrow she would begin to persuade Trader to leave. She was hardly aware that she was still standing by the table.

"He's not here," Basil said.

"Who?"

"Trader, my dear. Your . . . what you Americans call your ball and chain."

She saw the flute player, sitting alone in the corner. He smiled. No one had smiled at her all day. She ran over and sat down at his table.

Basil said to his friends, loudly enough for her to hear him, "Really, I must do something about them. They are quite pathetic. I befriended them and showed them around a bit and now they think they own me." They went back to planning the cruise on the ship with purple sails. "We ought to go to Crete. I know all about Knossos, if you care about that sort of thing."

Miranda's chair had fallen with a crash. She was standing over Basil again. "Have you also told them that we fed you and bought your drink for three months?" She wanted to scream at him but the words choked in her throat.

"My dear, I earned every penny," he told the others without bothering to look at her.

"Really, I must do something to protect myself. You can see that," he said after she had run out into the street. He saw the flute player follow her. "Scenes in bars, my dears. Not my sort of thing." Their heads went back to the Admiralty charts that were spread across the table, their glasses, water, and raki bottles set at the corners so the wind wouldn't lift it while they studied them.

"Inevitable," Basil sighed when he saw Trader in the doorway.

"She's gone to the boat," he called out before Trader had a chance to pull up a chair and bore them all.

"Oh?" He was still coming closer.

"She's looking for you. She wants to see you."

"Oh." Trader left the bar.

"You evil son of a bitch," David said when Basil went to the bar for another bottle of rakı.

"Oh that? Let her look after herself. You *can't* believe he doesn't *know*, David."

Trader didn't like the town or the crowds. He dodged his way through them, apologizing to people who didn't even look around when they bumped into him. He stopped at the bakal and slowly bought some food. He hoped that Miranda would let them eat on board, and be quiet for the evening. He told himself that he had to find a way to persuade her, finally, to leave. There were too many strangers and Trader let himself resent them. He wanted to find a small island where they could sit out the month until people became friendly again the way they had been before. The fishermen and sponge divers who had let him sit with them and drink were all gone to summer jobs at sea, and when they were ashore they were too busy to speak. Miranda was unhappy and he thought he knew why. There had been some quarrel with Basil that he couldn't understand and although Basil wasn't his kind of man, not at all, he didn't like to see his old girl hurt. He and Miranda, he had to admit, had been left high and dry.

By the time he got to the boat he had convinced himself that that was, of course, why Miranda was looking for him. He would let her tell him before he told her that she, too, wanted to find their island, the place where they could be happy alone until the fall was gentler and easier to live in.

He saw the flag up, their own sign that they had worked out together when one or the other of them wanted to be alone on the boat. He never used it, but

she did. She had explained so often that in the small
confines of the *Miranda* there were times when a person had to have it to themselves. He didn't know what
to do. Basil had told him that she wanted him, and the
flag was up. He lingered on the dock by the gangplank.
He could feel the margarine getting soft in the string
bag. He was worried about the meat. She told him he
worried too much about the meat. He decided that she
had forgotten to put the flag down.

He saw them through the door of her cabin. She
looked like someone he had never seen before. The
body that he had cared for, the proud muscles that he
had not been allowed to touch for so long, lay flattened
on the bunk. When the man rose out of her to plunge
again, he saw that she had much less pubic hair than
he had remembered. The man's eyes were closed as if
he didn't want to look at her, just plunge in and out.
She was giving orders, that strange woman. "Slow. Go
slower, yavash yavash," and obediently the plunging
slowed. The man came out too far and both their fingers fumbled. "Damn," he heard her say. He did not
look at the woman's face. "Shimdi. Shimdi. Now," she
yelled and they pumped faster and faster. Trader could
feel his own penis grow hard and he was ashamed.
They had gone wild in there, both groaning and
flailing. He turned away, calmer than he had ever been
in his life.

Poor girl. She was wrong. It was only that she was
wrong. He went quietly about what he had to do, careful and methodical. He had never felt so right about
things. He was surprised at himself. He didn't feel hurt,
just cold, and secure in what he had to do. He hung his
regulator around his neck. He found his weight belt
and attached more weights. He lowered his tanks over
the side and got into the dinghy. Just as he started the
motor he remembered that he had forgotten to put the
meat in the ice chest.

Miranda heard the spark and then the roar of the
outboard. She pushed the flute player off. "Git. Git,"
she said. "Git," she screamed at him. She was fumbling
with her shirt and jeans. She didn't bother to look at

him as he picked up money from the dressing table and put it in his trouser pocket.

She ran out on deck. The dinghy was already half-way across the inner harbor. She called and called, knowing he would not hear her.

Trader took the boat out through the outer harbor and steered it into the heavy sea and the high wind. He was afraid it would swamp before he got to the sunken island. It was his favorite dive. Fishing boats making for the harbor motioned him to turn around. He waved back, his friendly wave, by habit, and kept the boat into the wind.

At the sunken island he let the anchor go. It caught for long enough on one of the sunken columns on the crest of the island, eight meters below the water surface, for him to get into his tanks and fasten the weights. When he felt the boat and sank to the island, he saw that the anchor was already dragging across the sea moss. It didn't matter.

He thought, how beautiful it is. It doesn't change. It never changes. Who would have thought I would ever have a chance to see all this? Well, you never can tell, can you? He felt peaceful. Everything was in order. His insurance was paid up. He didn't owe anybody a damned thing, not a cent. He no longer felt guilty at having lied to Miranda about the house in Plainfield. He hadn't sold it. He had only rented it. He had thought that someday they would need a place to go back to.

He crawled along the island crest to where the steep side plunged down over seventy meters, deeper than he had ever gone. He let himself go over. He passed where the octopus hid, the hole where he had seen the moray eel, the two jutting rocks where the grouper hid that no one had managed to shoot. He made a slow descent so he wouldn't miss anything. His sneakers felt strange and he wished for a minute that he had bothered with his flippers.

He saw himself, tired and calm, but the tiredness and the calmness were not his own. No. He felt efficient. That was it, the old feeling. He was aware that he was not really thinking of Miranda at all, except in fragments, a face of thirty years before, as the dead are recalled. He went on letting himself sink through the lovely blue water, now darkening by evening and depth into bluer and bluer twilight. The only movement was the veil of his air bubbles. He turned away from them; he wanted to see everything. Far above him he could see the faint smudge of the sea ceiling where the meltem chopped it into waves, but where he was, all around him there was that sweet stillness like—oh nothing—nothing but itself. It occurred to him that he had never imagined things. He kept himself from doing it now.

His feet touched the sand floor. He looked around, pleased, knee-deep in the familiar eel grass of the nearly dark sea meadow. He saw a murex. He didn't pick it up. He was surprised at this. Miranda collected them. She called them Aphrodite shells. He turned around again slowly, a full turn, blue sea-space to rock wall to blue sea-space again. He unstrapped his tank, spat the regulator out of his mouth and unbuckled his weights. He felt one second of black panic. Then he dropped his gear.

The men on the fishing boat that had turned about to follow him spotted his boat adrift. It wasn't until they were nearly to the sunken island that they saw the body shoot up out of the sea like a flying fish.

The women said Mashallah, and August always brings death. It is a bad month. This will not be the last. They left bowls of yogurt and little cakes on the deck of the *Miranda*. It was as if Miranda herself had no name, no past. She was suffering a death. She was a new widow and they knew how to treat her. "Bashınız sağ olsun, health to your head," they said when they saw her sitting on the deck, not looking like the same woman anymore.

For a week she sat there like a stone, after they had taken her man to Izmir in the back of the truck, while she and her friends rode ahead of it in the town taxi.

The last view of him that anybody saw was the procession disappearing up the Izmir road, with the wooden box bouncing against the slat sides of the Ford pickup truck when it hit the bump at the road's turn. Trader lay inside it in his gray suit and his best shirt with the cuff links he had been given by the Lions Club.

Miranda wouldn't move away from the afterdeck or keep anything clean or try to eat. "Try to eat something," Ariadne kept saying until she hated the sound of the words. She fell into the formal movement of the death, cleaned the boat, opened the portholes, washed the linen. The boat shone when she finished, and then she started over again.

Miranda wouldn't come and stay at her house. She said that people would rob the boat while she was gone. Ariadne got tired of telling her she was wrong about that. She moved down with her, and washed and cooked and poured drinks for Horst and David when they turned up, and thanked the women when they brought their covered dishes.

Ariadne thought she was making new decisions about what to do, not knowing that the women smiled because she was doing exactly what they would do, moving into the house and doing all the things that women do until the dailiness returned to the lost mind and the madness of grief had passed. There were only two times they served each other in this way, at the wedding and at the funeral, both times recognized as ecstatic in their way, and in both cases they left when the dailiness returned to the woman's eyes.

It was Ariadne who found the insurance and the house deed and the careful list: banker, lawyer, the addresses of Miranda's mother, Trader's brother, and a broker in Athens who would sell the *Miranda*, "should for any reason the need arise," he had written beside the name. She put them in Miranda's lap.

Miranda turned them over and over in her hands. "He would do that. He would. Everything," she said, and began at last to cry. One of the women saw her start, and told the others and they stood in a semicircle just beyond being noticed and nodded to each other

that she would be all right now. The tears washed
away the grief madness. The next stage of mourning
had begun for them.

Miranda stumbled down into the cabin
and said to Ariadne, "It is time."

"For what?" Ariadne was making menemen, enough
for Horst and David and Munci if he turned up.

"To give the things away."

Trader as a person faded away. He became a series
of decisions, of objects that now spread over the town,
his neat tea shirts over the chests of a dozen boys, his
trousers to four old men, and his captain's cap to Kemal, who put it on solemnly and wore it for a few days
and then lost it. Miranda gave his electric shaver to
Munci. "He would want you to have that," she said,
and she sounded shy.

She stood looking at his toothbrush as if she didn't
know what it was, until Ariadne took it out of her
hand and dropped it in the trash. When she set the
trash bin on the quay to take it to the dump, she saw
one of the children run off with the toothbrush and a
pair of underpants too worn, she had decided, to give
away.

Gradually the woman Miranda had been or that she
would become, Ariadne didn't know which, began to
emerge from the dead shell of her week of mourning, if
that's what it had been. Was that what mourning
was—not grief, but a dead stunned shell without a person until the human emerged to survive, new somehow
and vulnerable, from the chrysalis? The woman who
was born wore clothes that Ariadne had never seen her
in before, dredged up from some deep safety cache of
her cabin, a sprigged blouse with a round collar, a
wash-and-wear skirt of blue denim that Ariadne
remembered from a *New Yorker* ad.

"It's too big for me," Miranda said, surprised,
watching herself in the mirror. Her dressing table was
as clean as if Trader had arranged it. She began to
wash her hairbrush every morning, and she kept a neat

box of Kleenex she had found in his locker set square below the mirror. The souvenirs were gone. When she had gotten rid of them, Ariadne didn't know. "We must," she kept saying, "keep everything shipshape."

Survival flowered in a series of practical considerations. She went to the Customs herself, although she took Munci to interpret for her. She hired him to sail the *Miranda* to Piraeus for her. "I will put her up for sale there," she said as if she had thought of it herself. "I'll get a better price and there is less trouble with the exchange," she told Ariadne. "The things you have to think of," she said with the faint resentment of the widow. "I have never had to do anything like this in my life."

On the night before she left she served them drinks, with meze she had learned to make in Turkey, and ice broken into the ice bucket. It was all very clean and formal. They sat on the deck while the time stretched and the evening came down over the harbor, not knowing what to say.

"I will come back," she said once, "for a visit. It was the place where Trader was happiest. I'll never forget that. I'll bring a friend." In the silences she dropped her plans. "I will go to my mother for a while," and then, "I will give notice to the people in our house. I'm sure they will understand." She mentioned Trader often. "He would like me to do that," or, "He would approve." He had entered her mind as a mentor, and she kept him there where she needed him.

In the last night, Ariadne woke and heard her sobbing, a sound monotonous and dry. In the morning she said as she stirred her Nescafé, "I just don't know what to do. I nearly have my master's. I could take that up again." She spoke as if she had put it down once like a half-knitted sweater.

When Ariadne asked her what she would study, she said, "I was in psych."

Ariadne could see her, coming back to a Ceramos that was strange to the woman she had become. She would come with a friend who looked like her. They would shop obsessively at the tourist shops, compare the bright baubles, and talk about cousins who would

like them. Trader's death would become, not a tragedy,
but a loss, conventional and inconvenient. She would
be a widow, fully fledged.

The woman they waved goodbye to as Munci slid
the *Miranda* out of its berth sat like a small passenger
in the stern of her own boat, already slightly dumpy in
her Braemar cardigan. She said when she put it on that
she had always disliked the channel wind. They stood,
letting her see them, until the boat disappeared beyond
the breakwater.

They wandered away through a crowd of tourists
who had come ashore from a large cruise ship. All
over the pavement of the quay the carpets of the souvenir sellers lay spread, piled with brass hookahs,
wooden camels, and embroidery.

Kachakchı Attila, the donkey driver, slapped the two
tourist camels behind their knees as they knelt and rose
and knelt again in their bright wedding saddles, raising
squealing tourists in the air to have their photographs
taken by each other. Over the bargaining, which here
and there had broken out into quarreling, the local
small boat owners called "Yazada, Yazada," to seduce
customers out to sea for the short voyage to the summer island. All around the edges of the crowd, the
people of Ceramos sat at faded wooden tables, laughing at the tourists' clothes and the clever bargaining.
Ariadne stopped in the middle of the crowd. "Goddammit," she said, "it ought to matter more."

"What are you going to do today?" David asked her.

"I don't know," she said, conscious that her job was
over. Everything was cleared away. The people she
had not much cared about were gone. Basil had left the
morning after Trader's death. He had taken his file
boxes and his trunk aboard the ship with the purple
sails to the next stop, the next betrayal, the next abandonment on the next island. It had been too early in the
morning to say goodbye.

When Munci came back into port three days later, a passenger with the new tourists who lined the ferry boat railings and stared up at the castle, the Captain of the Gendarmes was waiting for him. They walked up the quay together, the Captain's hand on Munci's arm, through the crowd of boys in their flared pants and their handmade sandals, who scanned the new crop of foreign girls and grinned at each other.

People who noticed them read their closeness and the way they were joking with each other as some strange new friendship. As they passed along they left arguments behind them. Munci's detractors said he had become a police spy because his business was bad. His defenders said he had been caught smuggling. The Captain of the Gendarmes nodded and smiled at men who were afraid not to nod and smile back.

"You think I bring two packs of cigarettes back on the ferry boat?" Munci was trying to joke information out of him. His stomach was cold with fear.

"Aheste beste, take it easy," the Captain said, enjoying himself. "You will find out soon enough." He believed in making people wait. It made interrogation easier, and he knew he had to be a little more diplomatic than he liked with Munci, whose father was important. "Gel, gel, come," he said, his hand on Munci's back. "You will know soon enough."

At the Gendarmerie he gave Munci coffee and passed his cigarettes across the desk. "How was it in Greece?" he asked as if he didn't care.

"Oh, the same. Full of Germans." Munci was very polite. "I think we get some more good business."

The Captain smiled. He knew that Munci had been to the bank again to borrow money now that the diving trips had stopped and he had his men to pay. "Let's see. You have Orhan from the village working for you. He is a good man," he said, blowing smoke at the ceiling.

"Yes. A good man." Munci's smoke met the Cap-

tain's. They watched it whirl in the evening breeze
through the open window.

"He has a son."

Munci's casualness was as elaborate as the smoke
swirls and as slow. "Oh, yes, poor man. His son is af-
flicted, but you know that. The mute one. He is a
smart boy and people do not know that. I think I will
train him for a sailor."

"Like you did the other?"

"Oh, many others. I am . . ."

"The older brother."

"Oh, him. He was a good sailor, but then he went
away to the University to be a doctor."

All of this was so familiar to them both that they
waited to get through it.

"I heard that he is back," the Captain said.

Munci had to listen hard for the tone that meant
knowledge, or the tone that was just a shot at the back
of his head.

"No." He leaned forward and took a long time putting ash into the ashtray. He was glad to see that his
hand was steady. "He will not come back for a long
time. He is in the medical school and I think he must
always find work in the holidays."

"Oh, you did not know then?" The Captain was
very surprised. His eyebrows rose. "He was expelled
from the medical school."

"I am sorry to hear that. It will hurt his mother. After all the trouble he took to prepare, maybe he did not
study enough. You know these village boys when they
go first to the city . . ."

"Perhaps. I think so." Around and around the
smoke whirled. The ashtray was getting full. The Captain called to a Gendarme to empty it. They waited
without speaking until he had brought it back and shut
the door deliberately behind him.

The Captain seemed to have forgotten what he had
been saying. He changed the subject. "The foreign
woman you took to Greece . . . Aye, that was a sad
thing, for a man to die so far from home . . . I think
there would have been good jobs on that boat. She
talked to Huseyin Bey about a crew."

Munci took a longer drag of his cigarette. They leaned forward together and put their cigarettes out side by side in the clean ashtray.

"Now you must smoke mine." Munci grinned and pulled out the Dunhills he had bought in Piraeus. They laughed together. "Here, take the rest. I have more, two, three packs." He left the box on the desk.

"Your uncle, the old man at English Harbor. She told Huseyin Bey there was a boy there she would like to hire. Did you know he has a boy there?"

"No." Munci leaned back, trying to recall if he had an uncle at English Harbor. "Oh, I know the old man. He has no one there. He is a tariki dünya, a hermit, and he is also a hadji. A long time ago he went to jail. He found Allah in his soul. He said there was nothing else to do in jail.

"When he came out he went to Mecca, two or three times. He is very holy. I will take you there. Maybe you would like to go in my boat. We will take your wife and your sons . . . they would like to sleep on the boat."

"You are so kind." The Captain waved his hands in the air. "But I think you are not allowed to take your boat that far with the compressor aboard. Besides, it is the tourist season. How would you have the time?"

"I would make time for my friend. And the compressor. I am taking it off. It is no problem."

"Perhaps later on. I will tell my wife of your kindness. She is lonely here because of my job, you understand; she will be pleased."

He offered Munci one of the Dunhills from his new pack.

"I wonder who it was she meant when she talked to Huseyin Bey," the Captain mused. "She probably meant a boy someplace else. They get things wrong. They do not bother to learn our language." The Captain launched into his series of complaints about the foreigners.

"Tabiî. Tabiî," Munci said every time he paused, until it was dark outside.

But what about love?" Lisa blinked.
"Love is the most important . . . you know, between
people and everything."

"Non. The least. You are a silly bitch. How is it?
Bruta."

"Oh shut your mouth Giglio. What is more, eh?
Amour." His friend leaned around her hair to tell him
this.

"Shit." Giglio could feel tears mingled with the taste
of aniseed from the rakı in his mouth. "Revolution?"
He put his arm around Lisa. "It is not that I don't
love."

The sound of all their words had become one roar of
drink and money to keep him through the winter.
David could wait. He was doing that now. A sense of
waiting filled his body. He shut his ears to them all and
listened only to the sound of his own waiting. He had
seen the circle completed and broken once again.

He smiled his listening smile at a man in a captain's
cap, who was telling him something, part of the roar,
his arms stretched out straight in front of him on the
bar, his wife plucking at his sleeve. Her voice was a soprano counterpoint to his story, whatever it was.
"George, please. Please George. Jesus, I don't want to
see the Aegean with him drunk all the time." She
turned to a young Italian boy on her other side. "He's
been drunk ever since we left Piraeus. I thought it
would be different here."

Three more weeks to go, and they would be cleared
out and forgotten. David let Ariadne and Horst come
into the sound of his waiting. He knew they were ready
to go, too, before they knew it themselves, and it made
him sad. He had read the signs.

No room for them in the bars, the discotheques, the
shops owned by firms from Istanbul or Ankara, the
new expensive food shops and the restaurants with
their fine modern lighting that went out with all the
rest when the power failed. What had Ariadne called

it? A midway. He liked that—midway between spring
and fall and the counting up.

"I am going to leave. I have wasted my whole summer waiting. The days passed and I didn't know. How
could I do that?" For a second he thought it was still
the man in the captain's cap talking and then he heard
Horst. His face hung in the crowded air, one line back
from the bar. David motioned him to the serving hatch
at the end of the bar.

"Ağabey, I have had enough. Now my Zeiss binoculars have been commandeered. Foreigners are not allowed strong binoculars. It is the new law," he grinned,
"made up today and for today because someone
wanted my binoculars. Bosh ver. I am not even angry
so I know that it is time to leave."

"The permission? The mountain?"

"The permission? The permission will not come."

David listened without argument. They were alone
at the end of the bar, under the crowd roar.

"I have a feeling. All the things that have happened
to me this summer make a pattern. I have lost my
mountain."

"When you see too much a pattern, that is
paranoia," David told him.

Horst laughed. The people near them thought they
were joking together. They looked like it. "Who needs
paranoia here? That is for people who want to play.
Here it is real."

David looked around. No one seemed interested after the laugh. He saw only backs of heads.

"I have a feeling."

"Yes. I know." It had come, then. They were so
used to the grapevine, the life under words, the sense
of things happening or going to happen, like animals.
David knew the sense. It was a new language, or an
old language picked up and learned again, forgotten for
a long time from his childhood.

"I will go back and teach this winter at the University of Minnesota." Horst said this too loudly.

"Hey boy, how do you know Minnesota?" the man
in the captain's cap called over the bar.

Horst lowered his voice again. "It's no use, David. I know."

Through the tangles of her hair Lisa watched Giglio as he smiled. "I am glad you have decided," he said. "We will find you a place to live."

"I don't have much money," she said. It made her sad to think that.

"No matter. We will find you a cheap place."

"It's the funniest thing," she said, and her breath blew her hair, "when I first came here I thought I was going to stay forever. I just had this real thing. I related to it. But, you know, there's nothing really here. Nobody's alive. Nothing happens. I have been so unhappy," she confided to Giglio.

It was danger, pure, dark danger, undersea danger of watchers outside the periphery of light. Munci did not look behind him. He did not dare. He walked casually toward the tea kahve where the old men sat. He was slow. He searched among the strange faces to find familiar ones to stop and pass a few minutes of the evening with. He was conscious of his habits, using them carefully. He knew he was being watched. He dared not even frown. He remembered to strut, be Munci, own the street a little but not too much. That would be elaborate. It would be noticed. His chest was full of fear. He passed Ariadne in the crowd and pretended not to notice her or hear her when she called out. He could not speak to her, not to a foreigner.

The police spy who was following him saw her turn, surprised, hurt, and stare after Munci. He filed this in his mind to tell the Captain of the Gendarmes. "Any deviation of behavior," he had ordered him. "Watch for that."

Munci turned into the old fisherman's kahve and sat facing the door, quickly enough to see the police spy come in. He almost smiled. It was Demir, one the stupidest of them, not a stranger he would have to watch, but he knew better than to let himself relax.

After the noise of the street, it was quiet in the kahve where the foreigners did not come. Munci listened to it, the quietness of men with no sound of women's voices. There was only a low murmur, and the click of tavla chips and dice. Far in a corner a man told a story to low laughter.

Munci sat alone, waiting for someone to sit down with him, trusting only chance to tell him what to do. A hand set a glass of tea down in front of him. He stared at it. Allah, that woman! He did not let himself dwell on her. She was gone and she had done her harm and he did not welcome her in his mind.

He tried to begin to sort out what he had to do—somehow, first, get a message to Timur. His mind began to lift out of fear into planning. Kurnaz, hile, all the cunning, all the tricks; he waited for them to come to him. He knew he had to think slowly because there was so little time. He dared not go himself. He, or anyone he sent, would be watched. He prayed a little and made his will patient so that when Hizir came he would recognize him.

He smiled a little, too; Hizir, the stranger who always came to help in time of trouble, had not been in his mind since he was a child and believed such things. Hizir has many faces, you have to learn to recognize him, his mother had told him. Ariadne had said once that you met him twelve times in your life, only twelve, only she said he was a teacher. He knew the fear was making his mind flutter around memories. So he sat for a long time, until he was in a flat calm, waiting for Hizir, and drinking tea. He felt peace begin in him. It was the only place in Ceramos in summer where he could hear men breathe.

He was suddenly struck with a message, but he kept himself from reacting to the thought. Of course, Hizir would not come to him in the tea kahve, not with Demir there, watching him with his boiled eyes, which kept closing because he was so bored with his job. I must put this silliness about Hizir out of my mind, Munci told himself. There is not room for that. Death can come, he added to remind himself, through a long chain of stupidities.

He got up very slowly, just late-night-tired slow, paid
for his tea, talked to one of his cousins, and walked out
of the kahve. He strolled toward home, conscious of
Demir, sat down for a long time on a bench beyond the
quay lights, to watch the moon throw wriggling snakes
of light into the water. He wondered who it was who
would be at his door, what face Hizir would have. He
could almost feel him in the darkness, waiting with the
answer. When he finally turned toward his gate, he let
himself look around. Demir had gone home for the
night.

There was no one at his door. He waited until he
knew no one would come. In the night, watching and
listening, he threw away a hundred plans. When his
waiting drifted toward dreams with himself as hero, he
woke himself with the sleep jerk of his head. With the
first dawn, when the black thread could be distin-
guished from the white thread, the knock that he had
waited for all night came, as part of him had known it
would, the smuggler's tap. He knew it was Hizir before
he opened the door. He nearly laughed aloud.

Hizir had the face of old Kachakchı Attila, the donkey driver, a man of instinct who knew when to be in
Ceramos and when to leave. How could Hizir look so
disreputable? He was a pile of dirty clothes. His shalvar hung down between his legs. He had taken the
scarf off the stump of his arm, and it was shriveled and
dirty. He told the tourists he had blown off his hand
with dynamite, fishing illegally, but he was an old man,
and everyone in Ceramos knew that it had been lopped
off in the Sultan's time for thievery, but they did not
tell strangers about that. It was none of their business.
His only comment, he was young then, had been,
"How wise of Allah to give a man two hands, one for
the law and one to do his job."

"I will see uncle. You send him some English cigarettes?" he said while Munci made coffee.

"Tamam. Did anyone see you come here?"

"Son of a donkey! What do you think I am?" The
old man slurped his coffee, rolling it around his gums.

"You take cigarettes, and you take a message."
Munci wrote the message. It was safe with Attila. He

could not read. Out of politeness, and to keep him from getting curious enough to have someone read it to him, Munci read it to him, word for word. "Please prepare for three tourist boats for next Thursday and let Attila know what supplies you will need. I will come in the first boat."

It was a beautiful morning in the first dawn. The new Zeiss binoculars were beautiful. The sea was beautiful. The Captain of the Gendarmes was happy. He had waited so long, while lesser men shot down the pigeons, and he had to put the crosses over the faces on the poster in his office, each cross giving credit to another man. This was not one of the pictured pigeons, he had to admit that, but he was on the list that the Captain kept in his drawer and studied like a love letter.

How long it had taken, and by what slim chance . . . he did not like to think of it. It was only when he had finally, out of despair, shown the list to Huseyin that a name had been recognized, a local name. He hadn't wanted Huseyin's help. He had wanted the whole thing to be his own, if it ever happened.

He almost thought of it as his own anyway, his own time, his own watchfulness, his own passion, and now the next step; suddenly he wanted to sing. There in the circle of his binoculars, so near he could not believe he was so far away, the old thief Attila was framed, a tiny clear picture, moving slowly out of Munci's street on his donkey and turning west. The Captain put the binoculars back in their case with great care so that he would not scratch the glass, and stepped back from the oriel high on the castle wall.

There is no time. All this has been done too often. Step by step through the beginning of the day, between rock and sun, Attila's shadow is long. It follows him east, along the north shore of the gulf. It

twists and flows over the rocky camel trail. His own
breathing and sighing, and the animal's, and the click
of stones disturbed by the donkey's feet are the only
interruption to the silence. He is not thinking. He
smokes. He exists in the moment as he has for fifty of
his seventy years since he came down from the Taurus
Mountains after the Greeks left, along this same path
or another like it, around the mountain passes.

By the calculations of life, accident, and starvation
in drought times, he has had seven donkeys between
his legs and only one he was in love with and never
beat. He can be tracked only by the turned stones, and
those could have been turned by goats moving the
same way, existent and mindless. This is why he is
such a good smuggler. Who can follow him? He is too
slow.

He has already forgotten the cigarettes and the note
in his shalvar, but he will remember them when the
restful antprogress stops. For now he is a cheteji, out-
lawed, alone. It does not matter. He wears the coat
given to him at the death of his father-in-law thirty
years before over an old sweat shirt with the word
HARVARD in faint brackish letters across the front. He
has no idea what the word means. The sweat shirt is a
good one. He is old enough to need the coat in the
growing dry hell-heat of the morning, but he does not
know that he has changed. He only senses that the
days are cooler than when he was young.

He moves beyond any reactions, black against the
gray and dun pathways through the camel thorn and
mountain desert, past the rock piles of ancient villages,
past the white domes of water cisterns, past the dry
bones of Greek churches where the goats and the
sheep leave their dung, past glimpses, over and over, of
the blue sea.

He is in a sweet pine forest. He crosses a stream. He
brushes past the lovely pink poison oleanders. It all
moves past him. Tangerine groves move past him. The
second and then the third of the alluvial valleys move
under the donkey's feet. Green fingers of valleys run
down from the mountain rock to touch the sea, each
valley worth an old war.

He sings a little song. The donkey slips into keeping time, or he is keeping time with the donkey. It doesn't matter. The sun is reaching its triumph. His shadow disappears under the donkey's belly. It is noon.

He stops to pray. First, he glances around for scorpions, then in the shadow of a rock he spreads the threadbare prayer rug which his mother wove. He hardly remembers her. She exists in his mind, not as word memory, but as a vague picture. He has been a father long ago but that is finished and all of them are dead. He killed men and women in the old wars. He liked the war, and would like it if there were another before he dies. It is all pictures, faded, unjudged or contemplated. He has been in prison. He liked that too. He bragged. In those days there was a lot to brag about. He has been a brave man, sheytanlik, only caught once—a donkey but not a son of a donkey.

He is where he intended to be, at the edge of the village at the head of the gulf. He goes in to the kahve and eats his cheese and olives and bread from an old plastic bag. It is time for a little doze.

When the sun is where he wants it to be, he rides west on the south side of the gulf. The sun is in front of him again. His shadow follows him. It lengthens toward the evening.

The Captain of the Gendarmes waited all morning for the engine of the Gendarme boat to be fixed. Waiting did not bother him. Why should it, he told himself. There is time. He savored it. He was a hunter and understood the necessity for slowness with his whole self. He had read the signs. Munci's casualness was a certain sign of hidden knowledge, or why would he not tell anyone that he had been with the Gendarme and why would he cut dead his best foreign friend? The old man going east at dawn—he drew in his mind the direction as if with calipers.

Excitement is a bad emotion for a hunter, he reminded himself. He knew that he would find something worthy of his time and the sea voyage. Finally he bor-

rowed Huseyin's tirandıl and put to sea in the afternoon, lulled by the fine sound of the diesel. He scorned
the sails when the sailors pointed out that they had a
following wind. He liked the power of the fine
Mercedes motor that made a purr that sounded as expensive as he knew it was. He rode the round stern of
the boat, reared back against the carved railing like a
sultan, his face turned toward the stern to catch the afternoon sun.

Slowly, pacing one another, the donkey and the boat
raced from opposite directions toward English Harbor.

When the boat moored, the old man, the uncle, had
already made tea, almost as though he were expecting
it. Out over the water a popular song on the transistor
welcomed them. The Captain sat drinking tea while his
men fanned out over the clearing. It was blue evening
when he finally recognized that there was nothing
there. The old man was alone. There was not even a
contraband cigarette to capture for all his time.

He waited until the meltem had died down. Then he
thanked the man for his hospitality and left. He was not
disappointed. The fact that he had found nothing, not
a trace, told him that much had been hidden. Where
there is no carelessness there is much to hide. It was a
rule with him. The arama tarama, the search and sei-
zure, had gone on for three hours. It was enough. It
was only the first day, after all, and all the signs were
right.

When the boat was once again a small black dot in
the evening sea, three men watched it from the shore.
They were smoking the Dunhills sent by Munci. Attila
had been asleep in a tree all evening. The young man
who helped Uncle had come back down from the hills
where he had taken the donkey. All three of them were
hungry, cheteji, outlaw hungry after the hours of patience. They made a feast to celebrate once again having beaten the Gendarmes, but the young man did not
eat or drink much.

At dawn, two men on donkeys rode out from English Harbor. Attila knew he must say nothing. He
glanced at the young man behind him with some admiration. Uncle had told him that the young man had

smuggled hashish and gold, and had killed four Gendarmes. That was good. He had long since given up hope that such men were made anymore. Pig-eaters and schoolteachers, that was all the young were good for.

The second morning was cool and sweet through the vines outside the Gendarmerie. The Captain was in a good mood. He had worked out the movement pattern that a man would follow, more and more animal-like as he tired, toward a center point, a lair. It was the homing instinct. The Captain prided himself on knowing this. Put yourself in the place of the hunted, let his pulse be yours. It was another of his rules. The center point—he had known it to be a kahve, a boat, a village. Find the center point, the point which in his daymind a man hardly realizes that he has, and you will find the man. He knew this. It had worked before.

The Chief of Police did not like what he had to do. He walked through the morning toward the Gendarmerie. It was time to discuss the reports for the dossiers. His nervous crowded town smelled of trouble. The Chief of Police did not know who would suffer. It was just that in that atmosphere, as catching as disease, he knew it would be hard for someone like the Captain not to find a victim. He knew he could protect people so long as they were within the town limits, but when the dossier grew, stuffed with rumors, and overheard remarks, and police reports, and the instructions came from that impersonal font called higher-up, there was little he could do.

So he was surprised and relieved to find the Captain in such a good mood.

They discussed Horst over their coffee. "It is now four months since he has been waiting for his permission. Poor Horst, what is holding it up?" The Chief of Police glanced over the reports. He did not need to read them. There was nothing new.

"A German to wait so long without working!" They

both smiled, but the Captain added, "This in itself is suspicious. I know this. My brother's brother-in-law works in Essen. Allah Allah, how they work, he says."

"Tabiî. Tabiî." The Chief of Police sighed.

"There is something here not quite right. I think he is a spy or he is smuggling antiquities. I have not decided which." The Captain whirled the coffee grounds around his cup, and then set it upside down in his saucer to read his fortune. "Olani biteni birbirini ekle." He pointed his finger with each word, and then made a circle to show how the past and the present were usually the same. "It is simple." He lifted the coffee cup and began to read it.

"I am sorry, he is a nice boy," the Chief of Police said. "I am sorry you have come to this unhappy conclusion . . ."

Why was there a bird in the coffee grounds? A tall thin man? Money? He saw the man as himself, the bird, oh, that was easy, and money, well, honor more than money. Were there women there, veils of women and a tree? It was a tree, not a man. He saw the bird flying toward the tree. Nest? Woman? The mother? The Captain put the cup down.

"I think we must make a negative report." He had already promised Horst's radio to the Customs Inspector. It had many stations, and short wave. Only a spy could afford such a radio.

"But what can you use? There is nothing new to report."

"Ah, but there is. I have a conversation reported. Anti-Turkish remarks. He says the new hotel is being built too quickly and that the sand has salt in it and that they are not following the earthquake rules. This is an anti-Turkish remark. Also he is guilty of excessive copulation."

"Bosh ver," the Chief of Police tried to smile, "what is there to do while he waits? He sits on the mountain all day."

"I am sorry but I already know this. This is why we have already commandeered his dangerously powerful binoculars. Excessive copulation. I will send the report. Next, his friend, David . . ."

"No. No. He is innocent," the Chief of Police said. "He is my friend." He knew this was not enough. "He brings money to the town." The Captain of the Gendarmes still had his pen poised over the report. "He is the only man in Ceramos who speaks four languages." The Captain put the dossier aside and lit a Dunhill. "Alas," the Chief of Police went on, "Horst is my friend, too. This makes me very unhappy," he groaned. "You know, I did not want to be a policeman, but my father took a stick to me. I am an artist. I wanted to sing. One time . . ."

After the story of his father, which was long and soothing, the Captain of the Gendarmes looked again at his list.

"The two American women."

"The older one is my friend," the Chief of Police said again. "That is all, nothing, nothing against her. As for the young one. Do not bother with her." He spread his arms. "She is a little fool but she is not dangerous. Besides that, she has picked up two Italians and she is planning to leave with them."

"How do you know this?" The Captain looked up from inspecting his coffee cup again. The Chief of Police was relieved to see how peaceful he looked.

"I know the signs. I have seen too much in my life," he sighed.

"But she has invested money . . ."

"What does that mean? They have so much. It is nothing, bombok, shit to them."

They went through the rest of the list quickly. It was nearly time to go to the kahve.

At the door, the Captain stopped, pleased with his timing. He had seen such a thing in a movie. "I have a new report on the American woman."

The Chief of Police's heart sank as he listened. He knew where it had come from, as wind rises and whirls, at first only lifting the dust, then faster and faster, the single mote nothing but the dust cloud, dangerous and blinding.

". . . an orgy," the Captain finished. "They kept the neighbors awake. Shameful."

"But she has not been there. She has been on the

boat helping the widow. There are no drugs. She is kind . . . and foolish. It is nothing." The Captain had walked ahead of him down the street, and he had to lose dignity by nearly running after him.

"Politics," the Captain said when he caught up with him, "are not nothing." He felt good. He kicked a dog. The dull, long-growing anger he called patience sang in him, an old song, older than this or that. They stopped to watch a butterfly.

Under the shadow of the central mosque, the late-comers to the Pazar had spread their kerchiefs to display their lettuce and packets of wild mountain herbs. The women made a small oasis among the parked dol-mushes and the shuffling feet of people going to and fro from the main Pazar. At first the Captain thought she was one of them, another still pile of clothes. He looked again. It was the American woman, squatted down there like a peasant, her face close to Kemal. She looked as if she were questioning him, the old fool, when he could not answer. She was obviously trying to find out something. He let the Chief of Police walk ahead of him, and then let the crowd push him closer until he was within hearing distance.

"Hele. Hele," she was saying slowly and they smiled at each other's mouths.

He was right. "Tell me. Tell me the truth," she meant when she said it slowly and with such a smile. If she had been frowning, and said it faster, it would have meant, "What have you been up to, you naughty boy." How often he had heard his mother say it, fast, shaking his shoulders. No, but she was slow, slow and smiling, the pig-eating seducer of secrets. Something between them about the brother, that much was certain. The Captain walked on. Demir could at least follow the idiot boy. It would, the Captain thought, be better exercise for him than sitting in the café and watching Munci, which he did so badly. He complained that Munci made a fool of him. Let him watch the boy, the dummy, at least he could do that.

It was the evening of the third day. Timur had to keep reminding himself to be conscious of what he was doing. It was dangerous to let running become automatic, animal-like, and a running man should do nothing by habit. He squatted under a cliff beyond his village, high in the mountain pass, to wait for Munci as he had told him to do in his note. He knew that Munci would come when it was dark enough to shelter his movements.

The weeks of working in Uncle's garden had made his muscles hard again, and his mind, he had to admit, soft. Tears, he discovered with some surprise, came easily, the tears of a man who has run toward home by instinct when he is in danger, to find that home is locked away from him, the most dangerous place of all. Like Paradise, he could only glimpse it from afar, a cluster below him, startling white in the dusk.

Before he realized what he was doing, he had let himself think of daily things, his mother rolling börek dough on the table he made for her, his father smoking and listening to the news on the transistor, Kemal, always Kemal in his area of watchful silence, following every movement as the dough grew thinner and thinner under the sweep of his mother's arms. Against the vision, all that had happened since seemed new and far away, Lale unreal, the names of streets in Istanbul gone. He was nearly asleep.

Someone touched his shoulder. He lunged at the man. It was Munci, feinting out of his way until he recognized him.

"Ağabey, I was asleep I think." He could hardly see Munci in the deep dusk. He hunkered down beside him.

"It was easy to get away. Demir is now following Kemal and Kemal is making him thin," Munci told him. "Now I have been thinking. Wait until midnight. Then go down to the Izmir road. Be there where the old Alexander road goes under the new one, at the broken bridge. The truck to Izmir that my cousin drives will pass at four o'clock. It will go very slowly around the curve. He has promised me that, but he does not know why. He asks nothing about it. Tomorrow it will be taking fish to the Pazar in Izmir. It will also carry some crates of machinery that were unloaded from the islands today. One of the crates will be empty. All of them are marked with the name of Dürüst Osman. It is written on them. He is to deliver them at Bashmane station. Just before Bashmane the truck will stop in traffic. It is always bad there. You get down and go to the Pazar. My cousin Ismet has sold the coins. You will pick up the money from his shop. It will keep you for a while. Then . . ."

It was the dark of the moon. Munci's voice went on, whispering his instructions. When he had finished he brought out bread and cheese and they ate together and talked of the things they had always talked about, the sea, ambition, people.

Once Timur said, "Why can't I go home like other men?"

There was no answer. Munci stared into the darkness. It was time for him to leave.

At midnight Timur began to move. He had slept a little. His body felt light. He allowed himself no luxury of easy movement in the dark. If his path took him nearer the village then he had meant it to, he told himself it was the most convenient of the goat paths. The village lay slightly below him, now faintly white, anonymous under the great depth of stars. It was poised in sleep.

Nothing moved. It could have been deserted for a thousand years. He knew better than to go closer and set the dogs barking. He moved a few steps, just to get near enough to pick out his family's house from the others. He knew it was a glimpse he would have to carry with him until, by some caprice of a ministry, some slight change in the political wind, in a few months or a few years he was safe and could return— he smiled—return to the quarrels of his father, to all he had run from in the past, unchanged. For a minute he let all that be sweet in his memory.

One path lay north of the great rock that had once

been the acropolis of the village; it was the path to the
Izmir road, five miles over the hills and down into the
valleys. Timur had no time to make a mistake in the
dark. He kept close in to the shadow of the rock, even
though he had seen from higher on the mountain there
was no one standing on it. That, the fact that the dogs
were not barking as they would do if a stranger were
there, the thought that he was not important enough
for a sentinel to stand all night to watch over the town,
and the black starry night were all signs of safety. A
body jumped down on him from above and knocked
him to the ground.

They rolled over and over, out of the shadow of the
rock and into the south path. The arms locked over his
shoulders, and he kicked at something heavy in the
dark. They wrestled without noise until one of their
feet dislodged a rock and it tumbled down the hill and
the dogs heard it. The air was full of barking. A voice
yelled in his ear, "Haydi gel!" He was nearly free,
slithering along the path. He managed to pick up a
rock and throw it back into the center of the heavy
panting bulk that still clutched at his ankle.

He heard running feet. His body was jerked upward
by the hair and one arm. Bright round torchlight
blinded him. A hand slapped his face.

"Timur! Timur!" He heard someone call out, the
hysterical voice of his mother, then silence, and breathing, and the dark bulks of men. His mind was ice-cold.
Usually in mob violence the victim is unconscious before major damage is done to the body. He had learned
that somewhere.

The light column turned away to the Gendarme who
was turning his body to get up. The rock had hit his
square dark face. There was blood at the edge of his
eye. One arm hung, useless. He was grinning.

The light swung back. It hurt Timur's eyes. He
closed them.

Something hit the side of his head.

The Captain of the Gendarmes swung the torch
down following the body as it fell. He let the circle of
strong light bore along it from head to foot. In this,

this rag bundle, dirty, unshaven, he checked the recognitions of the enemy.

The man was young, he was wearing the remains of those tight flared jeans he hated. He had seen such tight shirts new, moving over the muscles of the zamparalar, the boy whores, the imitators of the west. This was no man, only an enemy fallen, a dog in his path.

He felt very clean. He could sense his own certainty. A rigidity of dreams he didn't know he had kept his shoulders stiff. He felt cool. He had forgotten that the success, the bringing down of quarry, bird or animal or man, made him feel that way, poised and weightless. He was surprised.

The body did not move, only a slight rise and fall of the chest showed that it was alive. A thread of blood from its mouth muddied the dirt of its scruffy face. But the muscles of his arm were still tense, ready to respond. The Captain thought he might be shamming. He had been afraid that this thing in the path had been hit too soon and hit too hard, and might be beyond questioning. He showed the torch around at the dull faces of his men. "Which one of you hit him?"

One of the men, a Kurd, straightened up, proud.

The Captain slapped him across the face.

"Put that man under arrest," he said. It was almost a whisper. The torch was on the body again. The light shook a little. He hated them all, hated the grin on the now swollen face of the Gendarme who had caught the quarry, hated the sadistic lout who would not wait for orders, who had hit too soon. There was one way to find out if the scruff that lay at his feet was forever beyond him. It stirred once, a twitch.

He snapped his fingers into the dark. "Your gun. Haydi. Hold the light." He was instantly ashamed of having clicked his fingers. It showed an unseemly impatience.

He lifted the gun and brought it down, butt first, splitting the genitals. Blood spread. The man was not shamming. He was unconscious. The Captain was disgusted. He drove the butt again into the body. He could not tell if its movement was the blow or some animal reaction. He lifted the gun. He battered his way through the prison wall of the figure on the ground, its secrets, its arrogance. He went on like a woman churning.

Released finally from whatever it was that drove his arms, and exhausted, he stopped, handed the rifle into the dark, and turned away from them so they could not see the sweat on his face. No one said a word. The dogs had stopped barking. He grabbed the torch and tried to walk away calmly.

His men stared after him. They had watched him acting on his own in some private war they had no part in, that stunned them into a stupidity of watching as at disasters, street fights, or acts of God. Out of the dark he called, now calm.

"Well, pick him up."

There was no light in the village street as they passed through it, no sound, but the sense and glimpse of people crowded behind doors. A woman ran between the Gendarmes and tried to clutch at the body, but they pushed her off, and rolled it into the back of the jeep. It lay on the jeep floor, its dirty feet dangled over the edge.

The last that Kemal and his mother saw of it was the feet, swinging in time to the bumps as the jeep disappeared down the mountain.

Dogs lapped at the trail of blood.

For a long time Kemal watched the lights of the jeep wind down the mountain in and out of sight, and listened to the noise of it.

The Captain of the Gendarmes sat in his office. It was the fourth morning of the hunt. He had just had the satisfaction of drawing a red line, not through a picture, but at least through a name. He had sent the necessary telegrams. He began to write his report. One less, one less, was all he wanted to say, but that was unofficial. He let the old villager outside wait until he was finished. Then he gave orders to let him in.

The man stood before him, his hands clasped together, his head down, whether in grief or fear he could not tell. He felt sorry for him. Orhan was old, and his eldest son Timur had been a disappointment to him. The Captain explained carefully how the son's name had been on the list, a name on a list, you understand. The old man barely nodded. He said that the Gendarme the boy had attacked had a broken arm. A wild boy. What could he do? He spread his arms. He offered coffee but the old man clicked his tongue. He was like one dumb. The Captain released the body to him and offered him the jeep to take it to the village. The jeep floor had been cleaned. He gave orders to wrap the body neatly in a tarpaulin. Neatly, he stressed that. It was the least he could do.

When the old man shuffled to the door, he followed him. He lifted the old fingers to his mouth and then to his forehead. After all, he was old, and one owed respect to the old in their grief.

Ariadne felt lost. No one had been near her house for days, not Munci, not anybody. She sensed a new change, not a change in rhythm as there had been through the summer, but the change after an accident when nothing is the same. She thought of how a woman must feel who has been raped, and who wanders from room to room with no one to tell.

Lisa had gone, simply picked up and gone when she was on Miranda's boat. She had left a note. It was polite, the kind of note she would have left after a weekend in Virginia. It had the American Express in Florence as her forwarding address; Lisa wrote it Firenze. She had worn Ariadne's clothes. Ariadne's djallabah, stained with Lisa's menstrual blood, hung on her cupboard door. Her bed was unmade. The sheets were filthy, but thrown back properly, as one is taught to do when there are servants.

"I must go," Lisa had written, "to Firenze."

"And who must not, sometime?" Ariadne said, and tore the note across.

It was ending. Her house, her haven, was strange. It

and she had been used—used up. Oh, not the child.
The child was unimportant, and that was the saddest
thing about her. Ariadne stood in the middle of the
kitchen, and waited for the energy to clean it, trying to
figure out something without a name. Fear? No. Fear
was active. Fear changed the temperature and
heightened the awareness. It was just the exhausting
necessity for change when she did not want it and age
when she was not ready for it. She saw the blue bowl,
piled with the other dishes in the sink. She got it out
carefully. It was stained with dried olive juice. In the
middle of the mess she cleaned the bowl until it shined
again.

It released her at last into action. She scrubbed the
kitchen floor and walls, killed the bugs that had
gathered and crawled blindly around the counter now
that the dishes were clean and the trash thrown out.

There was no food. She put on her kerchief and left
the house. It was only when she reached the street
through the now familiar silence and the turned heads
of the women, that she realized that she had forgotten
to lock her door, and that she didn't care.

She turned, not toward the Pazar, but toward the
hills for peace and cleanliness and the white village of
simplicities. She thought, I will move up to the village.
They like me there, and she heard the thought as an
old refrain of returned illusion. She wanted still to have
dreams, switch time, think brightly, swing and strut
through mental complications, more interesting if more
painful than the empty plodding after too much had
happened. At least she sensed that she had borne too
much of something—a nameless weight, isolation or
neglect—but she did not know, only felt it, the sweat
of knowing on her skin.

Up ahead of her at last, after the hour's walk that
still brought peace of mind, peace that was leaving
something behind, unsettled, but no longer important
in the afternoon, she came to Eskiköy. The street was
empty. No men sat under the plane tree. No women
gathered at the pump.

She looked around and then she saw them. At the
wooden door of the cliff wall of the house where she

had tea with Meral when her man was not there, the whole village was gathered, pressed together, their backs to her. A woman turned and saw her and turned away again. She was left standing in the dusty road. Someone was pushing through the crowd, making it eddy. It was Munci. She was happy to see him.

"Go back," he said, and took her arm. "There is nothing for you here." He had been crying, she thought.

"Can I help?"

"Go back, just go back."

"Please tell me what's happened."

But Munci, even Munci, they were all like that, even he, changeable, disappeared through the huddle of people at the gate, shutting her out, after the way she had loved them. Whatever had happened or was happening was for them and not for her. She felt as though she were looking at them through a glass.

The Chief of Police had moved his work out under the vines of the veranda. He liked to watch the people. He was sad. There were things that had to be done that deepened a man's anger. He pushed the papers aside and got up and stretched himself.

Down below him in the street he could see Horst with his hands full of papers. He looked reasonably happy, a young man with a future who has only failed once and is not a fool. He was glad at least that he had been able to warn Horst. Now he was leaving before his equipment could be confiscated. He was glad of that. He could see the Customs Inspector watching Horst. He looked glum. The Chief of Police smiled. He knew that if Horst got away before the official orders came they could do nothing. They were not equipped to deal with surprise moves. He sat down again. You had to fight, always fight . . .

He was disgusted with himself. He had not been able to find Ariadne Hanim. He had gone to her house. The gate was swinging open. She was not there. Only the kitchen was clean. He had walked through the mess of

the other rooms, shaking his head. He had not known
she would fall to this, this squalor: bottles, stained
table tops, a broken plate in the fireplace. She, too, dis-
integrated like the rest after too long—the foreigners
with nothing to do. He sighed. The room had been so
lovely. Now it was dusty with boredom and defeat. He
told himself he would find her later and warn her before the Captain of Gendarmes got the orders he
sought, and the knock came to her door.

How they can live here under that threat, I do not
know, he told himself, and stretched and watched the
vines and let peace take over and release his bones before the next action, before he faced, once again, the
troubled surly town. He knew that the tension would
not be released until the funeral was over.

Rumors were flying, of course. He had been sent to
Ceramos too late to meet Timur, but he had heard first
that he was an erkek adam, then that he was the only
one from the village at the University, then silence,
then the Captain, showing his name on the damned
list.

He had no respect for the list. It was an Arapbashi,
an Arab's head of misguided students, criminals, terrorists, intellectuals, all lumped together indiscrimi-
nately, a mess of whispers, secret police reports, gossip,
and CIA. He hated it. He had seen too much of how
the dossier grew, a rankling insult told to a brother-in-
law, told to the kaymakam, then to the Ministry, one
or another of them, a series of unimportant fragments
and minor revenges.

Now they were saying in the kahve that Timur had
killed a Gendarme. Tomorrow it would be two Gendarmes. Some would praise him for the killing of a Gendarme that never happened, and remember their pride
in him when he was a boy and ruled the street, and
strutted after Munci. He had seen the body. It looked
like nothing human. When they lifted him off of the
jeep floor his bones had seemed to come apart. The
Captain of the Gendarmes had waked him and made
him come to watch.

He had tried, the Captain told him, to escape.

Above all, the Chief of Police told himself, these private matters must be kept from the tourists.

It was cooler by five o'clock. The Chief of Police had finished working on his reports and he stacked the papers neatly. He found his car keys. The feel of them turning in his hand was a pleasure. It was a gesture he had seen on the American cinema, that twisting and playing with car keys. In his hand, used to a different movement, they turned into prayer beads, or now that there was no recognized state religion, he preferred to call them worry beads.

He got slowly into the new police car, aware that it was beautiful—the plastic seats, the gleaming new paint of the white hood that caught the sun, the evil eye swinging from the rearview mirror, the finely painted gold insignia on the car door. He wished there were a turning light on the roof—what did they call it?—a cherry. He liked that. But the car had been a gift to the police from the new hotel owners; it was a civilian car and they could only afford to have it painted. It had been Turgut Bey's Chevrolet Impala. After he had taken away the body of his daughter in it, he said he could never ride in it again. Ah well, good from evil grows as flowers from dung.

The Chief of Police started the engine and let it idle a while. As when he turned his saz, he listened, keen to the nuances of its purring. He turned it around on the wide quay slowly, nudging the evening crowds back, and started along the narrow street, blowing the horn. He drove the Impala fast, watching the people run aside. It was a pleasure to see them flatten themselves against the walls. It was good that they should do this. It taught the children how dangerous cars were. The automobile, he liked to tell them from time to time, has no fear. Remember that. It is up to you to get out of the way.

It is a strange thing, he thought as he drove, there are always three deaths—the drowned girl, the American, and now the boy. Always three. He had seen this happen often.

He drew the car to a stop at the foot of Ariadne's street. He did not like what he had to do. She had been there so long, and there was, suddenly, so little time, now that her dossier had overweighted and toppled. Hayat böyle. He could have been a compassionate vizier of the Sultan on a work of personal kindness, one of those gestures that made authority bearable and spawned fairy tales. He felt strong and kind and sorry.

Ariadne's gate was open. White-kerchiefed women flowed along the terrace, circled the rooms, as instinctive and formal as ants or birds. The Chief of Police was surprised to notice first that there was not much noise. He watched a curtain tear slowly down from a window. A woman struggled by carrying a large terra-cotta amphora filled with green plants. Another, they had no faces, they all looked the same, was trailing a bundle of women's garments. A thin white cotton djallabah, sweeping the stones behind her, was splattered with dried blood.

He was afraid, not of their violence, there was none. It was their single-mindedness. He stood there, the Chief of Police in his cap, and the women circled around him, not seeing him. He swam through them to the door, thrust back once against the wall by a woman carrying very carefully an armful of dishes. He had seen rats once overrunning an empty house. They gave him the same sick twinge of disgust and fear.

In the center of the living room two women wrestled for a piece of blue silk, a great flowing thing that half engulfed them both. He stepped between them and grabbed their shoulders. One of the women was Ariadne and she was laughing.

"Yok! Yok! Olmaz!" she kept saying. She gathered the silk thing that the other had dropped when she saw who the man was. "She cannot have this," Ariadne told him. "It is my evening coat. I wear it in the evening."

He forced himself out of his shock into action. "Git! Haydi! Git!" He waded among the women, using his stick. They poured through the narrow outer door. No one dropped anything, not a spoon, not a pair of underpants. Behind him he could still hear Ariadne's voice, laughing and calling, "Here, take this. Chabuk chabuk! Quickly."

He saw an old woman struggling under a pile of wood, and started toward her. Someone touched his arm. "Leave her alone," Ariadne said. She spoke softly. The whole thing was so quiet. "I told her she could have the wood. In the winter I see her searching the road for sticks of wood to make her fire. She crosses them and blows them to life." She spoke like a woman who was dreaming.

The garden terrace was empty, except for the old woman who was too intent on moving the wood to look at them.

"That is Fatma, my friend," Ariadne told him.

There was nothing he could think to say.

"Something made them afraid," Ariadne said. What it was she could not know, deep memories of the invasion of forces like the winds of God, invasion of horsemen, of authority reaching down from its heights to slit and destroy? What memory, aroused by Timur's death, had set them whirling? She thought it was their way of grasping, through the wet surges of their fear, a way to tomorrow—to use the single shoe, the torn curtain, the few sticks to keep whatever it was away. It was a battle for life, not with her, but between them and something unknown. She had no part in it. They had forgotten her existence. There were only, for them, her fragments.

She and the Chief of Police walked together through the dead, dismantled living room, shoddy now, and almost empty. One mattress had been left on the floor. It was strange, she saw, how the abandonment of a mattress, naked of its cover, killed a house.

"I fought, though," she said with some pride. "I fought for what I really wanted." She pointed to a shelf where books had been and flowers. It was piled high. "That's all," she said, "a bowl I made myself, and some clothes."

"They will be punished for this."

"No. No they won't," she wandered away from him, that dream voice again. It worried him. "To them I

was as rich as King Croesus. Don't you see? They were
my entertainment. I was theirs. We didn't really touch
each other much. I thought we might . . ." This last
he hardly heard. She had walked into the kitchen and
left him standing there in women's wrack and ruin. It
was too personal. He was embarrassed. What was it?

I can help a woman who is crying but a woman who
is laughing is already too far away. He thought of that,
thought he might say it, but when he followed to the
kitchen and then to the terrace, she sat down and began to watch the street as if he were not there.

He said instead, "Where will you stay tonight? My
mother will welcome you."

"Oh, that is kind, and you do mean it. It is kinder
than you know. It breaks the glass for a minute."

He did not know what she meant.

"No," she said, "I will stay with David. Maybe I
should have done that before." She did not mention it
again.

The street below them was completely empty, except
for the new police car. Away in the distance they heard
the revving of motorcycles, that and nothing more.

"Why is it so still?" Ariadne's attention flickered.
"You know, they took all my photographs, all of them.
They passed them around like cards."

The Chief of Police was listening to the engine
sounds. "They wanted to remember you," he said.
"You are our friend."

"Good God." Ariadne opened her closed fist. She
still held a fragment of a belt she had failed to pull
away from a woman. "Then why . . ." she could
hardly speak through her sudden tears, "why do they
want to do that?"

"Remember you?" The Chief of Police felt more secure now that Ariadne Haním was crying as she should
be. At last he could comfort his friend. "We have had
so many come and go and they do not try to see us at
all, and they go away and talk and talk. You must
. . ." Here he stumbled for words. The English of
what he wanted to say was hard for him and he had
never before opened his heart to a foreigner, not the
way he did to the judge or in the old days to his wife.

He cleared his throat. "I think you people must live in strange places, very far apart from each other, without friends. You come here very lonely. You make acquaintances and you make love but not to make friendly, you understand. Friend is a big word with us. You, Ariadne Hanım, come here and you see us the way we are. We see a friend. We have feelings and pride. We show you these things you have not seen. It is not . . ."

Here he was lost. He prayed for her to wait, as a Turk would wait, for him to find his thoughts. "It is inside and outside, you see. A way we are taught to be and a way we are, two things. You do not do what the others do. They fall in love with our ways and when they find out some of us are as big son-of-a-bitches as anybody else, they get mad at us . . . It is unfair."

The motorcycles were coming nearer, revving hard to keep their speed down. There was only a gap between the houses where they could see the street. A pickup truck passed it, slowly. In the back of it was a wooden box. An old man sat beside it, and a young boy bowed over the box, crouched, his face hidden. The truck bed jostled along the stones of the pavement, laid down by the soldiers of Alexander.

Behind it one motorcycle after another passed the gap. Every motor in Ceramos followed, coughing and revving and groaning gears, a procession of all their riches, AID tractors almost too old to move, cars that had been patched and painted, dolmushes with fringed curtains. There was not a woman in sight.

The Chief of Police got up from the balustrade. "I must follow them to the cemetery in the new police car," he said. "It is only honorable."

"Is it Meral's son?" Ariadne asked.

"A foolish boy." The Chief of Police was too angry to stop himself. "Many of the men down there honor him for the wrong reasons, because he was brave, an erkek adam, because he was a good fighter. I," he paused and adjusted his cap, "I will follow him for the right reasons. Because he fought his way to the University."

Ariadne caught him at the gate. "What really happened?"

All the stories that he had prepared to tell fled from his mind. He was too furious and ashamed to lie. "He was beaten to death by a sadist."

"Who?" She bothered him. A funeral was no place for a woman's questions.

"The Captain of the Gendarmes," he said. "They have a list. They say it was prepared by the Ministry and the CIA. They all work together to make a list." At last she had stopped looking at him. "Have you no sadists in your own country? Have you no lists?"

He walked down toward the street. The steep lane was deserted. There was not even, as there had always been, a sense of people watching. The women had disappeared. Ariadne saw him hesitate, then stop. He turned again. She watched him climb back up the lane. He was looking at his feet as they moved.

He lifted his head when he got back to the gate. "Ariadne Hanim," he said formally, "I am distressed that this has happened. We are a poor country. We value your garbage. And I think, I think you should go soon, before . . ." It was not the way he had meant to tell her, he had meant to be gentle.

"Gechmish olsun, it has passed. So be it." He muttered the formal words of comfort, and turned away.

"Sağ ol," she called after him, as she should, her deepest formal thanks. Sağ ol. Be strong? For the first time in her life she refused to let words carry more than their own weight. Whether it had all been a clarity of blue or a three-year spell of enchantment, she no longer knew. It had passed. It wasn't as important to know as it was to begin packing. What? One rose medallion ashtray, one blue bowl. She felt that she was neither saint nor sinner, neither lost nor found. She was not needed, and it did not matter.

If there was "hope" it was that her passport was in order.

Her first acceptance of herself alone on earth—humus—humility—she sensed as a balance between poise and fatigue.

She watched the procession go on, a waste of sorrow. At the end, the Chief of Police swung the white Impala with the gold insignia into line.

She went on watching, long after the motor sounds had disappeared. The wind had died. The sea was flat calm. She found that she was smiling, and she was unprepared for that.

It was the thirtieth of August. An early rain had come, only one, but there was water again in Salmakis fountain, and the temple hill was lightly brushed with green. The rain had washed the tamarisk fronds and they lifted again out of their dusty summer exhaustion as if they had been decorated for the Zafer Bayram, the bayram of victory. There was the bustle of sea departures around the foreign yachts; fresh ropes lay coiled on the quay in front of them, dinghies were bottom up with new paint drying.

Frank Proctor was doing his duty, and, for once, he liked it. He came every year to the Zafer Bayram. The old man thought somebody ought to. Besides, this year they were sending a piece of the Sixth Fleet and somebody had to be around to cool things down in case there were incidents—usually, Frank told himself, over cultural misunderstandings about women.

He thought of how much earlier each successive year he had to get up to walk in the sweet timeless town. But he had to admit that he was being romantic about that. Even in the dawn washing of the sun, there was a sense of prosperous bustle in the air.

All over the town, wherever he passed, they were hanging out the red flag, the star and crescent, until the white walls were splashed with red. He passed three people, a woman standing in the street yelling "Yok, yok" and waving her arm to the right while her two sons centered the flag on a balcony above her, laughing at her, and calling "Anne, anne, olmaz!" "Tabiî tabiî," she yelled and laughed back, and then, over her shoulder, screamed "Hoshgeldin!" to Frank and began to laugh again, showing her teeth and not caring.

Frank knew that for a little while he was safe. He

had had his necessary and unpleasant meeting with the Captain of the Gendarmes the night before. They sat together down along the breakwater of the outer harbor in the dark, and Frank tried to listen to the sea run while the Captain of the Gendarmes bragged and lied. Frank wasn't surprised. He had never really liked the man very much, even though he was efficient at his job, unlike the local police chief who was one of those Middle Eastern officials who shrugged his shoulders and let things slide—sometimes damned important things.

There were not four anarchists caught. There was only one—a medical student from Istanbul, suspected of guilt by association with a group of terrorists. Poor bastard. If we could only *get* to them, Frank thought. We could spread some scholarship money. That's where some of our aid would *really* show a profit. He began to dream and plan.

He was so intent on his hopes that he didn't realize he had walked to where the street widened out onto the Customs House quay.

He had to laugh.

Someone in the night had spread a huge banner across the quay. It must have taken secret hours to make it. It read, in English and Turkish: SINCE IT WAS UNJUST THAT I SHOULD BE PUT INTO PRISON IT IS MY DUTY TO CORRECT THE REASONS AND MOTIVES WHICH CAUSED THIS INJUSTICE. THIS IS HOW A TURKISH YOUNG MAN AND THE YOUTH OF TURKEY SHOULD BEHAVE. MUSTAFA KEMAL ATATURK.

He ran to find the Captain of the Gendarmes. At first the Captain couldn't understand. Frank had to point out that although they were the Gazi's words they were disruptive.

"I am sure," the Captain of the Gendarmes said as they rolled up the banner, "this is not what the Gazi meant at all."

He said he would keep it at the Gendarmerie and investigate it later. "It should not be hard to find who has done this. The work is very beautiful," he had added. Frank agreed, even though it might have been an embarrassment for the crews of the two small ships of the Sixth Fleet which lay out to sea beyond the outer harbor.

What Frank did not know was that the whole of Ceramos was honoring a double holiday, the public one for the fiftieth birthday of the new nation, and the private secret one, a ceremony of mutual forgiveness and relief. They celebrated the coming of sweet kayf, that peace of unused time passing, and daily worries, and, inshallah, more normal ways of dying.

Ceramos was receding already back into its ever-moving stalemate with Dürüst Osman, and the dignified concerns of winter men, leaving the dithering preoccupations of summer, the clowning, the entertaining of the foreign adult children behind it. It was returning to its centuries, already beginning to forget the dangerous hints of summer shame.

The young judge agreed that it was a perfect day, a day when all divisions could be forgotten. He and the Chief of Police were standing at the rail of the terrace at the Police Station. From below they looked like two sileni, draped in summer vines. Beyond the terrace, Ceramos lay like an ancient theater around the harbor.

The parades were over. The local boats had raced, and Munci had won. That amused the Chief of Police. Without the weight of the compressor, the boat had flown through the water like a bird, leaving the ponderous tırandıl of Huseyin far behind. Now the small boats lay side by side along the quay, already working again, their brass catching the afternoon sun, their racing sails furled. For once the water of the harbor was so still that they could see, as under glass, the great stones of the ancient quay.

The whole town looked like a huge red and white patchwork quilt, dotted with gold stars and crescents. From every loudspeaker, music to celebrate their victory in the old war of independence met to make a pleasing cacophony of noise over the streets. The ferry that lay in the dock ready to take its passengers to the Greek islands blared its great klaxon over and over, loud enough for the Greeks to hear it over the silent sea. It was not a memorial of the war, it was a reliving of the victory itself, the day the sick old man of the Ottoman Empire had become a boy again, had spilled the Greeks, the French, the English who would have spoiled and divided it into the sea.

A fine white cruise ship lay out beyond the breakwater, its passengers ashore to watch the celebration. On the quay the crowd had formed a circle. Some at the back stood on chairs from the kahve, or perched along the lowest castle wall. The balconies hung with flags and people. In the center of the quay a troup of Mevlevi dervishes sent from the Ministry of Tourism whirled in their hypnotic dance, calling down Allah to their bodies for the foreigners to watch. Their skirts made huge whirling white flowers.

On the largest balcony opposite, Dürüst Osman and his entourage sat watching the dancers. The Chief of Police smiled. It was the one time of the year when the old man unbent and joined a celebration. He was the last man left alive in the town who had been a soldier of the Gazi. He wore his black kalpak, the gray blanket coat, the black boots of the army of the Gazi. Crisscrossed across his breast were cartridge belts. He wore a dagger that flashed when he turned to speak to Turgut Bey, who looked hot and fretful.

Behind them, standing, the Chief of Police could see the young man from Izmir, the American. Proctor Bey, they called him. They were too polite to call him Frank to his face. It could be taken as an insult after all, like saying pig-eater. He looked glum, trapped between the Captain of the Gendarmes on one side, and the müdür, Huseyin Bey, on the other, as if they were guarding him. The Chief of Police knew his feeling and his look as if the man were his ağabey, his brother. They in their way were both victims of the lists too. He wanted to kiss his brother, Proctor Bey, because he could read his poor young mind, and because it was, after all, a ceremony of forgiveness.

The Captain of the Gendarmes was another matter.

If the time were more propitious, he would have killed
him. He wanted, anyway, to spit when he saw him, but
that would have been rude, to spit where people could
see him. He had read the Captain of the Gendarmes'
report. It was eloquent: three terrorists, no less, caught
in the mountains. The town, he reported, had been
cleansed of disruptive elements.

The dervishes whirled to a stop. The white flowers
of their skirts billowed down. They were replaced by a
long line of school girls and boys, forming to dance,
the girls in their nylon shalvars, the boys' wide sashes
pregnant with old weapons. They began the old war
dance, solemn and graceful.

An English voice pierced the air from below the terrace, "It isn't at all like the Greek dances. It's fright-
fully solemn. I thought it would be like the Greek
dances."

The dancers wove in and out. They swept the
ground with their hands, the motions controlled and
slow. The Chief of Police could feel the music from
their movement, although he could not hear it. He
could feel himself, poised, his body silent, the arc of his
dignity as he knelt, the slow click of his fingers.

The judge was saying something.

"Efendim?" The Chief of Police stopped his secret
dancing.

"I said, it is everything we have tried to get rid of
. . . the dagger and the dervish. Now it is a tourist at-
traction."

"They seek what they know," the Chief said wisely.
He meant at least to be wise. He wanted to drift into
the dance again.

"When you make a world for tourists you make a
lie, a patchwork from all the coats you have shed."

The Chief of Police agreed, and later they would
talk, and he looked forward to that as to cool water—
but now, now was not the time. He wanted to enjoy
the dancing and feel his fingers clicking.

"Opium and harems, that is all they know," the
judge, who was not a dancer, complained as the dance
ended. He looked around carefully to be sure that no
one was listening.

"Belekler kan ichinde, dishler kenetli," he declaimed almost in a whisper, loving the words. "Our wrists are bloody, our teeth clenched, our feet bare, and the earth looks like a fine silk carpet. This hell, this heaven is ours. To know how to live free and alone as a tree, and close to our brothers as a forest, this longing is ours." There were tears in his voice when he finished, ". . . bu hasret bizim."

The Chief of Police was ashamed of the fact that he had liked the dancing, then he was ashamed of his shame. He wished the judge would keep his sadness for later when he could be part of it.

They went on standing in the silence the judge had created, watching the crowds fill the space the dancers had left—the hippies with their knapsacks, and without a nationality until you looked at their grubby passports, the wash-and-wear ladies, here and there small groups of American sailors, being overwatchful and overpolite. Gradually they drifted into their separate colors, among their own. The sailors began to disappear into the door of David's bar in the distance, the ladies toward the shops for a last nervous twitch among the silks.

The opposite balcony had emptied. The aghas had stopped gracing the ceremony. The Chief of Police could see Dürüst Osman's car, insulated from the crowd with its windows shut in the heat, nudging its slow way through the clotted street toward the mosque.

The ferry hooted its warning that it was time to leave. Late passengers huddled at the foot of the gangplank. Among them the Chief of Police could see Ariadne Hanim, the sun on her coiled hair. There was only David to see her off. He was sorry about that. It was wrong. All the time she had been there, there should have been more friends to wave her goodbye. It was a mark of affection in Ceramos, a ceremony of sadness to stand at the gangplank until the ferry left, and then to stand to be counted, waving until the boat was beyond the breakwater.

She had picked an inconvenient day to go. Even Munci waited at the stern of his boat to take tourists on a tour around the big ships, and back and forth to

Yazada. He could see him, waving people onto his
boat, overcrowding it, the more enterprising, the more
tourists, the more money. He could even hear his voice
now that the crowd had thinned, crying above the others, "Yazada! Yazada! Summer island. Hot springs.
Very old."

It was too bad he had to do that, but it was all part
of the sameness and the change, Eski hamam, eski
tosh, yenliz tellâklar değishmish. Same old bath, same
old water jug, only the attendants change.

Anyway, inchallah, the Captain of the Gendarmes
had not put Munci on the list. "He is a good Turk,"
the Captain had said. "He helped his friend. I would
have done the same, whatever his politics. He is," he
added, "a part of old Ceramos."

There was some rumor of making a historic monument of Ceramos, as if it could freeze in a day, to keep
the houses that had not already been torn down and
put the other new hotels beyond the town so that the
tourists could wander through a remnant of the past. It
made the Chief of Police laugh to think of this, and the
judge turned toward him when he heard the sound.

"What is it?" he asked.

"Nothing," the Chief of Police told him. He did not
want to hear what he had to say about it, not just yet;
he wanted to think about it some more.

Already the new hotel at Yazada had half risen out
of its foundations. He had not ever seen anything built
so fast. He was still smiling. Allah disposes. Yazada
was on an earthquake fault. Everyone seemed to have
forgotten.

There was a movement in the group below around
the passengers for the ferry. It was old Fatma, the one
who had carried the wood from Ariadne Hanım's
house. The Chief of Police saw her bend down and
pour water from a glass onto the pavement. He saw
Ariadne Hanım turn, surprised, and their colors mingle
as they hugged each other.

"I ought to say goodbye, but I can't. I have a
guest," he thought, and did not move.

Out beyond the bay the half-built hotel walls were mirrored in the water of the blue sea hole. The water reflected its always disintegrating image and drifting fall, as it had for six thousand years, mirroring what men had built around it, its rising and its dying, as rhythmic as the water's breathing. Forty meters below, the lipstick that had fallen from Lale's handbag lay among the fragments of amphorae and the sea urchin skeletons, already covered with the first camouflage of tiny sea animals.

High on the mountain at the eye window of his brother's tomb, Kemal watched the evening come down over the town. His eyes followed the toy ferry as it left the quay, its klaxon a wisp of sound taking Ariadne Hanım away. He kept on watching until it passed the new hotel at Yazada and disappeared behind the island. Soon the night would come and the fireworks the American fleet had given to Ceramos for its celebration would burst through the night and mingle with the deep stars. Kemal was sorry that he would have to see it from so far away, but there was no choice. He had waited for the bayram to do what he had to do, so that there would be no chance of anyone else being on the mountain.

There had not been much for him to bring and seal in the tomb, but he had done what he could. There was the kerchief that he had dipped in Timur's blood. He had seen the women do the same thing so he knew that it was right. They brought their blood-dipped kerchiefs to the cave mouth near the old church after the Kurban Bayram, the bayram of sacrifice when the sheep were killed. There were the books that Timur had loved so much, and that he had found where Timur had dropped them. That public body, its face swollen twice its size, the ugly thing that had been dumped out of its box into the ground because his father could not pay for a coffin and would not let Munci pay, though Munci had argued—that thing like a dog run over in the road was not Timur. Timur was here, and secret.

Kemal had not cried. He knew Timur would not want him to. Behave as if nothing has happened. It was the last thing he had told him. Besides, Munci was going to make a sailor of him. He had told his father. Sailors did not cry.

The tiny town in the distance below him was dotted with red patches on the white walls, just like the patches of blood on the kerchief he grasped in his hand. He turned back from the window. He made Timur's bed of skins as straight as if he were going to come back and sleep there again. He put the books on the stone tomb ready for him to study.

At first he did not know where to leave the kerchief. He laid it in front of one of the bull's heads. It was not right there. He picked it up again and looked around in the half-darkness. He was ashamed at not knowing what to do. He finally laid it down in front of the statue of the woman.

At least Timur had said it was a woman. It was not, it was just a rock, but he could see that it had had a face. He didn't like the shadowy thing that was left of its face though. Where the eyes ought to be there were only holes. The holes always seemed to be looking someplace else beyond him.

He was hitting the stone and he didn't know when he had started. It hurt. He hit again and again and it hurt the way he wanted it to. He kept on hitting the stone until the hurt didn't work anymore.

Slowly he lowered himself into the black smooth tunnel.

When he came out into the third chamber, he put the round stone back into its niche. He turned it until it dropped into its perfect fit. More careful than he had ever been, even to protect Timur, he arranged the stones and dust over it. Horst had gone and would not come back, but someone else would. There was always another one of them. He carried more dirt and stones.

When he had finished he was sure that not even an animal could find the entrance and they were more sensible than men.

He climbed down to the lowest chamber and walked to the entrance to scan the circle of the sea, the mountain, the paths for strangers, as a habit. Nothing moved, not even a goat or a sheep on the grass patches terraced below him.

The first purple of evening had come and the lights of the town were beginning to shine like reflections of the new stars as the sky darkened. Soon it would be dark enough for the fireworks. It was time to go and not come back. He could not move. He made himself sit down, his legs hanging over the edge of the chamber floor.

Timur had said that there were circles you could see but they were not real. They were a way to measure. There was the one from the distant islands, around to the shore, around the mountains behind Ceramos, and back again around to the far islands. He could see that. There was one that fitted it, that started if you chose to, Timur had told him, at the stars, flowed down the sky, down the mountainside through the water to the sea floor, and up the horizon through the darkness to the stars again. The bowl of the sea and the bowl of the sky and us between it he had said sitting here in the evening. It was called, he said, a sphere. Timur said it wasn't real. He was usually right but that time he was wrong. It was real. It was the whole world and people disappeared out of it like Ariadne Hanım on the boat. Timur disappeared out of it, the sphere that he could see.

His hand hurt where he had hit the stone. It hurt badly.

Something was happening to his throat. It was swelling. He had to disobey Timur. He had to cry. Something seemed to be breaking in his throat. It hurt. It hurt too much. Somebody howled like a dog.

He could feel his mouth stretching wide, somebody pulling it, a voice in it too big for it. It hurt.

"HELE HELE!" the voice howled out to the valley.

It was his own, his own voice. He could hear it echo on the rocks. He sounded like a frog.

He began to run down the mountain to tell his mother.